PENGUIN CLASSICS

# THE TRUMPET-MAJOR

Thomas Hardy was born at Higher Bockhampton, near Dorchester, on 2 June 1840. He was educated locally at the village school and later in Dorchester. At sixteen he was articled to the Dorchester architect and church restorer John Hicks, although he continued his studies under the guidance of Horace Moule, a Cambridge graduate, whose later suicide affected Hardy and his writing deeply. In 1862 he went to London to pursue his architectural career and also began writing at this time. In 1870 Hardy was sent to St Juliot in Cornwall and it was here that he met his first wife, Emma Gifford, whom he married in 1874; in the same year *Far from the Madding Crowd* was published and met with considerable success. In the previous three years he had published *Desperate Remedies* (1871), *Under the Greenwood Tree* (1872), and *A Pair of Blue Eyes* (1873). In 1878 Hardy moved back to London and in this year *The Return of the Native* appeared. His reputation as a writer grew and in 1885 he returned to Dorset to live at Max Gate. Over the next three years he published *The Mayor of Casterbridge* (1886), *The Woodlanders* (1887), and his first collection of short stories, *Wessex Tales* (1888). In 1891 *Tess of the d'Urbervilles* appeared and in 1895 his last novel, *Jude the Obscure*. During the latter part of his life Hardy devoted himself to poetry, publishing his first collection of verse, *Wessex Poems*, in 1898. Emma died in 1912, after a period of increasing marital discord. In 1914 Hardy married Florence Dugdale, who had been acting as his secretary. With her help, Hardy began work on his autobiography, *The Early Life of Thomas Hardy* (published posthumously in 1928). Thomas Hardy died on 11 January 1928.

Roger Ebbatson studied at the universities of Sheffield and London. After teaching at colleges in London he moved to the University of Sokoto in Nigeria. He is now Senior Lecturer in English at Worcester College of Higher Education. Roger Ebbatson is the author of a number of articles on nineteenth- and twentieth-century English literature and of two books, *Lawrence and the Nature Tradition* (1980) and *The Evolutionary Self: Hardy, Forster, Lawrence* (1983). He has contributed a book on *The Mill on the Floss* to the Penguin Masterstudies series and has edited Thomas Hardy's *A Pair of Blue Eyes* for Penguin Classics.

*Thomas Hardy*

# THE TRUMPET-MAJOR

## AND

# ROBERT HIS BROTHER

*Edited by*

## ROGER EBBATSON

PENGUIN BOOKS

Penguin Books Ltd, Harmondsworth, Middlesex, England
Viking Penguin Inc., 40 West 23rd Street, New York, New York 10010, U.S.A.
Penguin Books Australia Ltd, Ringwood, Victoria, Australia
Penguin Books Canada Limited, 2801 John Street, Markham, Ontario,
Canada L3R 1B4
Penguin Books (N.Z.) Ltd, 182–190 Wairau Road, Auckland 10, New Zealand

First published 1880
Published in the Penguin English Library 1984
Reprinted in Penguin Classics 1986
Reprinted with an Introduction, Notes and other editorial matter 1987

Typeset, printed and bound in Great Britain by
Hazell Watson & Viney Limited,
Member of the BPCC Group,
Aylesbury, Bucks
Set in Bembo

# CONTENTS

# ACKNOWLEDGEMENTS

THE preparation of this edition of *The Trumpet-Major* has been facilitated by reference to Denys Kay-Robinson's *Hardy's Wessex Re-appraised* (David & Charles, 1972), F. B. Pinion's *A Hardy Companion* (Macmillan, 1968), R. L. Purdy's *Thomas Hardy: A Bibliographical Study* (OUP, 1968), and the New Wessex edition of the novel, general editor P. N. Furbank (Macmillan, 1974). The map of the locality of *The Trumpet-Major* is reproduced by kind permission from the Students' Hardy edition (Macmillan, 1975). Study of the evolution of the text and of Hardy's use of historical sources has been greatly aided by reference to M. G. Edwards's invaluable 'The Making of Hardy's *The Trumpet-Major*' (MA thesis, University of Birmingham, 1967). I am grateful to the Royal Librarian for permission to study the manuscript of the novel in the Royal Library at Windsor. I should like to thank my colleagues Mick Burton and Catherine Neale for their advice.

# HARDY'S LIFE AND WORKS:
## A CHRONOLOGY

1839      Thomas Hardy, builder and mason of Higher Bockhampton near Dorchester, marries Jemima Hand, cook and servantmaid, at Melbury Osmund on 22 December.

1840      Their eldest son Thomas Hardy born at Higher Bockhampton, 2 June.

1848      He attends village school at Bockhampton built by the lady of the manor, Mrs Julia Martin of Kingston Maurward. His mother gives him Dryden's *Virgil*, Johnson's *Rasselas*. First visit to London about this time.

1849–56      Goes to school at Dorchester to learn Latin. Sees traditional harvest-supper and dance in Kingston Maurward barn. Plays fiddle at weddings and dances; begins learning French and German; reads the novels of Harrison Ainsworth and Dumas père.

1856–62      He is articled to one of his father's employers, the architect and church-restorer John Hicks, whose office in Dorchester is next door to the school kept by the Rev. William Barnes, the Dorset poet and philologist. Witnesses the public execution of Martha Brown outside Dorchester County Gaol. Horace Moule, a university-educated classical scholar and eight years Hardy's senior, becomes his mentor. Studies Greek dramatists with Moule. Reads Darwin's *Origin of Species* (1859). Writes his first poem, *Domicilium*.

1862–7      Leaves Dorchester for London in the year of the exhibition of 1862. Works as assistant-architect to Arthur Blomfield. Attends operas and theatre, explores London, visits National Gallery almost daily, dances at Willis's Rooms, sees Cremorne and the Argyle. Reads Spencer, Huxley, J. S. Mill, Shelley, Browning, Scott and Swinburne. In 1865 publishes his first article, 'How I Built Myself a House' (*Chambers' Journal*). Buys Walker's *Rhyming Dictionary* and begins sending poems to periodicals (they are rejected).

1867–70    Returns to Higher Bockhampton to assist Hicks at Dorchester. Begins his first novel (now lost) *The Poor Man and the Lady*. May have had an understanding with his cousin Tryphena Sparks, the model for Fancy Day and Sue Bridehead. (She went to London to train as a teacher in 1870, married seven years later, and died in 1890.) Completes *The Poor Man* in 1868; it is accepted by Chapman & Hall, but their reader, George Meredith, advises Hardy not to publish. Hicks dies, and Hardy moves to Weymouth to work for his successor, Crickmay. Begins writing *Desperate Remedies*. In 1870 Crickmay sends Hardy to St Juliot, Cornwall, to make plans for the restoration of the church. Here he meets his future wife, Emma Lavinia Gifford, the rector's sister-in-law.

1870–85    Publishes *Desperate Remedies* in 1871, followed by *Under the Greenwood Tree*, 1872, and *A Pair of Blue Eyes*, 1873. Leslie Stephen serializes *Far from the Madding Crowd* in the *Cornhill Magazine*. Horace Moule commits suicide at Cambridge. Publication and success of *Far from the Madding Crowd* in 1874. Hardy marries Emma Lavinia Gifford at St Peter's Church, Paddington, and encouraged by her abandons architecture for novel-writing. They take a short continental honeymoon and after brief residences at Surbiton, Swanage and Yeovil, settle at Sturminster Newton in 1876. In this year *The Hand of Ethelberta* is published. 1879 sees publication of *The Return of the Native* and the end of Hardy's 'Sturminster Newton idyll'. They remove to Upper Tooting. Hardy joins Savile Club and becomes a well-known literary figure in London, attending parties and 'crushes'. In 1880 publishes *The Trumpet-Major*, falls seriously ill and is bedridden for six months while writing *A Laodicean*. In 1881 Hardy publishes *A Laodicean*, and take a house at Wimborne Minster. Visits Paris in 1882 after publication of *Two on a Tower*. Moves to Dorchester in 1883 to supervise the building of his house at Max Gate, taking occupation in 1885.

1885–97    The next three years see the publication of *The Mayor of Casterbridge*, 1886, *The Woodlanders*, 1887, and his first collection of short stories, *Wessex Tales*, 1888. In the spring of 1887 the Hardys tour Italy, visiting Genoa, Pisa, Florence, Rome, Venice, and Milan, returning via London, where Hardy meets Browning and Arnold. From now on they usually visit London in the spring, and sometimes the Continent or Scotland. *A Group of Noble Dames* and *Tess of the D'Urbervilles* are published in 1891; and in the following year Hardy's father dies. In 1893 the Hardys visit Dublin at the invitation of Mrs Henniker (authoress, a daughter of Richard Monckton Milnes). In 1894 publishes *Life's Little Ironies*. About this time strain manifests itself in Hardy's home life, especially during the writing of *Jude the Obscure* (published 1896). Hardy resolves to write no more novels, though he publishes *The Well-Beloved* (written ten years earlier) in 1897.

1898–
1912
In 1898 Hardy publishes his first collection of verse, *Wessex Poems*, and in 1902 *Poems of the Past and the Present*. In this year he begins *The Dynasts*, of which the first part appears in 1904, the year of his mother's death. Two subsequent parts are published in 1906 and 1908, in which year he also brings out a selection of William Barnes's poems. In 1909 he publishes *Time's Laughingstocks*, and in the following year is awarded the Order of Merit and the freedom of Dorchester. He makes a final revision of his novels in 1912, and in November his wife suddenly dies.

1913–28
In March 1913 Hardy makes a pilgrimage to St Juliot and his wife's birthplace at Plymouth. He marries in February 1914 Florence Emily Dugdale, whom he had met through Mrs Henniker in 1904 and who had acted as his secretary and general assistant since 1912. In 1913 receives honorary degree of Litt. D. from Cambridge University (in 1920 Oxford University was to follow suit) and publishes *A Changed Man and Other Tales*. In 1914 publishes *Satires of Circumstance* (including 'Poems of 1912–13'). In 1915 his sister Mary dies. *Moments of Vision* published 1917; *Late Lyrics and Earlier*, 1922; and in 1923 a verse play, *The Famous Tragedy of the Queen of Cornwall*. *Human Shows*, the last collection of poems to appear in his lifetime, is published in 1925. During these years he works at his autobiography, *The Early Life of Thomas Hardy*, supposedly written by Florence Emily Hardy (published posthumously in 1928); at the same time burning his old letters, notebooks and private papers. Dies 11 January 1928, and his ashes are laid in Poets' Corner of Westminster Abbey at the same time that his heart is buried in the grave of his first wife at Stinsford, next to the tombs of his parents. This year sees the publication of his posthumous collection of poems, *Winter Words*.

# INTRODUCTION

## HARDY AND HISTORY: THE BAFFLEMENT OF DESIRE

On Waterloo Day, 18 June 1875, Thomas Hardy visited Chelsea Hospital to talk to survivors of the battle sixty years before. It was one of several such visits, and the novelist was fascinated to hear from a veteran how the only things visible in the haze of battle were the shining surfaces of 'bayonets, helmets, and swords'.[1] The following year the novelist made a pilgrimage to the battlefield itself. From the moment of his childhood discovery of a Napoleonic scrapbook compiled by his grandfather, a private in the Puddletown Volunteer Light Infantry, Hardy's youthful imagination had been fired by stories of the Napoleonic era. Indeed, the sources of *The Trumpet-Major* and *The Dynasts* lay far back in the stories of the invasion scare in Dorset with which his paternal grandmother, Mary Head Hardy, had regaled the family. The oral record of that exciting time formed part of what the novel calls 'the unwritten history of England' (p. 67). Material for the composition of the novel was assembled not only in the British Museum but also in the houses, lanes and fields of Dorset, 'collected from old people still living or recently deceased', as Hardy informed the Royal Librarian in 1880. In fictionalizing the scenes of war preparation *The Trumpet-Major* drew fruitfully upon oral sources in folk memory; it also, through the figure of Captain Hardy, stressed familial links and communal enterprise in the defence of the south coast. In his poem 'One We Knew', dedicated to his grandmother, Hardy affectionately recalled her stories:

> She told of that far-back day when they learnt astounded
> Of the death of the King of France:

13

Of the Terror; and then of Buonaparte's unbounded
  Ambition and arrogance.

Of how his threats woke warlike preparations
  Along the southern strand,
And how each night brought tremors and trepidations
  Lest morning should see him land.

It is this stress of immediacy and uncertainty which the novel,
with the historian's perspective of hindsight, finely dramatizes in
its impact upon a remote rural community invaded by a defending
army. Trivial incidents take on a historical significance and gravity
beyond the consciousness of the participants. Thus the 'cheerful,
careless, unpremeditated half-hour', when the troops enjoy Miller
Loveday's cherries, is to return to the memory of the participants
'when they lay wounded and weak in foreign lands' (p. 76). The
stability and continuity of rural life is both endorsed and undercut
by the historical omniscience of the narrative voice, as in the fine
evocation of the downs at the close of the military review (p. 100):

> They still spread their grassy surface to the sun as on that beautiful
> morning not, historically speaking, so very long ago; but the King
> and his fifteen thousand armed men, the horses, the bands of music,
> the princesses, the cream-coloured teams – the gorgeous centre-
> piece, in short, to which the downs were but the mere mount or
> margin – how entirely have they all passed and gone! – lying scat-
> tered about the world as military and other dust, some at Talavera,
> Albuera, Salamanca, Vittoria, Toulouse, and Waterloo; some in
> home churchyards; and a few small handfuls in royal vaults.

This premonitory note is sounded with most foreboding in the
carefully revised ending, when John Loveday, with his companions, departs to 'blow his trumpet till silenced for ever upon
one of the bloody battle-fields of Spain' (p. 377).

It is a note which signifies not only heroic martial deeds. There
is also a sense in the novel of the invasion of ordinary lives, an
unsettlement of the agricultural round, by forces of change dra-
matically embodied in the arrival of royalty at Budmouth. The
everyday people at the centre of the action are touched by historical

events, as Anne recognizes when she sees the King walking on the esplanade (p. 152):

> Anne now felt herself close to and looking into the stream of recorded history, within whose banks the littlest things are great, and outside which she and the general bulk of the human race were content to live on as an unreckoned, unheeded superfluity.

History, Hardy was to note a few years later, 'is rather a stream than a tree',[2] and it is in the antithetical images of stream and mill that the novel makes its central binary opposition between stability and change. The scrupulous description of Overcombe Mill foregrounds the symbolic role of the mill as a workplace embodying an immemorial agrarian way of life (p. 67):

> Overcombe Mill presented at one end the appearance of a hard-worked house slipping into the river, and at the other of an idle, genteel place, half-cloaked with creepers at this time of the year, and having no visible connection with flour. It had hips instead of gables, giving it a round-shouldered look, four chimneys with no smoke coming out of them, two zigzag cracks in the wall, several open windows, with a looking-glass here and there inside, showing its warped back to the passer-by; snowy dimity curtains waving in the draught; two mill doors, one above the other, the upper enabling a person to step out upon nothing at a height of ten feet from the ground; a gaping arch vomiting the river, and a lean, long-nosed fellow looking out from the mill doorway, who was the hired grinder, except when a bulging fifteen-stone man occupied the same place, namely, the miller himself.

It is significant that both the mill, anthropomorphically described here, and Oxwell Hall are perceived in a state of 'declension'. The emphasis, in the people who 'stood to smoke and consider things', and the cats who 'slept on the clean surfaces' (p. 68), is upon quietism and continuity. This accords with Hardy's reading of history, as revealed in a note of 1884:

> Is not the present quasi-scientific system of writing history mere charlatanism? Events and tendencies are traced as if they were rivers of voluntary activity, and courses reasoned out from the circumstances in which natures, religions, or what-not, have found them-

selves. But are they not in the main the outcome of *passivity* – acted upon by unconscious propensity?[3]

Rustic passivity, massively embodied in Miller Loveday, is jolted and shaken by the arrival of the military; and yet the text simultaneously urges the absorbent powers of the old way of life, as when the cavalrymen cross the threshold of the mill-house, 'the paving of which was worn into a gutter by the ebb and flow of feet that had been going on there ever since Tudor times' (p. 81). Once snugly ensconced in the mill-house, the soldiery are enveloped by an ancient cycle which frames the urgency of the national peril, so that the swarming of the miller's bees, 'the number of his chickens, and the fatness of his pigs, were matters of infinitely greater concern' than military questions (p. 92).

This evocation of the local and customary within the larger cycles of history is typical of the aims and concerns of a time-haunted novelist like Hardy. As Raymond Williams has pointed out, the strategy of the backward glance commonly enabled the nineteenth-century novelist to recreate an illusion of a society which was harmonious and continuous:

> A valuing society, the common condition of a knowable community, belongs ideally in the past. It can be recreated there for a widely ranging moral action. But the real step that has been taken is withdrawal from any full response to an existing society.[4]

The pressures and contradictions of contemporary rural society which inform and energize Hardy's most potent texts in their polyphonic richness are notably absent from *The Trumpet-Major*. Withdrawal into a warlike past paradoxically produces a text of anodyne smoothness. Yet contradictions working against the collusion in an agrarian myth of community are discernible in the texture of the prose at the very point where Hardy evokes the rustic symbolism of the mill. The opening of the second chapter unconsciously reveals, in its tracing of the lineage of the miller, the economic reality beneath the myth (p. 67):

> Miller Loveday was the representative of an ancient family of corn-grinders whose history is lost in the mists of antiquity. His ancestral line was contemporaneous with that of De Ros, Howard,

and De La Zouche; but, owing to some trifling deficiency in the possessions of the house of Loveday, the individual names and intermarriages of its members were not recorded during the Middle Ages, and thus their private lives in any given century were uncertain. But it was known that the family had formed matrimonial alliances with farmers not so very small, and once with a gentleman-tanner, who had for many years purchased after their death the horses of the most aristocratic persons in the county – fiery steeds that earlier in their career had been valued at many hundred guineas.

As George Wotton has observed, this passage is one of those 'nodal points' in Hardy's writing, where 'the unity of allusion to recorded history' and 'the imaginary history of Wessex' coalesce to reveal 'the "real" history of England'. Presence in the historical record, Wotton argues, 'depends on land *ownership*':

> The *apparent* history of England is thus nothing more than the record of the private lives of the large owners of property, a record which conceals the *real* but unwritten history of the Lovedays and the class they represent.[5]

This is not to belittle Hardy's aims in writing *The Trumpet-Major*, though the comparison with another mill-owning family, the Tullivers in *The Mill on the Floss*, may suggest how modest its achievement is in the recreation of an 'unwritten history' of the people. Yet the project of *The Trumpet-Major*, in connecting the Garlands, Lovedays and Derrimans with historical forces, could scarely be of greater significance. Georg Lukács, in analysing the genesis of the historical novel, observed that it was the French Revolution, and the rise and fall of Napoleon, 'which for the first time made history a *mass experience*, and moreover on a European scale'.[6] In effecting 'an extraordinary broadening of horizons', Lukács suggested, the Napoleonic wars brought into being 'the concrete possibilities for men to comprehend their own experience as something historically conditioned, for them to see in history something which deeply affects their daily lives and immediately concerns them'.[7] This is precisely the aim of *The Trumpet-Major*, one of that series of works inhabited, as Hardy wrote in his General Preface of 1912, by 'beings in whose hearts and minds that which is apparently local' is 'really universal'.

But to invoke Lukács is implicitly to call up memories of *War and Peace* and thus to expose with pitiless clarity the narrow range of Hardy's achievement here. In its painstaking documentation *The Trumpet-Major* hovers on the verge of what Lukács characterized as 'a deadening preponderance of antiquarianism'[8] in the historical novel of the later nineteenth century. Certainly the action of the novel does little to endorse Lukács's belief that history is a gradual realization of the full potential of man. The comparison with *War and Peace* is invidious but instructive. What Hazlitt said of Scott might also refer to Hardy's conscientious fact-gathering for the composition of *The Trumpet-Major*: 'Our historical novelist firmly thinks that nothing *is* but what *has* been.'

Nevertheless, though the story was evidently conceived at low pressure, the writer's imagination was fired by the events and traces of the Napoleonic period in Wessex – the door riddled with bullet holes, the hut of the beacon-watchers, the decaying pikes, and the ridges of the encampment to which he refers in the Preface – and by that less tangible record available to the novelist through 'oral relation' (p. 58). The difficulty in such writing, as the Preface acknowledges, is 'to construct a coherent narrative of past times' out of such 'fragmentary information' (p. 57). Much of the interest of *The Trumpet-Major* derives from Hardy's shaping of these miscellaneous materials into a narrative for his magazine audience.

In his examination of the processes of the nineteenth-century historical imagination, *Metahistory*, Hayden White offers some illuminating comments upon the relations of fictional narrative to historical source material. White designates chronicle and story as 'primitive elements' in the historical account. The arrangement of material entailed by a narrative such as Hardy's represents a 'process of selection and arrangement of data from the *unprocessed historical record* in the interest of rendering that record more comprehensible to an *audience* of a particular kind'.[9] Story is structured, White argues, in terms of inaugural, transitional and terminating motifs, and historical studies thus trace 'the sequence of events that lead from inaugurations to (provisional) terminations of social and cultural processes'.[10] A novel like *The Trumpet-Major* consists of a conjunction of real and imagined events arranged in some kind of hierarchy of significance, and its tone and structure conform to White's definition of comedy. In comedy, he argues, 'hope is held out for the temporary triumph of man over his world by the prospect of occasional *reconciliations* of the forces at play', and these reconciliations are 'symbolized in the festive occasions' which terminate 'dramatic accounts of change and transformation'.[11] Thus the marriages of Miller Loveday and Mrs Garland and Festus and Matilda, the victory of Trafalgar, the final coming together of Anne and Bob, and Anne's inheritance of the miser's wealth and property effectively limit and terminate the destabilizing effects of the invasion threat. At the same time, White justly insists upon the way comedy allows for the emergence of 'new forces or conditions out of processes that appear at a glance to be changeless in their essence'.[12] Beneath the placid surface of Wessex life there is radical unsettlement, a dynamic of change symbolized by the arrival of the soldiery and royalty, but also signalled by the status changes suffered or enjoyed by the protagonists. Thus Mrs Garland falls socially by her second marriage, whilst the miller paradoxically gains respectability; Anne, having fallen through her mother's alliance and her own connection with Bob, rises through her unexpected inheritance to a position of wealth and power; Matilda escapes from the low status and nomadic life of the actress through her liaison with Festus, whilst the latter falls through the demise of his large expectations. Wessex is shot through with change, just as Budmouth is transformed from its status as a modest resort by the arrival of the royal family.

As White sees it, historical explanation may be categorized in a variety of paradigms, and his definition of the 'organicist' model is of some relevance to *The Trumpet-Major*. An organicist reading of history arises out of a 'desire to see individual entities as components or processes which aggregate into wholes that are greater than, or qualitatively different from, the sum of their parts'. Thus the Dorset of the Napoleonic era may be characterized as an 'integrated entity whose importance is greater than that of any individual entities analysed or described in the course of the narrative'.[13]

Narrative implies continuity, and continuity implies memory. As a novel founded in familial and communal memories of a great crisis, *The Trumpet-Major* celebrates the potency of memory and expresses that potency in its warmly idyllic tone of voice. Yet communal memory and the immediacy of oral transmission appear to be curiously threatened in the novel. There is a remarkable degree of emphasis here upon the written record which is insidiously replacing speech. Anne's readings of the newspaper to Uncle Benjy, and the reliance upon letters and newspapers at the mill as guarantors of truth and reality, attest to a subtle shift in this society from speech to writing, from presence to absence, plenitude to emptiness. Language here, as elsewhere in the Wessex novels, is losing its dialectal vitality and substance as it becomes increasingly embalmed in the formality of script. It is no accident that the central relationships for Anne Garland, those with John and Bob Loveday, are marked by prolonged periods of absence and silence, or that the overwhelming presence in the novel is that of the absent Napoleon. A movement in the community from speech to writing prefigures an alienation of relationship which Hardy will finally dissect in the highly literary text of *Jude the Obscure*. The easygoing virtues of *The Trumpet-Major* as a novel which mutedly celebrates love, patriotism and traditional life conceal underlying dissonances which lurk beneath the text.

History, Michel Foucault has written, 'is that which transforms *documents* into *monuments*'.[14] Hardy, in his careful preparation for the novel, consciously sought such a transformation. Covertly, the text also seeks to aggrandize the Hardys and their place in Dorset history by claiming kinship with Captain Hardy, whose physical monument dominated the south-west of the county. The documents consulted at the British Museum provided foundations for the novelist's sly erection of his own familial monument, a monument built out of the primacy of writing over an older oral culture whose disappearance it records. Beneath the smoothly homogeneous discourse of *The Trumpet-Major* may be discerned other discourses: the novel operates like history in transforming and suppressing its own sources. As Foucault remarks, history can 'lend speech to those traces which, in themselves, are often not verbal, or which say in silence something other than what they actually say'.[15] The writer's imagination, exercising mastery over the historical material, utilizes that material to assert and validate its own existence. The narrative background of *The Trumpet-Major* fascinates its creator as part of his own prehistory. Foucault has argued that the writing of history is 'the indispensable correlative of the founding function of the subject'.[16] The mastery evinced by the narrative voice in the novel, with its grasp of wide historical movements, its foreknowledge of the course of individual lives, and its sure command of uncertainties, endorses Foucault's claim as to the underlying project of the historical writer:

> . . . the guarantee that everything that has eluded him may be restored to him; the certainty that time will disperse nothing without restoring it in a reconstituted unity; the promise that one day the subject – in the form of historical consciousness – will once again be able to appropriate . . . all those things that are kept at a distance by difference, and find in them what might be called his abode.[17]

The relationship of a fictional narrative like *The Trumpet-Major* to its historical sources is a complex matter of continuous reinterpretation and 'creative misprision'.

In the midst of history, yet marginal to it, the novelist places his love story. But, dwarfed and drained of significance by the Napoleonic manoeuvres around them, the protagonists of *The Trumpet-Major* are pallid and uninvolved, as if the novelist's eye is fascinatedly held upon the 'shining surfaces' observed by the veteran of Waterloo. As characters the people are all surface. The ill-fated passions of previous novels have here dwindled into timidity and self-interest, the riddling metaphoric richness of earlier texts thinned out to produce a carefully controlled and processed story. Hardy turns the plot upon his favourite motif of a woman pursued by a number of men, but the resultant drama of mismatching is tepid and manufactured, the heroine constrained to exist silently in a world dominated and preserved by the male implements of sword and pen. Anne Garland is an absent centre, and her suitors exert little power over heroine or reader. The trumpet-major himself functions through repression and self-abnegation to such a degree that the heroism upon which the narrator insists begins to feel psychotic. The extrovert Bob Loveday, by contrast, vacillates between a range of unsuitable partners in an arbitrary manner suggested by exigencies of plot rather than character. The third suitor, Festus Derriman, never rises above his origins as *miles gloriosus*, and his fate is wholly predictable. The textual effect of these machinations is a curious emptiness of characterization, as if the narrator has hidden the key to the characters' actions as stealthily as the old miser hides his guineas.

Hardy's deepest imaginative investment is in the conjuring up of the invasion scare, but the novel does bear traces of characteristic effects and devices in its handling of relationships. The characters of *The Trumpet-Major* are at once transparently simple and bafflingly opaque, and the situations into which they are thrown by the narrative gain in resonance through the prevalent notion of perception as the generating principle of relationship. Anne Garland, significantly deprived of a protective father and provided with a girlishly irresponsible mother, is, in the originating moment of the novel, sitting at a window of the mill-house working at a hearth-rug. Looking out from the open casement towards the mill-pond and the bare downland beyond, the heroine is surprised by the sudden arrival of two cavalry soldiers, followed by 'a whole column of cavalry in marching order' (p. 62), arriving, as soon becomes clear, to camp on the downs. This crucial scenario, with the isolated heroine looking outwards from her casement upon the soldiery beyond, will be repeated later in her observation of the 'panoramic procession' of the troops wheeling off on parade (p. 76). It is a moment which inscribes the status and role of the heroine as a girl deprived of 'thriving male relatives' (p. 113), simultaneously drawn towards, and withdrawing ' "prim and stiff" ' (p. 77) from, the events outside. Anne Garland, like other Hardy heroines, conforms to a kind of Lady of Shalott syndrome. The soldiers attract the passive female observer through colourful display, a change at the manuscript stage emphasizing the 'burnished chains, buckles, and plates' which 'shone like little looking-glasses', accoutrements reflecting 'the sun through the haze' (as Hardy visualized Waterloo), 'in faint flashes, stars, and streaks of light' (p. 62–3). Tennyson's heroine, similarly circumstanced, abandons her weaving to observe the glinting surfaces of Sir Lancelot's equipage:

> All in the blue unclouded weather
> Thick-jewell'd shone the saddle-leather,
> The helmet and the helmet-feather
> Burn'd like one burning flame together,
> As he rode down to Camelot.

Analysis of the recurrent Lady of Shalott situation in Victorian fiction has usefully identified a number of motifs associated with Anne Garland's posture at the opening of the novel. It is suggested that the heroine in this situation is commonly imprisoned 'in the midst of an expansive landscape that sustains a working community'.[18] It is a state of entrapment which may be characterized as one of 'self-enclosed gentility', imposed as much 'by the values ascribed' to the heroine as 'by the deprivations of a diminished life'.[19] There is a dramatic division, therefore, between the glamorized exterior world of male energy and the withdrawn inner space of an onlooking female passivity. The warlike sphere of masculine endeavour (parodied and thus endorsed by Festus Derriman) allows for the changefulness and instability emblematized in the weathercock which displays the figure of a soldier (John Loveday) transformed into the figure of a sailor (Bob Loveday). Indeed, the 'variable currents in the wind' (p. 68) aptly characterize the motivation both of 'that weathercock, Master Bob' (p. 343), and of the comically volcanic Festus. In the world of *The Trumpet-Major*, 'greedy carnivorous man' (p. 69) predominates, and this domination, desire and mastery are expressed through sight.

Hardy once observed that 'Love lives on propinquity, but dies of contact',[20] and the sexual chess-games of *The Trumpet-Major* are predicated upon this notion. Hillis Miller has drawn attention to the way, in Hardy, that the 'direct encounter, eye to eye in open reciprocity, is often only the final stage before sexual possession in a drama of looks which begins with some form of spying or the look unreturned'.[21] The plot turns upon misalliances founded in perception. As Hillis Miller remarks, 'Once the situation of desire has been established, often a tangled one involving a criss-cross of mismatching loves, the form of each novel is determined by the development of these loves.'[22] Desire is mediated through the glance, and as Hillis Miller's analysis indicates, the pattern of courtship in Hardy is often of the kind of approach and withdrawal which typifies Bob's behaviour.

Looking, seeing and being seen, and spying predominate as modes of relationship in *The Trumpet-Major*. Anne, protected by her casement, is alarmed to see Festus Derriman standing below in the mill-pond. Knocking on her lattice with his whip, he 'looked up, and their eyes met' (p. 118). He then strikes another blow against her window. The impatient suggestion of attempted penetration here is characteristic and is one which the story unconsciously mobilizes later. The scene is further complicated in its 'conjunction of incidents' by John Loveday's astounded sighting of Festus beneath Anne's window. Such erotic conjunctions have been prepared in the previous scene when Anne, reading the newspaper to Squire Derriman, becomes conscious of 'the bothering yeoman's eyes . . . creeping over her shoulders, up to her head, and across her arms and hands' (p. 114). Later in the novel the trumpet-major himself is voyeuristically to watch in the darkness as Anne enters her bedroom and closes her casement (p. 211). The final turn of events is engineered through a reversal in which the female secretly watches the 'pretty spectacle' of Bob Loveday ludicrously parading in full uniform in the garden (p. 362), a scene whose sexual implications feebly echo Troy's sword-play before Bathsheba. Bob, indeed, as an able-bodied seaman comes to feel entrapped into this dalliance: the ' "pleasure of sighting that young girl forty times a day, and letting her sight me" ', he feels, is little compensation for his absence from the male world of ships and action (p. 305). ' "Womankind has hampered me" ', he explains to Captain Hardy (p. 312), an explanation which both captain and novel endorse.

Elsewhere, images of sight also serve to dramatize the enforced passivity of the hidden female, as when Anne is constrained to watch the village flirtations from her window (p. 129). Even the dynamic Matilda Johnson is secretly observed by the trumpet-major, 'standing before the looking-glass, apparently lost in thought' (p. 189), her witty self-preservation evaporating at the news of his knowledge of her compromised past. The sense of complication, and of the acquisition of secret power and knowledge, is communicated in various scenes of spying, or in a network of reciprocal glances. John Loveday, having boxed Festus's ears to avenge the insult to Anne, is then humiliatingly forced to hide in the granary whilst below Bob and Anne exchange endearments (p. 274). Later, Anne will watch the feints and counterfeints of Festus and Uncle Benjy through a knot-hole in the floor of the mill-house (p. 274). But the most complex web of erotic contingency is traced in the theatre scene. Here, Bob and Anne, believing John to be in love with an actress, watch his face for signs of emotion. A 'deadlock of awkward suspense' occurs when Matilda Johnson appears on stage and sights both her former fiancé and the trumpet-major in the audience (p. 286). The scene is handled lightly for its comic potential, but it serves to concentrate and highlight the predominance of sight as the defining metaphor for sexuality, passivity and domination in *The Trumpet-Major*.

The paradoxical construction of meanings in the novel through this shifting drama of eye, glance and gaze may be more fully explored by reference to the theory of 'scopic drive' propounded by Jacques Lacan.[23] Lacan bases his theory of the constitution of the person or subject in desire upon the act of seeing. Through the gaze, the subject maintains and establishes himself 'in a function of desire'. The gaze is the 'underside of consciousness', and in the gaze of the male (John Loveday, Bob Loveday, Festus Derriman) through Anne Garland's casement window *The Trumpet-Major* metaphorically enacts a phallic penetration. The unconscious flow of desire in looking, Lacan asserts, causes a *méconnaissance* or mistaken seeing in the perceiving subject, since every act of visualization is founded in a conflictual play of repression of the unconscious, a dialectic of desire and lack, presence and absence. The kind of display in which the uniformed Bob Loveday indulges in the garden below Anne's window acts out the way, in Lacanian theory, the exhibitionist seeks through his behaviour the confirmation of his desire in the imagined desire of the other. Similarly, the voyeurism which marks this and other Hardy novels formulates and emphasizes desire as looking. Speaking of the gaze of the lover, Lacan asserts, 'You never look at me from the place from which I see you.' The lover thus narcissistically projects the desire of the other as completion of his own incompleteness. Reality, in

Lacan as in Hardy, does not correspond to wish: 'What I look at is never what I wish to see.' Absence and difference are at the heart of such transactions, just as the meaning of the plot of *The Trumpet-Major* is founded in the absence of lover or invader. Feminist responses to Lacan, stressing the way in which the male eye objectifies and masters what it sees, are also germane to the patriarchal world of *The Trumpet-Major*. The female looking out on to the world as subject at the opening is rapidly transformed through plot into an object of the excited male gaze. The female body, set in a carefully eroticized topography of (female) mill-pond and (male) downland, is transmuted into a fetish which is stared at voyeuristically by the controlling male with his weaponry.

The female is thus equated with passivity and lack, an equation which the narrative endorses in the erased presence of Anne as heroine. By positing a series of binary oppositions – male/female, war/peace, active/passive – the novel is able to define the female as a negative opposite to the male, a figure characterized by acquiescence and invisibility. In Matilda Johnson the novel displaces, focuses and revives Anne Garland's censored sexuality with revealing ambiguity. Matilda is a free-wheeling opportunist whose role-playing wit and energy threaten male power and the patriarchal values of the plot. She acts as the silent Anne's *alter ego*, but is placed judgementally through the stern moralism of John Loveday and casually paired off with Festus Derriman. Having disposed of the threat posed by Matilda's openly declared sexuality and freedom, the brothers collude over the disposal of Anne, passing the girl between them like a parcel of goods. As D. H. Lawrence remarked, the women Hardy's plots approve 'are not Female in any real sense', but are rather 'passive subjects to the male', whilst 'all exceptional or strong individual traits he holds up as weaknesses or wicked faults'.[24]

*The Trumpet-Major* is a text marked by a timidity and censorship produced jointly by the low pressure of the writer's imagination and the proprieties of magazine publication. The contingency of history spells death to the erotic. But at one critical juncture this textual self-effacement collapses to allow a dissonant scene which erupts disturbingly into the rural idyll. Festus Derriman's 'uncontrollable affection' (p. 226) is typically blocked by the heroine, as when she converses with him from behind the hedge (p. 203). But this blocking stratagem fails her at the crisis. The scene where, locked in the deserted house, the heroine is threatened by the enraged Festus Derriman takes the form of a covert rape scene which enacts the secret desires of the text in its bafflement with the passivity of its heroine. Festus is 'brimful of suppressed passion' (p. 265), a passion inflamed by the docility of his quarry. The fascinated but inconclusive scrutinies or earlier window scenes give way to a direct confrontation which unbalances the neutral narrative voice and destroys the equilibrium achieved elsewhere through the seeping away of energy and passion from the text. Anne's characteristic reaction of barricading herself from the proffered transaction, and her vacillation about accepting Festus's attentions, serve only to arouse and inflame. Derriman seeks to penetrate the inner space of the house in order to enact those desires which the book as a whole muffles and distorts. What is repressed in the narrative returns here with a vengeance. In Derriman's final desperate act the text, radically unaware of its own gesture, unites wished-for phallic penetration with unconsciously feared castration (p. 264):

> . . . peeping over the window-sill, she saw her tormentor drive his sword between the joints of the shutters, in an attempt to rip them open. The sword snapped off in his hand. With an imprecation he pulled out the piece, and returned the two halves to the scabbard.

It is a revealing moment, the secret signification of the pervasive imagery of weapons and war momentarily leaping out of hiding in the text's unavowed fascination with violence. The bragging Volunteer seeks to penetrate the heroine just as the absently threatening figure of the 'Corsican Ogre' seeks, through his armies, to penetrate the English defences.

Anne escapes, as plot and readership demand, and Hardy disentangles the love imbroglio with a burst of 'patriotic cheerfulness' (p. 313).[25] With the introduction of Captain Hardy, and Bob's subsequent departure on board the *Victory*, Hardy invokes national myth as plot resolution, just as Tennyson had done in 'Maud' and 'Locksley Hall'. From the nicely observed realities of mill life, the novel turns towards a world of naval derring-do owing little to historical reality. *The Trumpet-Major* feeds upon and sustains a potently shared communal myth to fake the direct energy and passion it so patently lacks.

The keynote of *The Trumpet-Major* is absence: Anne's dead father, Squire Derriman's fortune, Bob Loveday, the trumpet-major, all are made significant through absence. Over the entire narrative broods the absent Napoleon, expected at every moment, like Godot, but destined never to appear. Hardy's art thrives upon postponement, bafflement, absence, to the extent that the principle of deferral becomes the structural law of the novel: deferral of military action ramifies into deferral of erotic action, and both embody a society and a text remarkably addicted to deferral of meaning. History, in the novelist's homespun philosophical scheme, was driven forward by the Immanent Will. Yet the salient point about this brooding Will, as Hillis Miller has recognized, is its very immanence:

> It is visible only at a distance from itself, in the signs or traces of it, for example in Hardy's writings. Its coming to consciousness exists only within the images of his work. Its actual coming to consciousness is always deferred. The Will is the principle of distance, its writing always signs of itself, not its real self.[26]

*The Trumpet-Major*, in its repression of conflict and contradiction and its determined effacement of the female, is a Barthesian 'prattling text' which appears impervious to interpretation. Its undeniable strengths and beauties derive from its intimate relationship with a felt and recorded historical context. The novel grew almost somnambulistically out of tap-roots deep in Wessex folk consciousness and family memory. In this story, with its curiously hypnotic blend of warlike activity and erotic passivity, Hardy mobilizes the past in service of his own myth. The narrator fascinatedly controls, and is controlled by, his story, so that the final sense the reader is left with is of a history which writes (and reads) itself.

## COMPOSITION AND PUBLICATION

Hardy began making notes for *The Trumpet-Major* in the British Museum between May 1878 and November 1879. He and his wife were then living in London. By February 1879, when he visited Portland and Weymouth to obtain local colour, Hardy had planned out the action sufficiently to send a résumé of the plot to Leslie Stephen, editor of the *Cornhill Magazine*. Stephen was unable to consider the story at that time and Hardy was compelled to look elsewhere. In May he appears to have sent part of the manuscript to Macmillan with the idea of serialization in *Macmillan's Magazine*, and early the following month John Blackwood was offered 'a cheerful story, without views or opinions'. At the end of June 1879 Hardy finally arranged for his new novel to appear in the Edinburgh magazine *Good Words*. The editor of this journal, the Rev. Donald MacLeod, instructed the novelist that his story should be 'free at once from *Goody-goodyism* – and from anything – direct or indirect – which a healthy *Parson* like myself would not care to read to his bairns at the fireside'. By early August Hardy was working regularly on the narrative. In 1925, when Sydney Smith was seeking reminiscences for his biography of MacLeod, Hardy wrote: 'If I remember my arrangements with him were carried on through Mr Isbister the publisher, though I met Dr MacLeod whenever he came to London and discussed small points with him.' By the beginning of September 1879 the first fourteen chapters were in proof and the manuscript of Chapters XV to XXI almost completed. A few weeks later Hardy supplied the illustrator, John Collier, with sketches of military and domestic details, and at the end of November the novelist made some further investigations at the British Museum. It would seem that the novel was virtually finished before the first episode appeared in December, in the issue of *Good Words* for January 1880, a luxury which Hardy had not always enjoyed. The serial was accompanied by thirty-two illustrations by John Collier in which Hardy took a keen interest.

*The Trumpet-Major* ran in *Good Words* from January to December 1880. The monthly instalments ran as follows: Chapters I to IV, January; Chapters V to VII, February; Chapters VIII to X, March; Chapters XI to XIV, April; Chapters XV to XVII, May; Chapters XVIII to XXI, June; Chapters XXII to XXIV, July; Chapters XXV to XXVII, August; Chapters XXVIII to XXX, September; Chapters XXXI to XXXIV (part), October; Chapters XXXIV (continued) to XXXVII, November; Chapters XXXVIII to XLI, December. The novel was also published serially in the New York journal *Demorest's Monthly Magazine* from January 1880 to January 1881. In July 1880, as episode seven was appearing in *Good Words*, Smith, Elder and Co. agreed to publish a three-volume edition for which the author was to be paid £200. The first book edition of 1,000 copies appeared on 26 October 1880 with a cover design by the author showing the military camp and the mill connected by a winding path. It retailed at 31s 6d. The novel was subsequently published in book form in the USA in December 1880 by Henry Holt & Co. Three further editions appeared in Hardy's lifetime: the Osgood, McIlvaine edition of 1895; the Wessex edition of 1912; and the Mellstock edition of 1920, the last two both published by Macmillan. In 1911 Hardy presented the manuscript of the novel to King George V, and it is now housed in the Royal Library, Windsor Castle.

## HISTORICAL SOURCES

In *The Trumpet-Major* Hardy drew upon material whose interest dates back to his own childhood. The novelist's grandfather, the first Thomas Hardy, had acted as a Volunteer in Weymouth during the Napoleonic era, and had later served as a church musician in Stinsford church, where members of the Grey and Pitt families were buried. The same grandfather possessed an old deal box which he had carried on his way to fight Napoleon, as he and his fellow Dorset men assumed, and had compiled a scrapbook of the Weymouth seasons of the period. As a child Hardy had access to people and places affected by the Napoleonic scare in which his grandfather had been marginally involved. The king's summer residence, Gloucester Lodge, stood on the sea-front at Weymouth. It was later converted into an hotel, and nearby a statue of George III was erected in 1810. A little way inland, the White Horse at Preston, begun in 1808, depicted the monarch riding away from his favourite watering-place. Other topographical reminders, such as the footpath made by troopers on Bincombe Hill, still existed when Hardy was an old man. As a boy of eight he had discovered a history of the Napoleonic period in a closet at Bockhampton and, as described in the *Life*, 'these contemporary numbers with their melodramatic prints of serried ranks, crossed bayonets, huge knapsacks, and dead bodies, were the first to set him on the train of ideas that led to *The Trumpet-Major* and *The Dynasts*'.[27] At this time legends about 'Boney' appearing in Dorset in person, and the participation of the figure of the 'Corsican Ogre' in puppet-shows, kept the invasion scare alive in folk memory. Perusing Hutchins's *History of Dorset* in search of the family history of the Hardys, the novelist found evidence of his connections with Nelson's Captain Hardy, whose monument had been erected upon Blackdown in 1846, when the writer was a boy. This respectably heroic 'connection' is perhaps the first link between Hardy and the imaginary world of *The Trumpet-Major* and *The Dynasts*.

If the family and local environment served as a repository of Napoleonic memories, it was a reservoir which remained untapped until the late 1870s, when Hardy began to contemplate a work set in the Napoleonic period. This work, issuing first in *The Trumpet-Major* and later in *The Dynasts* (1903–8), was to become an abiding passion, a passion reinforced by Hardy's sense of the uncanny Napoleonic family resemblance he commented upon at Louis Napoleon's funeral at Chislehurst in 1879.[28] The compilation of the '*Trumpet-Major* Notebook', which Hardy undertook at the British Museum between the spring of 1878 and the autumn of 1879, is the clearest indication of the novelist's immersion in recorded detail of the period. That immersion was already becoming evident in the Napoleonic memories with which Grandfer Cantle regales the rustics in *The Return of the Native* (1877–8), the novel which immediately preceded *The Trumpet-Major*.

The '*Trumpet-Major* Notebook', which is now in the Dorset County Museum, comprises three separate gatherings bound together. Here, Hardy may be observed reading newspaper accounts of the period of the invasion scare, notably the *True Briton*, the *Morning Chronicle*, the *Naval Chronicle*, *St James's Chron-*

*icle* and the *Morning Post*. He copied extracts from local histories such as George Bankes's *Story of Corfe Castle* (1853) and James Dallaway's *History of the Western Division of the County of Sussex* (1815–30), and from personal biographies such as George Landmann's *Adventures and Recollections of Colonel Landmann* (1852). In the Notebook Hardy may be discerned noting advertisements for contemporary conveyances, and for styles and fashions of clothing. In pursuit of accuracy for his civilian costumes he consulted such periodicals of the day as the *Gentleman's Magazine*, and his study of military costume led him to the *Soldier's Companion* of 1803. Some of the notes he made at the British Museum are not fully worked up in the subsequent novel. Hardy's interest in contemporary duels, for instance, only appears vestigially in the threats involving John Loveday and Festus Derriman in Chapter XXVIII. Accounts of the hoarding of money during the invasion scare may have fed in to the conception of Uncle Benjy, and the late Mr Garland's career as a painter may have originated in a landscape painter depicted in Dallaway's history of Sussex. Hardy listed many contemporary plays and made copious notes on actors and actresses of the day, and on the regular attendance of the royal family at the Theatre Royal, Weymouth. In the manuscript of the novel the king watches *The Heir-at-Law*, which has become 'one of Colman's' in the novel; another play referred to in the text is *No Song, No Supper* (Chapter XXX), which was first put on at Weymouth in 1805. The descriptions of the royal progress and the review on the downs derive equally clearly from Hardy's habit of note-taking. His careful accounts of the soldiery and their regulations, including the duties, dress and status of a trumpet-major, are based upon such works as the Army Regulations of 1788–93, Instructions and Regulations of the Cavalry, 1799, and the Standing Orders of the Dragoon Guards, 1795. A full analysis of the transformation of this material into fictional terms is given in Edwards's study[29] to which this note is indebted. Some of the salient features of this process of adaptation are summarized below.

## i. The Review

Hardy made notes about six different reviews on the downs above Weymouth from the *Morning Post* and the *Morning Chronicle* for 1804 and 1805. The review in the novel is held on 15 August 1804, though in fact the king did not enter Weymouth until 25 August in that year. Hardy derived various features such as the sham fight, the blocking of the roads, and the arrival of the queen and princesses from various reviews.

## ii. Rumour and Alarm

The alarm registered by various characters – Mrs Garland, Corporal Tullidge, Cripplestraw, Benjamin and Festus Derriman – is discernible in the newspapers of the time. Hardy's notes from the *Morning Chronicle* for the autumn of 1803 read:

> Oct 10, and some weeks following – Enemy expected every moment – Margate people one day expected the expedition had sailed – seeing a large fleet.
> Nov 9. Confidently affirmed that a large body of the enemy has landed on our coasts – and other rumours.
> Nov 14. Ship news, Plymouth. An invasion of the western ports from Brest is deemed probable.

Equally strong fears were voiced in the summer of 1804, when the action of *The Trumpet-Major* begins, and again in 1805. Hardy increased the sense of apprehension from the serial to the first edition by having John Loveday speak of 1500 boats instead of 1000 in the French flotilla. In his account of the English watching Napoleon, and themselves being spied upon, Hardy combined reports of Pitt's visit to Deal in 1803, and a boat sailing close to the port of Boulogne, and the story of a mysterious foreigner who hired a boat to sail into the Channel, both incidents from 1805. In the matter of the lighting of the beacon Hardy also carefully perused his written sources. Signal stations had been established in 1794, but after the breakdown of the Peace of Amiens in 1803 the older fire beacons were once more resorted to. Hardy learnt in Bankes of the beacon at Badbury Rings, near Corfe, and utilized this in his portrayal of Burden and Tullidge, also retaining the oral tradition of the flight to Bere Regis.

### iii. George III at Weymouth

The king first visited Melcombe Regis (later Weymouth) in June 1789, and his summer visitations continued until 1805, when the Duke of Gloucester died. On these occasions the king and his entourage stayed at Gloucester Lodge on the sea-front. Hardy's narrative centres upon the final regal visits of 1804 and 1805. The first part of the novel, where John Loveday fails to gain Anne's favour whilst his father successfully gains the hand of Mrs Loveday, adheres closely to the timetable of the king's stay in Weymouth in 1804, as Hardy learnt about it in contemporary newspapers and in Landmann's memoirs. Whilst in reality the king stayed on in Weymouth until the end of October 1804, in the novel he departs at the end of August with the result that John's enforced absence allows Bob the freedom to approach Anne on his own account. In 1805 the king arrived in Weymouth on 13 July, and Hardy took John's description of the royal entry from the *Morning Post* for 16 July of that year. Bob and Anne share in the general excitement, and watch the king land after a sea-cruise, an activity whose popularity with the king is attested by Landmann. Captain Hardy's visit to George III was historically based upon an account in the *Morning Chronicle* for 5 September 1805. Likewise, the king's fondness for the theatre at Weymouth was well attested in the public prints which Hardy studied. Although there was no factual basis for the interruption of the play with news of Calder's action against Villeneuve in Chapter XXX, there was a tradition that the victory of the Battle of the Nile in October 1798 had been announced from the stage of the Weymouth theatre.

### iv. Nelson and Trafalgar

Hardy was at pains to adhere to exact chronology in recounting the sailing of the *Victory* and the reception of the news of Trafalgar at home. Bob Loveday leaves home on 4 September, the morning after his visit to Captain Hardy. A short time later John arrives with the news that the Captain has left his home at Portisham, and a letter is received from Bob stating that the ship will leave Portsmouth in two days' time. Hardy took this timing from the *Morning Chronicle* for 16 and 17 September 1805. Anne's telescopic view of the *Victory* from Portland Bill, and the old mariner's disquisition on the course of the fleet, were also firmly based upon the *Morning Chronicle* account.

### v. Military Procedure

The novel presents an imaginative synthesis of a wide range of prosaic army manuals in its realization of the procedures of the period in question. Hardy, for instance, copied out the duties and dress of a trumpet-major from the Standing Orders of Queen's Dragoon Guards, which explain that the trumpet-major ranks as a sergeant, and earns an extra allowance of six guineas per annum in regard to his disciplinary duties. The novel is painstaking in its approach to military matters, as it is in the account of the operations of the press-gang which Hardy likewise composed from a variety of contemporary evidence.

In addition to the sources drawn upon from the Notebook, the novel is also indebted to other written materials. Indeed, as Hardy later told William Archer, few of the novels were 'so closely founded in fact' as *The Trumpet-Major*. Thackeray's *The Four Georges* (1862) furnished a few details of George III, and Southey's *Life of Nelson* (1813) described Nelson taking his coffin on board the *Victory*, and provided the detail of Captain Hardy's shoe-buckle being shot off. In the *Diary and Letters of Madame d'Arblay* (1842–6), Vol. IV, Hardy seems to have picked up Fanny Burney's account of a visit of the royal family to Weymouth in 1789, and to have noted the description of how a band of musicians played the National Anthem whilst the king emerged from a dip in the sea.

The most problematic use of source-material in *The Trumpet-Major* arose in connection with C. H. Gifford's *History of the Wars Occasioned by the French Revolution* (1817). When *The Trumpet-Major* was published in the United States Hardy was accused of plagiarism. C. P. Jacobs of Indianapolis remarked upon similarities between Hardy's comic drilling scene and similar scenes in Augustus Longstreet's *Georgia Scenes* of 1835. Jacobs communicated this parallel to the New York journal the *Critic*, which published his allegations on 28 January 1882. The charge was repeated in the London *Academy* for the following month. In his 1895 Preface Hardy characteristically prevaricated. He acknowledged his debt to Gifford, but remained evasive as to the provenance of Gifford's own account. As a result the *Critic* for May 1896 returned to the accusation of plagiarism from *Georgia Scenes*. On 4 July 1896 Hardy responded, denying that he had known Longstreet's work, and reiterating that Gifford and the Army Regulations 'were the only printed matter' utilized in the composition of the drilling scene. Despite the fact that Gifford clearly states that his description relates to American army discipline, the matter was allowed to rest there. It seems possible that both Gifford and Longstreet were quoting an anonymous American sketch of 1807 reprinted in John Lambert's *Travel through Lower Canada and the United States, 1806, 1807 & 1808* (1810).

*The Trumpet-Major* also contains one self-plagiarism. The opening of Chapter XXIII, descriptive of the passage of winter into spring, closely resembles Chapter XII of Hardy's first published novel, *Desperate Remedies* (1871). Both passages probably derive from Hardy's first novel, the unpublished 'The Poor Man and the Lady' of 1867–8.

### HISTORICAL BACKGROUND

George III, born in 1738, began his reign in 1760. A year later he married Charlotte, daughter of the Duke of Mecklenburg. After signs of incipient madness in the king, England was ruled by the Prince Regent from 1811 until the king's death in 1820. The crucial ministries involved in the period of the Napoleonic campaigns were those of Pitt, 1783–1801 and 1804–6, and Addington 1801–4.

### Campaigns:

1793    France, already at war with Austria, Prussia and Piedmont, declared war on Britain and Holland, and then on

Spain. In August Admiral Hood captured Toulon.

1793–5   Campaign in the Netherlands. The Duke of York was sent to the Low Countries but was defeated, and in 1794 France reoccupied Brussels. Austria retreated towards the Rhine, and Britain towards Holland. In April 1795 Britain evacuated from Bremen after the French had overrun Holland.

1793–8   Campaign in the West Indies. In November 1793 7,000 men sailed under Grey, but in 1798 the campaign ended with the evacuation of San Domingo.

1797   In February the British fleet under Jervis defeated the Spanish fleet at Cape St Vincent. In October Duncan defeated the Dutch fleet at Camperdown.

1798   In August Nelson defeated the French fleet in the Battle of the Nile.

1799   In August the British army landed in Holland, and the Dutch army surrendered. A Russo-British force under the Duke of York planned an advance which was checked at Bergen-op-Zoom. In October under the Convention of Alkmaar the allies agreed to evacuate.

1801   A campaign against the French in Egypt led to the withdrawal of Napoleon's forces. In April Nelson defeated the Danes at Copenhagen.

1805   In October Nelson defeated a Franco-Spanish fleet at Trafalgar.

1808–14   Peninsular Campaign in Spain.

1815   The deposed Napoleon landed in France and entered Paris in March. He was finally deposed after the Battle of Waterloo in June.

## NOTES

1. F. E. Hardy, *The Life of Thomas Hardy* (Macmillan, 1972), p. 106.
2. ibid., p. 172.
3. ibid., p. 168.
4. Raymond Williams, *The Country and the City* (Chatto and Windus, 1973), p. 180.
5. George Wotton, *Thomas Hardy: Towards a Materialist Criticism* (Gill and Macmillan, 1985), p. 47.

6. George Lukács, *The Historical Novel* (Penguin Books, 1969), p. 20.

7. ibid., pp. 21–2.

8. ibid., p. 294.

9. Hayden White, *Metahistory* (Johns Hopkins University Press, 1973), p. 5.

10. ibid., p. 6.

11. ibid., p. 9.

12. ibid., p. 11.

13. ibid., p. 15.

14. Michel Foucault, *The Archaeology of Knowledge*, transl. A. Sheridan Smith (Tavistock Publications, 1974), p. 7.

15. ibid., p. 7.

16. ibid., p. 12.

17. ibid., p. 12.

18. Jennifer Gribble, *The Lady of Shalott in the Victorian Novel* (Macmillan, 1983), p. 2.

19. ibid., pp. 5, 12.

20. Hardy, op. cit., p. 220.

21. J. Hillis Miller, *Thomas Hardy: Distance and Desire* (Harvard University Press, 1970), p. 120.

22. ibid., pp. 146–7.

23. See especially Jacques Lacan, 'Seminar on "The Purloined Letter" ', *Yale French Studies*, 48 (1972), pp. 39–72, and 'Of the gaze as *Objet petit a*', in *The Four Fundamental Concepts of Psychoanalysis*, transl. A. Sheridan (Hogarth Press, 1977).

24. D. H. Lawrence, *Study of Thomas Hardy and Other Essays*, ed. B. Steele (Cambridge University Press, 1985), pp. 47, 95.

25. A glance at naval history confirms the gap between a jointly produced and consumed national myth and the reality of the naval service. The Draconian discipline enforced through flogging at the yard-arm, the low wages, lack of shore leave, poor victuals and ill-health are all well attested. It was these and other complaints that led to the mutinies at Spithead and the Nore in 1797, a few years prior to the action of the novel. Seen in this context, Bob Loveday's exploits on the *Victory* and later ships take on the aura of a magazine story for boys. The text similarly averts its eyes from the evidence in its treatment of the sexual life of the sailor. Bob excuses his roving eye thus: ' "when you come ashore after having been shut up in a ship for eighteen months, women-folks seem so new and nice that you can't help liking them, one and all in a body" ' (p. 196). The book here slides disingenuously over the real situation. When a ship docked after a long voyage it was common practice for it to be met by boat-loads of

prostitutes, as the 1822 'Statement of Certain Immoral Practices in H.M. Ships' vividly reveals: 'Let those who have never seen a ship of war picture to themselves a very large low room . . . with five hundred men and probably three or four hundred women of the vilest description shut up in it, and giving way to every excess of debauchery that the grossest passions of human nature can lead them to' (see Christopher Lloyd, *The British Seaman*, Collins, 1968). The cultivation of the 'cheerful' myth of naval glory serves to create an imaginary unified national history in the manufacture of which the text exercises a considerable degree of censorship and silence.

26. Hillis Miller, op. cit., p. 268.
27. Hardy, op. cit., pp. 16–17.
28. ibid., p. 128.
29. M. G. Edwards, 'The Making of Hardy's *The Trumpet-Major*' (M.A. thesis, Birmingham, 71967), Chapter 3.

## FURTHER READING

Hardy, Barbara, *Forms of Feeling in Victorian Fiction*, Peter Owen, 1985

Sanders, Andrew, *The Victorian Historical Novel, 1840–1880*, Macmillan, 1979

Taylor, Richard H., *The Neglected Hardy: Thomas Hardy's Lesser Novels*, Macmillan, 1982

White, R. J., *Thomas Hardy and History*, Macmillan, 1974

# A NOTE ON THE TEXT

FIVE versions of the novel are extant: the manuscript, the serial, and the book editions of 1880, 1895 and 1912. The 1920 Mellstock edition took the form of a reprint of the 1912 Wessex edition. The manuscript consists of a first draft overwritten by revisions, some of which have been added in the actual process of composition and others made later for the serial version. There are 306 leaves, with some interleaving; folios 238–51 are missing. At first, as M. G. Edwards observes in his study, it would seem that Hardy 'did not have a carefully worked-out, preconceived plan for his episodes, but sometimes wrote on and on until perhaps he suddenly realized that the chapter was overlong' (op. cit., p. 69). Various stages of composition are deducible in the manuscript: initial ideas immediately superseded; minor and major emendations made later; and some adjustments in pencil which relate to the serial version. The question of the textual emendations is fully discussed in Edwards, pp. 79ff. Some of the more significant changes are outlined below.

## I. CHANGES IN THE MANUSCRIPT

In the early part of the manuscript Anne Garland's father was conceived of as a schoolmaster. Only after Chapter IX was he described as a landscape painter, and as a result the social distinction between the Garlands and the Lovedays pointed up. A first reference to Anne's youthful affair with the younger Loveday was added to the text during the homecoming party, thus serving to arouse the reader's anticipation of later fraternal rivalry. The past history of Uncle Benjy was filled in to prepare the reader more fully for the old man's dislike of his nephew Festus. In the manuscript Festus himself began life as the frivolous-sounding Captain

Delalynde, a character unrelated to the old miser. Generally, the character of Festus Derriman as *miles gloriosus* was greatly amplified during the course of composition. Festus did not at first mistake John Loveday for Bob when challenged at the inn, and it may be that Festus's role as betrayer of Bob to the press-gang was a late addition to the plot. Three major additions to the manuscript were the scene in which Bob prepares a meal for himself before his father returns, the activities prompted by the lighting of the beacon, and the scene in which Matilda and Anne carry the unconscious Bob Loveday into hiding.

### II. THE SERIAL

Minor linguistic changes from the manuscript included a slight diminishing of dialect in favour of standard usage. Old Derriman's social status was improved from farmer to squireen, and Bob Loveday increased in height, age and nautical turns of speech. The Rev. MacLeod's strictures about the readership of *Good Words* led to changes to the manuscript made on the grounds of propriety. Swearing and any hints of blasphemy were excised, and the amatory passages between Bob and Anne, Festus and Anne, and Festus and Matilda were toned down, as was Festus's threatening behaviour towards Anne. Hardy also felt impelled to change Matilda's arrival by coach from Sunday to Monday, and thus to delete Bob's ironic observations of the town on the sabbath. In the manuscript Uncle Benjy's declaration of affection for Anne had been fundamentally serious and he had accordingly left her half his fortune in his will. In the serial a more comic note intruded as the old man replaced his gift of twenty guineas in the box whence they came, 'for safe-keeping'.

### III. FIRST EDITION

For the first book edition of 1880 Hardy continued the process of stylistic polishing. A redundant passage in which Miller Loveday discussed the characters of his two sons with the Garlands was omitted, whilst the dramatic effect of the York Hussars on the girls of Overcombe was emphasized, as was the episode where the ingenuous Mrs Garland looks back at the amorous Festus Derriman. Festus's appearance was more fully fleshed in, and most of the material excised from *Good Words* was now restored to the narrative. The arrival of the aristocracy in Weymouth and its impact upon Anne, which had been fully delineated at the end of Chapter XII in the serial, was now deleted (see note 77). Some specific dates were also omitted in the first edition so as to gain a greater feeling of universality for the story.

## IV. THE 1895 AND 1912 EDITIONS

Hardy added a preface for the Osgood, McIlvaine edition, and undertook minor stylistic changes for both editions. A few grammatical errors were corrected, and the density of dialect usage was increased at some points and diminished at others. The character of Matilda Johnson was more fully limned in and she was made a more dynamic agent within the plot. Perhaps the most significant alteration was the general substitution of actual place-names by the fictional ones which Hardy now attributed to his imaginary kingdom of Wessex.

## V. THE ENDING

In successive versions Hardy can be observed pointing up John Loveday's future so as to anticipate the way his heroic death would counterpoint his failure in love. Whilst the trumpet-major's fate is unclear in the manuscript, subsequent revisions served to increase the tragic shadowing of the end of the novel:

> But alas for that: Of the seven [who] upon whom these wishes were bestowed [three] four were dead men within the five following years, and their bones [laid for ever in a foreign land.] left to moulder in the land of their [exile] campaigns. [MS, f. 305]

> But, alas, for that! Battles and skirmishes, advances and retreats, fevers and fatigues, told hard on Anne's gallant friends in the coming time. Of the seven upon whom these wishes

were bestowed, five were dead within the few following years, and their bones left to moulder in the land of their campaigns. [*Good Words*, 1880, p. 806]

Of the seven upon whom these wishes were bestowed, five, including the trumpet-major, were dead men within the few following years. [1st edn. vol. III, p. 257]

But [you said] I thought you were going to look in again before leaving? she said. [MS, f. 305]

'But I thought you were going to look in again before leaving?' she said. (*Good Words*, 1880, p. 806)

'But I thought you were going to look in again before leaving?' she said gently. (1st edn, vol. III, p. 257)

Anne . . . smiled her reply. Then he . . . (MS, f. 306)

Anne . . . smiled her reply, not knowing the adieu was for evermore. Then he went out of the door . . . (*Good Words*, 1880, pp. 806–7)

Anne . . . smiled her reply, not knowing that the farewell was for ever more. Then, with a tear in his eye he . . . (1st edn, vol. III, p. 258)

. . . he joined his waiting companions-in-arms, and went off to blow his trumpet over the bloody/battle-/fields of Spain. (MS, f. 306)

. . . he joined his waiting companions-in-arms, and went off to blow his trumpet over the bloody battlefields of Spain. (*Good Words*, p. 807)

. . . he joined his waiting companions-in-arms, and went off to blow his trumpet till silenced for ever upon one of the bloody battle-fields of Spain. (1st edn, vol. III, p. 259)

The present edition is based upon the final revised text of the 1912 Wessex edition.

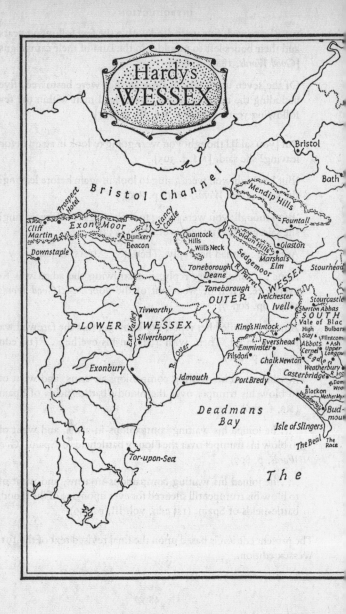

Hardy's WESSEX

Bristol Channel

Bristol

Bath

Mendip Hills

Fountall

Prospect Hotel

Cliff Martin

Exon Moor

Dunkery Beacon

Stancy Castle

Quantock Hills

Will's Neck

Poldon Hills

Glaston

Downstaple

Sedgemoor

R. Parret

Marshal's Elm

Stourhead

Toneborough Deane

WESSEX

Toneborough

OUTER

Ivelchester

Ivell

Stourcastle

Sherton Abbas

SOUTH

Tivworthy

LOWER WESSEX

Exe Valley

Silverthorn

King's Hintock

Vale of Blac

High Stoy

Bulbar

Flintcom

Ash

Upper Longpu

Evershead

Abbots Cernel

Egdo

Emminster

Pilsdon

Chalk Newton

Weatherbury

Exonbury

Otter

Casterbridge

Idmouth

Port Bredy

Blackon

Nether

Budmou

Deadmans Bay

Isle of Slingers

Tor-upon-Sea

The Beal

The Race

The

Fictitious names: Exonbury
Real names: Portsmouth

The Locality of *The Trumpet-Major*

# KEY TO PLACE NAMES

| Hardy's Name | Real Name |
|---|---|
| Abbotsea | Abbotsbury |
| Black'on | Blackdown, near Portisham |
| Budmouth | Weymouth |
| Casterbridge | Dorchester |
| Damer's Wood | Came Wood, south of Dorchester |
| Duddle Hole | Duddle Farm, near Bockhampton |
| Exonbury | Exeter |
| Greenhill | Woodbury Hill, near Bere Regis |
| King's Bere | Bere Regis |
| Longpuddle | The villages of Piddlehinton and Piddletrenthide |
| Mai-Dun Castle | Maiden Castle, near Dorchester |
| Melchester | Salisbury |
| Nether-Moynton | Owermoigne, south-east of Dorchester |
| Overcombe | Sutton Poyntz |
| Oxwell Hall | Poxwell Hall, north of Dorchester |
| Po'sham | Portisham |
| St Aldhelm's Head | St Alban's Head, near Corfe Castle |
| Shottsford Forum | Blandford Forum |
| Springham | Warmwell |

*Note:* In *Hardy's Wessex Re-appraised* Denys Kay-Robinson clears up the confusion surrounding the identity of Overcombe Mill. Although Hardy knew the mill at Upwey, Kay-Robinson argues convincingly that the Loveday mill is 'a largely imaginary creation' which draws upon features of both the upper and lower mills at Sutton Poyntz (pp. 169–70).

# GENERAL PREFACE TO THE
# WESSEX EDITION OF 1912

In accepting a proposal for a definite edition of these productions in prose and verse I have found an opportunity of classifying the novels under heads that show approximately the author's aim, if not his achievement, in each book of the series at the date of its composition. Sometimes the aim was lower than at other times; sometimes, where the intention was primarily high, force of circumstances (among which the chief were the necessities of magazine publication) compelled a modification, great or slight, of the original plan. Of a few, however, of the longer novels, and of many of the shorter tales, it may be assumed that they stand today much as they would have stood if no accidents had obstructed the channel between the writer and the public. That many of them, if any, stand as they would stand if written *now* is not to be supposed.

In the classification of these fictitious chronicles – for which the name of 'The Wessex Novels' was adopted, and is still retained – the first group is called 'Novels of Character and Environment', and contains those which approach most nearly to uninfluenced works; also one or two which, whatever their quality in some few of their episodes, may claim a verisimilitude in general treatment and detail.

The second group is distinguished as 'Romances and Fantasies', a sufficiently descriptive definition. The third class – 'Novels of Ingenuity' – show a not infrequent disregard of the probable in the chain of events, and depend for their interest mainly on the incidents themselves. They might also be characterized as 'Experiments', and were written for the nonce simply; though despite the artificiality of their fable some of their scenes are not without fidelity to life.

It will not be supposed that these differences are distinctly perceptible in every page of every volume. It was inevitable that blendings and alternations should occur in all. Moreover, as it was not thought desirable in every instance to change the arrangement of the shorter stories to which readers have grown accustomed, certain of these may be found under headings to which an acute judgment might deny appropriateness.

It has sometimes been conceived of novels that evolve their action on a circumscribed scene – as do many (though not all) of these – that they cannot be so inclusive in their exhibition of human nature as novels wherein the scenes cover large extents of country, in which events figure amid towns and cities, even wander over the four quarters of the globe. I am not concerned to argue this point further than to suggest that the conception is an untrue one in respect of the elementary passions. But I would state that the geographical limits of the stage here trodden were not absolutely forced upon the writer by circumstances; he forced them upon himself from judgment. I considered that our magnificent heritage from the Greeks in dramatic literature found sufficient room for a large proportion of its action in an extent of their country not much larger than the half-dozen counties here reunited under the old name of Wessex, that the domestic emotions have throbbed in Wessex nooks with as much intensity as in the palaces of Europe, and that, anyhow, there was quite enough human nature in Wessex for one man's literary purpose. So far was I possessed by this idea that I kept within the frontiers when it would have been easier to overlap them and give more cosmopolitan features to the narrative.

Thus, though the people in most of the novels (and in much of the shorter verse) are dwellers in a province bounded on the north by the Thames, on the south by the English Channel, on the east by a line running from Hayling Island to Windsor Forest, and on the west by the Cornish coast, they were meant to be typically and essentially those of any and every place where – 'Thought's the slave of life, and life time's fool'* – beings in whose hearts and minds that which is apparently local should be really universal.

But whatever the success of this intention, and the value of these novels as delineations of humanity, they have at least a humble supplementary quality of which I may be justified in reminding the reader, though it is one that was quite unintentional and unforeseen. At the dates represented in the various narrations things were like that in Wessex: the inhabitants lived in certain ways, engaged in certain occupations, kept alive certain customs, just as they are shown doing in these pages. And in particularizing such I have often been reminded of Boswell's remarks on the trouble to which he was put and the pilgrimages he was obliged to make to authenticate some detail, though the labour was one which would bring him no praise. Unlike his achievement, however, on which an error would as he says have brought discredit, if these country customs and vocations, obsolete and obsolescent, had been detailed wrongly, nobody would have discovered such errors to the end of Time. Yet I have instituted inquiries to correct tricks of memory, and striven against temptations to exaggerate, in order to preserve for my own satisfaction a fairly true record of a vanishing life.

It is advisable also to state here, in response to inquiries from readers interested in landscape, prehistoric antiquities, and especially old English architecture, that the description of these backgrounds has been done from the real – that is to say, has something real for its basis, however illusively treated. Many features of the first two kinds have been given under their existing names; for instance, the Vale of Blackmoor or Blakemore, Hambledon Hill, Bulbarrow, Nettlecombe Tout, Dogbury Hill, High-Stoy, Bubb-Down Hill, The Devil's Kitchen, Cross-in-Hand, Long-Ash Lane, Benvill Lane, Giant's Hill, Crimmercrock Lane, and Stonehenge. The rivers Froom, or Frome, and Stour, are, of course, well known as such. And the further idea was that large towns and points tending to mark the outline of Wessex – such as Bath, Plymouth, The Start, Portland Bill, Southampton, etc. –

* Shakespeare, *Henry IV*, Pt.I, V.iv. 81

should be named clearly. The scheme was not greatly elaborated, but, whatever its value, the names remain still.

In respect of places described under fictitious or ancient names in the novels – for reasons that seemed good at the time of writing them – and kept up in the poems – discerning people have affirmed in print that they clearly recognize the originals: such as Shaftesbury in 'Shaston', Sturminster Newton in 'Stourcastle', Dorchester in 'Casterbridge', Salisbury Plain in 'The Great Plain', Cranborne Chase in 'The Chase', Beaminster in 'Emminster', Bere Regis in 'Kingsbere', Woodbury Hill in 'Greenhill', Wool Bridge in 'Wellbridge', Harfoot or Harput Lane in 'Stagfoot Lane', Hazlebury in 'Nuttlebury', Bridport in 'Port Bredy', Maiden Newton in 'Chalk Newton', a farm near Nettlecombe Tout in 'Flintcomb Ash', Sherborne in 'Sherton Abbas', Milton Abbey in 'Middleton Abbey', Cerne Abbas in 'Abbot's Cernel', Evershot in 'Evershed', Taunton in 'Toneborough', Bournemouth in 'Sandbourne', Winchester in 'Wintoncester', Oxford in 'Christminster', Reading in 'Aldbrickham', Newbury in 'Kennetbridge', Wantage in 'Alfredston', Basingstoke in 'Stoke Barehills', and so on. Subject to the qualifications above given, that no detail is guaranteed – that the portraiture of fictitiously named towns and villages was only suggested by certain real places, and wantonly wanders from inventorial descriptions of them – I do not contradict these keen hunters for the real; I am satisfied with their statements as at least an indication of their interest in the scenes.

Thus much for the novels. Turning now to the verse – to myself the more individual part of my literary fruitage – I would say that, unlike some of the fiction, nothing interfered with the writer's freedom in respect of its form or content. Several of the poems – indeed many – were produced before novel-writing had been thought of as a pursuit; but few saw the light till all the novels had been published. The limited stage to which the majority of the latter confine their exhibitions has not been adhered to here in the same proportion, the dramatic part especially having a very broad theatre of action. It may thus relieve the circumscribed areas treated in the prose, if such relief be needed. To be sure, one might argue that by surveying Europe from a celestial point of vision –

as in *The Dynasts* – that continent becomes virtually a province – a Wessex, an Attica, even a mere garden – and hence is made to conform to the principle of the novels, however far it outmeasures their region. But that may be as it will.

The few volumes filled by the verse cover a producing period of some eighteen years first and last, while the seventeen or more volumes of novels represent correspondingly about four-and-twenty years. One is reminded by this disproportion in time and result how much more concise and quintessential expression becomes when given in rhythmic form than when shaped in the language of prose.

One word on what has been called the present writer's philosophy of life, as exhibited more particularly in this metrical section of his compositions. Positive views on the Whence and the Wherefore of things have never been advanced by this pen as a consistent philosophy. Nor is it likely, indeed, that imaginative writings extending over more than forty years would exhibit a coherent scientific theory of the universe even if it had been attempted – of that universe concerning which Spencer owns to the 'paralysing thought' that possibly there exists no comprehension of it anywhere. But such objectless consistency never has been attempted, and the sentiments in the following pages have been stated truly to be mere impressions of the moment, and not convictions or arguments.

That these impressions have been condemned as 'pessimistic' – as if that were a very wicked adjective – shows a curious muddle-mindedness. It must be obvious that there is a higher characteristic of philosophy than pessimism, or than meliorism, or even than the optimism of these critics – which is truth. Existence is either ordered in a certain way, or it is not so ordered, and conjectures which harmonize best with experience are removed above all comparison with other conjectures which do not so harmonize. So that to say one view is worse than other views without proving it erroneous implies the possibility of a false view being better or more expedient than a true view; and no pragmatic proppings can make that *idolum specus* stand on its feet, for it postulates a prescience denied to humanity.

And there is another consideration. Differing natures find their tongue in the presence of differing spectacles. Some natures become vocal at tragedy, some are made vocal by comedy, and it seems to me that to whichever of these aspects of life a writer's instinct for expression the more readily responds, to that he should allow it to respond. That before a contrasting side of things he remains undemonstrative need not be assumed to mean that he remains unperceiving.

It was my hope to add to these volumes of verse as many more as would make a fairly comprehensive cycle of the whole. I had wished that those in dramatic, ballad, and narrative form should include most of the cardinal situations which occur in social and public life, and those in lyric form a round of emotional experiences of some completeness. But

> The petty done, the undone vast!*

The more written the more seems to remain to be written; and the night cometh. I realize that these hopes and plans, except possibly to the extent of a volume or two, must remain unfulfilled.

*October 1911*                                                          T.H.

* Browning, 'The Last Ride Together', l. 53

*The Trumpet-Major*
*and*
*Robert His Brother*

# PREFACE

THE present tale is founded more largely on testimony – oral and written – than any other in this series. The external incidents which direct its course are mostly an unexaggerated reproduction of the recollections of old persons well known to the author in childhood, but now long dead, who were eye-witnesses of those scenes. If wholly transcribed their recollections would have filled a volume thrice the length of *The Trumpet-Major*.[1]

Down to the middle of this century, and later, there were not wanting, in the neighbourhood of the places more or less clearly indicated herein, casual relics of the circumstances amid which the action moves – our preparations for defence against the threatened invasion of England by Buonaparte. An outhouse door riddled with bullet-holes, which had been extemporized by a solitary man as a target for firelock[2] practice when the landing was hourly expected, a heap of bricks and clods on a beacon-hill, which had formed the chimney and walls of the hut occupied by the beacon-keeper, worm-eaten shafts and iron heads of pikes for the use of those who had no better weapons, ridges on the down thrown up during the encampment, fragments of volunteer uniform, and other such lingering remains, brought to my imagination in early childhood the state of affairs at the date of the war more vividly than volumes of history could have done.

Those who have attempted to construct a coherent narrative of past times from the fragmentary information furnished by survivors, are aware of the difficulty of ascertaining the true sequence of events indiscriminately recalled. For this purpose the newspapers of the date were indispensable. Of other documents consulted I may mention, for the satisfaction of those who love a true story, that the 'Address to all Ranks and Descriptions of

Englishmen' was transcribed from an original copy in a local museum; that the hieroglyphic portrait of Napoleon existed as a print down to the present day in an old woman's cottage near 'Overcombe'; that the particulars of the King's doings at his favourite watering-place were augmented by details from records of the time. The drilling scene of the local militia received some additions from an account given in so grave a work as Gifford's *History of the Wars of the French Revolution* (London, 1817). But on reference to the History I find I was mistaken in supposing the account to be advanced as authentic, or to refer to rural England. However, it does in a large degree accord with the local traditions of such scenes that I have heard recounted, times without number, and the system of drill was tested by reference to the Army Regulations of 1801, and other military handbooks. Almost the whole narrative of the supposed landing of the French in the Bay is from oral relation as aforesaid. Other proofs of the veracity of this chronicle have escaped my recollection.

*October 1895*                                                T.H.

# * I *

## What was Seen from the Window Overlooking the Down

IN the days of high-waisted and muslin-gowned women, when the vast amount of soldiering going on in the country was a cause of much trembling to the sex, there lived in a village near the Wessex coast two ladies of good report, though unfortunately of limited means. The elder was a Mrs Martha Garland, a landscape-painter's widow, and the other was her only daughter Anne.

Anne was fair, very fair, in a poetical sense; but in complexion she was of that particular tint between blonde and brunette which is inconveniently left without a name. Her eyes were honest and inquiring, her mouth cleanly cut and yet not classical, the middle point of her upper lip scarcely descending so far as it should have done by rights, so that at the merest pleasant thought, not to mention a smile, portions of two or three white teeth were uncovered whether she would or not. Some people said that this was very attractive. She was graceful and slender, and, though but little above five feet in height, could draw herself up to look tall. In her manner, in her comings and goings, in her 'I'll do this,' or 'I'll do that,' she combined dignity with sweetness as no other girl could do; and any impressionable stranger youths who passed by were led to yearn for a windfall of speech from her, and to see at the same time that they would not get it. In short, beneath all that was charming and simple in this young woman there lurked a real firmness, unperceived at first, as the speck of colour lurks unperceived in the heart of the palest parsley flower.

She wore a white handkerchief to cover her white neck, and a cap on her head with a pink ribbon round it, tied in a bow at the front. She had a great variety of these cap-ribbons, the young men being fond of sending them to her as presents until they fell definitely in love with a special sweetheart elsewhere, when they left off doing so. Between the border of her cap and her forehead were ranged a row of round brown curls, like swallows' nests under eaves.

She lived with her widowed mother in a portion of an ancient building formerly a manor-house, but now a mill, which, being too large for his own requirements, the miller had found it convenient to divide and appropriate in part to these highly respectable tenants. In this dwelling Mrs Garland's and Anne's ears were soothed morning, noon, and night by the music of the mill, the wheels and cogs of which, being of wood, produced notes that might have borne in their minds a remote resemblance to the wooden tones of the stopped diapason[3] in an organ. Occasionally, when the miller was bolting,[4] there was added to these continuous sounds the cheerful clicking of the hopper,[5] which did not deprive them of rest except when it was kept going all night; and over and above all this they had the pleasure of knowing that there crept in through every crevice, door, and window of their dwelling, however tightly closed, a subtle mist of superfine flour from the grinding-room, quite invisible, but making its presence known in the course of time by giving a pallid and ghostly look to the best furniture. The miller frequently apologized to his tenants for the intrusion of this insidious dry fog; but the widow was of a friendly and thankful nature, and she said that she did not mind it at all, being as it was, not nasty dirt, but the blessed staff of life.

By good-humour of this sort, and in other ways, Mrs Garland acknowledged her friendship for her neighbour, with whom Anne and herself associated to an extent which she never could have anticipated when, tempted by the lowness of the rent, they first removed thither after her husband's death from a larger house at the other end of the village. Those who have lived in remote places where there is what is called no society will comprehend the gradual levelling of distinctions that went on in this case at some sacrifice of gentility on the part of one household. The widow was sometimes sorry to find with what readiness Anne caught up some dialect-word or accent from the miller and his friends; but he was so good and true-hearted a man, and she so easy-minded, unambitious a woman, that she would not make life a solitude for fastidious reasons. More than all, she had good ground for thinking that the miller secretly admired her, and this added a piquancy to the situation.

On a fine summer morning, when the leaves were warm under the sun, and the more industrious bees abroad, diving into every blue and red cup that could possibly be considered a flower, Anne was sitting at the back window of her mother's portion of the house, measuring out lengths of worsted for a fringed rug that she was making, which lay, about three-quarters finished, beside her. The work, though chromatically brilliant, was tedious: a hearth-rug was a thing which nobody worked at from morning to night; it was taken up and put down; it was in the chair, on the floor, across the hand-rail, under the bed, kicked here, kicked there, rolled away in the closet, brought out again, and so on, more capriciously perhaps than any other home-made article. Nobody was expected to finish a rug within a calculable period, and the wools of the beginning became faded and historical before the end was reached. A sense of this inherent nature of worsted-work rather than idleness led Anne to look rather frequently from the open casement.

Immediately before her was the large, smooth mill-pond, over-full, and intruding into the hedge and into the road. The water, with its flowing leaves and spots of froth, was stealing away, like Time, under the dark arch, to tumble over the great slimy wheel within. On the other side of the mill-pond was an open place called the Cross, because it was three-quarters of one, two lanes and a cattle-drive meeting there. It was the general rendezvous and arena of the surrounding village. Behind this a steep slope rose high into the sky, merging in a wide and open down, now littered with sheep newly shorn. The upland by its height completely sheltered the mill and village from north winds, making summers of springs, reducing winters to autumn temperatures, and permitting myrtle to flourish in the open air.

The heaviness of noon pervaded the scene, and under its influence the sheep had ceased to feed. Nobody was standing at the Cross, the few inhabitants being indoors at their dinner. No human being was on the down, and no human eye or interest but

Anne's seemed to be concerned with it. The bees still worked on, and the butterflies did not rest from roving, their smallness seeming to shield them from the stagnating effect that this turning moment of day had on larger creatures. Otherwise all was still.

The girl glanced at the down and the sheep for no particular reason; the steep margin of turf and daisies rising above the roofs, chimneys, apple-trees, and church tower of the hamlet around her, bounded the view from her position, and it was necessary to look somewhere when she raised her head. While thus engaged in working and stopping her attention was attracted by the sudden rising and running away of the sheep squatted on the down; and there succeeded sounds of a heavy tramping over the hard sod which the sheep had quitted, the tramp being accompanied by a metallic jingle. Turning her eyes further she beheld two cavalry soldiers on bulky grey chargers, armed and accoutred throughout, ascending the down at a point to the left where the incline was comparatively easy. The burnished chains, buckles, and plates of their trappings shone like little looking-glasses, and the blue, red, and white about them was unsubdued by weather or wear.

The two troopers rode proudly on, as if nothing less than crowns and empires ever concerned their magnificent minds. They reached that part of the down which lay just in front of her, where they came to a halt. In another minute there appeared behind them a group containing some half-dozen more of the same sort. These came on, halted, and dismounted likewise.

Two of the soldiers then walked some distance onward together, when one stood still, the other advancing further, and stretching a white line of tape between them. Two more of the men marched to another outlying point, where they made marks in the ground. Thus they walked about and took distances, obviously according to some preconcerted scheme.

At the end of this systematic proceeding one solitary horseman – a commissioned officer, if his uniform could be judged rightly at that distance – rode up the down, went over the ground, looked at what the others had done, and seemed to think that it was good. And then the girl heard yet louder tramps and clankings, and she beheld rising from where the others had risen a whole column of cavalry in marching order. At a distance behind these came a cloud of dust enveloping more and more troops, their arms and accoutrements reflecting the sun through the haze in faint flashes, stars, and streaks of light. The whole body approached slowly towards the plateau at the top of the down.

Anne threw down her work, and letting her eyes remain on the nearing masses of cavalry, the worsteds getting entangled as they would, said, 'Mother, mother; come here! Here's such a fine sight! What does it mean? What can they be going to do up there?'

The mother thus invoked ran upstairs and came forward to the window. She was a woman of sanguine mouth and eye, unheroic manner, and pleasant general appearance; a little more tarnished as to surface, but not much worse in contour than the girl herself.

Widow Garland's thoughts were those of the period. 'Can it be the French?' she said, arranging herself for the extremest form of consternation. 'Can that arch-enemy of mankind have landed at last?' It should be stated that at this time there were two arch-enemies of mankind – Satan as usual, and Buonaparte, who had sprung up and eclipsed his elder rival altogether. Mrs Garland alluded, of course, to the junior gentleman.

'It cannot be he,' said Anne. 'Ah! there's Simon Burden, the man who watches at the beacon. He'll know!'

She waved her hand to an aged form of the same colour as the road, who had just appeared beyond the mill-pond, and who, though active, was bowed to that degree which almost reproaches a feeling observer for standing upright. The arrival of the soldiery had drawn him out from his drop of drink at the Duke of York as it had attracted Anne. At her call he crossed the mill-bridge, and came towards the window.

Anne inquired of him what it all meant; but Simon Burden, without answering, continued to move on with parted gums, staring at the cavalry on his own private account with a concern that people often show about temporal phenomena when such matters can affect them but a short time longer. 'You'll walk into the mill-pond!' said Anne. 'What are they doing? You were a soldier many years ago, and ought to know.'

'Don't ask me, Mis'ess Anne,' said the military relic, depositing his body against the wall one limb at a time. 'I were only in the foot, ye know, and never had a clear understanding of horses. Ay,

I be a old man, and of no judgement now.' Some additional pressure, however, caused him to search further in his worm-eaten magazine of ideas, and he found that he did know in a dim irresponsible way. The soldiers must have come there to camp: those men they had seen first were the markers: they had come on before the rest to measure out the ground. He who had accompanied them was the quartermaster. 'And so you see they have got all the lines marked out by the time the regiment have come up,' he added. 'And then they will – well-a-deary! who'd ha' supposed that Overcombe would see such a day as this!'

'And then they will –'

'Then – Ah, it's gone from me again!' said Simon. 'O, and then they will raise their tents, you know, and picket their horses.[6] That was it; so it was.'

By this time the column of horse had ascended into full view, and they formed a lively spectacle as they rode along the high ground in marching order, backed by the pale blue sky, and lit by the southerly sun. Their uniform was bright and attractive; white buckskin pantaloons, three-quarter boots, scarlet shakos[7] set off with lace, mustachios waxed to a needle point; and above all, those richly ornamented blue jackets mantled with the historic pelisse[8] – that fascination to women, and encumbrance to the wearers themselves.

' 'Tis the York Hussars!' said Simon Burden, brightening like a dying ember fanned. 'Foreigners to a man, and enrolled long since my time. But as good hearty comrades, they say, as you'll find in the King's service.'

'Here are more and different ones,' said Mrs Garland.

Other troops had, during the last few minutes, been ascending the down at a remoter point, and now drew near. These were of different weight and build from the others; lighter men, in helmet hats, with white plumes.

'I don't know which I like best,' said Anne. 'These, I think, after all.'

Simon, who had been looking hard at the latter, now said that they were the —th Dragoons.

'All Englishmen they,' said the old man. 'They lay at Budmouth barracks a few years ago.'

'They did. I remember it,' said Mrs Garland.

'And lots of the chaps about here 'listed at the time,' said Simon. 'I can call to mind that there was – ah, 'tis gone from me again! However, all that's of little account now.'

The dragoons passed in front of the lookers-on as the others had done, and their gay plumes, which had hung lazily during the ascent, swung to northward as they reached the top, showing that on the summit a fresh breeze blew. 'But look across there,' said Anne. There had entered upon the down from another direction several battalions of foot, in white kerseymere⁹ breeches and cloth gaiters. They seemed to be weary from a long march, the original black of their gaiters and shoes being white-brown with dust. Presently came regimental waggons, and the private canteen carts which followed at the end of a convoy.

The space in front of the mill-pond was now occupied by nearly all the inhabitants of the village, who had turned out in alarm, and remained for pleasure, their eyes lighted up with interest in what they saw; for trappings and regimentals, war horses and men, in towns an attraction, were here almost a sublimity.

The troops filed to their lines, dismounted, and in quick time took off their accoutrements, rolled up their sheep-skins, picketed and unbitted their horses, and made ready to erect the tents as soon as they could be taken from the waggons and brought forward. When this was done, at a given signal the canvases flew up from the sod; and thenceforth every man had a place in which to lay his head.

Though nobody seemed to be looking on but the few at the window and in the village street, there were, as a matter of fact, many eyes converging upon that military arrival in its high and conspicuous position, not to mention the glances of birds and other wild creatures. Men in distant gardens, women in orchards and at cottage-doors, shepherds on remote hills, turnip-hoers in blue-green enclosures miles away, captains with spy-glasses out at sea, were regarding the picture keenly. Those three or four thousand men of one machine-like movement, some of them swashbucklers by nature; others, doubtless, of a quiet shop-keeping disposition who had inadvertently got into uniform – all of them had arrived from nobody knew where, and hence were matter of great curiosity. They seemed to the mere eye to belong to a different order of beings from those who inhabited the valleys below. Apparently unconscious and careless of what all the world was doing elsewhere, they remained picturesquely engrossed in the business of making themselves a habitation on the isolated spot which they had chosen.

Mrs Garland was of a festive and sanguine turn of mind, a woman soon set up and soon set down, and the coming of the regiments quite excited her. She thought there was reason for putting on her best cap, thought that perhaps there was not; that she would hurry on the dinner and go out in the afternoon; then that she would, after all, do nothing unusual, nor show any silly excitements whatever, since they were unbecoming in a mother and a widow. Thus circumscribing her intentions till she was toned down to an ordinary person of forty, Mrs Garland accompanied her daughter downstairs to dine, saying, 'Presently we will call on Miller Loveday, and hear what he thinks of it all.'

# * II *

## Somebody Knocks and Comes In

MILLER Loveday was the representative of an ancient family of corn-grinders whose history is lost in the mists of antiquity. His ancestral line was contemporaneous with that of De Ros, Howard, and De La Zouche; but, owing to some trifling deficiency in the possessions of the house of Loveday, the individual names and intermarriages of its members were not recorded during the Middle Ages, and thus their private lives in any given century were uncertain. But it was known that the family had formed matrimonial alliances with farmers not so very small, and once with a gentleman-tanner, who had for many years purchased after their death the horses of the most aristocratic persons in the county – fiery steeds that earlier in their career had been valued at many hundred guineas.

It was also ascertained that Mr Loveday's great-grandparents had been eight in number, and his great-great-grandparents sixteen, every one of whom reached to years of discretion: at every stage backwards his sires and gammers thus doubled and doubled till they became a vast body of Gothic[10] ladies and gentlemen of the rank known as ceorls or villeins,[11] full of importance to the country at large, and ramifying throughout the unwritten history of England. His immediate father had greatly improved the value of their residence by building a new chimney, and setting up an additional pair of mill-stones.

Overcombe Mill presented at one end the appearance of a hard-worked house slipping into the river, and at the other of an idle, genteel place, half-cloaked with creepers at this time of the year, and having no visible connection with flour. It had hips instead of gables, giving it a round-shouldered look, four chimneys with no smoke coming out of them, two zigzag cracks in the wall, several

67

open windows, with a looking-glass here and there inside, showing its warped back to the passer-by; snowy dimity curtains waving in the draught; two mill doors, one above the other, the upper enabling a person to step out upon nothing at a height of ten feet from the ground; a gaping arch vomiting the river, and a lean, long-nosed fellow looking out from the mill doorway, who was the hired grinder, except when a bulging fifteen-stone man occupied the same place, namely, the miller himself.

Behind the mill door, and invisible to the mere wayfarer who did not visit the family, were chalked addition and subtraction sums, many of them originally done wrong, and the figures half rubbed out and corrected, noughts being turned into nines, and ones into twos. These were the miller's private calculations. There were also chalked in the same place rows and rows of strokes like open palings, representing the calculations of the grinder, who in his youthful ciphering studies had not gone so far as Arabic figures.

In the court in front were two worn-out mill-stones, made useful again by being let in level with the ground. Here people stood to smoke and consider things in muddy weather; and cats slept on the clean surfaces when it was hot. In the large stubbard-tree at the corner of the garden was erected a pole of larch fir, which the miller had bought with others at a sale of small timber in Damer's Wood one Christmas week. It rose from the upper boughs of the tree to about the height of a fisherman's mast, and on the top was a vane in the form of a sailor with his arm stretched out. When the sun shone upon this figure it could be seen that the greater part of his countenance was gone, and the paint washed from his body so far as to reveal that he had been a soldier in red before he became a sailor in blue. The image had, in fact, been John, one of our coming characters, and was then turned into Robert, another of them. This revolving piece of statuary could not, however, be relied on as a vane, owing to the neighbouring hill, which formed variable currents in the wind.

The leafy and quieter wing of the mill-house was the part occupied by Mrs Garland and her daughter, who made up in summer-time for the narrowness of their quarters by overflowing into the garden on stools and chairs. The parlour or dining-room had a stone floor – a fact which the widow sought to disguise by double carpeting, lest the standing of Anne and herself should be lowered in the public eye. Here now the midday meal went lightly and mincingly on, as it does where there is no greedy carnivorous man to keep the dishes about, and was hanging on the close when somebody entered the passage as far as the chink of the parlour door, and tapped. This proceeding was probably adopted to kindly avoid giving trouble to Susan, the neighbour's pink daughter, who helped at Mrs Garland's in the mornings, but was at that moment particularly occupied in standing on the water-butt and gazing at the soldiers, with an inhaling position of the mouth and circular eyes.

There was a flutter in the little dining-room – the sensitiveness of habitual solitude makes hearts beat for preternaturally small reasons – and a guessing as to who the visitor might be. It was some military gentleman from the camp perhaps? No; that was impossible. It was the parson? No; he would not come at dinner-time. It was the well-informed man who travelled with drapery and the best Birmingham earrings? Not at all; his time was not till Thursday at three. Before they could think further the visitor moved forward another step, and the diners got a glimpse of him through the same friendly chink that had afforded him a view of the Garland dinner-table.

'O! it is only Loveday.'

This approximation to nobody was the miller above mentioned, a hale man of fifty-five or sixty – hale all through, as many were in those days, and not merely veneered with purple by exhilarating victuals and drinks, though the latter were not at all despised by him. His face was indeed rather pale than otherwise, for he had just come from the mill. It was capable of immense changes of expression: mobility was its essence, a roll of flesh forming a buttress to his nose on each side, and a deep ravine lying between his lower lip and the tumulus represented by his chin. These fleshy lumps moved stealthily, as if of their own accord, whenever his fancy was tickled.

His eyes having lighted on the table-cloth, plates, and viands, he found himself in a position which had a sensible awkwardness for a modest man who always liked to enter only at seasonable

69

times the presence of a girl of such pleasantly soft ways as Anne Garland, she who could make apples seem like peaches, and throw over her shillings the glamour of guineas when she paid him for flour.

'Dinner is over, neighbour Loveday; please come in,' said the widow, seeing his case. The miller said something about coming in presently; but Anne pressed him to stay, with a tender motion of her lip as it played on the verge of a solicitous smile without quite lapsing into one – her habitual manner when speaking.

Loveday took off his low-crowned hat and advanced. He had not come about pigs or fowls this time. 'You have been looking out, like the rest o' us, no doubt, Mrs Garland, at the mampus[12] of soldiers that have come upon the down? Well, one of the horse regiments is the —th Dragoons, my son John's regiment, you know.'

The announcement, though it interested them, did not create such an effect as the father of John had seemed to anticipate; but Anne, who liked to say pleasant things, replied, 'The dragoons looked nicer than the foot, or the German cavalry either.'

'They are a handsome body of men,' said the miller in a disinterested voice. 'Faith! I didn't know they were coming, though it may be in the newspaper all the time. But old Derriman keeps it so long that we never know things till they be in everybody's mouth.'

This Derriman was a squireen living near, who was chiefly distinguished in the present warlike time by having a nephew in the yeomanry.[13]

'We were told that the yeomanry went along the turnpike road yesterday,' said Anne; 'and they say that they were a pretty sight, and quite soldierly.'

'Ah! well – they be not regulars,' said Miller Loveday, keeping back harsher criticism as uncalled for. But inflamed by the arrival of the dragoons, which had been the exciting cause of his call, his mind would not go to yeomanry. 'John has not been home these five years,' he said.

'And what rank does he hold now?' said the widow.

'He's trumpet-major, ma'am; and a good musician.' The miller, who was a good father, went on to explain that John had seen some service, too. He had enlisted when the regiment was lying in this neighbourhood, more than eleven years before, which put his father out of temper with him, as he had wished him to follow on at the mill. But as the lad had enlisted seriously, and as he had often said that he would be a soldier, the miller had thought that he would let Jack take his chance in the profession of his choice.

Loveday had two sons, and the second was now brought into the conversation by a remark of Anne's that neither of them seemed to care for the miller's business.

'No,' said Loveday in a less buoyant tone. 'Robert, you see, must needs go to sea.'

'He is much younger than his brother?' said Mrs Garland.

About four years, the miller told her. His soldier son was two-and-thirty, and Bob was twenty-eight. When Bob returned from his present voyage, he was to be persuaded to stay and assist as grinder in the mill, and go to sea no more.

'A sailor-miller!' said Anne.

'O, he knows as much about mill business as I do,' said Loveday; 'he was intended for it, you know, like John. But, bless me!' he continued, 'I am before my story. I'm come more particularly to ask you, ma'am, and you, Anne my honey, if you will join me and a few friends at a leetle homely supper that I shall gi'e to please the chap now he's come? I can do no less than have a bit of a randy, as the saying is, now that he's here safe and sound.'

Mrs Garland wanted to catch her daughter's eye; she was in some doubt about her answer. But Anne's eye was not to be caught, for she hated hints, nods, and calculations of any kind in matters which should be regulated by impulse; and the matron replied, 'If so be 'tis possible, we'll be there. You will tell us the day?'

He would, as soon as he had seen son John. ' 'Twill be rather untidy, you know, owing to my having no womenfolks in the house; and my man David is a poor dunder-headed feller for getting up a feast. Poor chap! his sight is bad, that's true, and he's very good at making the beds, and oiling the legs of the chairs and other furniture, or I should have got rid of him years ago.'

'You should have a woman to attend to the house, Loveday,' said the widow.

'Yes, I should, but – Well, 'tis a fine day, neighbours. Hark! I fancy I hear the noise of pots and pans up at the camp, or my ears deceive me. Poor fellows, they must be hungry! Good-day t'ye, ma'am.' And the miller went away.

All that afternoon Overcombe continued in a ferment of interest in the military investment, which brought the excitement of an invasion without the strife. There were great discussions on the merits and appearance of the soldiery. The event opened up to the girls unbounded possibilities of adoring and being adored, and to the young men an embarrassment of dashing acquaintances which quite superseded falling in love. Thirteen of these lads incontinently stated within the space of a quarter of an hour that there was nothing in the world like going for a soldier. The young women stated little, but perhaps thought the more; though, in justice, they glanced round towards the encampment from the corners of their blue and brown eyes in the most demure and modest manner that could be desired.

In the evening the village was lively with soldiers' wives; a tree full of starlings would not have rivalled the chatter that was going on. These ladies were very brilliantly dressed, with more regard for colour than for material. Purple, red, and blue bonnets were numerous, with bunches of cocks' feathers; and one had on an Arcadian hat[14] of green sarcenet,[15] turned up in front to show her cap underneath. It had once belonged to an officer's lady, and was not so much stained, except where the occasional storms of rain, incidental to a military life, had caused the green to run and stagnate in curious watermarks like peninsulas and islands. Some of the prettiest of these butterfly wives had been fortunate enough to get lodgings in the cottages, and were thus spared the necessity of living in huts and tents on the down. Those who had not been so fortunate were not rendered more amiable by the success of their sisters-in-arms, and called them names which brought forth retorts and rejoinders; till the end of these alternative remarks seemed dependent upon the close of the day.

One of these new arrivals, who had a rosy nose and a slight thickness of voice, which, as Anne said, she couldn't help, poor thing, seemed to have seen so much of the world, and to have been in so many campaigns, that Anne would have liked to take her into their own house, so as to acquire some of that practical knowledge of the history of England which the lady possessed, and which could not be got from books. But the narrowness of Mrs Garland's rooms absolutely forbade this, and the houseless treasury of experience was obliged to look for quarters elsewhere.

That night Anne retired early to bed. The events of the day, cheerful as they were in themselves, had been unusual enough to give her a slight headache. Before getting into bed she went to the window, and lifted the white curtains that hung across it. The moon was shining, though not as yet into the valley, but just peeping above the ridge of the down, where the white cones of the encampment were softly touched by its light. The quarter-guard[16] and foremost tents showed themselves prominently; but the body of the camp, the officers' tents, kitchens, canteen, and appurtenances in the rear were blotted out by the ground, because of its height above her. She could discern the forms of one or two sentries moving to and fro across the disc of the moon at intervals. She could hear the frequent shuffling and tossing of the horses tied to the pickets; and in the other direction the miles-long voice of the sea, whispering a louder note at those points of its length where hampered in its ebb and flow by some jutting promontory or group of boulders. Louder sounds suddenly broke this approach to silence; they came from the camp of dragoons, were taken up further to the right by the camp of the Hanoverians,[17] and further on still by the body of infantry. It was tattoo.[18] Feeling no desire to sleep, she listened yet longer, looked at Charles's Wain[19] swinging over the church tower, and the moon ascending higher and higher over the right-hand streets of tents, where, instead of parade and bustle, there was nothing going on but snores and dreams, the tired soldiers lying by this time under their proper canvases, radiating like spokes from the pole of each tent.

At last Anne gave up thinking, and retired like the rest. The night wore on, and, except the occasional 'All's well' of the sentries, no voice was heard in the camp or in the village below.

# * III *

## The Mill Becomes
## an Important Centre of Operations

THE next morning Miss Garland awoke with an impression that something more than usual was going on, and she recognized as soon as she could clearly reason that the proceedings, whatever they might be, lay not far away from her bedroom window. The sounds were chiefly those of pickaxes and shovels. Anne got up, and, lifting the corner of the curtain about an inch, peeped out.

A number of soldiers were busily engaged in making a zigzag path down the incline from the camp to the river-head at the back of the house, and judging from the quantity of work already got through they must have begun very early. Squads of men were working at several equidistant points in the proposed pathway, and by the time that Anne had dressed herself each section of the length had been connected with those above and below it, so that a continuous and easy track was formed from the crest of the down to the bottom of the steep.

The down rested on a bed of solid chalk, and the surface exposed by the roadmakers formed a white ribbon, serpenting from top to bottom.

Then the relays of working soldiers all disappeared; and, not long after, a troop of dragoons in watering order rode forward at the top and began to wind down the new path. They came lower and closer, and at last were immediately beneath her window, gathering themselves up on the space by the mill-pond. A number of the horses entered it at the shallow part, drinking and splashing and tossing about. Perhaps as many as thirty, half of them with riders on their backs, were in the water at one time; the thirsty animals drank, stamped, flounced, and drank again, letting the clear, cool water dribble luxuriously from their mouths. Miller

Loveday was looking on from over his garden hedge, and many admiring villagers were gathered around.

Gazing up higher, Anne saw other troops descending by the new road from the camp, those which had already been to the pond making room for these by withdrawing along the village lane and returning to the top by a circuitous route.

Suddenly the miller exclaimed, as in fulfilment of expectation, 'Ah, John, my boy; good morning!' And the reply of 'Morning, father,' came from a well-mounted soldier near him, who did not, however, form one of the watering party. Anne could not see his face very clearly, but she had no doubt that this was John Loveday.

There were tones in the voice which reminded her of old times, those of her very infancy, when Johnny Loveday had been top boy in the village school, and had wanted to learn painting of her father. The deeps and shallows of the mill-pond being better known to him than to any other man in the camp, he had apparently come down on that account, and was cautioning some of the horsemen against riding too far in towards the mill-head.

Since her childhood and his enlistment Anne had seen him only once, and then but casually, when he was home on a short furlough. His figure was not much changed from what it had been; but the many sunrises and sunsets which had passed since that day, developing her from a comparative child to womanhood, had abstracted some of his angularities, reddened his skin, and given him a foreign look. It was interesting to see what years of training and service had done for this man. Few would have supposed that the white and the blue coats of miller and soldier covered the forms of father and son.

Before the last troop of dragoons rode off they were welcomed in a body by Miller Loveday, who still stood in his outer garden, this being a plot lying below the mill-tail,[20] and stretching to the water-side. It was just the time of year when cherries are ripe, and hang in clusters under their dark leaves. While the troopers loitered on their horses, and chatted to the miller across the stream, he gathered bunches of the fruit, and held them up over the garden hedge for the acceptance of anybody who would have them; whereupon the soldiers rode into the water to where it had washed holes in the garden bank, and, reining their horses there, caught the cherries in their forage-caps, or received bunches of them on the ends of their switches, with the dignified laugh that became martial men when stooping to slightly boyish amusement. It was a cheerful, careless, unpremeditated half-hour, which returned like the scent of a flower to the memories of some of those who enjoyed it, even at a distance of many years after, when they lay wounded and weak in foreign lands.

Then dragoons and horses wheeled off as the others had done; and troops of the German Legion[21] next came down and entered in panoramic procession the space below Anne's eyes, as if on purpose to gratify her. These were notable by their mustachios, and queues[22] wound tightly with brown ribbon to the level of their broad shoulder-blades. They were charmed, as the others had been, by the head and neck of Miss Garland in the little square window overlooking the scene of operations, and saluted her with devoted foreign civility, and in such overwhelming numbers that the modest girl suddenly withdrew herself into the room, and had a private blush between the chest of drawers and the washing-stand.

When she came downstairs her mother said, 'I have been thinking what I ought to wear to Miller Loveday's tonight.'

'To Miller Loveday's?' said Anne.

'Yes. The party is tonight. He has been in here this morning to tell me that he has seen his son, and they have fixed this evening.'

'Do you think we ought to go, mother?' said Anne slowly, and looking at the smaller features of the window-flowers.

'Why not?' said Mrs Garland.

'He will only have men there except ourselves, will he? And shall we be right to go alone among 'em?'

Anne had not recovered from the ardent gaze of the gallant York Hussars, whose voices reached her even now in converse with Loveday.

'La, Anne, how proud you are!' said Widow Garland. 'Why, isn't he our nearest neighbour and our landlord? and don't he always fetch our faggots from the wood, and keep us in vegetables for next to nothing?'

'That's true,' said Anne.

'Well, we can't be distant with the man. And if the enemy land next autumn, as everybody says they will, we shall have quite to depend upon the miller's waggon and horses. He's our only friend.'

'Yes, so he is,' said Anne. 'And you had better go, mother; and I'll stay at home. They will be all men; and I don't like going.'

Mrs Garland reflected. 'Well, if you don't want to go, I don't,' she said. 'Perhaps, as you are growing up, it would be better to stay at home this time. Your father was a professional man, certainly.' Having spoken as a mother, she sighed as a woman.

'Why do you sigh, mother?'

'You are so prim and stiff about everything.'

'Very well – we'll go.'

'O no – I am not sure that we ought. I did not promise, and there will be no trouble in keeping away.'

Anne apparently did not feel certain of her own opinion, and, instead of supporting or contradicting, looked thoughtfully down, and abstractedly brought her hands together on her bosom, till her fingers met tip to tip.

As the day advanced the young woman and her mother became aware that great preparations were in progress in the miller's wing of the house. The partitioning between the Lovedays and the Garlands was not very thorough, consisting in many cases of a simple screwing up of the doors in the dividing walls; and thus when the mill began any new performances they proclaimed themselves at once in the more private dwelling. The smell of Miller Loveday's pipe came down Mrs Garland's chimney of an evening with the greatest regularity. Every time that he poked his fire they knew from the vehemence or deliberateness of the blows the precise state of his mind; and when he wound his clock on Sunday nights the whirr of that monitor reminded the widow to wind hers. This transit of noises was most perfect where Loveday's lobby adjoined Mrs Garland's pantry; and Anne, who was occupied for some time in the latter apartment, enjoyed the privilege of hearing the visitors arrive and of catching stray sounds and words without the connecting phrases that made them entertaining, to judge from the laughter they evoked. The arrivals passed through the house and went into the garden, where they had tea in a large summer-house, an occasional blink of bright colour, through the foliage, being all that was visible of the assembly from Mrs Garland's windows. When it grew dusk they all could be heard coming indoors to finish the evening in the parlour.

Then there was an intensified continuation of the above-mentioned signs of enjoyment, talkings and haw-haws, runnings upstairs and runnings down, a slamming of doors and a clinking of cups and glasses; till the proudest adjoining tenant without friends on his own side of the partition might have been tempted to wish for entrance to that merry dwelling, if only to know the cause of these fluctuations of hilarity, and to see if the guests were really so numerous, and the observations so very amusing as they seemed.

The stagnation of life on the Garland side of the party-wall began to have a very gloomy effect by the contrast. When, about half past nine o'clock, one of these tantalizing bursts of gaiety had resounded for a longer time than usual, Anne said, 'I believe, mother, that you are wishing you had gone.'

'I own to feeling that it would have been very cheerful if we had joined in,' said Mrs Garland, in a hankering tone. 'I was rather too nice in listening to you and not going. The parson never calls upon us except in his spiritual capacity. Old Derriman is hardly genteel; and there's nobody left to speak to. Lonely people must accept what company they can get.'

'Or do without it altogether.'

'That's not natural, Anne; and I am surprised to hear a young woman like you say such a thing. Nature will not be stifled in that way . . .' (Song and powerful chorus heard through partition.) 'I declare the room on the other side of the wall seems quite a paradise compared with this.'

'Mother, you are quite a girl,' said Anne in slightly superior accents. 'Go in and join them by all means.'

'O no – not now,' said her mother, resignedly shaking her head. 'It is too late now. We ought to have taken advantage of the invitation. They would look hard at me as a poor mortal who had no real business there, and the miller would say, with his broad smile, "Ah, you be obliged to come round." '

While the sociable and unaspiring Mrs Garland continued thus to pass the evening in two places, her body in her own house and her mind in the miller's, somebody knocked at the door, and directly after the elder Loveday himself was admitted to the room. He was dressed in a suit between grand and gay, which he used for such occasions as the present, and his blue coat, yellow and red waistcoat with the three lower buttons unfastened, steel-buckled shoes and speckled stockings, became him very well in Mrs Martha Garland's eyes.

'Your servant, ma'am,' said the miller, adopting as a matter of propriety the raised standard of politeness required by his higher costume. 'Now, begging your pardon, I can't hae this. 'Tis unnatural that you two ladies should be biding here and we under the same roof making merry without ye. Your husband, poor man – lovely picters that a' would make to be sure – would have been in with us long ago if he had been in your place. I can take no nay from ye, upon my honour. You and maidy Anne must come in, if it be only for half an hour. John and his friends have got passes till twelve o'clock tonight, and, saving a few of our own village folk, the lowest visitor present is a very genteel German corporal. If you should hae any misgivings on the score of respectability, ma'am, we'll pack off the underbred ones into the back kitchen.'

Widow Garland and Anne looked yes at each other after this appeal.

'We'll follow you in a few minutes,' said the elder, smiling; and she rose with Anne to go upstairs.

'No, I'll wait for ye,' said the miller doggedly; 'or perhaps you'll alter your mind again.'

While the mother and daughter were upstairs dressing, and saying laughingly to each other, 'Well, we *must* go now,' as if they hadn't wished to go all the evening, other steps were heard in the passage; and the miller cried from below, 'Your pardon, Mrs Garland; but my son John has come to help fetch ye. Shall I ask him in till ye be ready?'

'Certainly; I shall be down in a minute,' screamed Anne's mother in a slanting voice towards the staircase.

When she descended, the outline of the trumpet-major appeared half-way down the passage. 'This is John,' said the miller simply. 'John, you can mind Mrs Martha Garland very well?'

'Very well, indeed,' said the dragoon, coming in a little further. 'I should have called to see her last time, but I was only home a week. How is your little girl, ma'am?'

Mrs Garland said Anne was quite well. 'She is grown up now. She will be down in a moment.'

There was a slight noise of military heels without the door, at which the trumpet-major went and put his head outside, and said, 'All right – coming in a minute,' when voices in the darkness replied, 'No hurry.'

'More friends?' said Mrs Garland.

'O, it is only Buck and Jones come to fetch me,' said the soldier. 'Shall I ask 'em in a minute, Mrs Garland, ma'am?'

'O yes,' said the lady; and the two interesting forms of Trumpeter Buck and Saddler-sergeant Jones then came forward in the most friendly manner; whereupon other steps were heard without, and it was discovered that Sergeant-master-tailor Brett and Farrier-extraordinary Johnson were outside, having come to fetch Messrs Buck and Jones, as Buck and Jones had come to fetch the trumpet-major.

As there seemed a possibility of Mrs Garland's small passage being choked up with human figures personally unknown to her, she was relieved to hear Anne coming downstairs.

'Here's my little girl,' said Mrs Garland, and the trumpet-major looked with a sort of awe upon the muslin apparition who came forward, and stood quite dumb before her. Anne recognized him as the trooper she had seen from her window, and welcomed him kindly. There was something in his honest face which made her feel instantly at home with him.

At this frankness of manner Loveday – who was not a ladies' man – blushed, and made some alteration in his bodily posture, began a sentence which had no end, and showed quite a boy's embarrassment. Recovering himself, he politely offered his arm, which Anne took with a very pretty grace. He conducted her through his comrades, who glued themselves perpendicularly to the wall to let her pass, and then they went out of the door, her mother following with the miller, and supported by the body of troopers, the latter walking with the usual cavalry gait, as if their thighs were rather too long for them. Thus they crossed the threshold of the mill-house and up the passage, the paving of which was worn into a gutter by the ebb and flow of feet that had been going on there ever since Tudor times.

# * IV *

## Who were Present at
## the Miller's Little Entertainment

WHEN the group entered the presence of the company a lull in the conversation was caused by the sight of new visitors, and (of course) by the charm of Anne's appearance; until the old men, who had daughters of their own, perceiving that she was only a half-formed girl, resumed their tales and toss-potting[23] with unconcern.

Miller Loveday had fraternized with half the soldiers in the camp since their arrival, and the effect of this upon his party was striking – both chromatically and otherwise. Those among the guests who first attracted the eye were the sergeants and sergeant-majors of Loveday's regiment, fine hearty men, who sat facing the candles, entirely resigned to physical comfort. Then there were other non-commissioned officers, a German, two Hungarians, and a Swede, from the foreign hussars – young men with a look of sadness on their faces, as if they did not much like serving so far from home. All of them spoke English fairly well. Old age was represented by Simon Burden the pensioner, and the shady side of fifty by Corporal Tullidge, his friend and neighbour, who was hard of hearing, and sat with his hat on over a red cotton handkerchief that was wound several times round his head. These two veterans were employed as watchers at the neighbouring beacon, which had lately been erected by the Lord-Lieutenant for firing whenever the descent on the coast should be made. They lived in a little hut on the hill, close by the heap of faggots; but tonight they had found deputies to watch in their stead.

On a lower plane of experience and qualifications came neighbour James Comfort, of the Volunteers,[24] a soldier by courtesy, but a blacksmith by rights; also William Tremlett and Anthony Cripplestraw, of the local forces. The two latter men of war were dressed merely as villagers, and looked upon the regulars from a humble position in the background. The remainder of the party was made up of a neighbouring dairyman or two, and their wives, invited by the miller, as Anne was glad to see, that she and her mother should not be the only women there.

The elder Loveday apologized in a whisper to Mrs Garland for the presence of the inferior villagers. 'But as they are learning to be brave defenders of their home and country, ma'am, as fast as they can master the drill, and have worked for me off and on these many years, I've asked 'em in, and thought you'd excuse it.'

'Certainly, Miller Loveday,' said the widow.

'And the same of old Burden and Tullidge. They have served well and long in the Foot, and even now have a hard time of it up at the beacon in wet weather. So after giving them a meal in the kitchen I just asked 'em in to hear the singing. They faithfully promise that as soon as ever the gunboats appear in view, and they have fired the beacon, to run down here first, in case we shouldn't see it. 'Tis worth while to be friendly with 'em, you see, though their tempers be queer.'

'Quite worth while, miller,' said she.

Anne was rather embarrassed by the presence of the regular military in such force, and at first confined her words to the dairymen's wives she was acquainted with, and to the two old soldiers of the parish.

'Why didn't ye speak to me afore, chiel?'[25] said one of these, Corporal Tullidge, the elderly man with the hat, while she was talking to old Simon Burden. 'I met ye in the lane yesterday,' he added reproachfully, 'but ye didn't notice me at all.'

'I am very sorry for it,' she said; but, being afraid to shout in such a company, the effect of her remark upon the corporal was as if she had not spoken at all.

'You was coming along with yer head full of some high notions or other no doubt,' continued the uncompromising corporal in the same loud voice. 'Ah, 'tis the young bucks that get all the notice nowadays, and old folks are quite forgot! I can mind well enough how young Bob Loveday used to lie in wait for ye.'

Anne blushed deeply, and stopped his too excursive discourse by hastily saying that she always respected old folks like him. The corporal thought she inquired why he always kept his hat on, and answered that it was because his head was injured at Valenciennes,[26] in July, Ninety-three. 'We were trying to bomb down the tower, and a piece of the shell struck me. I was no more nor less than a dead man for two days. If it hadn't a been for that and my smashed arm I should have come home none the worse for my five-and-twenty years' service.'

'You have got a silver plate let into yer head, haven't ye, corp'el?' said Anthony Cripplestraw, who had drawn near. 'I have heard that the way they morticed[27] yer skull was a beautiful piece of workmanship. Perhaps the young woman would like to see the place? 'Tis a curious sight, Mis'ess Anne; you don't see such a wownd every day.'

'No, thank you,' said Anne hurriedly, dreading, as did all the young people of Overcombe, the spectacle of the corporal uncovered. He had never been seen in public without the hat and the handkerchief since his return in Ninety-four; and strange stories were told of the ghastliness of his appearance bare-headed, a little boy who had accidentally beheld him going to bed in that state having been frightened into fits.

'Well, if the young woman don't want to see yer head, maybe she'd like to hear yer arm?' continued Cripplestraw, earnest to please her.

'Hey?' said the corporal.

'Your arm hurt too?' cried Anne.

'Knocked to a pummy[28] at the same time as my head,' said Tullidge dispassionately.

'Rattle yer arm, corp'el, and show her,' said Cripplestraw.

'Yes, sure,' said the corporal, raising the limb slowly, as if the glory of exhibition had lost some of its novelty, though he was willing to oblige. Twisting it mercilessly about with his right hand he produced a crunching among the bones at every motion, Cripplestraw seeming to derive great satisfaction from the ghastly sound.

'How very shocking!' said Anne, painfully anxious for him to leave off.

'O, it don't hurt him, bless ye. Do it, corp'el?' said Cripplestraw.

'Not a bit,' said the corporal, still working his arm with great energy.

'There's no life in the bones at all. No life in 'em, I tell her, corp'el!'

'None at all.'

'They be as loose as a bag of ninepins,' explained Cripplestraw in continuation. 'You can feel 'em quite plain, Mis'ess Anne. If ye would like to, he'll undo his sleeve in a minute to oblege ye?'

'O no, no, please not! I quite understand,' said the young woman.

'Do she want to hear or see any more, or don't she?' the corporal inquired, with a sense that his time was getting wasted.

Anne explained that she did not on any account; and managed to escape from the corner.

# * V *

## The Song and the Stranger

THE trumpet-major now contrived to place himself near her, Anne's presence having evidently been a great pleasure to him since the moment of his first seeing her. She was quite at her ease with him, and asked him if he thought that Buonaparte would really come during the summer, and many other questions which the gallant dragoon could not answer, but which he nevertheless liked to be asked. William Tremlett, who had not enjoyed a sound night's rest since the First Consul's menace had become known, pricked up his ears at sound of this subject, and inquired if anybody had seen the terrible flat-bottomed boats that the enemy were to cross in.

'My brother Robert saw several of them paddling about the shore the last time he passed the Straits of Dover,' said the trumpet-major; and he further startled the company by informing them that there were supposed to be more than fifteen hundred of these boats, and that they would carry a hundred men apiece. So that a descent of one hundred and fifty thousand men might be expected any day as soon as Boney had brought his plans to bear.

'Lord ha' mercy upon us!' said William Tremlett.

'The night-time is when they will try it, if they try it at all,' said old Tullidge, in the tone of one whose watch at the beacon must, in the nature of things, have given him comprehensive views of the situation. 'It is my belief that the point they will choose for making the shore is just over there,' and he nodded with indifference towards a section of the coast at a hideous nearness to the house in which they were assembled, whereupon Fencible[29] Tremlett, and Cripplestraw of the Locals, tried to show no signs of trepidation.

'When d'ye think 'twill be?' said Volunteer Comfort, the blacksmith.

'I can't answer to a day,' said the corporal, 'but it will certainly be in a down-channel tide; and instead of pulling hard against it, he'll let his boats drift, and that will bring 'em right into Budmouth Bay. 'Twill be a beautiful stroke of war, if so be 'tis quietly done!'

'Beautiful,' said Cripplestraw, moving inside his clothes. 'But how if we should be all abed, corp'el? You can't expect a man to be brave in his shirt, especially we Locals, that have only got so far as shoulder fire-locks.'

'He's not coming this summer. He'll never come at all,' said a tall sergeant-major decisively.

Loveday the soldier was too much engaged in attending upon Anne and her mother to join in these surmises, bestirring himself to get the ladies some of the best liquor the house afforded, which had, as a matter of fact, crossed the Channel as privately as Buonaparte wished his army to do, and had been landed on a dark night over the cliff. After this he asked Anne to sing; but though she had a very pretty voice in private performances of that nature, she declined to oblige him; turning the subject by making a hesitating inquiry about his brother Robert, whom he had mentioned just before.

'Robert is as well as ever, thank you, Miss Garland,' he said. 'He is now mate of the brig[30] *Pewit* – rather young for such a command; but the owner puts great trust in him.' The trumpet-major added, deepening his thoughts to a profounder view of the person discussed, 'Bob is in love.'

Anne looked conscious, and listened attentively; but Loveday did not go on.

'Much?' she asked.

'I can't exactly say. And the strange part of it is that he never tells us who the woman is. Nobody knows at all.'

'He will tell, of course?' said Anne, in the remote tone of a person with whose sex such matters had no connection whatever.

Loveday shook his head, and the *tête-à-tête* was put an end to by a burst of singing from one of the sergeants, who was followed at the end of his song by others, each giving a ditty in his turn; the singer standing up in front of the table, stretching his chin well into the air, as though to abstract every possible wrinkle from his throat, and then plunging into the melody. When this was over one of the foreign hussars – the genteel German of Miller Loveday's description, who called himself a Hungarian, and in reality belonged to no definite country – performed at Trumpet-major Loveday's request the series of wild motions that he denominated his national dance, that Anne might see what it was like. Miss Garland was the flower of the whole company; the soldiers one and all, foreign and English, seemed to be quite charmed by her presence, as indeed they well might be, considering how seldom they came into the society of such as she.

Anne and her mother were just thinking of retiring to their own dwelling when Sergeant Stanner of the —th Foot, who was recruiting at Budmouth, began a satirical song:

> When law'-yers strive' to heal' a breach',
> And par'-sons prac'-tise what' they preach';
> Then Boney he'll come pouncing down',
> And march' his men' on Lon'-don town'!
>
> *Chorus:* Rol'-li-cum ro'-rum, tol'-lol-lo'-rum,
> Rol'-li-cum ro'-rum, tol'-lol-lay.
>
> When jus'-ti-ces' hold e'qual scales',
> And rogues' are on'-ly found' in jails';
> Then Boney he'll come pouncing down',
> And march' his men' on Lon'don town'!
>
> *Chorus:* Rol'-li-cum ro'-rum, &c.
>
> When rich' men find' their wealth' a curse',
> And fill' there-with' the poor' man's purse';
> Then Boney he'll come pouncing down',
> And march' his men' on Lon'-don town'!
>
> *Chorus:* Rol'-li-cum ro'-rum, &c.[31]

Poor Stanner! In spite of his satire, he fell at the bloody battle of Albuera[32] a few years after this pleasantly spent summer at the Georgian watering-place, being mortally wounded and trampled down by a French hussar when the brigade was deploying into line under Beresford.[33]

While Miller Loveday was saying 'Well done, Mr Stanner!' at the close of the thirteenth stanza, which seemed to be the last, and Mr Stanner was modestly expressing his regret that he could do no better, a stentorian voice was heard outside the window shutter repeating,

> Rol'-li-cum ro'-rum, tol'-lol-lo'-rum,
> Rol'-li-cum ro'-rum, tol'-lol-lay'.

The company was silent in a moment at this reinforcement, and only the military tried not to look surprised. While all wondered who the singer could be somebody entered the porch; the door opened, and in came a young man, about the size and weight of the Farnese Hercules,[34] in the uniform of the yeomanry cavalry.

' 'Tis young Squire Derriman, old Mr Derriman's nephew,' murmured voices in the background.

Without waiting to address anybody, or apparently seeing who were gathered there, the colossal man waved his cap above his head and went on in tones that shook the window-panes:

> When hus'-bands with' their wives' agree',
> And maids' won't wed' from mod'-es-ty',
> Then Boney he'll come pouncing down',
> And march' his men' on Lon'-don town'!

*Chorus:* Rol'-li-cum ro'-rum, tol'-lol-lo'-rum, &c., &c.

It was a verse which had been omitted by the gallant Stanner, out of respect to the ladies.

The newcomer was red-haired and of florid complexion, and seemed full of a conviction that his whim of entering must be their pleasure, which for the moment it was.

'No ceremony, good men all,' he said; 'I was passing by, and my ear was caught by the singing. I like singing; 'tis warming and cheering, and shall not be put down. I should like to hear anybody say otherwise.'

'Welcome, Master Derriman,' said the miller, filling a glass and handing it to the yeoman. 'Come all the way from quarters, then? I hardly knowed ye in your soldier's clothes. You'd look more natural with a spud[33] in your hand, sir. I shouldn't ha' known ye at all if I hadn't heard that you were called out.'

'More natural with a spud! – have a care, miller,' said the young giant, the fire of his complexion increasing to scarlet. 'I don't mean anger, but – but – a soldier's honour, you know!'

The military in the background laughed a little, and the yeoman then for the first time discovered that there were more regulars present than one. He looked momentarily disconcerted, but expanded again to full assurance.

'Right, right, Master Derriman, no offence – 'twas only my joke,' said the genial miller. 'Everybody's a soldier nowadays. Drink a drap o' this cordial, and don't mind words.'

The young man drank without the least reluctance, and said, 'Yes, miller, I am called out. 'Tis ticklish times for us soldiers now; we hold our lives in our hands – What are those fellows grinning at behind the table? – I say, we do!'

'Staying with your uncle at the farm for a day or two, Mr Derriman?'

'No, no; as I told you, six mile off. Billeted at Casterbridge. But I have to call and see the old, old –'

'Gentleman?'

'Gentleman! – no, skinflint. He lives upon the sweepings of the barton;[36] ha, ha!' And the speaker's regular white teeth showed themselves like snow in a Dutch cabbage.[37] 'Well, well, the profession of arms makes a man proof against all that. I take things as I find 'em.'

'Quite right, Master Derriman. Another drop?'

'No, no. I'll take no more than is good for me – no man should; so don't tempt me.'

The yeoman then saw Anne, and by an unconscious gravitation went towards her and the other women, flinging a remark to John Loveday in passing. 'Ah, Loveday! I heard you were come; in short, I come o' purpose to see you. Glad to see you enjoying yourself at home again.'

The trumpet-major replied civilly, though not without grimness, for he seemed hardly to like Derriman's motion towards Anne.

'Widow Garland's daughter! – yes, 'tis! surely. You remember me? I have been here before. Festus Derriman, Yeomanry Cavalry.'

Anne gave a little curtsey. 'I know your name is Festus – that's all.'

'Yes, 'tis well known – especially latterly.' He dropped his voice to confidence pitch. 'I suppose your friends here are disturbed by my coming in, as they don't seem to talk much? I don't mean to interrupt the party; but I often find that people are put out by my coming among 'em, especially when I've got my regimentals on.'

'La! and are they?'

'Yes; 'tis the way I have.' He further lowered his tone, as if they had been old friends, though in fact he had only seen her three or four times. 'And how did you come to be here? Dash my wig, I don't like to see a nice young lady like you in this company. You should come to some of our yeomanry sprees in Casterbridge or Shottsford-Forum. O, but the girls do come! The yeomanry are respected men, men of good substantial families, many farming their own land; and every one among us rides his own charger, which is more than these cussed fellows do.' He nodded towards the dragoons.

'Hush, hush! Why, these are friends and neighbours of Miller Loveday, and he is a great friend of ours – our best friend,' said Anne with great emphasis, and reddening at the sense of injustice to their host. 'What are you thinking of, talking like that? It is ungenerous in you.'

'Ha, ha! I've affronted you. Isn't that it, fair angel, fair – what do you call it? – fair vestal? Ah, well! would you was safe in my own house! But honour must be minded now, not courting. Rollicum-rorum, tol-lol-lorum. Pardon me, my sweet, I like ye! It may be a come-down for me, owning land; but I do like ye.'

'Sir, please be quiet,' said Anne, distressed.

'I will, I will. Well, Corporal Tullidge, how's your head?' he said, going towards the other end of the room, and leaving Anne to herself.

The company had again recovered its liveliness, and it was a long time before the bouncing Rufus[38] who had joined them could find heart to tear himself away from their society and good liquors, although he had had quite enough of the latter before he entered. The natives received him at his own valuation, and the soldiers of the camp, who sat beyond the table, smiled behind their pipes at his remarks, with a pleasant twinkle of the eye which approached the satirical, John Loveday being not the least conspicuous in this bearing. But he and his friends were too courteous on such an occasion as the present to challenge the young man's large remarks, and readily permitted him to set them right on the details of camping and other military routine, about which the troopers seemed willing to let persons hold any opinion whatever, provided that they themselves were not obliged to give attention to it; showing, strangely enough, that if there was one subject more than another which never interested their minds, it was the art of war. To them the art of enjoying good company in Overcombe Mill, the details of the miller's household, the swarming of his bees, the number of his chickens, and the fatness of his pigs, were matters of infinitely greater concern.

The present writer, to whom this party has been described times out of number by members of the Loveday family and other aged people now passed away, can never enter the old living-room of Overcombe Mill without beholding the genial scene through the mists of the seventy or eighty years that intervene between then and now. First and brightest to the eye are the dozen candles, scattered about regardless of expense, and kept well snuffed by the miller, who walks round the room at intervals of five minutes, snuffers in hand, and nips each wick with great precision, and with something of an executioner's grim look upon his face as he closes the snuffers upon the neck of the candle. Next to the candle-light show the red and blue coats and white breeches of the soldiers – nearly twenty of them in all besides the ponderous Derriman – the head of the latter, and, indeed, the heads of all who are standing up, being in dangerous proximity to the black beams of the ceiling. There is not one among them who would attach any meaning to 'Vittoria',[39] or gather from the syllables 'Waterloo'[40] the remotest idea of his own glory or death. Next appears the correct and innocent Anne, little thinking what things Time has in store for her at no great distance off. She looks at Derriman with a half-uneasy smile as he clanks hither and thither, and hopes he will not single her out again to hold a private dialogue with – which, however, he does, irresistibly attracted by the white muslin figure. She must, of course, look a little gracious again now, lest his mood should turn from sentimental to quarrelsome – no impossible contingency with the yeoman-soldier, as her quick perception had noted.

'Well, well; this idling won't do for me, folks,' he at last said, to Anne's relief. 'I ought not to have come in, by rights; but I heard you enjoying yourselves, and thought it might be worth while to see what you were up to; I have several miles to go before bedtime'; and stretching his arms, lifting his chin, and shaking his head, to eradicate any unseemly curve or wrinkle from his person, the yeoman wished them an off-hand good night, and departed.

'You should have teased him a little more, father,' said the trumpet-major drily. 'You could soon have made him as crabbed as a bear.'

'I didn't want to provoke the chap – 'twasn't worth while. He came in friendly enough,' said the gentle miller without looking up.

'I don't think he was overmuch friendly,' said John.

' 'Tis as well to be neighbourly with folks, if they be not quite onbearable,' his father genially replied, as he took off his coat to go and draw more ale – this periodical stripping to the shirt-sleeves being necessitated by the narrowness of the cellar and the smeary effect of its numerous cobwebs upon best clothes.

Some of the guests then spoke of Fess Derriman as not such a bad young man if you took him right and humoured him; others said that he was nobody's enemy but his own; and the elder ladies mentioned in a tone of interest that he was likely to come into a deal of money at his uncle's death. The person who did not praise was the one who knew him best, who had known him as a boy years ago, when he had lived nearer to Overcombe than he did at present. This unappreciative person was the trumpet-major.

# * VI *

## Old Mr Derriman of Oxwell Hall

At this time in the history of Overcombe one solitary newspaper occasionally found its way into the village. It was lent by the postmaster at Budmouth (who, in some mysterious way, got it for nothing through his connection with the mail) to Mr Derriman at the Hall, by whom it was handed on to Mrs Garland when it was not more than a fortnight old. Whoever remembers anything about the old farmer-squire will, of course, know well enough that this delightful privilege of reading history in long columns was not accorded to the Widow Garland for nothing. It was by such ingenuous means that he paid her for her daughter's occasional services in reading aloud to him and making out his accounts, in which matters the farmer, whose guineas were reported to touch five figures – some said more – was not expert.

Mrs Martha Garland, as a respectable widow, occupied a twilight rank between the benighted villagers and the well-informed gentry, and kindly made herself useful to the former as letter-writer and reader, and general translator from the printing tongue. It was not without satisfaction that she stood at her door of an evening, newspaper in hand, with three or four cottagers standing round, and poured down their open throats any paragraph that she might choose to select from the stirring ones of the period. When she had done with the sheet Mrs Garland passed it on to the miller, the miller to the grinder, and the grinder to the grinder's boy, in whose hands it became subdivided into half pages, quarter pages, and irregular triangles, and ended its career as a paper cap, a flagon bung, or a wrapper for his bread and cheese.

Notwithstanding his compact with Mrs Garland, old Mr

Derriman kept the paper so long, and was so chary of wasting his man's time on a merely intellectual errand, that unless she sent for the journal it seldom reached her hands. Anne was always her messenger. The arrival of the soldiers led Mrs Garland to dispatch her daughter for it the day after the party; and away she went in her hat and pelisse, in a direction at right angles to that of the encampment on the hill.

Walking across the downs for the distance of a mile or two, she came out upon the high-road by a wicket-gate. On the same side of the way was the entrance to what at first sight looked like a neglected meadow, the gate being a rotten one, without a bottom rail, and broken-down palings lying on each side. The dry hard mud of the opening was marked with several horse and cow tracks, that had been half obliterated by fifty score sheep tracks, surcharged with the tracks of a man and a dog. Beyond this geological record appeared a carriage-road, nearly grown over with grass, which Anne followed as it turned and dived under dark-rinded elm and chestnut trees. Further on appeared the cottages of Oxwell village, and some stone quarries. As Anne moved forward the grey, weather-worn front of a building edged from behind the trees. It was Oxwell Hall, once the seat of a family now extinct, and of late years used as a farmhouse.

Benjamin Derriman, who owned the crumbling place, had originally been only the occupier and tenant-farmer of the fields around. His wife had brought him a small fortune, and during the growth of their only son there had been a partition of the Oxwell estate, giving the farmer, now a widower, the opportunity of acquiring the building and a small portion of the land attached on exceptionally low terms. But two years after the purchase the boy died, and Derriman's existence was paralysed forthwith. It was said that since that event he had devised the house and fields to a distant female relative, to keep them out of the hands of his detested nephew; but this was not certainly known.

The hall was as interesting as mansions in a state of declension usually are, as the excellent county history[41] showed. That popular work in folio contained an old plate dedicated to the last scion of the original owners, from which drawing it appeared that in 1774, the date of publication, the windows were covered with little scratches like black flashes of lightning; that a horn of hard smoke many came out of the chimneys; that a lady and a lap-dog stood on the lawn in a strenuously walking position; and a substantial cloud and nine flying birds of no known species hung over the trees to the north-east.

The rambling and neglected dwelling had all the romantic excellencies and practical drawbacks which such mildewed places share in common with caves, mountains, wildernesses, glens, and other homes of poesy that people of taste wish to live and die in. Mustard and cress could have been raised on the inner plaster of the dewy walls at any height not exceeding three feet from the floor; and mushrooms of the most refined and thin-stemmed kinds grew up through the chinks of the larder paving. As for the outside, Nature, in the ample time that had been given her, had so mingled her filings and effacements with the marks of human wear and tear upon the house, that it was often hard to say in which of the two or if in both, any particular obliteration had its origin. The keenness was gone from the mouldings of the doorways, but whether worn out by the rubbing past of innumerable people's shoulders, and the moving of their heavy furniture, or by Time in a grander and more abstract form, did not appear. The iron stanchions[42] inside the window-panes were eaten away to the size of wires at the bottom where they entered the stone, the condensed breathings of generations having settled there in pools and rusted them. The panes themselves had either lost their shine altogether or become iridescent as a peacock's tail. In the middle of the porch was a vertical sun-dial, whose gnomon[43] swayed loosely about when the wind blew, and cast its shadow hither and thither, as much as to say, 'Here's your fine model dial; here's any time for any man; I am an old dial; and shiftiness is the best policy.'

Anne passed under the arched gateway which screened the main front; over it was the porter's lodge, reached by a spiral staircase. Across the archway was fixed a row of wooden hurdles, one of which Anne opened and closed behind her. Their necessity was apparent as soon as she got inside. The quadrangle of the ancient pile was a bed of mud and manure, inhabited by calves, geese, ducks, and sow pigs surprisingly large, with young ones surprisingly small. In the enclosure some heifers were amusing themselves by stretching up their necks and licking the mouldings of any salient stonework. Anne went on to a second and open door, across which was another hurdle to keep the livestock from absolute community with the inmates. There being no knocker, she knocked by means of a short stick which was laid against the post for that purpose; but nobody attending, she entered the passage, and tried an inner door.

A slight noise was heard inside, the door opened about an inch, and a strip of decayed face, including the eye and some forehead wrinkles, appeared within the crevice.

'Please I have come for the paper,' said Anne.

'O, is it you, dear Anne?' whined the inmate, opening the door a little further. 'I could hardly get to the door to open it, I am so weak.'

The speaker was a wizened old gentleman, in a coat the colour of his farmyard, breeches of the same hue, unbuttoned at the knees, revealing a bit of leg above his stocking and a dazzlingly white shirt-frill to compensate for this untidiness below. The edge of his skull round his eye-sockets was visible through the skin, and he had a mouth whose corners made towards the back of his head on the slightest provocation. He walked with great apparent difficulty back into the room, Anne following him.

'Well, you can have the paper if you want it; but you never give me much time to see what's in en! Here's the paper.' He held it out, but before she could take it he drew it back again, saying, 'I have not had my share o' the paper by a good deal, what with my weak sight, and people coming so soon for en. I am a poor put-upon soul; but my "Duty of Man"[44] will be left to me when the newspaper is gone.' And he sank into a chair with an air of exhaustion.

Anne said that she did not wish to take the paper if he had not done with it, and that she was really later in the week than usual, owing to the soldiers.

'Soldiers, yes – rot the soldiers! And now hedges will be broke, and hens' nests robbed, and sucking-pigs stole, and I don't know what all. Who's to pay for't, sure? I reckon that because the soldiers be come you don't mean to be kind enough to read to me what I hadn't time to read myself.'

She would read if he wished, she said; she was in no hurry. And sitting herself down she unfolded the paper.

' "Dinner at Carlton House"?'[45]

'No, faith. 'Tis nothing to I.'

' "Defence of the country"?'

'Ye may read that if ye will. I hope there will be no billeting in this parish, or any wild work of that sort; for what would a poor old lamiger[46] like myself do with soldiers in his house, and nothing to feed 'em with?'

Anne began reading, and continued at her task nearly ten minutes, when she was interrupted by the appearance in the quadrangular slough without of a large figure in the uniform of the yeomanry cavalry.

'What do you see out there?' said the farmer with a start, as she paused and slowly blushed.

'A soldier – one of the yeomanry,' said Anne, not quite at her ease.

'Scrounch it all – 'tis my nephew!' exclaimed the old man, his face turning to a phosphoric pallor, and his body twitching with innumerable alarms as he formed upon his face a gasping smile of joy, with which to welcome the new-coming relative. 'Read on, prithee, Miss Garland.'

Before she had read far the visitor straddled over the door-hurdle into the passage and entered the room.

'Well, nunc, how do you feel?' said the giant, shaking hands with the farmer in the manner of one violently ringing a hand-bell. 'Glad to see you.'

'Bad and weakish, Festus,' replied the other, his person responding passively to the rapid vibrations imparted. 'O, be tender, please – a little softer, there's a dear nephew! My arm is no more than a cobweb.'

'Ah, poor soul!'

'Yes, I am not much more than a skeleton, and can't bear rough usage.'

'Sorry to hear that; but I'll bear your affliction in mind. Why, you are all in a tremble, Uncle Benjy!'

' 'Tis because I am so gratified,' said the old man. 'I always get all in a tremble when I am taken by surprise by a beloved relation.'

'Ah, that's it!' said the yeoman, bringing his hand down on the back of his uncle's chair with a loud smack, at which Uncle Benjy nervously sprang three inches from his seat and dropped into it again. 'Ask your pardon for frightening ye, uncle. 'Tis how we do in the army, and I forgot your nerves. You have scarcely expected to see me, I dare say, but here I am.'

'I am glad to see ye. You are not going to stay long, perhaps?'

'Quite the contrary. I am going to stay ever so long!'

'O I see! I am so glad, dear Festus. Ever so long, did ye say?'

'Yes, *ever* so long,' said the young gentleman, sitting on the slope of the bureau and stretching out his legs as props. 'I am going to make this quite my own home whenever I am off duty, as long as we stay out. And after that, when the campaign is over in the autumn, I shall come here, and live with you like your own son, and help manage your land and your farm, you know, and make you a comfortable old man.'

'Ah! How you do please me!' said the farmer, with a horrified smile, and grasping the arms of his chair to sustain himself.

'Yes; I have been meaning to come a long time, as I knew you'd like to have me, Uncle Benjy; and 'tisn't in my heart to refuse you.'

'You always were kind that way!'

'Yes; I always was. But I ought to tell you at once, not to disappoint you, that I shan't be here always – all day, that is, because of my military duties as a cavalry man.'

'O, not always? That's a pity!' exclaimed the farmer with a cheerful eye.

'I knew you'd say so. And I shan't be able to sleep here at night sometimes, for the same reason.'

'Not sleep here o' nights?' said the old gentleman, still more relieved. 'You ought to sleep here – you certainly ought; in short, you must. But you can't!'

'Not while we are with the colours. But directly that's over – the very next day – I'll stay here all day, and all night too, to oblige you, since you ask me so very kindly.'

'Th-thank ye, that will be very nice!' said Uncle Benjy.

'Yes; I knew 'twould relieve ye.' And he kindly stroked his uncle's head, the old man expressing his enjoyment at the affectionate token by a death's-head grimace. 'I should have called to see you the other night when I passed through here,' Festus continued; 'but it was so late that I couldn't come so far out of my way. You won't think it unkind?'

'Not at all, if you *couldn't*. I never shall think it unkind if you really *can't* come, you know, Festy.' There was a few minutes' pause, and as the nephew said nothing Uncle Benjy went on: 'I wish I had a little present for ye. But as ill-luck would have it we have lost a deal of stock this year, and I have had to pay away so much.'

'Poor old man – I know you have. Shall I lend you a seven-shilling piece, Uncle Benjy?'

'Ha, ha! – you must have your joke; well I'll think o' that. And so they expect Buonaparty to choose this very part of the coast for his landing, hey? And that the yeomanry be to stand in front as the forlorn hope?'

'Who says so?' asked the florid son of Mars, losing a little redness.

'The newspaper-man.'

'O, there's nothing in that,' said Festus bravely. 'The gover'ment thought it possible at one time; but they don't know.'

Festus turned himself as he talked, and now said abruptly: 'Ah, who's this? Why, 'tis our little Anne!' He had not noticed her till this moment, the young woman having at his entry kept her face over the newspaper, and then got away to the back part of the room. 'And are you and your mother always going to stay down there in the mill-house watching the little fishes, Miss Anne?'

She said that it was uncertain, in a tone of truthful precision which the question was hardly worth, looking forcedly at him as she spoke. But she blushed fitfully, in her arms and hands as much as in her face. Not that she was overpowered by the great boots, formidable spurs, and other fierce appliances of his person, as he imagined; simply she had not been prepared to meet him there.

'I hope you will, I am sure, for my own good,' said he, letting his eyes linger on the round of her cheek.

Anne became a little more dignified, and her look showed

reserve. But the yeoman on perceiving this went on talking to her in so civil a way that he irresistibly amused her, though she tried to conceal all feeling. At a brighter remark of his than usual her mouth moved, her upper lip playing uncertainly over her white teeth; it would stay still – no, it would withdraw a little way in a smile; then it would flutter down again; and so it wavered like a butterfly in a tender desire to be pleased and smiling, and yet to be also sedate and composed; to show him that she did not want compliments, and yet that she was not so cold as to wish to repress any genuine feeling he might be anxious to utter.

'Shall you want any more reading, Mr Derriman?' said she, interrupting the younger man in his remarks. 'If not, I'll go homeward.'

'Don't let me hinder you longer,' said Festus. 'I am off in a minute or two, when your man has cleaned my boots.'

'Ye don't hinder us, nephew. She must have the paper: 'tis the day for her to have 'n. She might read a little more, as I have had so little profit out o' en hitherto. Well, why don't ye speak? Will ye, or won't ye, my dear?'

'Not to two,' she said.

'Ho, ho! damn it, I must go then, I suppose,' said Festus, laughing; and unable to get a further glance from her he left the room and clanked into the back yard, where he saw a man; holding up his hand he cried, 'Anthony Cripplestraw!'

Cripplestraw came up in a trot, moved a lock of his hair and replaced it, and said, 'Yes, Maister Derriman.' He was old Mr Derriman's odd hand in the yard and garden, and like his employer had no great pretensions to manly beauty, owing to a limpness of backbone and speciality of mouth, which opened on one side only, giving him a triangular smile.

'Well, Cripplestraw, how is it today?' said Festus, with socially superior heartiness.

'Middlin', considering, Maister Derriman. And how's yerself?'

'Fairish. Well, now, see and clean these military boots of mine. I'll cock my foot up on this bench. This pigsty of my uncle's is not fit for a soldier to come into.'

'Yes, Maister Derriman, I will. No, 'tis not fit, Maister Derriman.'

'What stock has uncle lost this year, Cripplestraw?'

'Well, let's see, sir. I can call to mind that we've lost three chickens, a tom-pigeon, and a weakly sucking-pig, one of a fare[47] of ten. I can't think of no more, Maister Derriman.'

'H'm, not a large quantity of cattle. The old rascal!'

'No, 'tis not a large quantity. Old what did you say, sir?'

'O nothing. He's within there.' Festus flung his forehead in the direction of a right line towards the inner apartment. 'He's a regular sniche[48] one.'

'Hee, hee; fie, fie, Maister Derriman!' said Cripplestraw, shaking his head in delighted censure. 'Gentlefolks shouldn't talk so. And an officer, Mr Derriman! 'Tis the duty of all cavalry gentlemen to bear in mind that their blood is a knowed thing in the country, and not to speak ill o't.'

'He's close-fisted.'

'Well, maister, he is – I own he is a little. 'Tis the nater of some old venerable gentlemen to be so. We'll hope he'll treat ye well in yer fortune, sir.'

'Hope he will. Do people talk about me here, Cripplestraw?' asked the yeoman, as the other continued busy with his boots.

'Well, yes, sir; they do off and on, you know. They says you be as fine a piece of calvery flesh and bones as was ever growed on fallow-ground; in short, all owns that you be a fine fellow, sir. I wish I wasn't no more afraid of the French than you be; but being in the Locals, Maister Derriman, I assure ye I dream of having to defend my country every night; and I don't like the dream at all.'

'You should take it careless, Cripplestraw, as I do; and 'twould soon come natural to you not to mind it at all. Well, a fine fellow is not everything, you know. O no. There's as good as I in the army, and even better.'

'And they say that when you fall this summer, you'll die like a man.'

'When I fall?'

'Yes, sure, Maister Derriman. Poor soul o' thee! I shan't forget 'ee as you lie mouldering in yer soldier's grave.'

'Hey?' said the warrior uneasily. 'What makes 'em think I am going to fall?'

'Well, sir, by all accounts the yeomanry will be put in front.'

'Front! That's what my uncle has been saying.'

'Yes, and by all accounts 'tis true. And naterelly they'll be mowed down like grass; and you among 'em, poor young galliant officer!'

'Look here, Cripplestraw. This is a reg'lar foolish report. How can yeomanry be put in front? Nobody's put in front. We yeomanry have nothing to do with Buonaparte's landing. We shall be away in a safe place, guarding the possessions and jewels. Now, can you see, Cripplestraw, any way at all that the yeomanry can be put in front? Do you think they really can?'

'Well, maister, I am afraid I do,' said the cheering Cripplestraw. 'And I know a great warrior like you is only too glad o' the chance. 'Twill be a great thing for ye, death and glory! In short, I hope from my heart you will be, and I say so very often to volk – in fact, I pray at night for't.'

'O! cuss you! you needn't pray about it.'

'No, Maister Derriman, I won't.'

'Of course my sword will do its duty. That's enough. And now be off with ye.'

Festus gloomily returned to his uncle's room and found that Anne was just leaving. He was inclined to follow her at once, but as she gave him no opportunity for doing this he went to the window, and remained tapping his fingers against the shutter while she crossed the yard.

'Well, nephy, you are not gone yet?' said the farmer, looking dubiously at Festus from under one eyelid. 'You see how I am. Not by any means better, you see; so I can't entertain 'ee as well as I would.'

'You can't, nunc, you can't. I don't think you are worse – if I do, dash my wig. But you'll have plenty of opportunities to make me welcome when you are better. If you are not so brisk inwardly as you was, why not try change of air? This is a dull, damp hole.'

' 'Tis, Festus; and I am thinking of moving.'

'Ah, where to?' said Festus, with surprise and interest.

'Up into the garret in the north corner. There is no fireplace in the room; but I shan't want that, poor soul o' me.'

' 'Tis not moving far.'

' 'Tis not. But I have not a soul belonging to me within ten mile; and you know very well that I couldn't afford to go to lodgings that I had to pay for.'

'I know it – I know it, Uncle Benjy! Well, don't be disturbed. I'll come and manage for you as soon as ever this Boney alarm is over; but when a man's country calls he must obey, if he is a man.'

'A splendid spirit!' said Uncle Benjy, with much admiration on the surface of his countenance. 'I never had it. How could it have got into the boy?'

'From my mother's side, perhaps.'

'Perhaps so. Well, take care of yourself, nephy,' said the farmer, waving his hand impressively. 'Take care! In these warlike times your spirit may carry ye into the arms of the enemy; and you are the last of the family. You should think of this, and not let your bravery carry ye away.'

'Don't be disturbed, uncle; I'll control myself,' said Festus, betrayed into self-complacency against his will. 'At least I'll do what I can, but nature will out sometimes. Well, I'm off.' He began humming 'Brighton Camp',[49] and, promising to come again soon, retired with assurance, each yard of his retreat adding private joyousness to his uncle's form.

When the bulky young man had disappeared through the porter's lodge, Uncle Benjy showed preternatural activity for one in his invalid state, jumping up quickly without his stick, at the same time opening and shutting his mouth quite silently like a thirsty frog, which was his way of expressing mirth. He ran upstairs as quick as an old squirrel, and went to a dormer window which commanded a view of the downs beyond the grounds, and the footpath that stretched across them to the village.

'Yes, yes!' he said in a suppressed scream, dancing up and down, 'he's after her: she've hit en!' For there appeared upon the path the figure of Anne Garland, and, hastening on at some little distance behind her, the swaggering shape of Festus. She became conscious of his approach, and moved more quickly. He moved more quickly still, and overtook her. She turned as if in answer to a call from him, and he walked on beside her, till they were out of sight. The old man then played upon an imaginary fiddle for about half a minute; and, suddenly discontinuing these signs of pleasure, went downstairs again.

# * VII *

## How They Talked in the Pastures

'YOU often come this way?' said Festus to Anne, rather before he had overtaken her.

'I come for the newspaper and other things,' she said, perplexed by a doubt whether he were there by accident or design.

They moved on in silence, Festus beating the grass with his switch in a masterful way. 'Did you speak, Mis'ess Anne?' he asked.

'No,' said Anne.

'Ten thousand pardons. I thought you did. Now don't let me drive you out of the path. I can walk among the high grass and giltycups⁵⁰ – they will not yellow my stockings as they will yours. Well, what do you think of a lot of soldiers coming to the neighbourhood in this way?'

'I think it is very lively, and a great change,' she said with demure seriousness.

'Perhaps you don't like us warriors as a body?'

Anne smiled without replying.

'Why, you are laughing!' said the yeoman, looking searchingly at her and blushing like a little fire. 'What do you see to laugh at?'

'Did I laugh?' said Anne, a little scared at his sudden mortification.

'Why, yes; you know you did, you young sneerer,' he said like a cross baby. 'You are laughing at me – that's who you are laughing at! I should like to know what you would do without such as me if the French were to drop in upon ye any night?'

'Would you help to beat them off?' said she.

'Can you ask such a question? What are we for? But you don't think anything of soldiers.'

O yes, she liked soldiers, she said, especially when they came home from the wars, covered with glory; though when she thought what doings had won them that glory she did not like them quite so well. The gallant and appeased yeoman said he supposed her to mean chopping off heads, blowing out brains, and that kind of business, and thought it quite right that a tender-hearted thing like her should feel a little horrified. But as for him, he should not mind such another Blenheim[51] this summer as the army had fought a hundred years ago, or whenever it was – dash his wig if he should mind it at all. 'Hullo! now you are laughing again; yes, I saw you!' And the choleric Festus turned his blue eyes and flushed face upon her as though he would read her through. Anne strove valiantly to look calmly back; but her eyes could not face his, and they fell. 'You did laugh!' he repeated.

'It was only a tiny little one,' she murmured.

'Ah – I knew you did!' thundered he. 'Now what was it you laughed at?'

'I only – thought that you were – merely in the yeomanry,' she murmured slily.

'And what of that?'

'And the yeomanry only seem farmers that have lost their senses.'

'Yes, yes! I knew you meant some jeering o' that sort, Mistress Anne. But I suppose 'tis the way of women, and I take no notice. I'll confess that some of us are no great things: but I know how to draw a sword, don't I? – say I don't just to provoke me.'

'I am sure you do,' said Anne sweetly. 'If a Frenchman came up to you, Mr Derriman, would you take him on the hip, or on the thigh?'

'Now you are flattering!' he said, his white teeth uncovering themselves in a smile. 'Well, of course I should draw my sword – no, I mean my sword would be already drawn; and I should put spurs to my horse – charger, as we call it in the army; and I should ride up to him and say – no, I shouldn't say anything, of course – men never waste words in battle; I should take him with the third guard, low point, and then coming back to the second guard –'[52]

'But that would be taking care of yourself – not hitting at him.'

'How can you say that!' he cried, the beams upon his face

turning to a lurid cloud in a moment. 'How can you understand military terms who've never had a sword in your life? I shouldn't take him with the sword at all.' He went on with eager sulkiness, 'I should take him with my pistol. I should pull off my right glove, and throw back my goat-skin; then I should open my priming-pan,[53] prime, and cast about – no, I shouldn't that's wrong; I should draw my right pistol, and as soon as loaded, seize the weapon by the butt; then at the word "Cock your pistol" I should –'

'Then there is plenty of time to give such words of command in the heat of battle?' said Anne innocently.

'No!' said the yeoman, his face again in flames. 'Why, of course I am only telling you what *would* be the word of command *if* – there now! you la –'

'I didn't; 'pon my word I didn't!'

'No, I don't think you did; it was my mistake. Well, then I come smartly to Present, looking well along the barrel – along the barrel – and fire. Of course I know well enough how to engage the enemy! But I expect my old uncle has been setting you against me.'

'He has not said a word,' replied Anne; 'though I have heard of you, of course.'

'What have you heard? Nothing good, I dare say. It makes my blood boil within me!'

'O, nothing bad,' said she assuringly. 'Just a word now and then.'

'Now, come, tell me, there's a dear. I don't like to be crossed. It shall be a sacred secret between us. Come, now!'

Anne was embarrassed, and her smile was uncomfortable. 'I shall not tell you,' she said at last.

'There it is again!' said the yeoman, throwing himself into a despair. 'I shall soon begin to believe that my name is not worth sixpence about here!'

'I tell you 'twas nothing against you,' repeated Anne.

'That means it might have been for me,' said Festus, in a mollified tone. 'Well, though, to speak the truth, I have a good many faults, some people will praise me, I suppose. 'Twas praise?'

'It was.'

'Well, I am not much at farming, and I am not much in company, and I am not much at figures, but perhaps I must own, since it is forced upon me, that I can show as fine a soldier's figure on the Esplanade as any man of the cavalry.'

'You can,' said Anne; for though her flesh crept in mortal terror of his irascibility, she could not resist the fearful pleasure of leading him on. 'You look very well; and some say, you are –'

'What? Well, they say I am good-looking. I don't make myself, so 'tis no praise. Hullo! what are you looking across there for?'

'Only at a bird that I saw fly out of that tree,' said Anne.

'What? Only at a bird, do you say?' he heaved out in a voice of thunder. 'I see your shoulders a-shaking, young madam. Now don't you provoke me with that laughing! By God, it won't do!'

'Then go away!' said Anne, changed from mirthfulness to irritation by his rough manner. 'I don't want your company, you great bragging thing! You are so touchy there's no bearing with you. Go away!'

'No, no, Anne; I am wrong to speak to you so. I give you free liberty to say what you will to me. Say I am not a bit of a soldier, or anything! Abuse me – do now, there's a dear. I'm scum, I'm froth, I'm dirt before the besom – yes!'

'I have nothing to say, sir. Stay where you are till I am out of this field.'

'Well, there's such command in your looks that I ha'n't heart to go against you. You will come this way tomorrow at the same time? Now, don't be uncivil.'

She was too generous not to forgive him, but the short little lip murmured that she did not think it at all likely she should come that way tomorrow.

'Then Sunday?' he said.

'Not Sunday,' said she.

'Then Monday – Tuesday – Wednesday, surely?' he went on experimentally.

She answered that she should probably not see him on either day, and, cutting short the argument, went through the wicket[54] into the other field. Festus paused, looking after her; and when he could no longer see her slight figure he swept away his deliberations, began singing, and turned off in the other direction.

# * VIII *

## Anne Makes a Circuit of the Camp

WHEN Anne was crossing the last field, she saw approaching her an old woman with wrinkled cheeks, who surveyed the earth and its inhabitants through the medium of brass-rimmed spectacles. Shaking her head at Anne till the glasses shone like two moons, she said, 'Ah, ah; I zeed ye! If I had only kept on my short ones that I use for reading the Collect and Gospel I shouldn't have zeed ye; but thinks I, I be going out o' doors, and I'll put on my long ones, little thinking what they'd show me. Ay, I can tell folk at any distance with these – 'tis a beautiful pair for out o' doors; though my short ones be best for close work, such as darning, and catching fleas, that's true.'

'What have you seen, Granny Seamore?' said Anne.

'Fie, fie, Miss Nancy! you know,' said Granny Seamore, shaking her head still. 'But he's a fine young feller, and will have all his uncle's money when 'a's gone.' Anne said nothing to this, and looking ahead with a smile passed Granny Seamore by.

Festus, the subject of the remark, was at this time about three-and-twenty, a fine fellow as to feet and inches, and of a remarkably warm tone in skin and hair. Symptoms of beard and whiskers had appeared upon him at a very early age, owing to his persistent use of the razor before there was any necessity for its operation. The brave boy had scraped unseen in the out-house, in the cellar, in the wood-shed, in the stable, in the unused parlour, in the cow-stalls, in the barn, and wherever he could set up his triangular bit of looking-glass without observation, or extemporize a mirror by sticking up his hat on the outside of a window-pane. The result now was that, did he neglect to use the instrument he once had trifled with, a fine rust broke out upon his countenance on the first day, a golden lichen on the second, and a fiery stubble on the third to a degree which admitted of no further postponement.

His disposition divided naturally into two, the boastful and the cantankerous. When Festus put on the big pot, [55] as it is classically called, he was quite blinded *ipso facto* [56] to the diverting effect of that mood and manner upon others; but when disposed to be envious or quarrelsome he was rather shrewd than otherwise, and could do some pretty strokes of satire. He was both liked and abused by the girls who knew him, and though they were pleased by his attentions, they never failed to ridicule him behind his back. In his cups (he knew those vessels, though only twenty-three) he first became noisy, then excessively friendly, and then invariably nagging. During childhood he had made himself renowned for his pleasant habit of pouncing down upon boys smaller and poorer than himself, and knocking their birds' nests out of their hands, or overturning their little carts of apples, or pouring water down their backs; but his conduct became singularly the reverse of aggressive the moment the little boys' mothers ran out to him, brandishing brooms, frying-pans, skimmers, and whatever else they could lay hands on by way of weapons. He then fled and hid behind bushes, under faggots, or in pits till they had gone away; and on one such occasion was known to creep into a badger's hole quite out of sight, maintaining that post with great firmness and resolution for two or three hours. He had brought more vulgar exclamations upon the tongues of respectable parents in his native parish than any other boy of his time. When other youngsters snowballed him he ran into a place of shelter, where he kneaded snowballs of his own, with a stone inside, and used these formidable missiles in returning their pleasantry. Sometimes he got fearfully beaten by boys his own age, when he would roar most lustily, but fight on in the midst of his tears, blood, and cries.

He was early in love, and had at the time of the story suffered from the ravages of that passion thirteen distinct times. He could not love lightly and gaily; his love was earnest, cross-tempered, and even savage. It was a positive agony to him to be ridiculed by the object of his affections, and such conduct drove him into a frenzy if persisted in. He was a torment to those who behaved

humbly towards him, cynical with those who denied his super
ity, and a very nice fellow towards those who had the courag
ill-use him.

This stalwart gentleman and Anne Garland did not cross
other's paths again for a week. Then her mother began as be
about the newspaper, and, though Anne did not much like
errand, she agreed to go for it on Mrs Garland pressing her
unusual anxiety. Why her mother was so persistent on so sm
matter quite puzzled the girl; but she put on her hat and starte

As she had expected, Festus appeared at a stile over which
sometimes went for shortness' sake, and showed by his mar
that he awaited her. When she saw this she kept straight on,
she would not enter the down at all.

'Surely this is your way?' said Festus.

'I was thinking of going round by the road,' she said.

'Why is that?'

She paused, as if she were not inclined to say. 'I go that
when the grass is wet,' she returned at last.

'It is not wet now,' he persisted; 'the sun has been shining
these nine hours.' The fact was that the way by the path was
open than by the road, and Festus wished to walk with
uninterrupted. 'But, of course, it is nothing to me what you
He flung himself from the stile and walked away towards
house.

Anne, supposing him really indifferent, took the same
upon which he turned his head and waited for her with a
smile.

'I cannot go with you,' she said decisively.

'Nonsense, you foolish girl! I must walk along with you
to the corner.'

'No, please, Mr Derriman; we might be seen.'

'Now, now – that's shyness!' he said jocosely.

'No; you know I cannot let you.'

'But I must.'

'But I do not allow it.'

'Allow it or not, I will.'

'Then you are unkind, and I must submit,' she said, h
brimming with tears.

'Ho, ho; what a shame of me! My wig, I won't do any such thing for the world,' said the repentant yeoman. 'Haw, haw; why, I thought your "go away" meant "come on", as it does with so many of the women I meet, especially in these clothes. Who was to know you were so confoundedly serious?'

As he did not go Anne stood still and said nothing.

'I see you have a deal more caution and a deal less good-nature than I ever thought you had,' he continued emphatically.

'No, sir; it is not any planned manner of mine at all,' she said earnestly. 'But you will see, I am sure, that I could not go down to the hall with you without putting myself in a wrong light.'

'Yes; that's it, that's it. I am only a fellow in the yeomanry cavalry – a plain soldier, I may say; and we know what women think of such: that they are a bad lot – men you mustn't speak to for fear of losing your character – chaps you avoid in the roads – chaps that come into a house like oxen, daub the stairs wi' their boots, stain the furniture wi' their drink, talk rubbish to the servants, abuse all that's holy and righteous, and are only saved from being carried off by Old Nick because they are wanted for Boney.'

'Indeed, I didn't know you were thought so bad of as that,' said he simply.

'What! don't my uncle complain to you of me? You are a favourite of that handsome, nice old gaffer's, I know.'

'Never.'

'Well, what do we think of our nice trumpet-major, hey?'

Anne closed her mouth up tight, built it up, in fact, to show that no answer was coming to that question.

'O now, come, seriously, Loveday is a good fellow, and so is his father.'

'I don't know.'

'What a close little rogue you are! There is no getting anything out of you. I believe you would say "I don't know" to every mortal question, so very discreet as you are. Upon my heart, there are some women who would say "I don't know" to "Will ye marry me?" '

The brightness upon Anne's cheek and in her eyes during this remark showed that there was a fair quantity of life and warmth beneath the discretion he complained of. Having spoken thus, he drew aside that she might pass, and bowed very low. Anne formally inclined herself and went on.

She had been at vexation point all the time that he was present, from a haunting sense that he would not have spoken to her so freely had she been a young woman with thriving male relatives to keep forward admirers in check. But she had been struck, now as at their previous meeting, with the power she possessed of working him up either to irritation or to complacency at will; and this consciousness of being able to play upon him as upon an instrument disposed her to a humorous considerateness, and made her tolerate even while she rebuffed him.

When Anne got to the hall the farmer, as usual, insisted upon her reading what he had been unable to get through, and held the paper tightly in his skinny hand till she had agreed. He sent her to a hard chair that she could not possibly injure to the extent of a pennyworth by sitting in it a twelvemonth, and watched her from the outer angle of his near eye while she bent over the paper. His look might have been suggested by the sight that he had witnessed from his window on the last occasion of her visit, for it partook of the nature of concern. The old man was afraid of his nephew, physically and morally, and he began to regard Anne as a fellow-sufferer under the same despot. After this sly and curious gaze at her he withdrew his eye again, so that when she casually lifted her own there was nothing visible but his keen bluish profile as before.

When the reading was about half-way through, the door behind them opened, and footsteps crossed the threshold. The farmer diminished perceptibly in his chair, and looked fearful, but pretended to be absorbed in the reading, and quite unconscious of an intruder. Anne felt the presence of the swashing Festus, and stopped her reading.

'Please go on, Miss Anne,' he said, 'I am not going to speak a word.' He withdrew to the mantelpiece and leaned against it at his ease.

'Go on, do ye, maidy Anne,' said Uncle Benjy, keeping down his tremblings by a great effort to half their natural extent.

Anne's voice became much lower now that there were two

listeners, and her modesty shrank somewhat from exposing to Festus the appreciative modulations which an intelligent interest in the subject drew from her when unembarrassed. But she still went on that he might not suppose her to be disconcerted, though the ensuing ten minutes was one of disquietude. She knew that the bothering yeoman's eyes were travelling over her from his position behind, creeping over her shoulders, up to her head, and across her arms and hands. Old Benjy on his part knew the same thing, and after sundry endeavours to peep at his nephew from the corner of his eye, he could bear the situation no longer.

'Do ye want to say anything to me, nephew?' he quaked.

'No, uncle, thank ye,' said Festus heartily. 'I like to stay here, thinking of you and looking at your back hair.'

The nervous old man writhed under this vivisection, and Anne read on; till, to the relief of both, the gallant fellow grew tired of his amusement and went out of the room. Anne soon finished her paragraph and rose to go, determined never to come again as long as Festus haunted the precincts. Her face grew warmer as she thought that he would be sure to waylay her on her journey home today.

On this account, when she left the house, instead of going in the customary direction, she bolted round to the further side, through the bushes, along under the kitchen-garden wall, and through a door leading into a rutted cart-track, which had been a pleasant gravelled drive when the fine old hall was in its prosperity. Once out of sight of the windows she ran with all her might till she had quitted the grounds by a route directly opposite to that towards her home. Why she was so seriously bent upon doing this she could hardly tell; but the instinct to run was irresistible.

It was necessary now to clamber over the down to the left of the camp, and make a complete circuit round the latter – infantry, cavalry, sutlers, [57] and all – descending to her house on the other side. This tremendous walk she performed at a rapid rate, never once turning her head, and avoiding every beaten track to keep clear of the knots of soldiers taking a walk. When she at last got down to the levels again she paused to fetch breath, and murmured, 'Why did I take so much trouble? He would not, after all, have hurt me.'

As she neared the mill an erect figure with a blue body and white thighs descended before her from the down towards the village, and went past the mill to a stile beyond, over which she usually returned to her house. Here he lingered. On coming nearer Anne discovered this person to be Trumpet-major Loveday; and not wishing to meet anybody just now Anne passed quickly on, and entered the house by the garden door.

'My dear Anne, what a time you have been gone!' said her mother.

'Yes, I have been round by another road.'

'Why did you do that?'

Anne looked thoughtful and reticent, for her reason was almost too silly a one to confess. 'Well, I wanted to avoid a person who is very busy trying to meet me – that's all,' she said.

Her mother glanced out of the window. 'And there he is, I suppose,' she said, as John Loveday, tired of looking for Anne at the stile, passed the house on his way to his father's door. He could not help casting his eyes towards their window, and, seeing them, he smiled.

Anne's reluctance to mention Festus was such that she did not correct her mother's error, and the dame went on: 'Well, you are quite right, my dear. Be friendly with him, but no more at present. I have heard of your other affair, and think it is a very wise choice. I am sure you have my best wishes in it, and I only hope it will come to a point.'

'What's that?' said the astonished Anne.

'You and Mr Festus Derriman, dear. You need not mind me; I have known it for several days. Old Granny Seamore called here Saturday, and told me she saw him coming home with you across White Horse Hill last week, when you went for the newspaper; so I thought I'd send you again today, and give you another chance.'

'Then you didn't want the paper – and it was only for that!'

'He's a very fine young fellow; he looks a thorough woman's protector.'

'He may look it,' said Anne.

'He has given up the freehold farm his father held at Pitstock, and lives in independence on what the land brings him. And when Farmer Derriman dies, he'll have all the old man's, for certain.

He'll be worth ten thousand pounds, if a penny, in money, besides sixteen horses, cart and hack, a fifty-cow dairy, and at least five hundred sheep.'

Anne turned away, and instead of informing her mother that she had been running like a doe to escape the interesting heir-presumptive alluded to, merely said, 'Mother, I don't like this at all.'

# * IX *

## Anne is Kindly Fetched
by the Trumpet-Major

AFTER this, Anne would on no account walk in the direction of
the hall for fear of another encounter with young Derriman. In
the course of a few days it was told in the village that the old
farmer had actually gone for a week's holiday and change of air to
the Royal watering-place[58] near at hand, at the instance of his
nephew Festus. This was a wonderful thing to hear of Uncle
Benjy, who had not slept outside the walls of Oxwell Hall for
many a long year before; and Anne well imagined what extraordinary pressure must have been put upon him to induce him to
take such a step. She pictured his unhappiness at the bustling
watering-place, and hoped no harm would come to him.

She spent much of her time indoors or in the garden, hearing
little of the camp movements beyond the periodical Ta-ta-ta-taa
of the trumpeters sounding their various ingenious calls for watch-
setting, stables, feed, boot-and-saddle, parade, and so on, which
made her think how clever her friend the trumpet-major must be
to teach his pupils to play those pretty little tunes so well.

On the third morning after Uncle Benjy's departure, she was
disturbed as usual while dressing by the tramp of the troops down
the slope to the mill-pond, and during the now familiar stamping
and splashing which followed there sounded upon the glass of the
window a slight smack, which might have been caused by a whip
or switch. She listened more particularly, and it was repeated.

As John Loveday was the only dragoon likely to be aware that
she slept in that particular apartment, she imagined the signal to
come from him, though wondering that he should venture upon
such a freak of familiarity.

Wrapping herself up in a red cloak, she went to the window,
gently drew up a corner of the curtain, and peeped out, as she had

done many times before. Nobody who was not quite close beneath her window could see her face; but as it happened, somebody was close. The soldiers whose floundering Anne had heard were not Loveday's dragoons, but a troop of the York Hussars, quite oblivious of her existence. They had passed on out of the water, and instead of them there sat Festus Derriman alone on his horse, and in plain clothes, the water reaching up to the animal's belly, and Festus's heels elevated over the saddle to keep them out of the stream, which threatened to wash rider and horse into the deep mill-head just below. It was plainly he who had struck her lattice, for in a moment he looked up, and their eyes met. Festus laughed loudly, and slapped her window again; and just at that moment the dragoons began prancing down the slope in review order. She could not but wait a minute or two to see them pass. While doing so she was suddenly led to draw back, drop the corner of the curtain, and blush privately in her room. She had not only been seen by Festus Derriman, but by John Loveday, who, riding along with his trumpet slung up behind him, had looked over his shoulder at the phenomenon of Derriman beneath Anne's bedroom window and seemed quite astounded at the sight.

She was quite vexed at the conjunction of incidents, and went no more to the window till the dragoons had ridden far away and she had heard Festus's horse laboriously wade on to dry land. When she looked out there was nobody left but Miller Loveday, who usually stood in the garden at this time of the morning to say a word or two to the soldiers, of whom he already knew so many, and was in a fair way of knowing many more, from the liberality with which he handed round mugs of cheering liquor whenever parties of them walked that way.

In the afternoon of this day Anne walked to a christening party at a neighbour's in the adjoining parish of Springham, intending to walk home again before it got dark; but there was a slight fall of rain towards evening, and she was pressed by the people of the house to stay over the night. With some hesitation she accepted their hospitality; but at ten o'clock, when they were thinking of going to bed, they were startled by a smart rap at the door, and on it being unbolted a man's form was seen in the shadows outside.

'Is Miss Garland here?' the visitor inquired, at which Anne suspended her breath.

'Yes,' said Anne's entertainer, warily.

'Her mother is very anxious to know what's become of her. She promised to come home.' To her great relief Anne recognized the voice as John Loveday's, and not Festus Derriman's.

'Yes, I did, Mr Loveday,' said she, coming forward; 'but it rained, and I thought my mother would guess where I was.'

Loveday said with diffidence that it had not rained anything to speak of at the camp, or at the mill, so that her mother was rather alarmed.

'And she asked you to come for me?' Anne inquired.

This was a question which the trumpet-major had been dreading during the whole of his walk thither. 'Well, she didn't exactly ask me,' he said rather lamely, but still in a manner to show that Mrs Garland had indirectly signified such to be her wish. In reality Mrs Garland had not addressed him at all on the subject. She had merely spoken to his father on finding that her daughter did not return, and received an assurance from the miller that the precious girl was doubtless quite safe. John heard of this inquiry, and, having a pass that evening, resolved to relieve Mrs Garland's mind on his own responsibility. Ever since his morning view of Festus under her window he had been on thorns of anxiety, and his thrilling hope now was that she would walk back with him.

He shifted his foot nervously as he made the bold request. Anne felt at once that she would go. There was nobody in the world whose care she would more readily be under than the trumpet-major's in a case like the present. He was their nearest neighbour's son, and she had liked his single-minded ingenuousness from the first moment of his return home.

When they had started on their walk Anne said in a practical way way, to show that there was no sentiment whatever in her acceptance of his company, 'Mother was much alarmed about me, perhaps?'

'Yes; she was uneasy,' he said; and then was compelled by conscience to make a clean breast of it. 'I know she was uneasy, because my father said so. But I did not see her myself. The truth is, she doesn't know I am come.'

Anne now saw how the matter stood; but she was not offended with him. What woman could have been? They walked on in silence, the respectful trumpet-major keeping a yard off on her right as precisely as if that measure had been fixed between them. She had a great feeling of civility towards him this evening, and spoke again. 'I often hear your trumpeters blowing the calls. They do it beautifully, I think.'

'Pretty fair; they might do better,' said he, as one too well-mannered to make much of an accomplishment in which he had a hand.

'And you taught them how to do it?'

'Yes, I taught them.'

'It must require wonderful practice to get them into the way of beginning and finishing so exactly at one time. It is like one throat doing it all. How came you to be a trumpeter, Mr Loveday?'

'Well, I took to it naturally when I was a little boy,' said he, betrayed into quite a gushing state by her delightful interest. 'I used to make trumpets of paper, eldersticks, eltrot[59] stems, and even stinging-nettle stalks, you know. Then father set me to keep the birds off that little barley-ground of his, and gave me an old horn to frighten 'em with. I learnt to blow that horn so that you could hear me for miles and miles. Then he bought me a clarionet, and when I could play that I borrowed a serpent,[60] and I learned to play a tolerable bass. So when I 'listed I was picked out for training as trumpeter at once.'

'Of course you were.'

'Sometimes, however, I wish I had never joined the army. My father gave me a very fair education, and your father showed me how to draw horses – on a slate, I mean. Yes, I ought to have done more than I have.'

'What, did you know my father?' she asked with new interest.

'O yes, for years. You were a little mite of a thing then; and you used to cry when we big boys looked at you, and made pig's eyes at you, which we did sometimes. Many and many a time have I stood by your poor father while he worked. Ah, you don't remember much about him; but I do!'

Anne remained thoughtful; and the moon broke from behind

the clouds, lighting up the wet foliage with a twinkling brightness, and lending to each of the trumpet-major's buttons and spurs a little ray of its own. They had come to Oxwell village, and he said, 'Do you like going across, or round by the lane?'

'We may as well go by the nearest road,' said Anne.

They entered a gate, following a half-obliterated drive till they came almost opposite the hall, when they entered a footpath leading towards the downs. While hereabout they heard a shout, or chorus of exclamation, apparently from within the walls of the dark buildings near them.

'What was that?' said Anne.

'I don't know,' said her companion. 'I'll go and see.'

He went round some intervening buildings into a wilderness which had once been a flower-garden, crossed an orchard of aged trees, and advanced to the wall of the house. Boisterous noises were resounding from within, and he was tempted to go round the corner, where the low windows were, and look through a chink into the room whence the sounds proceeded.

It was the room in which the owner dined – traditionally called the great parlour – and within it sat about a dozen young men of the yeomanry cavalry, one of them being Festus. They were drinking, laughing, singing, thumping their fists on the tables, and enjoying themselves in the very perfection of confusion. The candles, blown by the breeze from the partly opened window, had guttered into coffin handles and shrouds, and, choked by their long black wicks for want of snuffing, gave out a smoky yellow light. One of the young men might possibly have been in a maudlin state, for he had his arm round the neck of his next neighbour. Another was making an incoherent speech to which nobody was listening. Some of their faces were red, some were sallow; some were sleepy, some wide awake. The only one among them who appeared in his usual frame of mind was Festus, whose huge, burly form rose at the head of the table, enjoying with a serene and triumphant aspect the difference between his own condition and that of his neighbours. While the trumpet-major looked, a young woman, niece of Anthony Cripplestraw, and one of Uncle Benjy's servants, was called in by one of the crew, and much against her will a fiddle was placed in her hands, from which they made her produce discordant screeches.

The absence of Uncle Benjy had, in fact, been contrived by young Derriman that he might make use of the hall on his own account. Cripplestraw had been left in charge, and Festus had found no difficulty in forcing from that dependent the keys of whatever he required. John Loveday turned his eyes from the scene to the neighbouring moonlit path, where Anne still stood waiting. Then he looked into the room, then at Anne again. It was an opportunity of advancing his own cause with her by exposing Festus, for whom he began to entertain hostile feelings of no mean force.

'No; I can't do it,' he said. ' 'Tis underhand. Let things take their chance.'

He moved away, and then perceived that Anne, tired of waiting, had crossed the orchard, and almost come up with him.

'What is the noise about?' she said.

'There's company in the house,' said Loveday.

'Company? Farmer Derriman is not at home,' said Anne, and went on to the window whence the rays of light leaked out, the trumpet-major standing where he was. He saw her face enter the beam of candlelight, stay there for a moment, and quickly withdraw. She came back to him at once. 'Let us go on,' she said.

Loveday imagined from her tone that she must have an interest in Derriman, and said sadly, 'You blame me for going across to the window, and leading you to follow me.'

'Not a bit,' said Anne, seeing his mistake as to the state of her heart, and being rather angry with him for it. 'I think it was most natural, considering the noise.'

Silence again. 'Derriman is sober as a judge,' said Loveday, as they turned to go. 'It was only the others who were noisy.'

'Whether he is sober or not is nothing whatever to me,' said Anne.

'Of course not. I know it,' said the trumpet-major, in accents expressing unhappiness at her somewhat curt tone, and some doubt of her assurance.

Before they had emerged from the shadow of the hall some

persons were seen moving along the road to the gate. Loveday was for going on just the same; but Anne, from a shy feeling that it was as well not to be seen walking alone with a man who was not her lover, said –

'Mr Loveday, let us wait here a minute till they have gone in.'

On nearer view the group was seen to comprise a man on a piebald horse, and another man walking beside him. When they were opposite the house they halted, and the rider dismounted, whereupon a dispute between him and the other man ensued, apparently on a question of money.

' 'Tis old Mr Derriman come home!' said Anne. 'He has hired that horse from the bathing-machine to bring him. Only fancy!'

Before they had gone many steps further the farmer and his companion had ended their dispute, and the latter mounted the horse and cantered away, Uncle Benjy coming on to the house at a nimble pace. As soon as he observed Loveday and Anne, he fell into a feebler gait; when they came up he recognized Anne.

'And you have torn yourself away from King George's Esplanade so soon, Farmer Derriman?' said she.

'Yes, faith! I couldn't bide at such a ruination place,' said the farmer. 'Your hand in your pocket every minute of the day. 'Tis a shilling for this, half-a-crown for that; if you only eat one egg, or even a poor windfall of an apple, you've got to pay; and a bunch o' radishes is a halfpenny, and a quart o' cider a good tuppence three-farthings at lowest reckoning. Nothing without paying! I couldn't even get a ride homeward upon that screw without the man wanting a shilling for it, when my weight didn't take a penny out of the beast. I've saved a penn'orth or so of shoe-leather to be sure; but the saddle was so rough wi' patches that it took twopence out of the seat of my best breeches. King George hev' ruined the town for other folks. More than that, my nephew promised to come there tomorrow to see me, and if I had stayed I must have treated en. Hey – what's that?'

It was a shout from within the walls of the building, and Loveday said –

'Your nephew is here, and has company.'

'My nephew *here*?' gasped the old man. 'Good folks, will you come up to the door with me? I mean – hee – hee – just for company! Dear me, I thought my house was as quiet as a church!'

They went back to the window, and the farmer looked in, his mouth falling apart to a greater width at the corners than in the middle, and his fingers assuming a state of radiation.

' 'Tis my best silver tankards they've got, that I've never used! O, 'tis my strong beer! 'Tis eight candles guttering away, when I've used nothing but twenties[61] myself for the last half-year!'

'You didn't know he was here, then?' said Loveday.

'O no!' said the farmer, shaking his head half-way. 'Nothing's known to poor I! There's my best rummers[62] jingling as careless as if 'twas tin cups; and my table scratched, and my chairs wrenched out of joint. See how they tilt 'em on the two back legs – and that's ruin to a chair! Ah! when I be gone he won't find another old man to make such work with, and provide goods for his breaking, and house-room and drink for his tear-brass[63] set!'

'Comrades and fellow-soldiers,' said Festus to the hot farmers and yeomen he entertained within, 'as we have vowed to brave danger and death together, so we'll share the couch of peace. You shall sleep here tonight, for it is getting late. My scram[64] blue-vinnied[65] gallicrow[66] of an uncle takes care that there shan't be much comfort in the house, but you can curl up on the furniture if beds run short. As for my sleep, it won't be much. I'm melan-choly! A woman has, I may say, got my heart in her pocket, and I have hers in mine. She's not much – to other folk, I mean – but she is to me. The little thing came in my way, and conquered me. I fancy that simple girl! I ought to have looked higher – I know it; what of that? 'Tis a fate that may happen to the greatest men.'

'Whash her name?' said one of the warriors, whose head occasionally drooped upon his epaulettes, and whose eyes fell together in the casual manner characteristic of the tired soldier. (It was really Farmer Stubb, of Duddle Hole.)

'Her name? Well, 'tis spelt A, N – but, by gad, I won't give ye her name here in company. She don't live a hundred miles off, however, and she wears the prettiest cap-ribbons you ever saw. Well, well; 'tis weakness! She has little, and I have much; but I do adore that girl, in spite of myself!'

'Let's go on,' said Anne.

'Prithee stand by an old man till he's got into his house!' implored Uncle Benjy. 'I only ask ye to bide within call. Stand back under the trees, and I'll do my poor best to give no trouble.'

'I'll stand by you for half an hour, sir,' said Loveday. 'After that I must bolt to camp.'

'Very well; bide back there under the trees,' said Uncle Benjy. 'I don't want to spite 'em!'

'You'll wait a few minutes, just to see if he gets in?' said the trumpet-major to Anne as they retired from the old man.

'I want to get home,' said Anne anxiously.

When they had quite receded behind the tree-trunks and he stood alone, Uncle Benjy, to their surprise, set up a loud shout, altogether beyond the imagined power of his lungs.

'Man a-lost! man a-lost!' he cried, repeating the exclamation several times; and then ran and hid himself behind a corner of the building. Soon the door opened, and Festus and his guests came tumbling out upon the green.

' 'Tis our duty to help folks in distress,' said Festus. 'Man a-lost, where are you?'

' 'Twas across there,' said one of his friends.

'No; 'twas here,' said another.

Meanwhile Uncle Benjy, coming from his hiding-place, had scampered with the quickness of a boy up to the door they had quitted, and slipped in. In a moment the door flew together, and Anne heard him bolting and barring it inside. The revellers, however, did not notice this, and came on towards the spot where the trumpet-major and Anne were standing.

'Here's succour at hand, friends,' said Festus. 'We are all king's men; do not fear us.'

'Thank you,' said Loveday; 'so are we.' He explained in two words that they were not the distressed traveller who had cried out, and turned to go on.

' 'Tis she! my life, 'tis she!' said Festus, now first recognizing Anne. 'Fair Anne, I will not part from you till I see you safe at your own dear door.'

'She's in my hands,' said Loveday civilly, though not without firmness, 'so it is not required, thank you.'

'Man, had I but my sword —'

'Come,' said Loveday, 'I don't want to quarrel. Let's put it to her. Whichever of us she likes best, he shall take her home. Miss Anne, which?'

Anne would much rather have gone home alone, but seeing the remainder of the yeomanry party staggering up she thought it best to secure a protector of some kind. How to choose one without offending the other and provoking a quarrel was the difficulty.

'You must both walk home with me,' she adroitly said, 'one on one side, and one on the other. And if you are not quite civil to one another all the time, I'll never speak to either of you again.'

They agreed to the terms, and the other yeomen arriving at this time said they would go also as rear-guard.

'Very well,' said Anne. 'Now go and get your hats, and don't be long.'

'Ah, yes; our hats,' said the yeomanry, whose heads were so hot that they had forgotten their nakedness till then.

'You'll wait till we've got 'em – we won't be a moment,' said Festus eagerly.

Anne and Loveday said yes, and Festus ran back to the house, followed by all his band.

'Now let's run and leave 'em,' said Anne, when they were out of hearing.

'But we've promised to wait!' said the trumpet-major in surprise.

'Promised to wait!' said Anne indignantly. 'As if one ought to keep such a promise to drunken men as that. You can do as you like, I shall go.'

'It is hardly fair to leave the chaps,' said Loveday reluctantly, and looking back at them. But she heard no more, and flitting off under the trees, was soon lost to his sight.

Festus and the rest had by this time reached Uncle Benjy's door, which they were discomfited and astonished to find closed. They began to knock, and then to kick at the venerable timber, till the old man's head, crowned with a tasselled nightcap, appeared at an upper window, followed by his shoulders, with apparently nothing on but his shirt, though it was in truth a sheet thrown over his coat.

'Fie, fie upon ye all for making such a hullaballoo at a weak old man's door,' he said, yawning. 'What's in ye to rouse honest folks at this time o' night?'

'Hang me – why – it's Uncle Benjy! Haw-haw-haw!' said Festus. 'Nunc, why how the devil's this? 'Tis I – Festus – wanting to come in.'

'O no, no, my clever man, whoever you be!' said Uncle Benjy in a tone of incredulous integrity. 'My nephew, dear boy, is miles away at quarters, and sound asleep by this time, as becomes a good soldier. That story won't do tonight, my man, not at all.'

'Upon my soul 'tis I,' said Festus.

'Not tonight, my man; not tonight! Anthony, bring my blunderbuss,' said the farmer, turning and addressing nobody inside the room.

'Let's break in the window-shutters,' said one of the others.

'My wig, and we will!' said Festus. 'What a trick of the old man!'

'Get some big stones,' said the yeomen, searching under the wall.

'No; forbear, forbear,' said Festus, beginning to be frightened at the spirit he had raised. 'I forget; we should drive him into fits, for he's subject to 'em, and then perhaps 'twould be manslaughter. Comrades, we must march! No, we'll lie in the barn. I'll see into this, take my word for't. Our honour is at stake. Now let's back to see my beauty home.'

'We can't, as we hav'n't got our hats,' said one of his fellow-troopers – in domestic life Jacob Noakes, of Nether Moynton Farm.

'No more we can,' said Festus, in a melancholy tone. 'But I must go to her and tell her the reason. She pulls me in spite of all.'

'She's gone. I saw her flee across the Knap[67] while we were knocking at the door,' said another of the yeomanry.

'Gone!' said Festus, grinding his teeth and putting himself into a rigid shape. 'Then 'tis my enemy – he has tempted her away with him! But I am a rich man, and he's poor, and rides the King's horse while I ride my own. Could I but find that fellow, that regular, that common man, I would –'

'Yes?' said the trumpet-major, coming up behind him.

'I,' – said Festus, starting round – 'I would seize him by the hand and say, "Guard her; if you are my friend, guard her from all harm!" '

'A good speech. And I will, too,' said Loveday heartily.

'And now for shelter,' said Festus to his companions.

They then unceremoniously left Loveday, without wishing him good night, and proceeded towards the barn. He crossed the field and ascended the down to the camp, grieved that he had given Anne cause of complaint, and fancying that she held him of slight account beside his wealthier rival.

# X

# The Match-making Virtues
## of a Double Garden

ANNE was so flurried by the military incidents attending her return home that she was almost afraid to venture alone outside her mother's premises. Moreover, the numerous soldiers, regular and other, that haunted Overcombe and its neighbourhood, were getting better acquainted with the villagers, and the result was that they were always standing at garden gates, walking in the orchards, or sitting gossiping just within cottage doors, with the bowls of their tobacco-pipes thrust outside for politeness' sake, that they might not defile the air of the household. Being gentlemen of a gallant and most affectionate nature, they naturally turned their heads and smiled if a pretty girl passed by, which was rather disconcerting to the latter if she were unused to society. Every belle in the village soon had a lover, and when the belles were all allotted those who scarcely deserved that title had their turn, many of the soldiers being not at all particular about half-an-inch of nose more or less, a trifling deficiency of teeth, or a larger crop of freckles than is customary in the Saxon race. Thus, with one and another, courtship began to be practised in Overcombe on rather a large scale, and the dispossessed young men who had been born in the place were left to take their walks alone, where, instead of studying the works of nature, they meditated gross outrages on the brave men who had been so good as to visit their village.

Anne watched these romantic proceedings from her window with much interest, and when she saw how triumphantly other handsome girls of the neighbourhood walked by on the gorgeous arms of Lieutenant Knockheelmann, Cornet Flitzenhart, and Captain Klaspenkissen, of the thrilling York Hussars, who swore the most picturesque foreign oaths, and had a wonderful sort of estate or property called the Vaterland in their country across the sea, she was filled with a sense of her own loneliness. It made her think of things which she tried to forget, and to look into a little drawer at something soft and brown that lay in a curl there, wrapped in paper. At last she could bear it no longer, and went downstairs.

'Where are you going?' said Mrs Garland.

'To see the folks, because I am so gloomy!'

'Certainly not at present, Anne.'

'Why not, mother?' said Anne, blushing with an indefinite sense of being very wicked.

'Because you must not. I have been going to tell you several times not to go into the street at this time of day. Why not walk in the morning? There's young Mr Derriman would be glad to –'

'Don't mention him, mother, don't!'

'Well then, dear, walk in the garden.'

So poor Anne, who really had not the slightest wish to throw her heart away upon a soldier, but merely wanted to displace old thoughts by new, turned into the inner garden from day to day, and passed a good many hours there, the pleasant birds singing to her, and the delightful butterflies alighting on her hat, and the horrid ants running up her stockings.

This garden was undivided from Loveday's, the two having originally been the single garden of the whole house. It was a quaint old place, enclosed by a thorn hedge so shapely and dense from incessant clipping that the mill-boy could walk along the top without sinking in – a feat which he often performed as a means of filling out his day's work. The soil within was of that intense fat blackness which is only seen after a century of constant cultivation. The paths were grassed over, so that people came and went upon them without being heard. The grass harboured slugs, and on this account the miller was going to replace it by gravel as soon as he had time; but as he had said this for thirty years without doing it, the grass and the slugs seemed likely to remain.

The miller's man attended to Mrs Garland's piece of the garden as well as to the larger portion, digging, planting, and weeding indifferently in both, the miller observing with reason that it was not worth while for a helpless widow lady to hire a man for her little plot when his man, working alongside, could tend it without much addition to his labour. The two households were on this account even more closely united in the garden than within the mill. Out there they were almost one family, and they talked from plot to plot with a zest and animation which Mrs Garland could never have anticipated when she first removed thither after her husband's death.

The lower half of the garden, furthest from the road, was the most snug and sheltered part of this snug and sheltered enclosure, and it was well watered as the land of Lot.[68] Three small brooks, about a yard wide, ran with a tinkling sound from side to side between the plots, crossing the path under wood slabs laid as bridges, and passing out of the garden through little tunnels in the hedge. The brooks were so far overhung at their brinks by grass and garden produce that, had it not been for their perpetual babbling, few would have noticed that they were there. This was where Anne liked best to linger when her excursions became restricted to her own premises; and in a spot of the garden not far removed the trumpet-major loved to linger also.

Having by virtue of his office no stable duty to perform, he came down from the camp to the mill almost every day; and Anne, finding that he adroitly walked and sat in his father's portion of the garden whenever she did so in the other half, could not help smiling and speaking to him. So his epaulettes and blue jacket, and Anne's yellow gipsy hat, were often seen in different parts of the garden at the same time; but he never intruded into her part of the enclosure, nor did she into Loveday's. She always spoke to him when she saw him there, and he replied in deep, firm accents across the gooseberry bushes, or through the tall rows of flowering peas, as the case might be. He thus gave her accounts at fifteen paces of his experiences in camp, in quarters, in Flanders, and elsewhere; of the difference between line and column, of forced marches, billeting, and such-like, together with his hopes of promotion. Anne listened at first indifferently; but knowing no one else so good-natured and experienced, she grew interested in him as in a brother. By degrees his gold lace, buckles, and spurs lost all their strangeness and were as familiar to her as her own clothes.

At last Mrs Garland noticed this growing friendship, and began to despair of her motherly scheme of uniting Anne to the moneyed Festus. Why she could not take prompt steps to check interference with her plans arose partly from her nature, which was the reverse of managing, and partly from a new emotional circumstance with which she found it difficult to reckon. The near neighbourhood that had produced the friendship of Anne for John Loveday was slowly effecting a warmer liking between her mother and his father.

Thus the month of July passed. The troop horses came with the regularity of clockwork twice a day down to drink under her window, and, as the weather grew hotter, kicked up their heels and shook their heads furiously under the maddening sting of the dun-fly.[69] The green leaves in the garden became of a darker dye, the gooseberries ripened, and the three brooks were reduced to half their winter volume.

At length the earnest trumpet-major obtained Mrs Garland's consent to take her and her daughter to the camp, which they had not yet viewed from any closer point than their own windows. So one afternoon they went, the miller being of the party. The villagers were by this time driving a roaring trade with the soldiers, who purchased of them every description of garden produce, milk, butter, and eggs at liberal prices. The figures of these rural sutlers could be seen creeping up the slopes, laden like bees, to a spot in the rear of the camp, where there was a kind of market-place on the greensward.

Mrs Garland, Anne, and the miller were conducted from one place to another, and on to the quarter where the soldiers' wives lived who had not been able to get lodgings in the cottages near. The most sheltered place had been chosen for them, and snug huts had been built for their use by their husbands, of clods, hurdles, a little thatch, or whatever they could lay hands on. The trumpet-major conducted his friends thence to the large barn which had been appropriated as a hospital, and to the cottage with its windows bricked up, that was used as the magazine; then they inspected the lines of shining dark horses (each representing the then high figure of two-and-twenty guineas purchase money), standing patiently at the ropes which stretched from one picket-post to another, a bank being thrown up in front of them as a protection at night.

They passed on to the tents of the German Legion, a well-grown and rather dandy set of men, with a poetical look about their faces which rendered them interesting to feminine eyes. Hanoverians, Saxons, Prussians, Swedes, Hungarians, and other foreigners were numbered in their ranks. They were cleaning arms, which they leant carefully against a rail when the work was complete.

On their return they passed the mess-house, a temporary wooden building with a brick chimney. As Anne and her companions went by, a group of three or four of the hussars were standing at the door talking to a dashing young man, who was expatiating on the qualities of a horse that one was inclined to buy. Anne recognized Festus Derriman in the seller, and Cripplestraw was trotting the animal up and down. As soon as she caught the yeoman's eye he came forward, making some friendly remark to the miller, and then turning to Miss Garland, who kept her eyes steadily fixed on the distant landscape till he got so near that it was impossible to do so longer. Festus looked from Anne to the trumpet-major, and from the trumpet-major back to Anne, with a dark expression of face, as if he suspected that there might be a tender understanding between them.

'Are you offended with me?' he said to her in a low voice of repressed resentment.

'No,' said Anne.

'When are you coming to the hall again?'

'Never, perhaps.'

'Nonsense, Anne,' said Mrs Garland, who had come near, and smiled pleasantly on Festus. 'You can go at any time, as usual.'

'Let her come with me now, Mrs Garland; I should be pleased to walk along with her. My man can lead home the horse.'

'Thank you, but I shall not come,' said Miss Anne coldly.

The widow looked unhappily in her daughter's face, distressed between her desire that Anne should encourage Festus, and her wish to consult Anne's own feelings.

'Leave her alone, leave her alone,' said Festus, his gaze blackening. 'Now I think of it I am glad she can't come with me, for I am engaged'; and he stalked away.

Anne moved on with her mother, young Loveday silently following, and they began to descend the hill.

'Well, where's Mr Loveday?' asked Mrs Garland.

'Father's behind,' said John.

Mrs Garland looked behind her solicitously; and the miller, who had been waiting for the event, beckoned to her.

'I'll overtake you in a minute,' she said to the younger pair, and went back, her colour, for some unaccountable reason, rising as she did so. The miller and she then came on slowly together, conversing in very low tones, and when they got to the bottom they stood still. Loveday and Anne waited for them, saying but little to each other, for the rencounter with Festus had damped the spirits of both. At last the widow's private talk with Miller Loveday came to an end, and she hastened onward, the miller going in another direction to meet a man on business. When she reached the trumpet-major and Anne she was looking very bright and rather flurried, and seemed sorry when Loveday said that he must leave them and return to the camp. They parted in their usual friendly manner, and Anne and her mother were left to walk the few remaining yards alone.

'There, I've settled it,' said Mrs Garland. 'Anne, what are you thinking about? I have settled in my mind that it is all right.'

'What's all right?' said Anne.

'That you do not care for Derriman, and mean to encourage John Loveday. What's all the world so long as folks are happy! Child, don't take any notice of what I have said about Festus, and don't meet him any more.'

'What a weathercock you are, mother! Why should you say that just now?'

'It is easy to call me a weathercock,' said the matron, putting on the look of a good woman; 'but I have reasoned it out, and at last, thank God, I have got over my ambition. The Lovedays are our true and only friends, and Mr Festus Derriman, with all his money, is nothing to us at all.'

'But,' said Anne, 'what has made you change all of a sudden from what you have said before?'

'My feelings and my reason, which I am thankful for!'

Anne knew that her mother's sentiments were naturally so

versatile that they could not be depended on for two days together; but it did not occur to her for the moment that a change had been helped on in the present case by a romantic talk between Mrs Garland and the miller. But Mrs Garland could not keep the secret long. She chatted gaily as she walked, and before they had entered the house she said, 'What do you think Mr Loveday has been saying to me, dear Anne?'

Anne did not know at all.

'Why, he has asked me to marry him.'

# XI

# Our People are Affected by the Presence of Royalty

To explain the miller's sudden proposal it is only necessary to go back to that moment when Anne, Festus, and Mrs Garland were talking together on the down. John Loveday had fallen behind so as not to interfere with a meeting in which he was decidedly superfluous; and his father, who guessed the trumpet-major's secret, watched his face as he stood. John's face was sad, and his eyes followed Mrs Garland's encouraging manner to Festus in a way which plainly said that every parting of her lips was tribulation to him. The miller loved his son as much as any miller or private gentleman could do, and he was pained to see John's gloom at such a trivial circumstance. So what did he resolve but to help John there and then by precipitating a matter which, had he himself been the only person concerned, he would have delayed for another six months.

He had long liked the society of his impulsive, tractable neighbour, Mrs Garland; had mentally taken her up and pondered her in connection with the question whether it would not be for the happiness of both if she were to share his home, even though she was a little his superior in antecedents and knowledge. In fact he loved her; not tragically, but to a very creditable extent for his years; that is, next to his sons, Bob and John, though he knew very well of that ploughed-ground appearance near the corners of her once handsome eyes, and that the little depression in her right cheek was not the lingering dimple it was poetically assumed to be, but a result of the abstraction of some worn-out nether mill-stones within the cheek by Rootle, the Budmouth man, who lived by such practices on the heads of the elderly. But what of that, when he had lost two to each one of hers, and exceeded her in age by some eight years! To do John a service, then, he quickened his designs, and put the question to her while they were standing under the eyes of the younger pair.

Mrs Garland, though she had been interested in the miller for a long time, and had for a moment now and then thought on this question as far as, 'Suppose he should', 'If he were to', and so on, had never thought much further; and she was really taken by surprise when the question came. She answered without affectation that she would think over the proposal; and thus they parted.

Her mother's infirmity of purpose set Anne thinking, and she was suddenly filled with a conviction that in such a case she ought to have some purpose herself. Mrs Garland's complacency at the miller's offer had, in truth, amazed her. While her mother had held up her head, and recommended Festus, it had seemed a very pretty thing to rebel; but the pressure being removed, an awful sense of her own responsibility took possession of her mind. As there was no longer anybody to be wise or ambitious for her, surely she should be wise and ambitious for herself, discountenance her mother's attachment, and encourage Festus in his addresses, for her own and her mother's good. There had been a time when a Loveday thrilled her own heart; but that was long ago, before she had thought of position or differences. To wake into cold daylight like this, when and because her mother had gone into the land of romance, was dreadful and new to her, and like an increase of years without living them.

But it was easier to think that she ought to marry the yeoman than to take steps for doing it; and she went on living just as before, only with a little more thoughtfulness in her eyes.

Two days after the visit to the camp, when she was again in the garden, Soldier Loveday said to her, at a distance of five rows of beans and a parsley-bed –

'You have heard the news, Miss Garland?'

'No,' said Anne, without looking up from a book she was reading.

'The King is coming tomorrow.'

'The King?' She looked up then.

'Yes; to Gloucester Lodge;[70] and he will pass this way. He can't arrive till long past the middle of the night, if what they say is true, that he is timed to change horses at Woodyates Inn – between

Mid and South Wessex – at twelve o'clock,' continued Loveday, encouraged by her interest to cut off the parsley-bed from the distance between them.

Miller Loveday came round the corner of the house.

'Have ye heard about the King coming, Miss Maidy Anne?' he said.

Anne said that she had just heard of it; and the trumpet-major, who hardly welcomed his father at such a moment, explained what he knew of the matter.

'And you will go with your regiment to meet 'en, I suppose?' said old Loveday.

Young Loveday said that the men of the German Legion were to perform that duty. And turning half from his father, and half towards Anne, he added, in a tentative tone, that he thought he might get leave for the night, if anybody would like to be taken to the top of the Ridgeway over which the royal party must pass.

Anne, knowing by this time of the budding hope in the gallant dragoon's mind, and not wishing to encourage it, said, 'I don't want to go.'

The miller looked disappointed as well as John.

'Your mother might like to!'

'Yes, I am going indoors, and I'll ask her if you wish me to,' said she.

She went indoors and rather coldly told her mother of the proposal. Mrs Garland, though she had determined not to answer the miller's question on matrimony just yet, was quite ready for this jaunt, and in spite of Anne she sailed off at once to the garden to hear more about it. When she re-entered, she said –

'Anne, I have not seen the King or the King's horses for these many years; and I am going.'

'Ah, it is well to be you, mother,' said Anne, in an elderly tone.

'Then you won't come with us?' said Mrs Garland, rather rebuffed.

'I have very different things to think of,' said her daughter with virtuous emphasis, 'than going to see sights at that time of night.'

Mrs Garland was sorry, but resolved to adhere to the arrangement. The night came on; and it having gone abroad that the King would pass by the road, many of the villagers went out to see the procession. When the two Lovedays and Mrs Garland were gone, Anne bolted the door for security, and sat down to think again on her grave responsibilities in the choice of a husband, now that her natural guardian could no longer be trusted.

A knock came to the door.

Anne's instinct was at once to be silent, that the comer might think the family had retired.

The knocking person, however, was not to be easily persuaded. He had in fact seen rays of light over the top of the shutter, and, unable to get an answer, went on to the door of the mill, which was still going, the miller sometimes grinding all night when busy. The grinder accompanied the stranger to Mrs Garland's door.

'The daughter is certainly at home, sir,' said the grinder. 'I'll go round to t'other side, and see if she's there, Master Derriman.'

'I want to take her out to see the King,' said Festus.

Anne had started at the sound of the voice. No opportunity could have been better for carrying out her new convictions on the disposal of her hand. But in her mortal dislike of Festus, Anne forgot her principles, and her idea of keeping herself above the Lovedays. Tossing on her hat and blowing out the candle, she slipped out at the back door, and hastily followed in the direction that her mother and the rest had taken. She overtook them as they were beginning to climb the hill.

'What! you have altered your mind after all?' said the widow. 'How came you to do that, my dear?'

'I thought I might as well come,' said Anne.

'To be sure you did,' said the miller heartily. 'A good deal better than biding at home there.'

John said nothing, though she could almost see through the gloom how glad he was that she had changed her mind. When they reached the ridge over which the highway stretched they found many of their neighbours who had got there before them idling on the grass border between the roadway and the hedge, enjoying a sort of midnight picnic, which it was easy to do, the air being still and dry. Some carriages were also standing near, though most people of the district who possessed four wheels, or even two, had driven into the town to await the King there. From this height could be seen in the distance the position of the watering-place, an additional number of lanterns, lamps, and candles having been lighted tonight by the loyal burghers to grace the royal entry, if it should occur before dawn.

Mrs Garland touched Anne's elbow several times as they walked, and the young woman at last understood that this was meant as a hint to her to take the trumpet-major's arm, which its owner was rather suggesting than offering to her. Anne wondered what infatuation was possessing her mother, declined to take the arm, and contrived to get in front with the miller, who mostly kept in the van to guide the others' footsteps. The trumpet-major was left with Mrs Garland, and Anne's encouraging pursuit of them induced him to say a few words to the former.

'By your leave, ma'am, I'll speak to you on something that concerns my mind very much indeed?'

'Certainly.'

'It is my wish to be allowed to pay my addresses to your daughter.'

'I thought you meant that,' said Mrs Garland simply.

'And you'll not object!'

'I shall leave it to her. I don't think she will agree, even if I do.'

The soldier sighed, and seemed helpless. 'Well, I can but ask her,' he said.

The spot on which they had finally chosen to wait for the King was by a field gate, whence the white road could be seen for a long distance northwards by day, and some little distance now. They lingered and lingered, but no King came to break the silence of that beautiful summer night. As half-hour after half-hour glided by, and nobody came, Anne began to get weary; she knew why her mother did not propose to go back, and regretted the reason. She would have proposed it herself, but that Mrs Garland seemed so cheerful, and as wide awake as at noonday, so that it was almost a cruelty to disturb her.

The trumpet-major at last made up his mind, and tried to draw Anne into a private conversation. The feeling which a week ago had been a vague and piquant aspiration, was today altogether too lively for the reasoning of this warm-hearted soldier to regulate.

So he persevered in his intention to catch her alone, and at last, in spite of her manœuvres to the contrary, he succeeded. The miller and Mrs Garland had walked about fifty yards further on, and Anne and himself were left standing by the gate.

But the gallant musician's soul was so much disturbed by tender vibrations and by the sense of his presumption that he could not begin; and it may be questioned if he would ever have broached the subject at all, had not a distant church clock opportunely assisted him by striking the hour of three. The trumpet-major heaved a breath of relief.

'That clock strikes in G sharp,' he said.

'Indeed – G sharp?' said Anne civilly.

'Yes. 'Tis a fine-toned bell. I used to notice that note when I was a boy.'

'Did you – the very same?'

'Yes; and since then I had a wager about that bell with the bandmaster of the North Wessex Militia. He said the note was G; I said it wasn't. When we found it G sharp we didn't know how to settle it.'

'It is not a deep note for a clock.'

'O no! The finest tenor bell about here is the bell of Peter's, Casterbridge[71] – in E flat. Tum-m-m-m – that's the note – tum-m-m-m.' The trumpet-major sounded from far down his throat what he considered to be E flat, with a parenthetic sense of luxury unquenchable even by his present distraction.

'Shall we go on to where my mother is?' said Anne, less impressed by the beauty of the note than the trumpet-major himself was.

'In one minute,' he said tremulously. 'Talking of music – I fear you don't think the rank of a trumpet-major much to compare with your own?'

'I do. I think a trumpet-major a very respectable man.'

'I am glad to hear you say that. It is given out by the King's command that trumpet-majors are to be considered respectable.'

'Indeed! Then I am, by chance, more loyal than I thought for.'

'I get a good deal a year extra to the trumpeters, because of my position.'

'That's very nice.'

'And I am not supposed ever to drink with the trumpeters who serve beneath me.'

'Naturally.'

'And, by the orders of the War Office, I am to exert over them (that's the government word) exert over them full authority; and if any one behaves towards me with the least impropriety, or neglects my orders, he is to be confined and reported.'

'It is really a dignified post,' she said, with, however, a reserve of enthusiasm which was not altogether encouraging.

'And of course some day I shall,' stammered the dragoon – 'shall be in rather a better position than I am at present.'

'I am glad to hear it, Mr Loveday.'

'And in short, Mistress Anne,' continued John Loveday bravely and desperately, 'may I pay court to you in the hope that – no, no, don't go away! – you haven't heard yet – that you may make me the happiest of men; not yet, but when peace is proclaimed and all is smooth and easy again? I can't put it any better, though there's more to be explained.'

'This is most awkward,' said Anne, evidently with pain. 'I cannot possibly agree; believe me, Mr Loveday, I cannot.'

'But there's more than this. You would be surprised to see what snug rooms the married trumpet- and sergeant-majors have in quarters.'

'Barracks are not all; consider camp and war.'

'That brings me to my strong point!' exclaimed the soldier hopefully. 'My father is better off than most non-commissioned officers' fathers; and there's always a home for you at his house in any emergency. I can tell you privately that he has enough to keep us both, and if you wouldn't hear of barracks, well, peace once established, I'd live at home as a miller and farmer – next door to your own mother.'

'My mother would be sure to object,' expostulated Anne.

'No; she leaves it all to you.'

'What! you have asked her?' said Anne, with surprise.

'Yes. I thought it would not be honourable to act otherwise.'

'That's very good of you,' said Anne, her face warming with a generous sense of his straightforwardness. 'But my mother is so entirely ignorant of a soldier's life, and the life of a soldier's wife

– she is so simple in all such matters, that I cannot listen to you any more readily for what she may say.'

'Then it is all over for me,' said the poor trumpet-major, wiping his face and putting away his handkerchief with an air of finality.

Anne was silent. Any woman who has ever tried will know without explanation what an unpalatable task it is to dismiss, even when she does not love him, a man who has all the natural and moral qualities she would desire, and only fails in the social. Would-be lovers are not so numerous, even with the best women, that the sacrifice of one can be felt as other than a good thing wasted, in a world where there are few good things.

'You are not angry, Miss Garland?' said he, finding that she did not speak.

'O no. Don't let us say anything more about this now.' And she moved on.

When she drew near to the miller and her mother she perceived that they were engaged in a conversation of that peculiar kind which is all the more full and communicative from the fact of definitive words being few. In short, here the game was succeeding which with herself had failed. It was pretty clear from the symptoms, marks, tokens, telegraphs, and general by-play between widower and widow, that Miller Loveday must have again said to Mrs Garland some such thing as he had said before, with what result this time she did not know.

As the situation was delicate, Anne halted awhile apart from them. The trumpet-major, quite ignorant of how his cause was entered into by the white-coated man in the distance (for his father had not yet told him of his designs upon Mrs Garland), did not advance, but stood still by the gate, as though he were attending a princess, waiting till he should be called up. Thus they lingered, and the day began to break. Mrs Garland and the miller took no heed of the time, and what it was bringing to earth and sky, so occupied were they with themselves; but Anne in her place and the trumpet-major in his, each in private thought of no bright kind, watched the gradual glory of the east through all its tones and changes. The world of birds and insects got lively, the blue and the yellow and the gold of Loveday's uniform again became distinct; the sun bored its way upward, the fields, the trees, and the distant landscape kindled to flame, and the trumpet-major, backed by a lilac shadow as tall as a steeple, blazed in the rays like a very god of war.

It was half past three o'clock. A short time after, a rattle of horses and wheels reached their ears from the quarter in which they gazed, and there appeared upon the white line of road a moving mass, which presently ascended the hill and drew near.

Then there arose a huzza from the few knots of watchers gathered there, and they cried, 'Long live King Jarge!' The *cortège*[72] passed abreast. It consisted of three travelling-carriages, escorted by a detachment of the German Legion. Anne was told to look in the first carriage – a post-chariot drawn by four horses – for the King and Queen, and was rewarded by seeing a profile reminding her of the current coin of the realm; but as the party had been travelling all night, and the spectators here gathered were few, none of the royal family looked out of the carriage windows. It was said that the two elder princesses were in the same carriage, but they remained invisible. The next vehicle, a coach and four, contained more princesses, and the third some of their attendants.

'Thank God, I have seen my King!' said Mrs Garland, when they had all gone by.

Nobody else expressed any thankfulness, for most of them had expected a more pompous procession than the bucolic tastes of the King[73] cared to indulge in; and one old man said grimly that that sight of dusty old leather coaches was not worth waiting for. Anne looked hither and thither in the bright rays of the day, each of her eyes having a little sun in it, which gave her glance a peculiar golden fire, and kindled the brown curls grouped over her forehead to a yellow brilliancy, and made single hairs, blown astray by the night, look like lacquered wires. She was wondering if Festus were anywhere near, but she could not see him.

Before they left the ridge they turned their attention towards the Royal watering-place, which was visible at this place only as a portion of the sea-shore, from which the night-mist was rolling slowly back. The sea beyond was still wrapped in summer fog, the ships in the roads[74] showing through it as black spiders suspended in the air. While they looked and walked a white jet of smoke burst from a spot which the miller knew to be the battery in front of the King's residence, and then the report of guns reached their ears. This announcement was answered by a salute from the Castle of the adjoining Isle,[75] and the ships in the neighbouring anchorage. All the bells in the town began ringing. The King and his family had arrived.

# XII

# How Everybody Great and Small Climbed to the Top of the Downs

As the days went on, echoes of the life and bustle of the town reached the ears of the quiet people in Overcombe hollow – exciting and moving those unimportant natives as a ground-swell moves the weeds in a cave. Travelling-carriages of all kinds and colours climbed and descended the road that led towards the seaside borough. Some contained those personages of the King's suite who had not kept pace with him in his journey from Windsor; others were the coaches of aristocracy, big and little, whom news of the King's arrival drew thither for their own pleasure: so that the highway, as seen from the hills about Overcombe, appeared like an ant-walk – a constant succession of dark spots creeping along its surface at nearly uniform rates of progress, and all in one direction.[76]

The traffic and intelligence between camp and town passed in a measure over the villagers' heads. It being summer time the miller was much occupied with business, and the trumpet-major was too constantly engaged in marching between the camp and Gloucester Lodge with the rest of the dragoons to bring his friends any news for some days.

At last he sent a message that there was to be a review on the downs by the King, and that it was fixed for the day following. This information soon spread through the village and country round, and next morning the whole population of Overcombe – except two or three very old men and women, a few babies and their nurses, a cripple, and Corporal Tullidge – ascended the slope with the crowds from afar, and awaited the events of the day.

The miller wore his best coat on this occasion, which meant a good deal. An Overcombe man in those days would have a best coat, and keep it as a best coat half his life. The miller's had seen five and twenty summers, chiefly through the chinks of a clothes-box, and was not at all shabby as yet, though getting singular. But that could not be helped; common coats and best coats were distinct species, and never interchangeable. Living so near the scene of the review he walked up the hill, accompanied by Mrs Garland and Anne as usual.

It was a clear day, with little wind stirring, and the view from the downs, one of the most extensive in the county, was unclouded. The eye of any observer who cared for such things swept over the wave-washed town, and the bay beyond, and the Isle, with its pebble bank, lying on the sea to the left of these, like a great crouching animal tethered to the mainland. On the extreme east of the marine horizon, St Aldhelm's Head closed the scene, the sea to the southward of that point glaring like a mirror under the sun. Inland could be seen Badbury Rings, where a beacon had been recently erected; and nearer, Rainbarrow, on Egdon Heath, where another stood: farther to the left Bulbarrow, where there was yet another. Not far from this came Nettlecombe Tout; to the west, Dogbury Hill, and Black'on near to the foreground, the beacon thereon being built of furze faggots thatched with straw, and standing on the spot where the monument[77] now raises its head.

At nine o'clock the troops marched upon the ground – some from the camps in the vicinity, and some from quarters in the different towns round about. The approaches to the down were blocked with carriages of all descriptions, ages, and colours, and with pedestrians of every class. At ten the royal personages were said to be drawing near, and soon after the King, accompanied by the Dukes of Cambridge and Cumberland,[78] and a couple of generals, appeared on horseback, wearing a round hat turned up at the side, with a cockade and military feather. (Sensation among the crowd.) Then the Queen and three of the princesses entered the field in a great coach drawn by six beautiful cream-coloured horses. Another coach, with four horses of the same sort, brought the two remaining princesses.[79] (Confused acclamations, 'There's King Jarge!' 'That's Queen Sharlett!' 'Princess 'Lizabeth!' 'Princesses Sophiar and Meelyer!' &c., from the surrounding spectators.)

Anne and her party were fortunate enough to secure a position on the top of one of the barrows which rose here and there on the down; and the miller having gallantly constructed a little cairn of flints, he placed the two women thereon, by which means they were enabled to see over the heads, horses, and coaches of the multitudes below and around. At the march-past the miller's eye, which had been wandering about for the purpose, discovered his son in his place by the trumpeters, who had moved forwards in two ranks, and were sounding the march.

'That's John!' he cried to the widow. 'His trumpet-sling is of two colours, d'ye see; and the others be plain.'

Mrs Garland too saw him now, and enthusiastically admired him from her hands upwards, and Anne silently did the same. But before the young woman's eyes had quite left the trumpet-major they fell upon the figure of Yeoman Festus riding with his troop, and keeping his face at a medium between haughtiness and mere bravery. He certainly looked as soldierly as any of his own corps, and felt more soldierly than half-a-dozen, as anybody could see by observing him. Anne got behind the miller, in case Festus should discover her, and, regardless of his monarch, rush upon her in a rage with, 'Why the devil did you run away from me that night – hey, madam?' But she resolved to think no more of him just now, and to stick to Loveday, who was her mother's friend. In this she was helped by the stirring tones which burst from the latter warrior and his subordinates from time to time.

'Well,' said the miller complacently, 'there's few of more consequence in a regiment than a trumpeter. He's the chap that tells 'em what to do, after all. Hey, Mrs Garland?'

'So he is, miller,' said she.

'They could no more do without Jack and his men than they could without generals.'

'Indeed they could not,' said Mrs Garland again, in a tone of pleasant agreement with any one in Great Britain or Ireland.

It was said that the line that day was three miles long, reaching from the high ground on the right of where the people stood to the turnpike road on the left. After the review came a sham fight, during which action the crowd dispersed more widely over the downs, enabling Widow Garland to get still clearer glimpses of the King, and his handsome charger, and the head of the Queen, and the elbows and shoulders of the princesses in the carriages, and fractional parts of General Garth and the Duke of Cumberland; which sights gave her great gratification. She tugged at her daughter at every opportunity, exclaiming, 'Now you can see his feather!' 'There's her hat!' 'There's her Majesty's India muslin shawl!' in a minor form of ecstasy, that made the miller think her more girlish and animated than her daughter Anne.

In those military manœuvres the miller followed the fortunes of one man; Anne Garland of two. The spectators, who, unlike our party, had no personal interest in the soldiery, saw only troops and battalions in the concrete, straight lines of red, straight lines of blue, white lines formed of innumerable knee-breeches, black lines formed of many gaiters, coming and going in kaleidoscopic change. Who thought of every point in the line as an isolated man, each dwelling all to himself in the hermitage of his own mind? One person did, a young man far removed from the barrow where the Garlands and Miller Loveday stood. The natural expression of his face was somewhat obscured by the bronzing effects of rough weather, but the lines of his mouth showed that affectionate impulses were strong within him – perhaps stronger than judgement well could regulate. He wore a blue jacket with little brass buttons, and was plainly a seafaring man.

Meanwhile, in the part of the plain where rose the tumulus on which the miller had established himself, a broad-brimmed tradesman was elbowing his way along. He saw Mr Loveday from the base of the barrow, and beckoned to attract his attention. Loveday went half-way down, and the other came up as near as he could.

'Miller,' said the man, 'a letter has been lying at the post-office for you for the last three days. If I had known that I should see ye here I'd have brought it along with me.'

The miller thanked him for the news, and they parted, Loveday returning to the summit. 'What a very strange thing!' he said to Mrs Garland, who had looked inquiringly at his face, now very grave. 'That was Budmouth postmaster, and he says there's a letter for me. Ah, I now call to mind that there *was* a letter in the candle[80] three days ago this very night – a large red one; but foolish-like I thought nothing o't. Who *can* that letter be from?'

A letter at this time was such an event for hamleteers, even of the miller's respectable standing, that Loveday thenceforward was thrown into a fit of abstraction which prevented his seeing any more of the sham fight, or the people, or the King. Mrs Garland imbibed some of his concern, and suggested that the letter might come from his son Robert.

'I should naturally have thought that,' said Miller Loveday; 'but he wrote to me only two months ago, and his brother John heard from him within the last four weeks, when he was just about starting on another voyage. If you'll pardon me, Mrs Garland, ma'am, I'll see if there's any Overcombe man here who is going to Budmouth today, so that I may get the letter by night-time. I cannot possibly go myself.'

So Mr Loveday left them for a while; and as they were so near home Mrs Garland did not wait on the barrow for him to come back, but walked about with Anne a little time, until they should be disposed to trot down the slope to their own door. They listened to a man who was offering one guinea to receive ten in case Buonaparte should be killed in three months, and to other entertainments of that nature, which at this time were not rare. Once during their peregrination the eyes of the sailor before-mentioned fell upon Anne; but he glanced over her and passed her unheedingly by. Loveday the elder was at this time on the other side of the line, looking for a messenger to the town. At twelve o'clock the review was over, and the King and his family left the hill. The troops then cleared off the field, the spectators followed, and by one o'clock the downs were again bare.

They still spread their grassy surface to the sun as on that beautiful morning not, historically speaking, so very long ago; but the King and his fifteen thousand armed men, the horses, the bands of music, the princesses, the cream-coloured teams – the gorgeous centre-piece, in short, to which the downs were but the mere mount or margin – how entirely have they all passed and gone! – lying scattered about the world as military and other dust, some at Talavera, Albuera, Salamanca, Vittoria, Toulouse, and Waterloo;[81] some in home churchyards; and a few small handfuls in royal vaults.

In the afternoon John Loveday, lightened of his trumpet and

trappings, appeared at the old mill-house door, and beheld Anne standing at hers.

'I saw you, Miss Garland,' said the soldier gaily.

'Where was I?' said she, smiling.

'On the top of the big mound – to the right of the King.'

'And I saw you; lots of times,' she rejoined.

Loveday seemed pleased. 'Did you really take the trouble to find me? That was very good of you.'

'Her eyes followed you everywhere,' said Mrs Garland from an upper window.

'Of course I looked at the dragoons most,' said Anne, disconcerted. 'And when I looked at them my eyes naturally fell upon the trumpets. I looked at the dragoons generally, no more.'

She did not mean to show any vexation to the trumpet-major, but he fancied otherwise, and stood repressed. The situation was relieved by the arrival of the miller, still looking serious.

'I am very much concerned, John; I did not go to the review for nothing. There's a letter a-waiting for me at Budmouth, and I must get it before bedtime, or I shan't sleep a wink.'

'I'll go, of course,' said John; 'and perhaps Miss Garland would like to see what's doing there today? Everybody is gone or going; the road is like a fair.'

He spoke pleadingly, but Anne was not won to assent.

'You can drive in the gig; 'twill do Blossom good,' said the miller.

'Let David drive Miss Garland,' said the trumpet-major, not wishing to coerce her; 'I would just as soon walk.'

Anne joyfully welcomed this arrangement, and a time was fixed for the start.

# * XIII *

## The Conversation in the Crowd

IN the afternoon they drove off, John Loveday being nowhere visible. All along the road they passed and were overtaken by vehicles of all descriptions going in the same direction; among them the extraordinary machines which had been invented for the conveyance of troops to any point of the coast on which the enemy should land; they consisted of four boards placed across a sort of trolly, thirty men of the volunteer companies riding on each.

The popular Georgian watering-place was in a paroxysm of gaiety. The town was quite overpowered by the country round, much to the town's delight and profit. The fear of invasion was such that six frigates lay in the roads to ensure the safety of the royal family, and from the regiments of horse and foot quartered at the barracks, or encamped on the hills round about, a picket of a thousand men mounted guard every day in front of Gloucester Lodge, where the King resided. When Anne and her attendant reached this point, which they did on foot, stabling the horse on the outskirts of the town, it was about six o'clock. The King was on the Esplanade, and the soldiers were just marching past to mount guard. The band formed in front of the King, and all the officers saluted as they went by.

Anne now felt herself close to and looking into the stream of recorded history, within whose banks the littlest things are great, and outside which she and the general bulk of the human race were content to live on as an unreckoned, unheeded superfluity.

When she turned from her interested gaze at this scene, there stood John Loveday. She had had a presentiment that he would turn up in this mysterious way. It was marvellous that he could have got there so quickly; but there he was – not looking at the King, or at the crowd, but waiting for the turn of her head.

'Trumpet-major, I didn't see you,' said Anne demurely. 'How is it that your regiment is not marching past?'

'We take it by turns, and it is not our turn,' said Loveday.

She wanted to know then if they were afraid that the King would be carried off by the First Consul.[82] Yes, Loveday told her; and his Majesty was rather venturesome. A day or two before he had gone so far to sea that he was nearly caught by some of the enemy's cruisers. 'He is anxious to fight Boney single-handed,' he said.

'What a good, brave King!' said Anne.

Loveday seemed anxious to come to more personal matters. 'Will you let me take you round to the other side, where you can see better?' he asked. 'The Queen and the princesses are at the window.'

Anne passively assented. 'David, wait here for me,' she said; 'I shall be back again in a few minutes.'

The trumpet-major then led her off triumphantly, and they skirted the crowd and came round on the side towards the sands. He told her everything he could think of, military and civil, to which Anne returned pretty syllables and parenthetic words about the colour of the sea and the curl of the foam – a way of speaking that moved the soldier's heart even more than long and direct speeches would have done.

'And that other thing I asked you?' he ventured to say at last.

'We won't speak of it.'

'You don't dislike me?'

'O no!' she said, gazing at the bathing-machines, digging children, and other common objects of the seashore, as if her interest lay there rather than with him.

'But I am not worthy of the daughter of a genteel professional man – that's what you mean?'

'There's something more than worthiness required in such cases, you know,' she said, still without calling her mind away from surrounding scenes. 'Ah, there are the Queen and princesses at the window!'

'Something more?'

'Well, since you will make me speak, I mean the woman ought to love the man.'

The trumpet-major seemed to be less concerned about this than about her supposed superiority. 'If it were all right on that point, would you mind the other?' he asked, like a man who knows he is too persistent, yet who cannot be still.

'How can I say, when I don't know? What a pretty chip hat the elder princess wears!'

Her companion's general disappointment extended over him almost to his lace and his plume. 'Your mother said, you know, Miss Anne –'

'Yes, that's the worst of it,' she said. 'Let us go back to David; I have seen all I want to see, Mr Loveday.'

The mass of the people had by this time noticed the Queen and princesses at the window, and raised a cheer, to which the ladies waved their embroidered handkerchiefs. Anne went back towards the pavement with her trumpet-major, whom all the girls envied her, so fine-looking a soldier was he; and not only for that, but because it was well known that he was not a soldier from necessity, but from patriotism, his father having repeatedly offered to set him up in business: his artistic taste in preferring a horse and uniform to a dirty, rumbling flour-mill was admired by all. She, too, had a very nice appearance in her best clothes as she walked along – the sarcenet hat, muslin shawl, and tight-sleeved gown being of the newest Overcombe fashion, that was only about a year old in the adjoining town, and in London three or four. She could not be harsh to Loveday and dismiss him curtly, for his musical pursuits had refined him, educated him, and made him quite poetical. Today he had been particularly well-mannered and tender; so, instead of answering, 'Never speak to me like this again', she merely put him off with a 'Let us go back to David'.

When they reached the place where they had left him David was gone.

Anne was now positively vexed. 'What *shall* I do?' she said.

'He's only gone to drink the King's health,' said Loveday, who had privately given David the money for performing that operation. 'Depend upon it, he'll be back soon.'

'Will you go and find him?' said she, with intense propriety in her looks and tone.

'I will,' said Loveday reluctantly; and he went.

Anne stood still. She could now escape her gallant friend, for, although the distance was long, it was not impossible to walk home. On the other hand, Loveday was a good and sincere fellow, for whom she had almost a sisterly feeling, and she shrank from such a trick. While she stood and mused, scarcely heeding the music, the marching of the soldiers, the King, the dukes, the brilliant staff, the attendants, and the happy groups of people, her eyes fell upon the ground.

Before her she saw a flower lying – a crimson sweet-william – fresh and uninjured. An instinctive wish to save it from destruction by the passengers' feet led her to pick it up; and then, moved by a sudden self-consciousness, she looked around. She was standing before an inn, and from an upper window Festus Derriman was leaning with two or three kindred spirits of his cut and kind. He nodded eagerly, and signified to her that he had thrown the flower.

What should she do? To throw it away would seem stupid, and to keep it was awkward. She held it between her finger and thumb, twirled it round on its axis and twirled it back again, regarding and yet not examining it. Just then she saw the trumpet-major coming back.

'I can't find David anywhere,' he said; and his heart was not sorry as he said it.

Anne was still holding out the sweet-william as if about to drop it, and, scarcely knowing what she did under the distressing sense that she was watched, she offered the flower to Loveday.

His face brightened with pleasure as he took it. 'Thank you, indeed,' he said.

Then Anne saw what a misleading blunder she had committed towards Loveday in playing to the yeoman. Perhaps she had sown the seeds of a quarrel.

'It was not my sweet-william,' she said hastily; 'it was lying on the ground. I don't mean anything by giving it to you.'

'But I'll keep it all the same,' said the innocent soldier, as if he knew a good deal about womankind; and he put the flower carefully inside his jacket, between his white waistcoat and his heart.

Festus, seeing this, enlarged himself wrathfully, got hot in the face, rose to his feet, and glared down upon them like a turnip-lantern.[83]

'Let us go away,' said Anne timorously.

'I'll see you safe to your own door, depend upon me,' said Loveday. 'But – I had near forgot – there's father's letter, that he's so anxiously waiting for! Will you come with me to the post-office? Then I'll take you straight home.'

Anne, expecting Festus to pounce down every minute, was glad to be off anywhere; so she accepted the suggestion, and they went along the parade together.

Loveday set this down as a proof of Anne's relenting. Thus in joyful spirits he entered the office, paid the postage, and received the letter.

'It is from Bob, after all!' he said. 'Father told me to read it at once, in case of bad news. Ask your pardon for keeping you a moment.' He broke the seal and read, Anne standing silently by.

'He is coming home *to be married*,' said the trumpet-major, without looking up.

Anne did not answer. The blood swept impetuously up her face at his words, and as suddenly went away again, leaving her rather paler than before. She disguised her agitation and then overcame it, Loveday observing nothing of this emotional performance.

'As far as I can understand he will be here Saturday,' he said.

'Indeed!' said Anne quite calmly. 'And who is he going to marry?'

'That I don't know,' said John, turning the letter about. 'The woman is a stranger.'

At this moment the miller entered the office hastily.

'Come, John,' he cried, 'I have been waiting and waiting for that there letter till I was nigh crazy!'

John briefly explained the news, and when his father had recovered from his astonishment, taken off his hat, and wiped the exact line where his forehead joined his hair, he walked with Anne up the street, leaving John to return alone. The miller was so absorbed in his mental perspective of Bob's marriage, that he saw nothing of the gaieties they passed through; and Anne seemed also so much impressed by the same intelligence, that she crossed before the inn occupied by Festus without showing a recollection of his presence there.

# * XIV *

## *Later in the Evening of the Same Day*

WHEN they reached home the sun was going down. It had already
been noised abroad that miller Loveday had received a letter, and,
his cart having been heard coming up the lane, the population of
Overcombe drew down towards the mill as soon as he had gone
indoors – a sudden flash of brightness from the window showing
that he had struck such an early light as nothing but the immediate
deciphering of literature could require. Letters were matters of
public moment, and everybody in the parish had an interest in the
reading of those rare documents; so that when the miller had
placed the candle, slanted himself, and called in Mrs Garland to
have her opinion on the meaning of any hieroglyphics that he
might encounter in his course, he found that he was to be
additionally assisted by the opinions of the other neighbours,
whose persons appeared in the doorway, partly covering each
other like a hand of cards, yet each showing a large enough piece
of himself for identification. To pass the time while they were
arranging themselves, the miller adopted his usual way of filling
up casual intervals, that of snuffing the candle.

'We heard you had got a letter, Maister Loveday,' they said.

'Yes; "Southampton, the twelfth of August, dear father",' said
Loveday; and they were as silent as relations at the reading of a
will. Anne, for whom the letter had a singular fascination, came
in with her mother and sat down.

Bob stated in his own way that having, since landing, taken
into consideration his father's wish that he should renounce a
seafaring life and become a partner in the mill, he had decided to
agree to the proposal; and with that object in view he would return
to Overcombe in three days from the time of writing.

He then said incidentally that since his voyage he had been in

158

lodgings at Southampton, and during that time had become acquainted with a lovely and virtuous young maiden, in whom he found the exact qualities necessary to his happiness. Having known this lady for the full space of a fortnight he had had ample opportunities of studying her character, and, being struck with the recollection that, if there was one thing more than another necessary in a mill which had no mistress, it was somebody who could play that part with grace and dignity, he had asked Miss Matilda Johnson to be his wife. In her kindness she, though sacrificing far better prospects, had agreed; and he could not but regard it as a happy chance that he should have found at the nick of time such a woman to adorn his home, whose innocence was as stunning as her beauty. Without much ado, therefore, he and she had arranged to be married at once, and at Overcombe, that his father might not be deprived of the pleasures of the wedding feast. She had kindly consented to follow him by land in the course of a few days, and to live in the house as their guest for the week or so previous to the ceremony.

' 'Tis a proper good letter,' said Mrs Comfort from the background. 'I never heerd true love better put out of hand in my life; and they seem 'nation fond of one another.'

'He haven't knowed her such a very long time,' said Job Mitchell dubiously.

'That's nothing,' said Esther Beach. ' 'Nater will find her way very rapid when the time's come for't. Well, 'tis good news for ye, miller.'

'Yes, sure, I hope 'tis,' said Loveday, without, however, showing any great hurry to burst into the frantic form of fatherly joy which the event should naturally have produced, seeming more disposed to let off his feelings by examining thoroughly into the fibres of the letter-paper.

'I was five years a-courting my wife,' he presently remarked. 'But folks were slower about everything in them days. Well, since she's coming we must make her welcome. Did any of ye catch by my reading which day it is he means? What with making out the penmanship, my mind was drawn off from the sense here and there.'

'He says in three days,' said Mrs Garland. 'The date of the letter will fix it.'

On examination it was found that the day appointed was the one nearly expired; at which the miller jumped up and said, 'Then he'll be here before bedtime. I didn't gather till now that he was coming afore Saturday. Why, he may drop in this very minute!'

He had scarcely spoken when footsteps were heard coming along the front, and they presently halted at the door. Loveday pushed through the neighbours and rushed out; and, seeing in the passage a form which obscured the declining light, the miller seized hold of him, saying, 'O my dear Bob; then you are come!'

'Scrounch it all,[84] miller, don't quite pull my poor shoulder out of joint! Whatever is the matter?' said the newcomer, trying to release himself from Loveday's grasp of affection. It was Uncle Benjy.

'Thought 'twas my son!' faltered the miller, sinking back upon the toes of the neighbours who had closely followed him into the entry. 'Well, come in, Mr Derriman, and make yerself at home. Why, you haven't been here for years! Whatever has made you come now, sir, of all times in the world?'

'Is he in there with ye?' whispered the farmer with misgiving.

'Who?'

'My nephew; after that maid that he's so mighty smit with?'

'O no; he never calls here.'

Farmer Derriman breathed a breath of relief. 'Well, I've called to tell ye,' he said, 'that there's more news of the French. We shall have 'em here this month as sure as a gun. The gunboats be all ready – near two thousand of 'em – and the whole army is at Boulogne. And, miller, I know ye to be an honest man.'

Loveday did not say nay.

'Neighbour Loveday, I know ye to be an honest man,' repeated the old squireen. 'Can I speak to ye alone?'

As the house was full, Loveday took him into the garden, all the while upon tenter-hooks, not lest Buonaparte should appear in their midst, but lest Bob should come whilst he was not there to receive him. When they had got into a corner Uncle Benjy said, 'Miller, what with the French, and what with my nephew Festus, I assure ye my life is nothing but wherrit from morning to night. Miller Loveday, you are an honest man.'

Loveday nodded.

'Well, I've come to ask a favour – to ask if you will take charge of my few poor title-deeds and documents and suchlike, while I am away from home next week, lest anything should befall me, and they should be stole away by Boney or Festus, and I should have nothing left in the wide world? I can trust neither banks nor lawyers in these terrible times; and I am come to you.'

Loveday after some hesitation agreed to take care of anything that Derriman should bring, whereupon the farmer said he would call with the parchments and papers alluded to in the course of a week. Derriman then went away by the garden gate, mounted his pony, which had been tethered outside, and rode on till his form was lost in the shades.

The miller rejoined his friends, and found that in the meantime John had arrived. John informed the company that after parting from his father and Anne he had rambled to the harbour, and discovered the *Pewit* by the quay. On inquiry he had learnt that she came in at eleven o'clock, and that Bob had gone ashore.

'We'll go and meet him,' said the miller. ' 'Tis still light out of doors.'

So, as the dew rose from the meads and formed fleeces in the hollows, Loveday and his friends and neighbours strolled out, and loitered by the stiles which hampered the footpath from Overcombe to the high-road at intervals of a hundred yards. John Loveday, being obliged to return to camp, was unable to accompany them, but Widow Garland thought proper to fall in with the procession. When she had put on her bonnet she called to her daughter. Anne said from upstairs that she was coming in a minute; and her mother walked on without her.

What was Anne doing? Having hastily unlocked a receptacle for emotional objects of small size, she took thence the little folded paper with which we have already become acquainted, and, striking a light from her private tinder-box, she held the paper, and curl of hair it contained, in the candle till they were burnt. Then she put on her hat and followed her mother and the rest of them across the moist grey fields, cheerfully singing in an undertone as she went, to assure herself of her indifference to circumstances.

# * XV *

## 'Captain' Bob Loveday of the
## Merchant Service

WHILE Loveday and his neighbours were thus rambling forth, full of expectancy, some of them, including Anne in the rear, heard the crackling of light wheels along the curved lane to which the path was the chord.[85] At once Anne thought, 'Perhaps that's he, and we are missing him.' But recent events were not of a kind to induce her to say anything; and the others of the company did not reflect on the sound.

Had they gone across to the hedge which hid the lane, and looked through it, they would have seen a light cart driven by a boy, beside whom was seated a seafaring man, apparently of good standing in the merchant service, with his feet outside on the shaft. The vehicle went over the main bridge, turned in upon the other bridge at the tail of the mill, and halted by the door. The sailor alighted, showing himself to be a well-shaped, active, and fine young man, with a bright eye, an anonymous nose, and of such a rich complexion by exposure to ripening suns that he might have been some connection of the foreigner who calls his likeness the Portrait of a Gentleman in galleries of the Old Masters. Yet in spite of this, and though Bob Loveday had been all over the world from Cape Horn to Pekin, and from India's coral strand to the White Sea, the most conspicuous of all the marks that he had brought back with him was an increased resemblance to his mother, who had lain all the time beneath Overcombe church wall.

Captain Loveday tried the house door; finding this locked he went to the mill door: this was locked also, the mill being stopped for the night.

'They are not at home,' he said to the boy. 'But never mind that. Just help to unload the things; and then I'll pay you, and you can drive off home.'

The cart was unloaded, and the boy was dismissed, thanking the sailor profusely for the payment rendered. Then Bob Loveday, finding that he had still some leisure on his hands, looked musingly east, west, north, south, and nadir;[86] after which he bestirred himself by carrying his goods, article by article, round to the back door, out of the way of casual passers. This done, he walked round the mill in a more regardful attitude, and surveyed its familiar features one by one – the panes of the grinding-room, now as heretofore clouded with flour as with stale hoar-frost; the meal lodged in the corners of the window-sills, forming a soil in which lichens grew without ever getting any bigger, as they had done since his dimmest infancy; the mosses on the plinth[87] towards the river, reaching as high as the capillary power of the walls would fetch up moisture for their nourishment, and the penned mill-pond, now as ever on the point of overflowing into the garden. Everything was the same.

When he had had enough of this it occurred to Loveday that he might get into the house in spite of the locked doors; and by entering the garden, placing a pole from the fork of an apple-tree to the window-sill of a bedroom on that side, and climbing across like a Barbary ape,[88] he entered the window and stepped down inside. There was something anomalous in being close to the familiar furniture without having first seen his father, and its silent, impassive shine was not cheering; it was as if his relations were all dead, and only their tables and chests of drawers left to greet him. He went downstairs and seated himself in the dark parlour. Finding this place, too, rather solitary, and the tick of the invisible clock preternaturally loud, he unearthed the tinder-box, obtained a light, and set about making the house comfortable for his father's return, divining that the miller had gone out to meet him by the wrong road.

Robert's interest in this work increased as he proceeded, and he bustled round and round the kitchen as lightly as a girl. David the indoor factotum having lost himself among the quart pots of Budmouth, there had been nobody left here to prepare supper, and Bob had it all to himself. In a short time a fire blazed up the chimney, a tablecloth was found, the plates were clapped down, and a search made for what provisions the house afforded, which, in addition to various meats, included some fresh eggs of the elongated shape that produces cockerels when hatched, and had been set aside on that account for putting under the next broody hen.

A more reckless cracking of eggs than that which now went on had never been known in Overcombe since the last large christening; and as Loveday gashed one on the side, another at the end, another longways, and another diagonally, he acquired adroitness by practice, and at last made every son of a hen of them fall into two hemispheres as neatly as if it opened by a hinge. From eggs he proceeded to ham, and from ham to kidneys, the result being a brilliant fry.

Not to be tempted to fall to before his father came back, the returned navigator emptied the whole into a dish, laid a plate over the top, his coat over the plate, and his hat over his coat. Thus completely stopping in the appetizing smell, he sat down to await events. He was relieved from the tediousness of doing this by hearing voices outside; and in a minute his father entered.

'Glad to welcome ye home, father,' said Bob. 'And supper is just ready.'

'Lard, lard – why, Captain Bob's here!' said Mrs Garland.

'And we've been out waiting to meet thee!' said the miller, as he entered the room, followed by representatives of the houses of Cripplestraw, Comfort, Mitchell, Beach, and Snooks, together with some small beginnings of Fencible Tremlett's posterity. In the rear came David, and quite in the vanishing-point of the composition, Anne the fair.

'I drove over; and so was forced to come by the road,' said Bob.

'And we went across the fields, thinking you'd walk,' said his father.

'I should have been here this morning; but not so much as a wheelbarrow could I get for my traps; everything was gone to the review. So I went too, thinking I might meet you there. I was then obliged to return to the harbour for the luggage.'

Then there was a welcoming of Captain Bob by pulling out his arms like drawers and shutting them again, smacking him on the back as if he were choking, holding him at arm's length as if he were of too large type to read close. All which persecution Bob bore with a wide, genial smile that was shaken into fragments and scattered promiscuously among the spectators.

'Get a chair for 'n!' said the miller to David, whom they had met in the fields and found to have got nothing worse by his absence than a slight slant in his walk.

'Never mind – I am not tired – I have been here ever so long,' said Bob. 'And I –' But the chair having been placed behind him, and a smart touch in the hollow of a person's knee by the edge of that piece of furniture having a tendency to make the person sit without further argument, Bob sank down dumb, and the others drew up other chairs at a convenient nearness for easy analytic vision and the subtler forms of good fellowship. The miller went about saying, 'David, the nine best glasses from the corner cupboard!' – 'David, the corkscrew!' – 'David, whisk the tail of thy smock-frock round the inside of these quart pots afore you draw drink in 'em – they be an inch thick in dust!' – 'David, lower that chimney-crook[89] a couple of notches that the flame may touch the bottom of the kettle, and light three more of the largest candles!' – 'If you can't get the cork out of the jar, David, bore a hole in the tub of Hollands[90] that's buried under the scroff[91] in the fuel-house; d'ye hear? – Dan Brown left en there yesterday as a return for the little porker I gied en.'

When they had all had a thimbleful round, and the superfluous neighbours had reluctantly departed, one by one, the inmates gave their minds to the supper, which David had begun to serve up.

'What be you rolling back the tablecloth for, David?' said the miller.

'Maister Bob have put down one of the under-sheets by mistake, and I thought you might not like it, sir, as there's ladies present!'

'Faith, 'twas the first thing that came to hand,' said Robert. 'It seemed a tablecloth to me.'

'Never mind – don't pull off the things now he's laid 'em down – let it bide,' said the miller. 'But where's Widow Garland and Maidy Anne?'

'They were here but a minute ago,' said David. 'Depend upon it they have slinked off 'cause they be shy.'

The miller at once went round to ask them to come back and

sup with him; and while he was gone David told Bob in confidence what an excellent place he had for an old man.

'Yes, Cap'n Bob, as I suppose I must call ye; I've worked for yer father these eight-and-thirty years, and we have always got on very well together. Trusts me with all the keys, lends me his sleeve-waistcoat, and leaves the house entirely to me. Widow Garland next door, too, is just the same with me, and treats me as if I was her own child.'

'She must have married young to make you that, David.'

'Yes, yes – I'm years older than she. 'Tis only my common way of speaking.'

Mrs Garland would not come in to supper, and the meal proceeded without her, Bob recommending to his father the dish he had cooked, in the manner of a householder to a stranger just come. The miller was anxious to know more about his son's plans for the future, but would not for the present interrupt his eating, looking up from his own plate to appreciate Bob's travelled way of putting English victuals out of sight, as he would have looked at a mill on improved principles.

David had only just got the table clear, and set the plates in a row under the bakehouse table for the cats to lick, when the door was hastily opened, and Mrs Garland came in, looking concerned.

'I have been waiting to hear the plates removed to tell you how frightened we are at something we hear at the back-door. It seems like robbers muttering; but when I look out there's nobody there!'

'This must be seen to,' said the miller, rising promptly. 'David, light the middle-sized lantern. I'll go and search the garden.'

'And I'll go too,' said his son, taking up a cudgel. 'Lucky I've come home just in time!'

They went out stealthily, followed by the widow and Anne, who had been afraid to stay alone in the house under the circumstances. No sooner were they beyond the door when, sure enough, there was the muttering, almost close at hand, and low upon the ground, as from persons lying down in hiding.

'Bless my heart!' said Bob, striking his head as though it were some enemy's: 'why, 'tis my luggage. I'd quite forgot it!'

'What!' asked his father.

'My luggage. Really, if it hadn't been for Mrs Garland it would have stayed there all night, and they, poor things! would have been starved. I've got all sorts of articles for ye. You go inside, and I'll bring 'em in. 'Tis parrots that you hear a-muttering, Mrs Garland. You needn't be afraid any more.'

'Parrots?' said the miller. 'Well, I'm glad 'tis no worse. But how couldst forget so, Bob?'

The packages were taken in by David and Bob, and the first unfastened were three, wrapped in cloths, which being stripped off revealed three cages, with a gorgeous parrot in each.

'This one is for you, father, to hang up outside the door, and amuse us,' said Bob. 'He'll talk very well, but he's sleepy tonight. This other one I brought along for any neighbour that would like to have him. His colours are not so bright; but 'tis a good bird. If you would like to have him you are welcome to him,' he said, turning to Anne, who had been tempted forward by the birds. 'You have hardly spoken yet, Miss Anne, but I recollect you very well. How much taller you have got, to be sure!'

Anne said she was much obliged, but did not know what she could do with such a present. Mrs Garland accepted it for her, and the sailor went on – 'Now this other bird I hardly know what to do with; but I dare say he'll come in for something or other.'

'He is by far the prettiest,' said the widow. 'I would rather have it than the other, if you don't mind.'

'Yes,' said Bob, with embarrassment. 'But the fact is, that bird will hardly do for ye, ma'am. He's a hard swearer, to tell the truth; and I am afraid he's too old to be broken of it.'

'How dreadful!' said Mrs Garland.

'We could keep him in the mill,' suggested the miller. 'It won't matter about the grinder hearing him, for he can't learn to cuss worse than he do already!'

'The grinder shall have him, then,' said Bob. 'The one I have given you, ma'am, has no harm in him at all. You might take him to church o' Sundays as far as that goes.'

The sailor now untied a small wooden box about a foot square, perforated with holes. 'Here are two marmosets,' he continued. 'You can't see them tonight; but they are beauties – the tufted sort.'

'What's a marmoset?' said the miller.

'O, a little kind of monkey. They bite strangers rather hard, but you'll soon get used to 'em.'

'They are wrapped up in something, I declare,' said Mrs Garland, peeping in through a chink.

'Yes, that's my flannel shirt,' said Bob apologetically. 'They suffer terribly from cold in this climate, poor things! and I had nothing better to give them. Well, now, in this next box I've got things of different sorts.'

The latter was a regular seaman's chest, and out of it he produced shells of many sizes and colours, carved ivories, queer little caskets, gorgeous feathers, and several silk handkerchiefs, which articles were spread out upon all the available tables and chairs till the house began to look like a bazaar.

'What a lovely shawl!' exclaimed Widow Garland, in her interest forestalling the regular exhibition by looking into the box at what was coming.

'O yes,' said the mate, pulling out a couple of the most bewitching shawls that eyes ever saw. 'One of these I am going to give to that young lady I am shortly to be married to, you know, Mrs Garland. Has father told you about it? Matilda Johnson, of Southampton, that's her name.'

'Yes, we know all about it,' said the widow.

'Well, I shall give one of these shawls to her – because, of course, I ought to.'

'Of course,' said she.

'But the other one I've got no use for at all; and,' he continued, looking round, 'will you have it, Miss Anne? You refused the parrot, and you ought not to refuse this.'

'Thank you,' said Anne calmly, but much distressed; 'but really I don't want it, and couldn't take it.'

'But do have it!' said Bob, in hurt tones, Mrs Garland being all the while on tenter-hooks lest Anne should persist in her absurd refusal.

'Why, there's another reason why you ought to!' said he, his face lighting up with recollections. 'It never came into my head till this moment that I used to be your beau in a humble sort of way. Faith, so I did, and we used to meet at places sometimes, didn't we? – that is, when you were not too proud; and once I gave you, or somebody else, a bit of my hair in fun.'

'It was somebody else,' said Anne quickly.

'Ah, perhaps it was,' said Bob innocently. 'But it was you I used to meet, or try to, I am sure. Well, I've never thought of that boyish time for years till this minute! I am sure you ought to accept some one gift, dear, out of compliment to those old times!'

Anne drew back and shook her head, for she would not trust her voice.

'Well, Mrs Garland, then you shall have it,' said Bob, tossing the shawl to that ready receiver. 'If you don't, upon my life I will throw it out to the first beggar I see. Now, here's a parcel of cap ribbons of the splendidest sort I could get. Have these – do, Anne!'

'Yes, do,' said Mrs Garland.

'I promised them to Matilda,' continued Bob; 'but I am sure she won't want 'em, as she has got some of her own: and I would as soon see them upon your head, my dear, as upon hers.'

'I think you had better keep them for your bride if you have promised them to her,' said Mrs Garland mildly.

'It wasn't exactly a promise. I just said, "Til, there's some cap ribbons in my box, if you would like to have them." But she's got enough things already for any bride in creation. Anne, now you shall have 'em – upon my soul you shall – or I'll fling them down the mill-tail!'

Anne had meant to be perfectly firm in refusing everything, for reasons obvious even to that poor waif, the meanest capacity; but when it came to this point she was absolutely compelled to give in, and reluctantly received the cap ribbons in her arms, blushing fitfully, and with her lip trembling in a motion which she tried to exhibit as a smile.

'What would Tilly say if she knew!' said the miller slily.

'Yes, indeed – and it is wrong of him!' Anne instantly cried, tears running down her face as she threw the parcel of ribbons on the floor. 'You'd better bestow your gifts where you bestow your l-l-love, Mr Loveday – that's what I say!' And Anne turned her back and went away.

'I'll take them for her,' said Mrs Garland, quickly picking up the parcel.

'Now that's a pity,' said Bob, looking regretfully after Anne.
'I didn't remember that she was a quick-tempered sort of girl at
all. Tell her, Mrs Garland, that I ask her pardon. But of course I
didn't know she was too proud to accept a little present – how
should I? Upon my life if it wasn't for Matilda I'd – Well, that
can't be, of course.'

'What's this?' said Mrs Garland, touching with her foot a large
package that had been laid down by Bob unseen.

'That's a bit of baccy for myself,' said Robert meekly.

The examination of presents at last ended, and the two families
parted for the night. When they were alone, Mrs Garland said to
Anne, 'What a close girl you are! I am sure I never knew that Bob
Loveday and you had walked together: you must have been mere
children.'

'O yes – so we were,' said Anne, now quite recovered. 'It was
when we first came here, about a year after father died. We did
not walk together in any regular way. You know I have never
thought the Lovedays high enough for me. It was only just –
nothing at all, and I had almost forgotten it.'

It is to be hoped that somebody's sins were forgiven her that
night before she fell asleep.

When Bob and his father were left alone, the miller said, 'Well,
Robert, about this young woman of thine – Matilda what's her
name?'

'Yes, father – Matilda Johnson. I was just going to tell ye about
her.'

The miller nodded, and sipped his mug.

'Well, she is an excellent body,' continued Bob; 'that can truly
be said – a real charmer, you know – a nice good comely young
woman, a miracle of genteel breeding, you know, and all that.
She can throw her hair into the nicest curls, and she's got splendid
gowns and headclothes. In short, you might call her a land
mermaid. She'll make such a first-rate wife as there never was.'

'No doubt she will,' said the miller; 'for I have never known
thee wanting in sense in a jineral way.' He turned his cup round
on its axis till the handle had travelled a complete circle. 'How
long did you say in your letter that you had known her?'

'A fortnight.'

'Not *very* long.'

'It don't sound long, 'tis true; and 'twas really longer – 'twas fifteen days and a quarter. But hang it, father, I could see in the twinkling of an eye that the girl would do. I know a woman well enough when I see her – I ought to, indeed, having been so much about the world. Now, for instance, there's Widow Garland and her daughter. The girl is a nice little thing; but the old woman – O no!' Bob shook his head.

'What of her?' said his father, slightly shifting in his chair.

'Well, she's, she's – I mean, I should never have chose her, you know. She's of a nice disposition, and young for a widow with a grown-up daughter; but if all the men had been like me she would never have had a husband. I like her in some respects; but she's a style of beauty I don't care for.'

'O, if 'tis only looks you are thinking of,' said the miller, much relieved, 'there's nothing to be said, of course. Though there's many a duchess worse-looking, if it comes to argument, as you would find, my son,' he added, with a sense of having been mollified too soon.

The mate's thoughts were elsewhere by this time.

'As to my marrying Matilda, thinks I, here's one of the very genteelest sort, and I may as well do the job at once. So I chose her. She's a dear girl; there's nobody like her, search where you will.'

'How many did you choose her out from?' inquired his father.

'Well, she was the only young woman I happened to know in Southampton, that's true. But what of that? It would have been all the same if I had known a hundred.'

'Her father is in business near the docks, I suppose?'

'Well, no. In short, I didn't see her father.'

'Her mother?'

'Her mother? No, I didn't. I think her mother is dead; but she has got a very rich aunt living at Melchester. I didn't see her aunt, because there wasn't time to go; but of course we shall know her when we are married.'

'Yes, yes, of course,' said the miller, trying to feel quite satisfied. 'And she will soon be here?'

'Ay, she's coming soon,' said Bob. 'She has gone to this aunt's at Melchester to get her things packed, and suchlike, or she would have come with me. I am going to meet the coach at the King's Arms, Casterbridge, on Sunday, at one o'clock. To show what a capital sort of wife she'll be, I may tell you that she wanted to come by the Mercury, because 'tis a little cheaper than the other. But I said, "For once in your life do it well, and come by the Royal Mail, and I'll pay." I can have the pony and trap to fetch her, I suppose, as 'tis too far for her to walk?'

'Of course you can, Bob, or anything else. And I'll do all I can to give you a good wedding feast.'

# * XVI *

## They Make Ready for the
## Illustrious Stranger

PREPARATIONS for Matilda's welcome, and for the event which was to follow, at once occupied the attention of the mill. The miller and his man had but dim notions of housewifery on any large scale; so the great wedding cleaning was kindly supervised by Mrs Garland, Bob being mostly away during the day with his brother, the trumpet-major, on various errands, one of which was to buy paint and varnish for the gig that Matilda was to be fetched in, which he had determined to decorate with his own hands.

By the widow's direction the old familiar incrustation of shining dirt, imprinted along the back of the settle by the heads of countless jolly sitters, was scrubbed and scraped away; the brown circle round the nail whereon the miller hung his hat, stained by the brim in wet weather, was whitened over; the tawny smudges of bygone shoulders in the passage were removed without regard to a certain genial and historical value which they had acquired. The face of the clock, coated with verdigris as thick as a diachylon plaister,[92] was rubbed till the figures emerged into day; while, inside the case of the same chronometer, the cobwebs that formed triangular hammocks, which the pendulum could hardly wade through, were cleared away at one swoop.

Mrs Garland also assisted at the invasion of worm-eaten cupboards, where layers of ancient smells lingered on in the stagnant air, and recalled to the reflective nose the many good things that had been kept there. The upper floors were scrubbed with such abundance of water that the old-established death-watches, wood-lice, and flour-worms were all drowned, the suds trickling down into the room below in so lively and novel a manner as to convey the romantic notion that the miller lived in a cave with dripping stalactites.

They moved what had never been moved before – the oak coffer, containing the miller's wardrobe – a tremendous weight, what with its locks, hinges, nails, dust, framework, and the hard stratification of old jackets, waistcoats, and knee-breeches at the bottom, never disturbed since the miller's wife died, and half pulverized by the moths, whose flattened skeletons lay amid the mass in thousands.

'It fairly makes my back open and shut!' said Loveday, as, in obedience to Mrs Garland's direction, he lifted one corner, the grinder and David assisting at the others. 'All together: speak when ye be going to heave. Now!'

The pot covers and skimmers were brought to such a state that, on examining them, the beholder was not conscious of utensils, but of his own face in a condition of hideous elasticity. The broken clock-line[93] was mended, the kettles rocked,[94] the creeper nailed up, and a new handle put to the warming-pan. The large household lantern was cleaned out, after three years of uninterrupted accumulation, the operation yielding a conglomerate of candle-snuffs, candle-ends, remains of matches, lamp-black, and eleven ounces and a half of good grease – invaluable as dubbing for skitty boots[95] and ointment for cart-wheels.

Everybody said that the mill residence had not been so thoroughly scoured for twenty years. The miller and David looked on with a sort of awe tempered by gratitude, tacitly admitting by their gaze that this was beyond what they had ever thought of. Mrs Garland supervised all with disinterested benevolence. It would never have done, she said, for his future daughter-in-law to see the house in its original state. She would have taken a dislike to him, and perhaps to Bob likewise.

'Why don't ye come and live here with me, and then you would be able to see to it at all times?' said the miller as she bustled about again. To which she answered that she was considering the matter, and might in good time. He had previously informed her that his plan was to put Bob and his wife in the part of the house that she, Mrs Garland, occupied, as soon as she chose to enter his, which relieved her of any fear of being incommoded by Matilda.

The cooking for the wedding festivities was on a proportionate scale of thoroughness. They killed the four supernumerary chickens that had just begun to crow, and the little curly-tailed barrow pig,[96] in preference to the sow; not having been put up fattening for more than five weeks it was excellent small meat, and therefore more delicate and likely to suit a town-bred lady's taste than the large one, which, having reached the weight of fourteen score, might have been a little gross to a cultured palate. There were also provided a cold chine, stuffed veal, and two pigeon pies. Also thirty rings of black-pot,[97] a dozen of white-pot,[98] and ten knots of tender and well-washed chitterlings,[99] cooked plain, in case she should like a change.

As additional reserves there were sweetbreads, and five milts,[100] sewed up at one side in the form of a chrysalis, and stuffed with thyme, sage, parsley, mint, groats, rice, milk, chopped egg, and other ingredients. They were afterwards roasted before a slow fire, and eaten hot.

The business of chopping so many herbs for the various stuffings was found to be aching work for women; and David, the miller, the grinder, and the grinder's boy being fully occupied in their proper branches, and Bob being very busy painting the gig and touching up the harness, Loveday called in a friendly dragoon of John's regiment who was passing by, and he, being a muscular man, willingly chopped all the afternoon for a quart of strong beer, judiciously administered, and all other victuals found, taking off his jacket and gloves, rolling up his shirt-sleeves and unfastening his stock in an honourable and energetic way.

All windfalls and maggot-cored codlins were excluded from the apple pies; and as there was no known dish large enough for the purpose, the puddings were stirred up in the milking-pail, and boiled in the three-legged bell-metal crock, of great weight and antiquity, which every travelling tinker for the previous thirty years had tapped with his stick, coveted, made a bid for, and often attempted to steal.

In the liquor line Loveday laid in an ample barrel of Casterbridge 'strong beer'. This renowned drink – now almost as much a thing of the past as Falstaff's favourite beverage[101] – was not only well calculated to win the hearts of soldiers blown dry and dusty by residence in tents on a hill-top, but of any wayfarer whatever in that land. It was of the most beautiful colour that the eye of an artist in beer could desire; full in body, yet brisk as a volcano; piquant, yet without a twang; luminous as an autumn sunset; free from streakiness of taste; but, finally, rather heady. The masses worshipped it, the minor gentry loved it more than wine, and by the most illustrious county families it was not despised. Anybody brought up for being drunk and disorderly in the streets of its natal borough, had only to prove that he was a stranger to the place and its liquor to be honourably dismissed by the magistrates, as one overtaken in a fault that no man could guard against who entered the town unawares.

In addition, Mr Loveday also tapped a hogshead of fine cider that he had had mellowing in the house for several months, having bought it of an honest down-country man, who did not colour,[102] for any special occasion like the present. It had been pressed from fruit judiciously chosen by an old hand – Horner and Cleeves apple for the body, a few Tom-Putts for colour, and just a dash of Old Five-corners for sparkle – a selection originally made to please the palate of a well-known temperate earl who was a regular cider-drinker, and lived to be eighty-eight.

On the morning of the Sunday appointed for her coming Captain Bob Loveday set out to meet his bride. He had been all the week engaged in painting the gig, assisted by his brother at odd times, and it now appeared of a gorgeous yellow, with blue streaks, and tassels at the corners, and red wheels outlined with a darker shade. He put in the pony at half past eleven, Anne looking at him from the door as he packed himself into the vehicle and drove off. There may be young women who look out at young men driving to meet their brides as Anne looked at Captain Bob, and yet are quite indifferent to the circumstances; but they are not often met with.

So much dust had been raised on the highway by traffic resulting from the presence of the Court at the town further on, that brambles hanging from the fence, and giving a friendly scratch to the wanderer's face, were dingy as church cobwebs; and the grass on the margin had assumed a paper-shaving hue. Bob's father had wished him to take David, lest, from want of recent experience at the whip, he should meet with any mishap; but, picturing to himself the awkwardness of three in such circumstances, Bob would not hear of this; and nothing more serious happened to his driving than that the wheel-marks formed two serpentine lines along the road during the first mile or two, before he had got his hand in, and that the horse shied at a milestone, a piece of paper, a sleeping tramp, and a wheelbarrow, just to make use of the opportunity of being in bad hands.

He entered Casterbridge between twelve and one, and, putting up at the Old Greyhound, walked on to the Bow.[103] Here, rather dusty on the ledges of his clothes, he stood and waited while the people in their best summer dresses poured out of the three churches round him. When they had all gone, and a smell of cinders and gravy had spread down the ancient high-street, and the pie-dishes from adjacent bakehouses[104] had all travelled past, he saw the mail coach rise above the arch of Grey's Bridge, a quarter of a mile distant, surmounted by swaying knobs, which proved to be the heads of the outside travellers.

'That's the way for a man's bride to come to him!' said Robert to himself with a feeling of poetry; and as the horn sounded and the horses clattered up the street he walked down to the inn. The knot of hostlers and inn-servants had gathered, the horses were dragged from the vehicle, and the passengers for Casterbridge began to descend. Captain Bob eyed them over, looked inside, looked outside again; to his disappointment Matilda was not there, nor her boxes, nor anything that was hers. Neither coachman nor guard had seen or heard of such a person at Melchester; and Bob walked slowly away.

Depressed by forebodings to an extent which took away nearly a third of his appetite, he sat down in the parlour of the Old Greyhound to a slice from the family joint of the landlord. This gentleman, who dined in his shirt-sleeves, partly because it was August, and partly from a sense that they would not be so fit for public view further on in the week, suggested that Bob should wait till three or four that afternoon, when the road-waggon[105] would arrive, as the lost lady might have preferred that mode of conveyance; and when Bob appeared rather hurt at the suggestion, the landlord's wife assured him, as a woman who knew good life, that many genteel persons travelled in that way during the present high price of provisions. Loveday, who knew little of travelling by land, readily accepted her assurance and resolved to wait.

Wandering up and down the pavement, or leaning against some hot wall between the waggon-office and the corner of the street above, he passed the time away. It was a still, sunny, drowsy afternoon, and scarcely a soul was visible in the length and breadth of the street. The office was not far from All Saints' Church, and the church-windows being open, he could hear the afternoon service from where he lingered as distinctly as if he had been one of the congregation. Thus he was mentally conducted through the Psalms, through the first and second lessons, through the burst of fiddles and clarionets which announced the evening-hymn, and well into the sermon, before any signs of the waggon could be seen upon the London road.

The afternoon sermons at this church being of a dry and metaphysical nature at that date, it was by a special providence that the waggon-office was placed near the ancient fabric, so that whenever the Sunday waggon was late, which it always was in hot weather, in cold weather, in wet weather, and in weather of almost every other sort, the rattle, dismounting, and swearing outside completely drowned the parson's voice within, and sustained the flagging interest of the congregation at precisely the right moment. No sooner did the charity children begin to writhe on their benches, and adult snores grow audible, than the waggon arrived.

Captain Loveday felt a kind of sinking in his poetry at the possibility of her for whom they had made such preparations being in the slow, unwieldy vehicle which crunched its way towards him; but he would not give in to the weakness. Neither would he walk down the street to meet the waggon, lest she should not be there. At last the broad wheels drew up against the kerb, the waggoner with his white smock-frock, and whip as long as a fishing-line, descended from the pony on which he rode alongside, and the six broad-chested horses backed from their collars and shook themselves. In another moment something showed forth, and he knew that Matilda was there.

Bob felt three cheers rise within him as she stepped down; but it being Sunday he did not utter them. In dress, Miss Johnson passed his expectations – a green and white gown, with long, tight sleeves, a green silk handkerchief round her neck and crossed in front, a green parasol, and green gloves. It was strange enough to see this verdant caterpillar turn out of a road-waggon, and gracefully shake herself free from the bits of straw and fluff which would usually gather on the raiment of the grandest travellers by that vehicle.

'But, my dear Matilda,' said Bob, when he had kissed her three times with much publicity – the practical step he had determined on seeming to demand that these things should no longer be done in a corner – 'my dear Matilda, why didn't you come by the coach, having the money for't and all?'

'That's my scrimping!' said Matilda in a delightful gush. 'I know you won't be offended when you know I did it to save against a rainy day!'

Bob, of course, was not offended, though the glory of meeting her had been less; and even if vexation were possible, it would have been out of place to say so. Still, he would have experienced no little surprise had he learnt the real reason of his Matilda's change of plan. That angel had, in short, so wildly spent Bob's and her own money in the adornment of her person before setting out, that she found herself without a sufficient margin for her fare by coach, and had scrimped from sheer necessity.

'Well, I have got the trap out at the Greyhound,' said Bob. 'I don't know whether it will hold your luggage and us too; but it looked more respectable than the waggon on a Sunday, and if there's not room for the boxes I can walk alongside.'

'I think there will be room,' said Miss Johnson mildly. And it was soon very evident that she spoke the truth; for when her property was deposited on the pavement, it consisted of a trunk about eighteen inches long, and nothing more.

'O – that's all!' said Captain Loveday, surprised.

'That's all,' said the young woman assuringly. 'I didn't want to give trouble, you know, and what I have besides I have left at my aunt's.'

'Yes, of course,' he answered readily. 'And as it's no bigger, I can carry it in my hand to the inn, and so it will be no trouble at all.'

He caught up the little box, and they went side by side to the Greyhound; and in ten minutes they were trotting up the Southern Road.

Bob did not hurry the horse, there being many things to say and hear, for which the present situation was admirably suited. The sun shone occasionally into Matilda's face as they drove on, its rays picking out all her features to a great nicety. Her eyes would have been called brown, but they were really eel-colour, like many other nice brown eyes; they were well-shaped and rather bright, though they had more of a broad shine than a sparkle. She had a firm, sufficient nose, which seemed to say of itself that it was good as noses go. She had rather a picturesque way of wrapping her upper in her lower lip, the red of these surpassing a mere flesh-pink. Whenever she gazed against the sun towards the distant hills, she brought into her forehead, without knowing it, three short vertical lines – not there at other times – giving her for the moment rather a hard look. And in turning her head round to a far angle, to stare at something or other that he pointed out, the drawn flesh of her neck became a mass of lines. But Bob did not look at these things, which, of course, were of no significance; for had she not told him, when they compared ages, that she was a little over two-and-twenty?

As Nature was hardly invented at this early point of the century, Bob's Matilda could not say much about the glamour of the hills, or the shimmering of the foliage, or the wealth of glory in the distant sea, as she would doubtless have done had she lived later on; but she did her best to be interesting, asking Bob about matters of social interest in the neighbourhood, to which she seemed quite a stranger.

'Is your watering-place a large city?' she inquired when they mounted the hill where the Overcombe folk had waited for the King.

'Bless you, my dear – no! 'Twould be nothing if it wasn't for the Royal Family, and the lords and ladies, and the regiments of soldiers, and the frigates, and the King's messengers, and the actors and actresses, and the games that go on.'

At the words 'actors and actresses', the innocent young thing pricked up her ears.

'Does Elliston[106] pay as good salaries this summer as in – ?'

'O, you know about it then? I thought –'

'O no, no! I have heard of Budmouth – read in the papers, you know, dear Robert, about the doings there, and the actors and actresses, you know.'

'Yes, yes, I see. Well, I have been away from England a long time, and don't know much about the theatre in the town; but I'll take you there some day. Would it be a treat to you?'

'O, an amazing treat!' said Miss Johnson, with an ecstasy in which a close observer might have discovered a tinge of ghastliness.

'You've never been into one perhaps, dear?'

'N-never,' said Matilda flatly. 'Whatever do I see yonder – a row of white things on the down?'

'Yes, that's a part of the encampment above Overcombe. Lots of soldiers are encamped about here; those are the white tops of their tents.'

He pointed to a wing of the camp that had become visible. Matilda was much interested.

'It will make it very lively for us,' he added, 'especially as John is there.'

She thought so too, and thus they chatted on.

# * XVII *

## Two Fainting Fits and a Bewilderment

MEANWHILE Miller Loveday was expecting the pair with interest; and about five o'clock, after repeated outlooks, he saw two specks the size of caraway seeds on the far line of ridge where the sunlit white of the road met the blue of the sky. Then the remainder parts of Bob and his lady became visible, and then the whole vehicle, end on, and he heard the dry rattle of the wheels on the dusty road. Miller Loveday's plan, as far as he had formed any, was that Robert and his wife should live with him in the mill-house until Mrs Garland made up her mind to join him there; in which event her present house would be made over to the young couple. Upon all grounds, he wished to welcome becomingly the woman of his son's choice, and came forward promptly as they drew up at the door.

'What a lovely place you've got here!' said Miss Johnson, when the miller had received her from the captain. 'A real stream of water, a real mill-wheel, and real fowls, and everything!'

'Yes, 'tis real enough,' said Loveday, looking at the river with balanced sentiments; 'and so you will say when you've lived here a bit as mis'ess, and had the trouble of claning the furniture.'

At this Miss Johnson looked modest, and continued to do so till Anne, not knowing they were there, came round the corner of the house, with her prayer-book in her hand, having just arrived from church. Bob turned and smiled to her, at which Miss Johnson looked glum. How long she would have remained in that phase is unknown, for just then her ears were assailed by a loud bass note from the other side, causing her to jump round.

'O la! what dreadful thing is it?' she exclaimed, and beheld a cow of Loveday's, of the name of Crumpler, standing close to her

182

shoulder. It being about milking-time, she had come to look up David and hasten on the operation.

'O, what a horrid bull! – it did frighten me so. I hope I shan't faint,' said Matilda.

The miller immediately used the formula which has been uttered by the proprietors of livestock ever since Noah's time. 'She won't hurt ye. Hoosh, Crumpler! She's as timid as a mouse, ma'am.'

But as Crumpler persisted in making another terrific inquiry for David, Matilda could not help closing her eyes and saying, 'O, I shall be gored to death!' her head falling back upon Bob's shoulder, which – seeing the urgent circumstances, and knowing her delicate nature – he had providentially placed in a position to catch her. Anne Garland, who had been standing at the corner of the house, not knowing whether to go back or come on, at this felt her womanly sympathies aroused. She ran and dipped her handkerchief into the splashing mill-tail, and with it damped Matilda's face. But as her eyes still remained closed, Bob, to increase the effect, took the handkerchief from Anne and wrung it out on the bridge of Matilda's nose, whence it ran over the rest of her face in a stream.

'O, Captain Loveday!' said Anne, 'the water is running over her green silk handkerchief, and into her pretty reticule!'

'There – if I didn't think so!' exclaimed Matilda, opening her eyes, starting up, and promptly pulling out her pocket handkerchief, with which she wiped away the drops and an unimportant trifle of her complexion, assisted by Anne, who, in spite of a background of antagonistic emotions, could not help being interested.

'That's right!' said the miller, his spirits reviving with the revival of Matilda. 'The lady is not used to country life; are you, ma'am?'

'I am not,' replied the sufferer. 'All is so strange about here!'

Suddenly there spread into the firmament, from the direction of the down:

Ra, ta, ta! Ta-ta-ta-ta-ta! Ra, ta, ta!

183

'O dear, dear! more hideous country sounds, I suppose?' she inquired, with another start.

'O no,' said the miller cheerfully. ' 'Tis only my son John's trumpeter chaps at the camp of dragoons just above us, a-blowing Mess, or Feed, or Picket, or some other of their vagaries. John will be much pleased to tell you the meaning on't when he comes down. He's trumpet-major, as you may know, ma'am.'

'O yes; you mean Captain Loveday's brother. Dear Bob has mentioned him.'

'If you come round to Widow Garland's side of the house, you can see the camp,' said the miller.

'Don't force her; she's tired with her long journey,' said Mrs Garland humanely, the widow having come out in the general wish to see Captain Bob's choice. Indeed, they all behaved towards her as if she were a tender exotic, which their crude country manners might seriously injure.

She went into the house, accompanied by Mrs Garland and her daughter; though before leaving Bob she managed to whisper in his ear, 'Don't tell them I came by waggon, will you, dear?' – a request which was quite needless, for Bob had long ago determined to keep that a dead secret; not because it was an uncommon mode of travel, but simply that it was hardly the usual conveyance for a gorgeous lady to her bridal.

As the men had a feeling that they would be superfluous indoors just at present, the miller assisted David in taking the horse round to the stables, Bob following, and leaving Matilda to the women. Indoors, Miss Johnson admired everything: the new parrots and marmosets, the black beams of the ceiling, the double-corner cupboard with the glass doors, through which gleamed the remainders of sundry china sets acquired by Bob's mother in her housekeeping – two-handled sugar-basins, no-handled tea-cups, a tea-pot like a pagoda, and a cream-jug in the form of a spotted cow. This sociability in their visitor was returned by Mrs Garland and Anne; and Miss Johnson's pleasing habit of partly dying whenever she heard any unusual bark or bellow added to her piquancy in their eyes. But conversation, as such, was naturally at first of a nervous, tentative kind, in which, as in the works of some hazy poets, the sense was considerably led by the sound.

'You get the sea-breezes here, no doubt?'

'O yes, dear; when the wind is that way.'

'Do you like windy weather?'

'Yes; though not now, for it blows down the young apples.'

'Apples are plentiful, it seems. You country-folk call St Swithin's their christening day, if it rains?'

'Yes, dear. Ah me! I have not been to a christening for these many years; the baby's name was George, I remember – after the King.'

'I hear that King George is still staying at the town here. I *hope* he'll stay till I have seen him!'

'He'll wait till the corn turns yellow; he always does.'

'How *very* fashionable yellow is getting for gloves just now!'

'Yes. Some persons wear them to the elbow, I hear.'

'Do they? I was not aware of that. I struck my elbow last week so hard against the door of my aunt's mansion that I feel the ache now.'

Before they were quite overwhelmed by the interest of this discourse the miller and Bob came in. In truth, Mrs Garland found the office in which he had placed her – that of introducing a strange woman to a house which was not the widow's own – a rather awkward one, and yet almost a necessity. There was no woman belonging to the house except that wondrous compendium of usefulness, the intermittent maid-servant, whom Loveday had, for appearances, borrowed from Mrs Garland, and Mrs Garland was in the habit of borrowing from the girl's mother. And as for the demi-woman David, he had been informed as peremptorily as Pharaoh's baker[107] that the office of housemaid and bedmaker was taken from him, and would be given to this girl till the wedding was over, and Bob's wife took the management into her own hands.

They all sat down to high tea, Anne and her mother included, and the captain sitting next to Miss Johnson. Anne had put a brave face upon the matter – outwardly, at least – and seemed in a fair way of subduing any lingering sentiment which Bob's return had revived. During the evening, and while they still sat over the meal, John came down on a hurried visit, as he had promised, ostensibly on purpose to be introduced to his intended sister-in-law, but much more to get a word and a smile from his beloved Anne. Before they saw him, they heard the trumpet-major's smart step coming round the corner of the house, and in a moment his form darkened the door. As it was Sunday, he appeared in his full-dress laced coat, white waistcoat and breeches, and towering plume, the latter of which he instantly lowered, as much from necessity as good manners, the beam in the mill-house ceiling having a tendency to smash and ruin all such head-gear without warning.

'John, we've been hoping you would come down,' said the miller, 'and so we have kept the tay about on purpose. Draw up, and speak to Mrs Matilda Johnson . . . Ma'am, this is Robert's brother.'

'Your humble servant, ma'am,' said the trumpet-major gallantly.

As it was getting dusk in the low, small-paned room, he instinctively moved towards Miss Johnson as he spoke, who sat with her back to the window. He had no sooner noticed her features than his helmet nearly fell from his hand; his face became suddenly fixed, and his natural complexion took itself off, leaving a greenish yellow in its stead. The young person, on her part, had no sooner looked closely at him than she said weakly, 'Robert's brother!' and changed colour yet more rapidly than the soldier had done. The faintness, previously half counterfeit, seized on her now in real earnest.

'I don't feel well,' she said, suddenly rising by an effort. 'This warm day has quite upset me!'

There was a regular collapse of the tea-party, like that of the Hamlet play scene. Bob seized his sweetheart and carried her upstairs, the miller exclaiming, 'Ah, she's terribly worn by the journey! I thought she was when I saw her nearly go off at the blare of the cow. No woman would have been frightened at that if she'd been up to her natural strength.'

'That, and being so very shy of men, too, must have made John's handsome regimentals quite overpowering to her, poor thing!' added Mrs Garland, following the catastrophic young lady upstairs, whose indisposition was this time beyond question. And yet, by some perversity of the heart, she was as eager now to make light of her faintness as she had been to make much of it two or three hours ago.

The miller and John stood like straight sticks in the room the others had quitted, John's face being hastily turned towards a caricature of Buonaparte on the wall that he had not seen more than a hundred and fifty times before.

'Come, sit down and have a dish of tay, anyhow,' said his father at last. 'She'll soon be right again, no doubt.'

'Thanks; I don't want any tea,' said John quickly. And, indeed, he did not, for he was in one gigantic ache from head to foot.

The light had been too dim for anybody to notice his amazement; and not knowing where to vent it, the trumpet-major said he was going out for a minute. He hastened to the bakehouse; but David being there, he went to the pantry; but the maid being there, he went to the cart-shed; but a couple of tramps being there, he went behind a row of French beans in the garden, where he let off an ejaculation the most pious that he had uttered that Sabbath day: 'By God! what's to be done!'

And then he walked wildly about the paths of the dusky garden, where the trickling of the brooks seemed loud by comparison with the stillness around; treading recklessly on the cracking snails that had come forth to feed, and entangling his spurs in the long grass till the rowels were choked with its blades. Presently he heard another person approaching, and his brother's shape appeared between the stubbard tree and the hedge.

'O, is it you?' said the mate.

'Yes. I am – taking a little air.'

'She is getting round nicely again; and as I am not wanted indoors just now, I am going into the village to call upon a friend or two I have not been able to speak to as yet: And they'll like me to see 'em first on a Sunday, and in their best clothes.'

John took his brother Bob's hand. Bob rather wondered why.

'All right, old boy,' he said. 'Going into the village? You'll be back again, I suppose, before it gets very late?'

'O yes,' said Captain Bob cheerfully, and passed out of the garden.

John allowed his eyes to follow his brother till his shape could not be seen, and then he turned and again walked up and down.

# * XVIII *

## The Night After the Arrival

JOHN continued his sad and heavy pace till walking seemed too old and worn-out a way of showing sorrow so new, and he leant himself against the fork of an apple-tree like a log. There the trumpet-major remained for a considerable time, his face turned towards the house, whose ancient, many-chimneyed outline rose against the darkened sky, and just shut out from his view the camp above. But faint noises coming thence from horses restless at the pickets, and from visitors taking their leave, recalled its existence, and reminded him that, in consequence of Matilda's arrival, he had obtained leave for the night – a fact which, owing to the startling emotions that followed his entry, he had not yet mentioned to his friends.

While abstractedly considering how he could best use that privilege under the new circumstances which had arisen, he heard Farmer Derriman drive up to the front door and hold a conversation with his father. The old man had at last apparently brought the tin box of private papers that he wished the miller to take charge of during Derriman's absence; and it being a calm night, John could hear, though he little heeded, Uncle Benjy's reiterated supplications to Loveday to keep it safe from fire and thieves. Then Uncle Benjy left, and John's father went upstairs to deposit the box in a place of security, the whole proceeding reaching John's preoccupied comprehension merely as voices during sleep.

The next thing was the appearance of a light in the bedroom which had been assigned to Matilda Johnson. This effectually aroused the trumpet-major, and with a stealthiness unusual in him he went indoors. No light was in the lower rooms, his father, Mrs Garland, and Anne having gone out on the bridge to look at the new moon. John went upstairs on tip-toe, and along the uneven passage till he came to her door. It was standing ajar, a band of candlelight shining across the passage and up the opposite wall. As soon as he entered the radiance he saw her. She was standing before the looking-glass, apparently lost in thought, her fingers being clasped behind her head in abstraction, and the light falling full upon her face.

'I must speak to you,' said the trumpet-major.

She started, turned, and grew paler than before; and then, as if moved by a sudden impulse, she swung the door wide open, and, coming out, said quite collectedly and with apparent pleasantness, 'O yes; you are my Bob's brother! I didn't, for a moment, recognize you.'

'But you do now?'

'As Bob's brother.'

'You have not seen me before?'

'I have not,' she answered, with a face as impassible as Talleyrand's.[108]

'Good God!'

'I have not!' she repeated.

'Nor any of the —th Dragoons? Captain Jolly, Captain Bearboy, Mr Plight, for instance?'

'No.'

'You mistake; I'll remind you of particulars,' he said drily. And he did remind her at some length.

'Never!' she said desperately.

But she had miscalculated her staying powers, and her adversary's character. Five minutes after that she was in tears, and the conversation had resolved itself into words, which, on the soldier's part, were of the nature of commands, tempered by pity, and were a mere series of entreaties on hers.

The whole scene did not last ten minutes. When it was over, the trumpet-major walked from the doorway where they had been standing, and brushed moisture from his eyes. Reaching a dark lumber-room, he stood still there to calm himself, and then descended by a Flemish-ladder[109] to the bakehouse, instead of by the front stairs. He found that the others, including Bob, had gathered in the parlour during his absence and lighted the candles.

Miss Johnson, having sent down some time before John re-entered the house to say that she would prefer to keep her room that evening, was not expected to join them, and on this account Bob showed less than his customary liveliness. The miller wishing to keep up his son's spirits, expressed his regret that, it being Sunday night, they could have no songs to make the evening cheerful; when Mrs Garland proposed that they should sing psalms which, by choosing lively tunes and not thinking of the words, would be almost as good as ballads.

This they did, the trumpet-major appearing to join in with the rest; but as a matter of fact no sound came from his moving lips. His mind was in such a state that he derived no pleasure even from Anne Garland's presence, though he held a corner of the same book with her, and was treated in a winsome way which it was not her usual practice to indulge in. She saw that his mind was clouded, and, far from guessing the reason why, was doing her best to clear it.

At length the Garlands found that it was the hour for them to leave, and John Loveday at the same time wished his father and Bob good night, and went as far as Mrs Garland's door with her.

He had said not a word to show that he was free to remain out of camp, for the reason that there was painful work to be done, which it would be best to do in secret and alone. He lingered near the house till its reflected window-lights ceased to glimmer upon the mill-pond, and all within the dwelling was dark and still. Then he entered the garden and waited there till the back door opened, and a woman's figure timorously came forward. John Loveday at once went up to her, and they began to talk in low yet dissentient tones.

They had conversed about ten minutes, and were parting as if they had come to some painful arrangement, Miss Johnson sobbing bitterly, when a head stealthily arose above the dense hedgerow, and in a moment a shout burst from its owner.

'Thieves! thieves! – my tin box! – thieves! thieves!'

Matilda vanished into the house, and John Loveday hastened to the hedge. 'For heaven's sake, hold your tongue, Mr Derriman!' he exclaimed.

'My tin box!' said Uncle Benjy. 'O, only the trumpet-major!'

'Your box is safe enough, I assure you. It was only' – here the trumpet-major gave vent to an artificial laugh – 'only a sly bit of courting, you know.'

'Ha, ha, I see!' said the relieved old squireen. 'Courting Miss Anne! Then you've ousted my nephew, trumpet-major! Well, so much the better. As for myself, the truth on't is that I haven't been able to go to bed easy, for thinking that possibly your father might not take care of what I put under his charge; and at last I thought I would just step over and see if all was safe here before I turned in. And when I saw your two shapes my poor nerves magnified ye to housebreakers, and Boneys, and I don't know what all.'

'You have alarmed the house,' said the trumpet-major, hearing the clicking of flint and steel in his father's bedroom, followed in a moment by the rise of a light in the window of the same apartment. 'You have got me into difficulty,' he added gloomily, as his father opened the casement.

'I am sorry for that,' said Uncle Benjy. 'But step back; I'll put it all right again.'

'What, for heaven's sake, is the matter?' said the miller, his tasselled nightcap appearing in the opening.

'Nothing, nothing!' said the farmer. 'I was uneasy about my few bonds and documents, and I walked this way, miller, before going to bed, as I start from home tomorrow morning. When I came down by your garden-hedge, I thought I saw thieves, but it turned out to be – to be –'

Here a lump of earth from the trumpet-major's hand struck Uncle Benjy in the back as a reminder.

'To be – the bough of a cherry-tree a-waving in the wind. Good night.'

'No thieves are like to try my house,' said Miller Loveday. 'Now don't you come alarming us like this again, farmer, or you shall keep your box yourself, begging your pardon for saying so. Good night t' ye!'

'Miller, will ye just look, since I am here – just look and see if the box is all right? there's a good man! I am old, you know, and my poor remains are not what my original self was. Look and see if it is where you put it, there's a good, kind man.'

'Very well,' said the miller good-humouredly.

'Neighbour Loveday! on second thoughts I will take my box

home again, after all, if you don't mind. You won't deem it ill of me? I have no suspicion, of course; but now I think on't there's rivalry between my nephew and your son; and if Festus should take it into his head to set your house on fire in his enmity, 'twould be bad for my deeds and documents. No offence, miller, but I'll take the box, if you don't mind.'

'Faith! I don't mind,' said Loveday. 'But your nephew had better think twice before he lets his enmity take that colour.' Receding from the window, he took the candle to a back part of the room and soon reappeared with the tin box.

'I won't trouble ye to dress,' said Derriman considerately; 'let en down by anything you have at hand.'

The box was lowered by a cord, and the old man clasped it in his arms. 'Thank ye!' he said with heartfelt gratitude. 'Good night!'

The miller replied and closed the window, and the light went out.

'There, now I hope you are satisfied, sir?' said the trumpet-major.

'Quite, quite!' said Derriman; and, leaning on his walking-stick he pursued his lonely way.

That night Anne lay awake in her bed, musing on the traits of the new friend who had come to her neighbour's house. She would not be critical, it was ungenerous and wrong; but she could not help thinking of what interested her. And were there, she silently asked, in Miss Johnson's mind and person such rare qualities as placed that lady altogether beyond comparison with herself? O yes, there must be; for had not Captain Bob singled out Matilda from among all other women, herself included? Of course, with his world-wide experience, he knew best.

When the moon had set, and only the summer stars threw their light into the great damp garden, she fancied that she heard voices in that direction. Perhaps they were the voices of Bob and Matilda taking a lover's walk before retiring. If so, how sleepy they would be next day, and how absurd it was of Matilda to pretend she was tired! Ruminating in this way, and saying to herself that she hoped they would be happy, Anne fell asleep.

# * XIX *

## Miss Johnson's Behaviour
## Causes No Little Surprise

PARTLY from the excitement of having his Matilda under the paternal roof, Bob rose next morning as early as his father and the grinder, and, when the big wheel began to patter and the little ones to mumble in response, went to sun himself outside the mill-front, among the fowls of brown and speckled kinds which haunted that spot, and the ducks that came up from the mill-tail.

Standing on the worn-out mill-stone inlaid in the gravel, he talked with his father on various improvements of the premises, and on the proposed arrangements for his permanent residence there, with an enjoyment that was half based upon this prospect of the future, and half on the penetrating warmth of the sun to his back and shoulders. Then the different troops of horses began their morning scramble down to the mill-pond, and, after making it very muddy round the edge, ascended the slope again. The bustle of the camp grew more and more audible, and presently David came to say that breakfast was ready.

'Is Miss Johnson downstairs?' said the miller; and Bob listened for the answer, looking at a blue sentinel aloft on the down.

'Not yet, maister,' said the excellent David.

'We'll wait till she's down,' said Loveday. 'When she is, let us know.'

David went indoors again, and Loveday and Bob continued their morning survey by ascending into the mysterious quivering recesses of the mill, and holding a discussion over a second pair of burr-stones,[110] which had to be re-dressed before they could be used again. This and similar things occupied nearly twenty minutes, and, looking from the window, the elder of the two was reminded of the time of day by seeing Mrs Garland's table-cloth

193

fluttering from her back door over the heads of a flock of pigeons that had alighted for the crumbs.

'I suppose David can't find us,' he said, with a sense of hunger that was not altogether strange to Bob. He put out his head and shouted.

'The lady is not down yet,' said his man in reply.

'No hurry, no hurry,' said the miller, with cheerful emptiness. 'Bob, to pass the time we'll look into the garden.'

'She'll get up sooner than this, you know, when she's signed articles and got a berth here,' Bob observed apologetically.

'Yes, yes,' said Loveday; and they descended into the garden.

Here they turned over sundry flat stones and killed the slugs sheltered beneath them from the coming heat of the day, talking of slugs in all their branches – of the brown and the black, of the tough and the tender, of the reason why there were so many in the garden that year, of the coming time when the grass-walks harbouring them were to be taken up and gravel laid, and of the relatively exterminatory merits of a pair of scissors and the heel of the shoe. At last the miller said, 'Well, really, Bob, I'm hungry; we must begin without her.'

They were about to go in, when David appeared with haste in his motions, his eyes wider vertically than crosswise, and his cheeks nearly all gone.

'Maister, I've been to call her; and as 'a didn't speak I rapped, and as 'a didn't answer I kicked, and not being latched the door opened, and – she's gone!'

Bob went off like a swallow towards the house, and the miller followed like the rather heavy man that he was. That Miss Matilda was not in her room, or a scrap of anything belonging to her, was soon apparent. They searched every place in which she could possibly hide or squeeze herself, every place in which she could not, but found nothing at all.

Captain Bob was quite wild with astonishment and grief. When he was fully sure that she was nowhere in his father's house, he ran into Mrs Garland's, and telling them the story so hastily that they hardly understood the particulars, he went on towards Comfort's house, intending to raise the alarm there, and also at Mitchell's, Beach's, Cripplestraw's, the parson's, the clerk's, the camp of dragoons, of hussars, and so on through the whole county. But he paused, and thought it would be hardly expedient to publish his discomfiture in such a way. If Matilda had left the house for any freakish reason he would not care to look for her, and if her deed had a tragic intent she would keep aloof from camp and village.

In his trouble he thought of Anne. She was a nice girl and could be trusted. To her he went, and found her in a state of excitement and anxiety which equalled his own.

' 'Tis so lonely to cruise for her all by myself!' said Bob disconsolately, his forehead all in wrinkles; 'and I've thought you would come with me and cheer the way?'

'Where shall we search?' said Anne.

'O, in the holes of rivers, you know, and down wells, and in quarries, and over cliffs, and like that. Your eyes might catch the loom of any bit of a shawl or bonnet that I should overlook, and it would do me a real service. Please do come!'

So Anne took pity upon him, and put on her hat and went, the miller and David having gone off in another direction. They examined the ditches of fields, Bob going round by one fence and Anne by the other, till they met at the opposite side. Then they peeped under culverts,[111] into outhouses, and down old wells and quarries, till the theory of a tragical end had nearly spent its force in Bob's mind, and he began to think that Matilda had simply run away. However, they still walked on, though by this time the sun was hot and Anne would gladly have sat down.

'Now, didn't you think highly of her, Miss Garland?' he inquired, as the search began to languish.

'O yes,' said Anne; 'very highly.'

'She was really beautiful; no nonsense about her looks, was there?'

'None. Her beauty was thoroughly ripe – not too young. We should all have got to love her. What can have possessed her to go away?'

'I don't know, and, upon my life, I shall soon be drove to say I don't care!' replied the mate despairingly. 'Let me pilot ye down over those stones,' he added, as Anne began to descend a rugged quarry. He stepped forward, leapt down, and turned to her.

She gave him her hand and sprang down. Before he relinquished his hold, Captain Bob raised her fingers to his lips and kissed them.

'O, Captain Loveday!' cried Anne, snatching away her hand in genuine dismay, while a tear rose unexpectedly to each eye. 'I never heard of such a thing! I won't go an inch further with you, sir; it is too barefaced!' And she turned and ran off.

'Upon my life I didn't mean it!' said the repentant captain, hastening after. 'I do love her best – indeed I do – and I don't love you at all! I am not so fickle as that! I merely just for the moment admired you as a sweet little craft, and that's how I came to do it. You know, Miss Garland,' he continued earnestly, and still running after, ' 'tis like this: when you come ashore after having been shut up in a ship for eighteen months, womenfolks seem so new and nice that you can't help liking them, one and all in a body; and so your heart is apt to get scattered and to yaw[112] a bit, as we call it; but of course I think of poor Matilda most, and shall always stick to her.' He heaved a sigh of tremendous magnitude, to show beyond the possibility of doubt that his heart was still in the place that honour required.

'I am glad to hear that – of course I am very glad!' said she, with quick petulance, keeping her face turned from him. 'And I hope we shall find her, and that the wedding will not be put off, and that you'll both be happy. But I won't look for her any more! No; I don't care to look for her – and my head aches. I am going home!'

'And so am I,' said Robert promptly.

'No, no; go on looking for her, of course – all the afternoon, and all night. I am sure you will, if you love her.'

'O yes; I mean to. Still, I ought to convey you home first?'

'No, you ought not; and I shall not accept your company. Good morning, sir!' And she went off over one of the stone stiles with which the spot abounded, leaving the friendly sailor standing in the field.

He sighed again, and, observing the camp not far off, thought he would go to his brother John and ask him his opinion on the sorrowful case. On reaching the tents he found that John was not at liberty just at that time, being engaged in practising the trumpeters; and leaving word that he wished the trumpet-major to come down to the mill as soon as possible, Bob went back again.

' 'Tis no good looking for her,' he said gloomily. 'She liked *me* well enough, but when she came here and saw the house, and the place, and the old horse, and the plain furniture, she was disappointed to find us all so homely, and felt she didn't care to marry into such a family!'

His father and David had returned with no news. 'Yes, 'tis as I've been thinking, father,' Bob said. 'We weren't good enough for her, and she went away in scorn!'

'Well, that can't be helped,' said the miller. 'What we be, we be, and have been for generations. To my mind she seemed glad enough to get hold of us!'

'Yes, yes – for the moment – because of the flowers, and birds, and what's pretty in the place,' said Bob tragically. 'But you don't know, father – how should you know, who have hardly been out of Overcombe in your life? – you don't know what delicate feelings are in a real refined woman's mind. Any little vulgar action unreaves[113] their nerves like a marline-spike.[114] Now I wonder if you did anything to disgust her?'

'Faith! not that I know of,' said Loveday, reflecting. 'I didn't say a single thing that I should naturally have said, on purpose to give no offence.'

'You was always very homely, you know, father.'

'Yes; so I was,' said the miller meekly.

'I wonder what it could have been,' Bob continued, wandering about restlessly. 'You didn't go drinking out of the big mug with your mouth full, or wipe your lips with your sleeve?'

'That I'll swear I didn't!' said the miller firmly. 'Thinks I, there's no knowing what I may do to shock her, so I'll take my solid victuals in the bakehouse, and only a crumb and a drop in her company for manners.'

'You could do no more than that, certainly,' said Bob gently.

'If my manners be good enough for well-brought-up people like the Garlands, they be good enough for her,' continued the miller, with a sense of injustice.

'That's true. Then it must have been David. David, come here!

How did you behave before that lady? Now, mind you speak the truth!'

'Yes, Mr Captain Robert,' said David earnestly. 'I assure ye she was served like a royal queen. The best silver spoons was put down, and yer poor grandfer's silver tanket, as you seed, and the feather cushion for her to sit on –'

'Now I've got it!' said Bob decisively, bringing down his hand upon the window-sill. 'Her bed was hard! – and there's nothing shocks a true lady like that. The bed in that room always was as hard as the Rock of Gibraltar!'

'No, Captain Bob! The beds were changed – wasn't they, maister? We put the goose bed in her room, and the flock one, that used to be there, in yours.'

'Yes, we did,' corroborated the miller. 'David and I changed 'em with our own hands, because they were too heavy for the women to move.'

'Sure I didn't know I had the flock bed,' murmured Bob. 'I slept on, little thinking what I was going to wake to. Well, well, she's gone; and search as I will I shall never find another like her! She was too good for me. She must have carried her box with her own hands, poor girl. As far as that goes, I could overtake her even now, I dare say; but I won't entreat her against her will – not I.'

Miller Loveday and David, feeling themselves to be rather a desecration in the presence of Bob's sacred emotions, managed to edge off by degrees, the former burying himself in the most floury recesses of the mill, his invariable resource when perturbed, the rumbling having a soothing effect upon the nerves of those properly trained to its music.

Bob was so impatient that, after going up to her room to assure himself once more that she had not undressed, but had only lain down on the outside of the bed, he went out of the house to meet John, and waited on the sunny slope of the down till his brother appeared. John looked so brave and shapely and warlike that, even in Bob's present distress, he could not but feel an honest and affectionate pride at owning such a relative. Yet he fancied that John did not come along with the same swinging step he had shown yesterday; and when the trumpet-major got nearer he looked anxiously at the mate and waited for him to speak first.

'You know our great trouble, John?' said Robert, gazing stoically into his brother's eyes.

'Come and sit down, and tell me all about it,' answered the trumpet-major, showing no surprise.

They went towards a slight ravine, where it was easier to sit down than on the flat ground, and here John reclined among the grasshoppers, pointing to his brother to do the same.

'But do you know what it is?' said Robert. 'Has anybody told ye?'

'I do know,' said John. 'She's gone; and I am thankful!'

'What!' said Bob, rising to his knees in amazement.

'I'm at the bottom of it,' said the trumpet-major slowly.

'You, John?'

'Yes; and if you will listen I'll tell you all. Do you remember what happened when I came into the room last night? Why, she turned colour and nearly fainted away. That was because she knew me.'

Bob stared at his brother with a face of pain and distrust.

'For once, Bob, I must say something that will hurt thee a good deal,' continued John. 'She was not a woman who could possibly be your wife – and so she's gone.'

'You sent her off?'

'Well, I did.'

'John! – Tell me right through – tell me!'

'Perhaps I had better,' said the trumpet-major, his blue eyes resting on the far distant sea, that seemed to rise like a wall as high as the hill they sat upon.

And then he told a tale of Miss Johnson and the —th Dragoons which wrung his heart as much in the telling as it did Bob's to hear, and which showed that John had been temporarily cruel to be ultimately kind. Even Bob, excited as he was, could discern from John's manner of speaking what a terrible undertaking that night's business had been for him. To justify the course he had adopted, the dictates of duty must have been imperative; but the trumpet-major, with a becoming reticence which his brother at the time was naturally unable to appreciate, scarcely dwelt distinctly enough upon the compelling cause of his conduct. It would, indeed, have been hard for any man, much less so modest a one as John, to do himself justice in that remarkable relation, when the listener was the lady's lover; and it is no wonder that Robert rose to his feet and put a greater distance between himself and John.

'And what time was it?' he asked in a hard, suppressed voice.

'It was just before one o'clock.'

'How could you help her to go away?'

'I had a pass. I carried her box to the coach-office. She was to follow at dawn.'

'But she had no money.'

'Yes, she had; I took particular care of that.' John did not add, as he might have done, that he had given her, in his pity, all the money he possessed, and at present had only eighteenpence in the world. 'Well, it is over, Bob; so sit ye down, and talk with me of old times,' he added.

'Ah, Jack, it is well enough for you to speak like that,' said the disquieted sailor; 'but I can't help feeling that it is a cruel thing you have done. After all, she would have been snug enough for me. Would I had never found out this about her! John, why did you interfere? You had no right to overhaul my affairs like this. Why didn't you tell me fairly all you knew, and let me do as I chose? You have turned her out of the house, and it's a shame! If she had only come to me! Why didn't she?'

'Because she knew it was best to do otherwise.'

'Well, I shall go after her,' said Bob firmly.

'You can do as you like,' said John; 'but I would advise you strongly to leave matters where they are.'

'I won't leave matters where they are,' said Bob impetuously. 'You have made me miserable, and all for nothing. I tell you she was good enough for me; and as long as I knew nothing about what you say of her history, what difference would it have made to me? Never was there a young woman who was better company; and she loved a merry song as I do myself. Yes, I'll follow her.'

'O, Bob,' said John; 'I hardly expected this!'

'That's because you didn't know your man. Can I ask you to do me one kindness? I don't suppose I can. Can I ask you not to say a word against her to any of them at home?'

'Certainly. The very reason why I got her to go off silently, as she has done, was because nothing should be said against her here, and no scandal should be heard of.'

'That may be; but I'm off after her. Marry that girl I will.'

'You'll be sorry.'

'That we shall see,' replied Robert with determination; and he went away rapidly towards the mill. The trumpet-major had no heart to follow – no good could possibly come of further opposition; and there on the down he remained like a graven image till Bob had vanished from his sight into the mill.

Bob entered his father's only to leave word that he was going on a renewed search for Matilda, and to pack up a few necessaries for his journey. Ten minutes later he came out again with a bundle in his hand, and John saw him go diagonally across the lower fields towards the high-road.

'And this is all the good I have done!' said John, musingly readjusting his stock where it cut his neck, and descending towards the mill.

# * XX *

## How They Lessened the Effect of the Calamity

MEANWHILE Anne Garland had gone home, and, being weary with her ramble in search of Matilda, sat silent in a corner of the room. Her mother was passing the time in giving utterance to every conceivable surmise on the cause of Miss Johnson's disappearance that the human mind could frame, to which Anne returned monosyllabic answers, the result, not of indifference, but of intense preoccupation. Presently Loveday, the father, came to the door; her mother vanished with him, and they remained closeted together a long time. Anne went into the garden and seated herself beneath the branching tree whose boughs had sheltered her during so many hours of her residence here. Her attention was fixed more upon the miller's wing of the irregular building before her than upon that occupied by her mother, for she could not help expecting every moment to see someone run out with a wild face and announce some awful clearing up of the mystery.

Every sound set her on the alert, and hearing the tread of a horse in the lane she looked round eagerly. Gazing at her over the hedge was Festus Derriman, mounted on such an incredibly tall animal that he could see to her very feet over the thick and broad thorn fence. She no sooner recognized him than she withdrew her glance; but as his eyes were fixed steadily upon her this was a futile manœuvre.

'I saw you look round!' he exclaimed crossly. 'What have I done to make you behave like that? Come, Miss Garland, be fair. 'Tis no use to turn your back upon me.' As she did not turn he went on – 'Well, now, this is enough to provoke a saint. Now I tell you what, Miss Garland; here I'll stay till you do turn round, if 'tis all the afternoon. You know my temper – what I say I mean.' He seated himself firmly in the saddle, plucked some leaves from the hedge, and began humming a song, to show how absolutely indifferent he was to the flight of time.

'What have you come for, that you are so anxious to see me?' inquired Anne, when at last he had wearied her patience, rising and facing him with the added independence which came from a sense of the hedge between them.

'There, I knew you would turn round!' he said, his hot angry face invaded by a smile in which his teeth showed like white hemmed in by red at chess.

'What do you want, Mr Derriman?' said she.

' "What do you want, Mr Derriman?" – now listen to that! Is that my encouragement?'

Anne bowed superciliously, and moved away.

'I have just heard news that explains all that,' said the giant, eyeing her movements with somnolent irascibility. 'My uncle has been letting things out. He was here late last night, and he saw you.'

'Indeed he didn't,' said Anne.

'O, now! He saw Trumpet-major Loveday courting somebody like you in that garden walk; and when he came you ran indoors.'

'It is not true, and I wish to hear no more.'

'Upon my life, he said so! How can you do it, Miss Garland, when I, who have enough money to buy up all the Lovedays, would gladly come to terms with ye? What a simpleton you must be, to pass me over for him! There, now you are angry because I said simpleton! – I didn't mean simpleton, I meant misguided – misguided rosebud! That's it – run off,' he continued in a raised voice, as Anne made towards the garden door. 'But I'll have you yet. Much reason you have to be too proud to stay with me. But it won't last long; I shall marry you, madam, if I choose, as you'll see.'

When he was quite gone, and Anne had calmed down from the not altogether unrelished fear and excitement that he always caused her, she returned to her seat under the tree, and began to wonder what Festus Derriman's story meant, which, from the earnestness of his tone, did not seem like a pure invention. It suddenly flashed upon her mind that she herself had heard voices in the garden, and that the persons seen by Farmer Derriman, of whose visit and reclamation of his box the miller had told her, might have been Matilda and John Loveday. She further recalled the strange agitation of Miss Johnson on the preceding evening, and that it occurred just at the entry of the dragoon, till by degrees suspicion amounted to conviction that he knew more than anyone else supposed of that lady's disappearance.

It was just at this time that the trumpet-major descended to the mill after his talk with his brother on the down. As fate would have it, instead of entering the house he turned aside to the garden and walked down that pleasant enclosure, to learn if he were likely to find in the other half of it the woman he loved so well.

Yes, there she was, sitting on the seat of logs that he had repaired for her, under the apple-tree; but she was not facing in his direction. He walked with a noisier tread, he coughed, he shook a bough, he did everything, in short, but the one thing that Festus did in the same circumstances – call out to her. He would not have ventured on that for the world. Any of his signs would have been sufficient to attract her a day or two earlier; now she would not turn. At last, in his fond anxiety, he did what he had never done before without an invitation, and crossed over into Mrs Garland's half of the garden, till he stood before her.

When she could not escape him she arose, and, saying 'Good afternoon, trumpet-major,' in a glacial manner unusual with her, walked away to another part of the garden.

Loveday, quite at a loss, had not the strength of mind to persevere further. He had a vague apprehension that some imperfect knowledge of the previous night's unhappy business had reached her; and, unable to remedy the evil without telling more than he dared, he went into the mill, where his father still was, looking doleful enough, what with his concern at events and the extra quantity of flour upon his face through sticking so closely to business that day.

'Well, John; Bob has told you all, of course? A queer, strange, perplexing thing, isn't it? I can't make it out at all. There must be something wrong in the woman, or it couldn't have happened. I haven't been so upset for years.'

'Nor have I. I wouldn't it should have happened for all I own in the world,' said the dragoon. 'Have you spoke to Anne Garland today – or has anybody been talking to her?'

'Festus Derriman rode by half-an-hour ago, and talked to her over the hedge.'

John guessed the rest, and, after standing on the threshold in silence awhile, walked away towards the camp.

All this time his brother Robert had been hastening along in pursuit of the woman who had withdrawn from the scene to avoid the exposure and complete overthrow which would have resulted had she remained. As the distance lengthened between himself and the mill, Bob was conscious of some cooling down of the excitement that had prompted him to set out; but he did not pause in his walk till he had reached the head of the river which fed the mill-stream. Here, for some indefinite reason, he allowed his eyes to be attracted by the bubbling spring whose waters never failed or lessened, and he stopped as if to look longer at the scene; it was really because his mind was so absorbed by John's story.

The sun was warm, the spot was a pleasant one, and he deposited his bundle and sat down. By degrees, as he reflected, first on John's view and then on his own, his convictions became unsettled; till at length he was so balanced between the impulse to go on and the impulse to go back, that a puff of wind either way would have been well-nigh sufficient to decide for him. When he allowed John's story to repeat itself in his ears, the reasonableness and good sense of his advice seemed beyond question. When, on the other hand, he thought of his poor Matilda's eyes, and her, to him, pleasant ways, their charming arrangements to marry, and her probable willingness still, he could hardly bring himself to do otherwise than follow on the road at the top of his speed.

This strife of thought was so well maintained that sitting and standing, he remained on the borders of the spring till the shadows had stretched out eastwards, and the chance of overtaking Matilda had grown considerably less. Still he did not positively go towards home. At last he took a guinea from his pocket, and resolved to put the question to the hazard. 'Heads I go; tails I don't.' The piece of gold spun in the air and came down heads.

'No, I won't go, after all,' he said. 'I won't be steered by accidents any more.'

He picked up his bundle and switch, and retraced his steps towards Overcombe Mill, knocking down the brambles and nettles as he went with gloomy and indifferent blows. When he got within sight of the house he beheld David in the road.

'All right – all right again, captain!' shouted that retainer. 'A wedding after all! Hurrah!'

'Ah – she's back again?' cried Bob, seizing David, ecstatically, and dancing round with him.

'No – but it's all the same! it is of no consequence at all, and no harm will be done! Maister and Mrs Garland have made up a match, and mean to marry at once, that the wedding victuals may not be wasted! They felt 'twould be a thousand pities to let such good things get blue-vinnied for want of a ceremony to use 'em upon, and at last they have thought of this.'

'Victuals – I don't care for the victuals!' bitterly cried Bob, in a tone of far higher thought. 'How you disappoint me!' and he went slowly towards the house.

His father appeared in the opening of the mill-door, looking more cheerful than when they had parted. 'What, Robert, you've been after her?' he said. 'Faith, then, I wouldn't have followed her if I had been as sure as you were that she went away in scorn of us. Since you told me that, I have not looked for her at all.'

'I was wrong, father,' Bob replied gravely, throwing down his bundle and stick. 'Matilda, I find, has not gone away in scorn of us; she has gone away for other reasons. I followed her some way; but I have come back again. She may go.'

'Why is she gone?' said the astonished miller.

Bob had intended, for Matilda's sake, to give no reason to a living soul for her departure. But he could not treat his father thus reservedly; and he told.

'She has made great fools of us,' said the miller deliberately; 'and she might have made us greater ones. Bob, I thought th' hadst more sense.'

'Well, don't say anything against her, father,' implored Bob. ' 'Twas a sorry haul, and there's an end on't. Let her down quietly, and keep the secret. You promise that?'

'I do.' Loveday the elder remained thinking awhile, and then went on – 'Well, what I was going to say is this: I've hit upon a plan to get out of the awkward corner she has put us in. What you'll think of it I can't say.'

'David has just given me the heads.'

'And do it hurt your feelings, my son, at such a time?'

'No – I'll bring myself to bear it, anyhow! Why should I object to other people's happiness because I have lost my own?' said Bob, with saintly self-sacrifice in his air.

'Well said!' answered the miller heartily. 'But you may be sure that there will be no unseemly rejoicing, to disturb ye in your present frame of mind. All the morning I felt more ashamed than I cared to own at the thought of how the neighbours, great and small, would laugh at what they would call your folly, when they knew what had happened; so I resolved to take this step to stave it off, if so be 'twas possible. And when I saw Mrs Garland I knew I had done right. She pitied me so much for having had the house cleaned in vain, and laid in provisions to waste, that it put her into the humour to agree. We mean to do it right off at once, afore the pies and cakes get mouldy and the black-pot stale. 'Twas a good thought of mine and hers, and I am glad 'tis settled,' he concluded cheerfully.

'Poor Matilda!' murmured Bob.

'There – I was afraid 'twould hurt thy feelings,' said the miller, with self-reproach: 'making preparations for thy wedding, and using them for my own!'

'No,' said Bob heroically; 'it shall not. It will be a great comfort in my sorrow to feel that the splendid grub, and the ale, and your stunning new suit of clothes, and the great table-cloths you've bought, will be just as useful now as if I had married myself. Poor Matilda! But you won't expect me to join in – you hardly can. I can sheer off that day very easily, you know.'

'Nonsense, Bob!' said the miller reproachfully.

'I couldn't stand it – I should break down.'

'Deuce take me if I would have asked her, then, if I had known 'twas going to drive thee out of the house! Now, come, Bob, I'll find a way of arranging it and sobering it down, so that it shall be as melancholy as you can require – in short, just like a funeral, if thou'lt promise to stay?'

'Very well,' said the afflicted one. 'On that condition I'll stay.'

# * XXI *

## 'Upon the Hill He Turned'

HAVING entered into this solemn compact with his son, the elder Loveday's next action was to go to Mrs Garland, and ask her how the toning down of the wedding had best be done. 'It is plain enough that to make merry just now would be slighting Bob's feelings, as if we didn't care who was not married, so long as we were,' he said. 'But then, what's to be done about the victuals?'

'Give a dinner to the poor folk,' she suggested. 'We can get everything used up that way.'

'That's true,' said the miller. 'There's enough of 'em in these times to carry off any extras whatsoever.'

'And it will save Bob's feelings wonderfully. And they won't know that the dinner was got for another sort of wedding and another sort of guests; so you'll have their good-will for nothing.'

The miller smiled at the subtlety of the view. 'That can hardly be called fair,' he said. 'Still, I did mean some of it for them, for the friends we meant to ask would not have cleared all.'

Upon the whole the idea pleased him well, particularly when he noticed the forlorn look of his sailor son as he walked about the place, and pictured the inevitably jarring effect of fiddles and tambourines upon Bob's shattered nerves at such a crisis, even if the notes of the former were dulled by the application of a mute, and Bob shut up in a distant bedroom – a plan which had at first occurred to him. He therefore told Bob that the surcharged larder was to be emptied by the charitable process above alluded to, and hoped he would not mind making himself useful in such a good and gloomy work. Bob readily fell in with the scheme, and it was at once put in hand and the tables spread.

The alacrity with which the substituted wedding was carried out seemed to show that the worthy pair of neighbours would have joined themselves into one long ago, had there previously occurred any domestic incident dictating such a step as an apposite expedient, apart from their personal wish to marry.

The appointed morning came, and the service quietly took place at the cheerful hour of ten, in the face of a triangular congregation, of which the base was the front pew, and the apex the west door. Mrs Garland dressed herself in the muslin shawl like Queen Charlotte's, that Bob had brought home, and her best plum-coloured gown, beneath which peeped out her shoes with red rosettes. Anne was present, but she considerately toned herself down, so as not to too seriously damage her mother's appearance. At moments during the ceremony she had a distressing sense that she ought not to be born, and was glad to get home again.

The interest excited in the village, though real, was hardly enough to bring a serious blush to the face of coyness. Neighbours' minds had become so saturated by the abundance of showy military and regal incident lately vouchsafed to them, that the wedding of middle-aged civilians was of small account, excepting in so far that it solved the question whether or not Mrs Garland would consider herself too genteel to mate with a grinder of corn.

In the evening, Loveday's heart was made glad by seeing the baked and boiled in rapid process of consumption by the kitchenful of people assembled for that purpose. Three-quarters of an hour were sufficient to banish for ever his fears as to spoilt food. The provisions being the cause of the assembly, and not its consequence, it had been determined to get all that would not keep consumed on that day, even if highways and hedges had to be searched for operators. And, in addition to the poor and needy, every cottager's daughter known to the miller was invited, and told to bring her lover from camp – an expedient which, for letting daylight into the inside of pie crust, was among the most happy ever known.

While Mr and Mrs Loveday, Anne, and Bob were standing in the parlour, discussing the progress of the entertainment in the next room, John, who had not been down all day, entered the house and looked in upon them through the open door.

'How's this, John? Why didn't you come before?'

'Had to see the captain, and – other duties,' said the trumpet-major, in a tone which showed no great zeal for explanations.

'Well, come in, however,' continued the miller, as his son remained with his hand on the door-post, surveying them reflectively.

'I cannot stay long,' said John, advancing. 'The Route[5] is come, and we are going away.'

'Going away! Where to?'

'To Exonbury.'

'When?'

'Friday morning.'

'All of you?'

'Yes; some tomorrow and some next day. The King goes next week.'

'I am sorry for this,' said the miller, not expressing half his sorrow by the simple utterance. 'I wish you could have been here today, since this is the case,' he added, looking at the horizon through the window.

Mrs Loveday also expressed her regret, which seemed to remind the trumpet-major of the event of the day, and he went to her and tried to say something befitting the occasion. Anne had not said that she was either sorry or glad, but John Loveday fancied that she had looked rather relieved than otherwise when she heard his news. His conversation with Bob on the down made Bob's manner, too, remarkably cool, notwithstanding that he had after all followed his brother's advice, which it was as yet too soon after the event for him to rightly value. John did not know why the sailor had come back, never supposing that it was because he had thought better of going, and said to him privately, 'You didn't overtake her?'

'I didn't try to,' said Bob.

'And you are not going to?'

'No; I shall let her drift.'

'I am glad indeed, Bob; you have been wise,' said John heartily.

Bob, however, still loved Matilda too well to be other than dissatisfied with John and the event that he had precipitated, which the elder brother only too promptly perceived; and it made his stay that evening of short duration. Before leaving he said with some hesitation to his father, including Anne and her mother by his glance, 'Do you think to come up and see us off?'

The miller answered for them all, and said that of course they would come. 'But you'll step down again between now and then?' he inquired.

'I'll try to.' He added after a pause, 'In case I should not, remember that Revalley will sound at half past five; we shall leave about eight. Next summer, perhaps, we shall come and camp here again.'

'I hope so,' said his father and Mrs Loveday.

There was something in John's manner which indicated to Anne that he scarcely intended to come down again; but the others did not notice it, and she said nothing. He departed a few minutes later, in the dusk of the August evening, leaving Anne still in doubt as to the meaning of his private meeting with Miss Johnson.

John Loveday had been going to tell them that on the last night, by an especial privilege, it would be in his power to come and stay with them until eleven o'clock, but at the moment of leaving he abandoned the intention. Anne's attitude had chilled him, and made him anxious to be off. He utilized the spare hours of that last night in another way.

This was by coming down from the outskirts of the camp in the evening, and seating himself near the brink of the mill-pond as soon as it was quite dark; where he watched the lights in the different windows till one appeared in Anne's bedroom, and she herself came forward to shut the casement, with the candle in her hand. The light shone out upon the broad and deep mill-head, illuminating to a distinct individuality every moth and gnat that entered the quivering chain of radiance stretching across the water towards him, and every bubble or atom of froth that floated into its width. She stood for some time looking out, little thinking what the darkness concealed on the other side of that wide stream; till at length she closed the casement, drew the curtains, and retreated into the room. Presently the light went out, upon which John Loveday returned to camp and lay down in his tent.

The next morning was dull and windy, and the trumpets of the —th sounded Réveille for the last time on Overcombe Down. Knowing that the Dragoons were going away, Anne had slept heedfully, and was at once awakened by the smart notes. She looked out of the window, to find that the miller was already astir, his white form being visible at the end of his garden, where he stood motionless, watching the preparations. Anne also looked on as well as she could through the dim grey gloom, and soon she saw the blue smoke from the cooks' fires creeping fitfully along the ground, instead of rising in vertical columns, as it had done during the fine weather season. Then the men began to carry their bedding to the waggons, and others to throw all refuse into the trenches, till the down was lively as an ant-hill. Anne did not want to see John Loveday again, but hearing the household astir, she began to dress at leisure, looking out at the camp the while.

When the soldiers had breakfasted, she saw them selling and giving away their superfluous crockery to the natives who had clustered round; and then they pulled down and cleared away the temporary kitchens which they had constructed when they came. A tapping of tent-pegs and wriggling of picket-posts followed, and soon the cones of white canvas, now almost become an intrinsic part of the landscape, fell to the ground. At this moment the miller came indoors and asked at the foot of the stairs if anybody was going up the hill with him.

Anne felt that, in spite of the cloud hanging over John in her mind, it would ill become the present moment not to see him off, and she went downstairs to her mother, who was already there, though Bob was nowhere to be seen. Each took an arm of the miller, and thus climbed to the top of the hill. By this time the men and horses were at the place of assembly, and, shortly after the mill-party reached level ground, the troops slowly began to move forward. When the trumpet-major, half buried in his uniform, arms, and horse-furniture, drew near to the spot where the Lovedays were waiting to see him pass, his father turned anxiously to Anne and said, 'You will shake hands with John?'

Anne faintly replied 'Yes,' and allowed the miller to take her forward on his arm to the trackway, so as to be close to the flank of the approaching column. It came up, many people on each side grasping the hands of the troopers in bidding them farewell; and as soon as John Loveday saw the members of his father's household, he stretched down his hand across his right pistol for the same performance. The miller gave his, then Mrs Loveday gave hers, and then the hand of the trumpet-major was extended towards Anne. But as the horse did not absolutely stop, it was a somewhat awkward performance for a young woman to undertake, and, more on that account than on any other, Anne drew back, and the gallant trooper passed by without receiving her adieu. Anne's heart reproached her for a moment; and then she thought that, after all, he was not going off to immediate battle, and that she would in all probability see him again at no distant date, when she hoped that the mystery of his conduct would be explained. Her thoughts were interrupted by a voice at her elbow: 'Thank heaven, he's gone! Now there's a chance for me.'

She turned, and Festus Derriman was standing by her.

'There's no chance for you,' she said indignantly.

'Why not?'

'Because there's another left!'

The words had slipped out quite unintentionally, and she blushed quickly. She would have given anything to be able to recall them; but he had heard, and said, 'Who?'

Anne went forward to the miller to avoid replying, and Festus caught her no more.

'Has anybody been hanging about Overcombe Mill except Loveday's son the soldier?' he asked of a comrade.

'His son the sailor,' was the reply.

'O – his son the sailor,' said Festus slowly. 'Damn his son the sailor!'

# * XXII *
## The Two Households United

AT this particular moment the object of Festus Derriman's fulmination was assuredly not dangerous as a rival. Bob, after abstractedly watching the soldiers from the front of the house till they were out of sight, had gone within doors and seated himself in the mill-parlour, where his father found him, his elbows resting on the table and his forehead on his hands, his eyes being fixed upon a document that lay open before him.

'What art perusing, Bob, with such a long face?'

Bob sighed, and then Mrs Loveday and Anne entered. ' 'Tis only a state-paper that I fondly thought I should have a use for,' he said gloomily. And, looking down as before, he cleared his voice, as if moved inwardly to go on, and began to read in feeling tones from what proved to be his nullified marriage licence:

> 'Timothy Titus Philemon, by permission Bishop of Bristol: To our well-beloved Robert Loveday, of the parish of Overcombe, Bachelor; and Matilda Johnson, of the same parish, Spinster. Greeting.'

Here Anne sighed, but contrived to keep down her sigh to a mere nothing.

'Beautiful language, isn't it!' said Bob. 'I was never greeted like that afore!'

'Yes; I have often thought it very excellent language myself,' said Mrs Loveday.

'Come to that, the old gentleman will greet thee like it again any day for a couple of guineas,' said the miller.

'That's not the point, father! You never could see the real meaning of these things . . . Well, then he goes on: "Whereas ye are, as it is alleged, determined to enter into the holy estate of matrimony —'' But why should I read on? It all means nothing now – nothing, and the splendid words are all wasted upon air. It seems as if I had been hailed by some venerable hoary prophet, and had turned away, put the helm hard up, and wouldn't hear.'

Nobody replied, feeling probably that sympathy could not meet the case, and Bob went on reading the rest of it to himself, occasionally heaving a breath like the wind in a ship's shrouds.

'I wouldn't set my mind so much upon her, if I was thee,' said his father at last.

'Why not?'

'Well, folk might call thee a fool, and say thy brains were turning to water.'

Bob was apparently much struck by this thought, and, instead of continuing the discourse further, he carefully folded up the licence, went out, and walked up and down the garden. It was startlingly apt what his father had said; and, worse than that, what people would call him might be true, and the liquefaction of his brains turn out to be no fable. By degrees he became much concerned, and the more he examined himself by this new light the more clearly did he perceive that he was in a very bad way.

On reflection he remembered that since Miss Johnson's departure his appetite had decreased amazingly. He had eaten in meat no more than fourteen or fifteen ounces a day, but one-third of a quartern pudding on an average, in vegetables only a small heap of potatoes and half a York cabbage, and no gravy whatever; which, considering the usual appetite of a seaman for fresh food at the end of a long voyage, was no small index of the depression of his mind. Then he had waked once every night, and on one occasion twice. While dressing each morning since the gloomy day he had not whistled more than seven bars of a hornpipe without stopping and falling into thought of a most painful kind; and he had told none but absolutely true stories of foreign parts to the neighbouring villagers when they saluted and clustered about him, as usual, for anything he chose to pour forth – except that story of the whale whose eye was about as large as the round pond in Derriman's ewe-lease[116] – which was like tempting fate to set a seal for ever upon his tongue as a traveller. All this enervation, mental and physical, had been produced by Matilda's departure.

He also considered what he had lost of the rational amusements of manhood during these unfortunate days. He might have gone to the neighbouring fashionable resort every afternoon, stood before Gloucester Lodge till the King and Queen came out, held his hat in his hand, and enjoyed their Majesties' smiles at his homage all for nothing – watched the picket-mounting, heard the different bands strike up, observed the staff; and, above all, have seen the pretty town girls go trip-trip-trip along the esplanade, deliberately fixing their innocent eyes on the distant sea, the grey cliffs, and the sky, and accidentally on the soldiers and himself.

'I'll raze out her image,' he said. 'She shall make a fool of me no more.' And his resolve resulted in conduct which had elements of real greatness.

He went back to his father, whom he found in the mill-loft. ' 'Tis true, father, what you say,' he observed: 'my brains will turn to bilge-water if I think of her much longer. By the oath of a – navigator, I wish I could sigh less and laugh more! She's gone – why can't I let her go, and be happy? But how begin?'

'Take it careless, my son,' said the miller, 'and lay yourself out to enjoy snacks and cordials.'

'Ah – that's a thought!' said Bob.

'Baccy is good for't. So is sperrits. Though I don't advise thee to drink neat.'

'Baccy – I'd almost forgot it!' said Captain Loveday.

He went to his room, hastily untied the package of tobacco that he had brought home, and began to make use of it in his own way, calling to David for a bottle of the old household mead that had lain in the cellar these eleven years. He was discovered by his father three-quarters of an hour later as a half-invisible object behind a cloud of smoke.

The miller drew a breath of relief. 'Why, Bob,' he said, 'I thought the house was a-fire!'

'I'm smoking rather fast to drown my reflections, father. 'Tis no use to chaw.'

To tempt his attenuated appetite the unhappy mate made David cook an omelet and bake a seed-cake, the latter so richly compounded that it opened to the knife like a freckled buttercup.

With the same object he stuck night-lines into the banks of the mill-pond, and drew up next morning a family of fat eels, some of which were skinned and prepared for his breakfast. They were his favourite fish, but such had been his condition that, until the moment of making this effort, he had quite forgotten their existence at his father's back-door.

In a few days Bob Loveday had considerably improved in tone and vigour. One other obvious remedy for his dejection was to indulge in the society of Miss Garland, love being so much more effectually got rid of by displacement than by attempted annihilation. But Loveday's belief that he had offended her beyond forgiveness, and his ever-present sense of her as a woman who by education and antecedents was fitted to adorn a higher sphere than his own, effectually kept him from going near her for a long time, notwithstanding that they were inmates of one house. The reserve was, however, in some degree broken by the appearance one morning, later in the season, of the point of a saw through the partition which divided Anne's room from the Loveday half of the house. Though she dined and supped with her mother and the Loveday family, Miss Garland had still continued to occupy her old apartments, because she found it more convenient there to pursue her hobbies of wool-work and of copying her father's old pictures. The division wall had not as yet been broken down.

As the saw worked its way downwards under her astonished gaze Anne jumped up from her drawing; and presently the temporary canvasing and papering which had sealed up the old door of communication was cut completely through. The door burst open, and Bob stood revealed on the other side, with the saw in his hand.

'I beg your ladyship's pardon,' he said, taking off the hat he had been working in, as his handsome face expanded into a smile. 'I didn't know this door opened into your private room.'

'Indeed, Captain Loveday!'

'I am pulling down the division on principle, as we are now one family. But I really thought the door opened into your passage.'

'It don't matter; I can get another room.'

'Not at all. Father wouldn't let me turn you out. I'll close it up again.'

But Anne was so interested in the novelty of a new doorway that she walked through it, and found herself in a dark low passage which she had never seen before.

'It leads to the mill,' said Bob. 'Would you like to go in and see it at work? But perhaps you have already.'

'Only into the ground floor.'

'Come all over it. I am practising as grinder, you know, to help my father.'

She followed him along the dark passage, in the side of which he opened a little trap, when she saw a great slimy cavern, where the long arms of the mill-wheel flung themselves slowly and distractedly round, and splashing water-drops caught the little light that strayed into the gloomy place, turning it into stars and flashes. A cold mist-laden puff of air came into their faces, and the roar from within made it necessary for Anne to shout as she said, 'It is dismal! let us go on.'

Bob shut the trap, the roar ceased, and they went on to the inner part of the mill, where the air was warm and nutty, and pervaded by a fog of flour. Then they ascended the stairs, and saw the stones lumbering round and round, and the yellow corn running down through the hopper. They climbed yet further to the top stage, where the wheat lay in bins, and where long rays like feelers stretched in from the sun through the little window, got nearly lost among cobwebs and timber, and completed their course by marking the opposite wall with a glowing patch of gold.

In his earnestness as an exhibitor Bob opened the bolter,[117] which was spinning rapidly round, the result being that a dense cloud of flour rolled out in their faces, reminding Anne that her complexion was probably much paler by this time than when she had entered the mill. She thanked her companion for his trouble, and said she would now go down. He followed her with the same deference as hitherto, and with a sudden and increasing sense that of all cures for his former unhappy passion this would have been the nicest, the easiest, and the most effectual, if he had only been fortunate enough to keep her upon easy terms. But Miss Garland showed no disposition to go further than accept his services as a guide; she descended to the open air, shook the flour from her like a bird, and went on into the garden amid the September sunshine, whose rays lay level across the blue haze which the earth gave forth. The gnats were dancing up and down in airy companies, the nasturtium flowers shone out in groups from the dark hedge over which they climbed, and the mellow smell of the decline of summer was exhaled by everything. Bob followed her as far as the gate, looked after her, thought of her as the same girl who had half encouraged him years ago, when she seemed so superior to him; though now they were almost equal she apparently thought him beneath her. It was with a new sense of pleasure that his mind flew to the fact that she was now an inmate of his father's house.

His obsequious bearing was continued during the next week. In the busy hours of the day they seldom met, but they regularly encountered each other at meals, and these cheerful occasions began to have an interest for him quite irrespective of dishes and cups. When Anne entered and took her seat she was always loudly hailed by Miller Loveday as he whetted his knife; but from Bob she condescended to accept no such familiar greeting, and they often sat down together as if each had a blind eye in the direction of the other. Bob sometimes told serious and correct stories about sea-captains, pilots, boatswains, mates, able seamen, and other curious fauna of the marine world; but these were directly addressed to his father and Mrs Loveday, Anne being included at the clinching-point by a glance only. He sometimes opened bottles of sweet cider for her, and then she thanked him; but even this did not lead to her encouraging his chat.

One day when Anne was paring an apple she was left at table with the young man. 'I have made something for you,' he said.

She looked all over the table; nothing was there save the ordinary remnants.

'O I don't mean that it is here; it is out by the bridge at the mill-head.'

He arose, and Anne followed with curiosity in her eyes, and with her firm little mouth pouted up to a puzzled shape. On reaching the mossy mill-head she found that he had fixed in the keen damp draught which always prevailed over the wheel an Æolian harp[118] of large size. At present the strings were partly covered with a cloth. He lifted it, and the wires began to emit a weird harmony which mingled curiously with the plashing of the wheel.

'I made it on purpose for you, Miss Garland,' he said.

She thanked him very warmly, for she had never seen anything like such an instrument before, and it interested her. 'It was very thoughtful of you to make it,' she added. 'How came you to think of such a thing?'

'O I don't know exactly,' he replied, as if he did not care to be questioned on the point. 'I have never made one in my life till now.'

Every night after this, during the mournful gales of autumn, the strange mixed music of water, wind, and strings met her ear, swelling and sinking with an almost supernatural cadence. The character of the instrument was far enough removed from anything she had hitherto seen of Bob's hobbies; so that she marvelled pleasantly at the new depths of poetry this contrivance revealed as existent in that young seaman's nature, and allowed her emotions to flow out yet a little further in the old direction, notwithstanding her late severe resolve to bar them back.

One breezy night, when the mill was kept going into the small hours, and the wind was exactly in the direction of the water-current, the music so mingled with her dreams as to wake her: it seemed to rhythmically set itself to the words, 'Remember me! think of me!' She was much impressed; the sounds were almost too touching; and she spoke to Bob the next morning on the subject.

'How strange it is that you should have thought of fixing that harp where the water gushes!' she gently observed. 'It affects me almost painfully at night. You are poetical, Captain Bob. But it is too – too sad!'

'I will take it away,' said Captain Bob promptly. 'It certainly is too sad; I thought so myself. I myself was kept awake by it one night.'

'How came you to think of making such a peculiar thing?'

'Well,' said Bob, 'it is hardly worth saying why. It is not a good place for such a queer noisy machine; and I'll take it away.'

'On second thoughts,' said Anne, 'I should like it to remain a little longer, because it sets me thinking.'

'Of me?' he asked with earnest frankness.

Anne's colour rose fast.

'Well, yes,' she said, trying to infuse much plain matter-of-fact into her voice. 'Of course I am led to think of the person who invented it.'

Bob seemed unaccountably embarrassed, and the subject was not pursued. About half-an-hour later he came to her again, with something of an uneasy look.

'There was a little matter I didn't tell you just now, Miss Garland,' he said. 'About that harp thing, I mean. I did make it, certainly, but it was my brother John who asked me to do it, just before he went away. John is very musical, as you know, and he said it would interest you; but as he didn't ask me to tell, I did not. Perhaps I ought to have, and not have taken the credit to myself.'

'O, it is nothing!' said Anne quickly. 'It is a very incomplete instrument after all, and it will be just as well for you to take it away as you first proposed.'

He said that he would, but he forgot to do it that day; and the following night there was a high wind, and the harp cried and moaned so movingly that Anne, whose window was quite near, could hardly bear the sound with its new associations. John Loveday was present to her mind all night as an ill-used man; and yet she could not own that she had ill-used him.

The harp was removed next day. Bob, feeling that his credit for originality was damaged in her eyes, by way of recovering it set himself to paint the summer-house which Anne frequented, and when he came out he assured her that it was quite his own idea.

'It wanted doing, certainly,' she said, in a neutral tone.

'It is just about troublesome.'

'Yes; you can't quite reach up. That's because you are not very tall; is it not, Captain Loveday?'

'You never used to say things like that.'

'O, I don't mean that you are much less than tall! Shall I hold the paint for you, to save your stepping down?'

'Thank you, if you would.'

She took the paint-pot, and stood looking at the brush as it moved up and down in his hand.

'I hope I shall not sprinkle your fingers,' he observed as he dipped.

'O, that would not matter! You do it very well.'

'I am glad to hear that you think so.'

'But perhaps not quite so much art is demanded to paint a summer-house as to paint a picture?'

Thinking that, as a painter's daughter, and a person of education superior to his own, she spoke with a flavour of sarcasm, he felt humbled and said –

'You did not use to talk like that to me.'

'I was perhaps too young then to take any pleasure in giving pain,' she observed daringly.

'Does it give you pleasure?'

Anne nodded.

'I like to give pain to people who have given pain to me,' she said smartly, without removing her eyes from the green liquid in her hand.

'I ask your pardon for that.'

'I didn't say I meant you – though I did mean you.'

Bob looked and looked at her side face till he was bewitched into putting down his brush.

'It was that stupid forgetting of 'ee for a time!' he exclaimed. 'Well, I hadn't seen you for so very long – consider how many years! O, dear Anne!' he said, advancing to take her hand, 'how well we knew one another when we were children! You was a queen to me then; and so you are now, and always.'

Possibly Anne was thrilled pleasantly enough at having brought the truant village lad to her feet again; but he was not to find the situation so easy as he imagined, and her hand was not to be taken yet.

'Very pretty!' she said, laughing. 'And only six weeks since Miss Johnson left.'

'Zounds, don't say anything about that!' implored Bob. 'I swear that I never – never deliberately loved her – for a long time together, that is; it was a sudden sort of thing, you know. But towards you – I have more or less honoured and respectfully loved you, off and on, all my life. There, that's true.'

Anne retorted quickly –

'I am willing, off and on, to believe you, Captain Robert. But I don't see any good in your making these solemn declarations.'

'Give me leave to explain, dear Miss Garland. It is to get you to be pleased to renew an old promise – made years ago – that you'll think o' me.'

'Not a word of any promise will I repeat.'

'Well, well, I won't urge 'ee today. Only let me beg of you to get over the quite wrong notion you have of me; and it shall be my whole endeavour to fetch your gracious favour.'

Anne turned away from him and entered the house, whither in the course of a quarter of an hour he followed her, knocking at her door, and asking to be let in. She said she was busy; whereupon he went away, to come back again in a short time and receive the same answer.

'I have finished painting the summer-house for you,' he said through the door.

'I cannot come to see it. I shall be engaged till supper-time.'

She heard him breathe a heavy sigh and withdraw, murmuring something about his bad luck in being cut away from the starn like this. But it was not over yet. When supper-time came and they sat down together, she took upon herself to reprove him for what he had said to her in the garden.

Bob made his forehead express despair.

'Now, I beg you this one thing,' he said. 'Just let me know your whole mind. Then I shall have a chance to confess my faults and mend them, or clear my conduct to your satisfaction.'

She answered with quickness, but not loud enough to be heard by the old people at the other end of the table – 'Then, Captain Loveday, I will tell you one thing, one fault, that perhaps would have been more proper to my character than to yours. You are too easily impressed by new faces, and that gives me a *bad opinion* of you – yes, a *bad opinion*.'

'O, that's it!' said Bob slowly, looking at her with the intense respect of a pupil for a master, her words being spoken in a manner so precisely between jest and earnest that he was in some doubt how they were to be received. 'Impressed by new faces. It is wrong, certainly, of me.'

The popping of a cork, and the pouring out of strong beer by the miller with a view to giving it a head, were apparently distractions sufficient to excuse her in not attending further to him; and during the remainder of the sitting her gentle chiding seemed to be sinking seriously into his mind. Perhaps her own heart ached to see how silent he was; but she had always meant to punish him. Day after day for two or three weeks she preserved the same demeanour, with a self-control which did justice to her character. And, on his part, considering what he had to put up with, how she eluded him, snapped him off, refused to come out when he called her, refused to see him when he wanted to enter the little parlour which she had now appropriated to her private use, his patience testified strongly to his good-humour.

# XXIII

# Military Preparations on an Extended Scale

CHRISTMAS had passed. Dreary winter with dark evenings had given place to more dreary winter with light evenings. Rapid thaws had ended in rain, rain in wind, wind in dust. Showery days had come – the season of pink dawns and white sunsets; and people hoped that the March weather was over.

The chief incident that concerned the household at the mill was that the miller, following the example of all his neighbours, had become a volunteer, and duly appeared twice a week in a red, long-tailed military coat, pipe-clayed breeches, black cloth gaiters, a heel-balled[119] helmet-hat, with a tuft of green wool, and epaulettes of the same colour and material. Bob still remained neutral. Not being able to decide whether to enrol himself as a sea-fencible, a local militia-man, or a volunteer, he simply went on dancing attendance upon Anne. Mrs Loveday had become awake to the fact that the pair of young people stood in a curious attitude towards each other; but as they were never seen with their heads together, and scarcely ever sat even in the same room, she could not be sure what their movements meant.

Strangely enough (or perhaps naturally enough), since entering the Loveday family herself, she had gradually grown to think less favourably of Anne doing the same thing, and reverted to her original idea of encouraging Festus; this more particularly because he had of late shown such perseverance in haunting the precincts of the mill, presumably with the intention of lighting upon the young girl. But the weather had kept her mostly indoors.

One afternoon it was raining in torrents. Such leaves as there were on trees at this time of year – those of the laurel and other evergreens – staggered beneath the hard blows of the drops which fell upon them, and afterwards could be seen trickling down the stems beneath and silently entering the ground. The surface of the mill-pond leapt up in a thousand spirts under the same downfall, and clucked like a hen in the rat-holes along the banks as it undulated under the wind. The only dry spot visible from the front windows of the mill-house was the inside of a small shed, on the opposite side of the courtyard. While Mrs Loveday was noticing the threads of rain descending across its interior shade, Festus Derriman walked up and entered it for shelter, which, owing to the lumber within, it but scantily afforded to a man who would have been a match for one of Frederick William's Patagonians.[120]

It was an excellent opportunity for helping on her scheme. Anne was in the back room, and by asking him in till the rain was over she would bring him face to face with her daughter, whom, as the days went on, she increasingly wished to marry other than a Loveday, now that the romance of her own alliance with the miller had in some respects worn off. She was better provided for than before; she was not unhappy; but the plain fact was that she had married beneath her. She beckoned to Festus through the window-pane; he instantly complied with her signal, having in fact placed himself there on purpose to be noticed; for he knew that Miss Garland would not be out-of-doors on such a day.

'Good afternoon, Mrs Loveday,' said Festus on entering. 'There now – if I didn't think that's how it would be!' His voice had suddenly warmed to anger, for he had seen a door close in the back part of the room, a lithe figure having previously slipped through.

Mrs Loveday turned, observed that Anne was gone, and said, 'What is it?' as if she did not know.

'O, nothing, nothing!' said Festus crossly. 'You know well enough what it is, ma'am; only you make pretence otherwise. But I'll bring her to book yet. You shall drop your haughty airs, my charmer! She little thinks I have kept an account of 'em all.'

'But you must treat her politely, sir,' said Mrs Loveday, secretly pleased at these signs of uncontrollable affection.

'Don't tell me of politeness or generosity, ma'am! She is more than a match for me. She regularly gets over me. I have passed by this house five-and-fifty times since last Martinmas,[121] and this is all my reward for't!'

'But you will stay till the rain is over, sir?'

'No. I don't mind rain. I'm off again. She's got somebody else in her eye!' And the yeoman went out, slamming the door.

Meanwhile the slippery object of his hopes had gone along the dark passage, passed the trap which opened on the wheel, and through the door into the mill, where she was met by Bob, who looked up from the flour-shoot inquiringly and said, 'You want me, Miss Garland?'

'O no,' said she. 'I only want to be allowed to stand here a few minutes.'

He looked at her to know if she meant it, and finding that she did, returned to his post. When the mill had rumbled on a little longer he came back.

'Bob,' she said, when she saw him move, 'remember that you are at work, and have no time to stand close to me.'

He bowed and went to his original post again, Anne watching from the window till Festus should leave. The mill rumbled on as before, and at last Bob came to her for the third time. 'Now, Bob –' she began.

'On my honour, 'tis only to ask a question. Will you walk with me to church next Sunday afternoon?'

'Perhaps I will,' she said. But at this moment the yeoman left the house, and Anne, to escape further parley, returned to the dwelling by the way she had come.

Sunday afternoon arrived, and the family was standing at the door waiting for the church bells to begin. From that side of the house they could see southward across a paddock to the rising ground further ahead, where there grew a large elm-tree, beneath whose boughs footpaths crossed in different directions, like meridians at the pole. The tree was old, and in summer the grass beneath it was quite trodden away by the feet of the many trysters and idlers who haunted the spot. The tree formed a conspicuous object in the surrounding landscape.

While they looked, a foot soldier in red uniform and white breeches came along one of the paths, and stopping beneath the elm, took from his pocket a paper, which he proceeded to nail up by the four corners to the trunk. He drew back, looked at it, and went on his way. Bob got his glass from indoors and levelled it at the placard, but after looking for a long time he could make out nothing but a lion and a unicorn[122] at the top. Anne, who was ready for church, moved away from the door, though it was yet early, and showed her intention of going by way of the elm. The paper had been so impressively nailed up that she was curious to read it even at this theological time. Bob took the opportunity of following, and reminded her of her promise.

'Then walk behind me not at all close,' she said.

'Yes,' he replied, immediately dropping behind.

The ludicrous humility of his manner led her to add playfully over her shoulder, 'It serves you right, you know.'

'I deserve anything, but I must take the liberty to say that I hope my behaviour about Matil—, in forgetting you awhile, will not make ye wish to keep me *always* behind?'

She replied confidentially, 'Why I am so earnest not to be seen with you is that I may appear to people to be independent of you. Knowing what I do of your weaknesses I can do no otherwise. You must be schooled into —'

'O, Anne,' sighed Bob, 'you hit me hard – too hard! If ever I do win you I am sure I shall have fairly earned you.'

'You are not what you once seemed to be,' she returned softly. 'I don't quite like to let myself love you.' The last words were not very audible, and as Bob was behind he caught nothing of them, nor did he see how sentimental she had become all of a sudden. They walked the rest of the way in silence, and coming to the tree read as follows:

## ADDRESS TO ALL RANKS AND DESCRIPTIONS OF ENGLISHMEN.

FRIENDS AND COUNTRYMEN, The French are now assembling the largest force that ever was prepared to invade this Kingdom, with the professed purpose of effecting our complete Ruin and Destruction. They do not disguise their intentions, as they have often done to other Countries; but openly boast that they will come over in such Numbers as cannot be resisted.

Wherever the French have lately appeared they have spared neither Rich nor Poor, Old nor Young; but like a Destructive Pestilence have laid waste and destroyed every Thing that before was fair and flourishing.

On this occasion no man's service is compelled, but you are invited voluntarily to come forward in defence of everything that is dear to you, by entering your Names on the Lists which are sent to the Tything-man[123] of every Parish, and engaging to act either as *Associated Volunteers bearing Arms, as Pioneers and Labourers*, or as *Drivers of Waggons*.

As Associated Volunteers you will be called out only once a week, unless the actual Landing of the Enemy should render your further Services necessary.

As Pioneers or Labourers you will be employed in Breaking up Roads to hinder the Enemy's advance.

Those who have Pickaxes, Spades, Shovels, Bill-hooks, or other Working Implements, are desired to mention them to the Constable or Tything-man of their Parish, in order that they may be entered on the Lists opposite their Homes, to be used if necessary . . .

It is thought desirable to give you this Explanation, that you may not be ignorant of the Duties to which you may be called. But if the love of true Liberty and honest Fame has not ceased to animate the Hearts of Englishmen, Pay, though necessary, will be the least Part of your Reward. You will find your best Recompense in having done your Duty to your King and Country by driving back or destroying your old and implacable Enemy, envious of your Freedom and Happiness, and therefore seeking to destroy them; in having protected your Wives and Children from Death, or worse than Death, which will follow the Success of such Inveterate Foes.

ROUSE, therefore, and unite as one man in the best of Causes! United we may defy the World to conquer us; but Victory will never belong to those who are slothful and unprepared.*

'I must go and join at once!' said Bob.

Anne turned to him, all the playfulness gone from her face. 'I wish we lived in the north of England, Bob, so as to be further away from where he'll land!' she murmured uneasily.

---

* *Vide* Preface.

'Where we are would be Paradise to me, if you would only make it so.'

'It is not right to talk so lightly at such a serious time,' she thoughtfully returned, going on towards the church.

On drawing near, they saw through the boughs of a clump of intervening trees, still leafless, but bursting into buds of amber hue, a glittering which seemed to be reflected from points of steel. In a few moments they heard above the tender chiming of the church bells the loud voice of a man giving words of command, at which all the metallic points suddenly shifted like the bristles of a porcupine, and glistened anew.

''Tis the drilling,' said Loveday. 'They drill now between the services, you know, because they can't get the men together so readily in the week. It makes me feel that I ought to be doing more than I am!'

When they had passed round the belt of trees, the company of recruits became visible, consisting of the able-bodied inhabitants of the hamlets thereabout, more or less known to Bob and Anne. They were assembled on the green plot outside the churchyard-gate, dressed in their common clothes, and the sergeant who had been putting them through their drill was the man who nailed up the proclamation. He was now engaged in untying a canvas money-bag, from which he drew forth a handful of shillings, giving one to each man in payment for his attendance.

'Men, I dismissed ye too soon – parade, parade again, I say,' he cried. 'My watch is fast, I find. There's another twenty minutes afore the worship of God commences. Now all of you that ha'n't got firelocks, fall in at the lower end. Eyes right and dress!'

As every man was anxious to see how the rest stood, those at the end of the line pressed forward for that purpose, till the line assumed the form of a bow.

'Look at ye now! Why, you are all a-crooking in! Dress, dress!'

They dressed forthwith; but impelled by the same motive they soon resumed their former figure, and so they were despairingly permitted to remain.

'Now, I hope you'll have a little patience,' said the sergeant, as he stood in the centre of the arc, 'and pay strict attention to the word of command, just exactly as I give it out to ye; and if I should go wrong, I shall be much obliged to any friend who'll put me right again, for I have only been in the army three weeks myself, and we are all liable to mistakes.'

'So we be, so we be,' said the line heartily.

''Tention, the whole, then. Poise fawlocks!'[124] Very well done!'

'Please, what must we do that haven't got no firelocks?' said the lower end of the line in a helpless voice.

'Now, was ever such a question! Why, you must do nothing at all, but think *how* you'd poise 'em *if* you had 'em. You middle men, that are armed with hurdle-sticks and cabbage-stumps just to make-believe, must of course use 'em as if they were the real thing. Now then, cock fawlocks! Present! Fire! (Pretend to, I mean, and the same time throw yer imagination into the field o' battle.) Very good – very good indeed; except that some of you were a *little* too soon, and the rest a *little* too late.'

'Please, sergeant, can I fall out, as I am master-player in the choir, and my bass-viol strings won't stand at this time o' year, unless they be screwed up a little before the passon comes in?'

'How can you think of such trifles as churchgoing at such a time as this, when your own native country is on the point of invasion?' said the sergeant sternly. 'And, as you know, the drill ends three minutes afore church begins, and that's the law, and it wants a quarter of an hour yet. Now, at the word *Prime*, shake the powder (supposing you've got it) into the priming-pan, three last fingers behind the rammer;[125] then shut your pans, drawing your right arm nimble-like towards your body. I ought to have told ye before this, that at *Hand your katridge*, seize it and bring it with a quick motion to your mouth, bite the top well off, and don't swaller so much of the powder as to make ye hawk and spet instead of attending to your drill. What's that man a-saying of in the rear rank?'

'Please, sir, 'tis Anthony Cripplestraw, wanting to know how he's to bite off his katridge, when he haven't a tooth left in 's head?'

'Man! Why, what's your genius for war? Hold it up to your right-hand man's mouth, to be sure, and let him nip it off for ye. Well, what have you to say, Private Tremlett? Don't ye understand English?'

'Ask yer pardon, sergeant; but what must we infantry of the awkward squad do if Boney comes afore we get our firelocks?'

'Take a pike, like the rest of the incapables. You'll find a store of them ready in the corner of the church tower. Now then – Shoulder-r-r-r-'

'There, they be tinging in the passon!' exclaimed David, Miller Loveday's man, who also formed one of the company, as the bells changed from chiming all three together to a quick beating of one. The whole line drew a breath of relief, threw down their arms, and began running off.

'Well, then, I must dismiss ye,' said the sergeant. 'Come back – come back! Next drill is Tuesday afternoon at four. And, mind, if your masters won't let ye leave work soon enough, tell me, and I'll write a line to Gover'ment! 'Tention! To the right – left wheel, I mean – no, no – right wheel. Mar-r-r-rch!'

Some wheeled to the right and some to the left, and some obliging men, including Cripplestraw, tried to wheel both ways.

'Stop, stop; try again! 'Cruits and comrades, unfortunately when I'm in a hurry I can never remember my right hand from my left, and never could as a boy. You must excuse me, please. Practice makes perfect, as the saying is; and, much as I've learnt since I 'listed, we always find something new. Now then, right wheel! march! halt! Stand at ease! dismiss! I think that's the order o't, but I'll look in the Gover'ment book afore Tuesday.'*

Many of the company who had been drilled preferred to go off and spend their shillings instead of entering the church; but Anne and Captain Bob passed in. Even the interior of the sacred edifice was affected by the agitation of the times. The religion of the country had, in fact, changed from love of God to hatred of Napoleon Buonaparte; and, as if to remind the devout of this alteration, the pikes for the pikemen (all those accepted men who were not otherwise armed) were kept in the church of each parish. There, against the wall, they always stood – a whole sheaf of them, formed of new ash stems, with a spike driven in at one end, the stick being preserved from splitting by a ferule. And there they remained, year after year, in the corner of the aisle, till they were removed and placed under the gallery stairs, and thence

* *Vide* Preface.

ultimately to the belfry, where they grew black, rusty, and worm-eaten, and were gradually stolen and carried off by sextons, parish clerks, whitewashers, window-menders, and other church servants for use at home as rake-stems, benefit-club staves,[126] and pick-handles, in which degraded situations they may still occasionally be found.

But in their new and shining state they had a terror for Anne, whose eyes were involuntarily drawn towards them as she sat at Bob's side during the service, filling her with bloody visions of their possible use not far from the very spot on which they were now assembled. The sermon, too, was on the subject of patriotism; so that when they came out she began to harp uneasily upon the probability of their all being driven from their homes.

Bob assured her that with the sixty thousand regulars, the militia reserve of a hundred and twenty thousand, and the three hundred thousand volunteers, there was not much to fear.

'But I sometimes have a fear that poor John will be killed,' he continued after a pause. 'He is sure to be among the first that will have to face the invaders, and the trumpeters get picked off.'

'There is the same chance for him as for the others,' said Anne.

'Yes – yes – the same chance, such as it is. You have never liked John since that affair of Matilda Johnson, have you?'

'Why?' she quickly asked.

'Well,' said Bob timidly, 'as it is a ticklish time for him, would it not be worth while to make up any differences before the crash comes?'

'I have nothing to make up,' said Anne, with some distress. She still fully believed the trumpet-major to have smuggled away Miss Johnson because of his own interest in that lady, which must have made his professions to herself a mere pastime; but that very conduct had in it the curious advantage to herself of setting Bob free.

'Since John has been gone,' continued her companion, 'I have found out more of his meaning, and of what he really had to do with that woman's flight. Did you know that he had anything to do with it?'

'Yes.'

'That he got her to go away?'

She looked at Bob with surprise. He was not exasperated with John, and yet he knew so much as this.

'Yes,' she said; 'what did it mean?'

He did not explain to her then; but the possibility of John's death, which had been newly brought home to him by the military events of the day, determined him to get poor John's character cleared. Reproaching himself for letting her remain so long with a mistaken idea of him, Bob went to his father as soon as they got home, and begged him to get Mrs Loveday to tell Anne the true reason of John's objection to Miss Johnson as a sister-in-law.

'She thinks it is because they were old lovers new met, and that he wants to marry her,' he exclaimed to his father in conclusion.

'Then *that's* the meaning of the split between Miss Nancy and Jack,' said the miller.

'What, were they any more than common friends?' asked Bob uneasily.

'Not on her side, perhaps.'

'Well, we must do it,' replied Bob, painfully conscious that common justice to John might bring them into hazardous rivalry, yet determined to be fair. 'Tell it all to Mrs Loveday, and get her to tell Anne.'

# * XXIV *

## A Letter, a Visitor and a Tin Box

THE result of the explanation upon Anne was bitter self-reproach.
She was so sorry at having wronged the kindly soldier that next
morning she went by herself to the down, and stood exactly where
his tent had covered the sod on which he had lain so many nights,
thinking what sadness he must have suffered because of her at the
time of packing up and going away. After that she wiped from
her eyes the tears of pity which had come there, descended to the
house, and wrote an impulsive letter to him, in which occurred
the following passages, indiscreet enough under the circumstances:

> I find all justice, all rectitude, on your side, John; and all
> impertinence, all inconsiderateness, on mine. I am so much
> convinced of your honour in the whole transaction, that I shall for
> the future mistrust myself in everything. And if it be possible,
> whenever I differ from you on any point I shall take an hour's time
> for consideration before I say that I differ. If I have lost your
> friendship, I have only myself to thank for it; but I sincerely hope
> that you can forgive.

After writing this she went to the garden, where Bob was
shearing the spring grass from the paths. 'What is John's direction?'
she said, holding the sealed letter in her hand.

'Exonbury Barracks,' Bob faltered, his countenance sinking.

She thanked him and went indoors. When he came in, later in
the day, he passed the door of her empty sitting-room and saw the
letter on the mantelpiece. He disliked the sight of it. Hearing
voices in the other room, he entered and found Anne and her
mother there, talking to Cripplestraw, who had just come in with
a message from Squire Derriman, requesting Miss Garland, as she

valued the peace of mind of an old and troubled man, to go at once and see him.

'I cannot go,' she said, not liking the risk that such a visit involved.

An hour later Cripplestraw shambled again into the passage, on the same errand.

'Maister's very poorly, and he hopes that you'll come, Mis'ess Anne. He wants to see 'ee very particular about the French.'

Anne would have gone in a moment, but for the fear that someone besides the farmer might encounter her, and she answered as before.

Another hour passed, and the wheels of a vehicle were heard. Cripplestraw had come for the third time, with a horse and gig; he was dressed in his best clothes, and brought with him on this occasion a basket containing raisins, almonds, oranges, and sweet cakes. Offering them to her as a gift from the old farmer, he repeated his request for her to accompany him, the gig and best mare having been sent as an additional inducement.

'I believe the old gentleman is in love with you, Anne,' said her mother.

'Why couldn't he drive down himself to see me?' Anne inquired of Cripplestraw.

'He wants you at the house, please.'

'Is Mr Festus with him?'

'No; he's away to Budmouth.'

'I'll go,' said she.

'And I may come and meet you?' said Bob.

'There's my letter – what shall I do about that?' she said, instead of answering him. 'Take my letter to the post-office, and you may come,' she added.

He said yes and went out, Cripplestraw retreating to the door till she should be ready.

'What letter is it?' said her mother.

'Only one to John,' said Anne. 'I have asked him to forgive my suspicions. I could do no less.'

'Do you want to marry *him*?' asked Mrs Loveday bluntly.

'Mother!'

'Well; he will take that letter as an encouragement. Can't you see that he will, you foolish girl?'

Anne did see instantly. 'Of course!' she said. 'Tell Robert that he need not go.'

She went to her room to secure the letter. It was gone from the mantelpiece, and on inquiry it was found that the miller, seeing it there, had sent David with it to Budmouth hours ago. Anne said nothing, and set out for Oxwell Hall with Cripplestraw.

'William,' said Mrs Loveday to the miller when Anne was gone and Bob had resumed his work in the garden, 'did you get that letter sent off on purpose?'

'Well, I did. I wanted to make sure of it. John likes her, and now 'twill be made up; and why shouldn't he marry her? I'll start him in business, if so be she'll have him.'

'But she is likely to marry Festus Derriman.'

'I don't want her to marry anybody but John,' said the miller doggedly.

'Not if she is in love with Bob, and has been for years, and he with her?' asked his wife triumphantly.

'In love with Bob, and he with her?' repeated Loveday.

'Certainly,' said she, going off and leaving him to his reflections.

When Anne reached the hall she found old Mr Derriman in his customary chair. His complexion was more ashen, but his movement in rising at her entrance, putting a chair and shutting the door behind her, were much the same as usual.

'Thank God you've come, my dear girl,' he said earnestly. 'Ah, you don't trip across to read to me now! Why did ye cost me so much to fetch you? Fie! A horse and gig, and a man's time in going three times. And what I sent ye cost a good deal in Budmouth market, now everything is so dear there, and 'twould have cost more if I hadn't bought the raisins and oranges some months ago, when they were cheaper. I tell you this because we are old friends, and I have nobody else to tell my troubles to. But I don't begrudge anything to ye since you've come.'

'I am not much pleased to come, even now,' said she. 'What can make you so seriously anxious to see me?'

'Well, you be a good girl and true; and I've been thinking that of all people of the next generation that I can trust, you are the best. 'Tis my bonds and my title-deeds, such as they be, and the leases, you know, and a few guineas in packets, and more than these, my will, that I have to speak about. Now do ye come this way.'

'O, such things as those!' she returned, with surprise. 'I don't understand those things at all.'

'There's nothing to understand. 'Tis just this. The French will be here within two months; that's certain. I have it on the best authority, that the army at Boulogne is ready, the boats equipped, the plans laid, and the First Consul only waits for a tide. Heaven knows what will become o' the men o' these parts! But most likely the women will be spared. Now I'll show 'ee.'

He led her across the hall to a stone staircase of semi-circular plan, which conducted to the cellars.

'Down here?' she said.

'Yes; I must trouble ye to come down here. I have thought and thought who is the woman that can best keep a secret for six months, and I say, "Anne Garland". You won't be married before then?'

'O no!' murmured the young woman.

'I wouldn't expect ye to keep a close tongue after such a thing as that. But it will not be necessary.'

When they reached the bottom of the steps he struck a light from a tinder-box, and unlocked the middle one of three doors which appeared in the whitewashed wall opposite. The rays of the candle fell upon the vault and sides of a long low cellar, littered with decayed woodwork from other parts of the hall, among the rest stair-balusters, carved finials,[127] tracery panels, and wainscoting. But what most attracted her eye was a small flagstone turned up in the middle of the floor, a heap of earth beside it, and a measuring-tape. Derriman went to the corner of the cellar, and pulled out a clamped box from under the straw. 'You be rather heavy, my dear, eh?' he said, affectionately addressing the box as he lifted it. 'But you are going to be put in a safe place, you know, or that rascal will get hold of ye, and carry ye off and ruin me.' He then with some difficulty lowered the box into the hole, raked in the earth upon it, and lowered the flagstone, which he was a long time in fixing to his satisfaction. Miss Garland, who was romantically interested, helped him to brush away the fragments of loose earth; and when he had scattered over the floor a little of the straw that lay about, they again ascended to upper air.

'Is this all, sir?' said Anne.

'Just a moment longer, honey. Will you come into the great parlour?'

She followed him thither.

'If anything happens to me while the fighting is going on – it may be on these very fields – you will know what to do,' he resumed. 'But first please sit down again, there's a dear, whilst I write what's in my head. See, there's the best paper, and a new quill that I've afforded myself for't.'

'What a strange business! I don't think I much like it, Mr Derriman,' she said, seating herself.

He had by this time begun to write, and murmured as he wrote –

' "Twenty-three and a half from N.W. Sixteen and three-quarters from N.E." – There, that's all. Now I seal it up and give it to you to keep safe till I ask ye for it, or you hear of my being trampled down by the enemy.'

'What does it mean?' she asked, as she received the paper.

'Clk! Ha! ha! Why, that's the distance of the box from the two corners of the cellar. I measured it before you came. And, my honey, to make all sure, if the French soldiery are after ye, tell your mother the meaning on't, or any other friend, in case they should put ye to death, and the secret be lost. But that I am sure I hope they won't do, though your pretty face will be a sad bait to the soldiers. I often have wished you was my daughter, honey; and yet in these times the less cares a man has the better, so I am glad you bain't. Shall my man drive you home?'

'No, no,' she said, much depressed by the words he had uttered. 'I can find my way. You need not trouble to come down.'

'Then take care of the paper. And if you outlive me, you'll find I have not forgot you.'

# * XXV *

## *Festus Shows His Love*

FESTUS Derriman had remained in the Royal watering-place all that day, his horse being sick at stables; but, wishing to coax or bully from his uncle a remount for the coming summer, he set off on foot for Oxwell early in the evening. When he drew near to the village, or rather to the hall, which was in advance of the village, he overtook a slim, quick-eyed woman, sauntering along at a leisurely pace. She was fashionably dressed in a green spencer,[128] with 'Mameluke' sleeves,[129] and wore a velvet Spanish hat and feather.

'Good afternoon t'ye, ma'am,' said Festus, throwing a sword-and-pistol air into his greeting. 'You are out for a walk?'

'I *am* out for a walk, captain,' said the lady, who had criticized him from the crevice of her eye, without seeming to do much more than continue her demure look forward, and gave the title as a sop to his apparent character.

'From the town? – I'd swear it, ma'am; 'pon my honour I would!'

'Yes, I am from the town, sir,' said she.

'Ah, you are a visitor! I know every one of the regular inhabitants; we soldiers are in and out there continually. Festus Derriman, Yeomanry Cavalry, you know. The fact is, the watering-place is under our charge; the folks will be quite dependent upon us for their deliverance in the coming struggle. We hold our lives in our hands, and theirs, I may say, in our pockets. What made you come here, ma'am, at such a critical time?'

'I don't see that it is such a critical time?'

'But it is, though; and so you'd say if you was as much mixed up with the military affairs of the nation as some of us.'

The lady smiled. 'The King is coming this year, anyhow,' said she.

'Never!' said Festus firmly. 'Ah, you are one of the attendants at court perhaps, come on ahead to get the King's chambers ready, in case Boney should not land?'

'No,' she said; 'I am connected with the theatre, though not just at the present moment. I have been out of luck for the last year or two; but I have fetched up again. I join the company when they arrive for the season.'

Festus surveyed her with interest. 'Faith! and is it so? Well, ma'am, what part do you play?'

'I am mostly the leading lady – the heroine,' she said, drawing herself up with dignity.

'I'll come and have a look at ye if all's well, and the landing is put off – hang me if I don't! – Hullo, hullo, what do I see?'

His eyes were stretched towards a distant field, which Anne Garland was at that moment hastily crossing, on her way from the hall to Overcombe.

'I must be off. Good day to ye, dear creature!' he exclaimed, hurrying forward.

The lady said, 'O, you droll monster!' as she smiled and watched him stride ahead.

Festus bounded on over the hedge, across the intervening patch of green, and into the field which Anne was still crossing. In a moment or two she looked back, and seeing the well-known herculean figure of the yeoman behind her felt rather alarmed, though she determined to show no difference in her outward carriage. But to maintain her natural gait was beyond her powers. She spasmodically quickened her pace; fruitlessly, however, for he gained upon her, and when within a few strides of her exclaimed, 'Well, my darling!' Anne started off at a run.

Festus was already out of breath, and soon found that he was not likely to overtake her. On she went, without turning her head, till an unusual noise behind compelled her to look round. His face was in the act of falling back; he swerved on one side, and dropped like a log upon a convenient hedgerow-bank which bordered the path. There he lay quite still.

Anne was somewhat alarmed; and after standing at gaze for

two or three minutes, drew nearer to him, a step and a half at a time, wondering and doubting, as a meek ewe draws near to some strolling vagabond who flings himself on the grass near the flock.

'He is in a swoon!' she murmured.

Her heart beat quickly, and she looked around. Nobody was in sight; she advanced a step nearer still and observed him again. Apparently his face was turning to a livid hue, and his breathing had become obstructed.

' 'Tis not a swoon; 'tis apoplexy!' she said, in deep distress. 'I ought to untie his neck.' But she was afraid to do this, and only drew a little closer still.

Miss Garland was now within three feet of him, whereupon the senseless man, who could hold his breath no longer, sprang to his feet and darted at her, saying, 'Ha! ha! a scheme for a kiss!'

She felt his arm slipping round her neck; but, twirling about with amazing dexterity, she wriggled from his embrace and ran away along the field. The force with which she had extricated herself was sufficient to throw Festus upon the grass, and by the time that he got upon his legs again she was many yards off. Uttering a word which was not exactly a blessing, he immediately gave chase; and thus they ran till Anne entered a meadow divided down the middle by a brook about six feet wide. A narrow plank was thrown loosely across at the point where the path traversed this stream, and when Anne reached it she at once scampered over. At the other side she turned her head to gather the probabilities of the situation, which were that Festus Derriman would overtake her even now. By a sudden forethought she stooped, seized the end of the plank, and endeavoured to drag it away from the opposite bank. But the weight was too great for her to do more than slightly move it, and with a desperate sigh she ran on again, having lost many valuable seconds.

But her attempt, though ineffectual in dragging it down, had been enough to unsettle the little bridge; and when Derriman reached the middle, which he did half a minute later, the plank turned over on its edge, tilting him bodily into the river. The water was not remarkably deep, but as the yeoman fell flat on his stomach he was completely immersed; and it was some time before he could drag himself out. When he arose, dripping on the bank, and looked around, Anne had vanished from the mead. Then Festus's eyes glowed like carbuncles, and he gave voice to fearful imprecations, shaking his fist in the soft summer air towards Anne, in a way that was terrible for any maiden to behold. Wading back through the stream, he walked along its bank with a heavy tread, the water running from his coat-tails, wrists, and the tips of his ears, in silvery dribbles, that sparkled pleasantly in the sun. Thus he hastened away, and went round by a by-path to the hall.

Meanwhile the author of his troubles was rapidly drawing nearer to the mill, and soon, to her inexpressible delight, she saw Bob coming to meet her. She had heard the flounce, and, feeling more secure from her pursuer, had dropped her pace to a quick walk. No sooner did she reach Bob than, overcome by the excitement of the moment, she flung herself into his arms. Bob instantly enclosed her in an embrace so very thorough that there was no possible danger of her falling, whatever degree of exhaustion might have given rise to her somewhat unexpected action; and in this attitude they silently remained, till it was borne in upon Anne that the present was the first time in her life that she had ever been in such a position. Her face then burned like a sunset, and she did not know how to look up at him. Feeling at length quite safe, she suddenly resolved not to give way to her first impulse to tell him the whole of what had happened, lest there should be a dreadful quarrel and fight between Bob and the yeoman, and great difficulties caused in the Loveday family on her account, the miller having important wheat transactions with the Derrimans.

'You seem frightened, dearest Anne,' said Bob tenderly.

'Yes,' she replied. 'I saw a man I did not like the look of, and he was inclined to follow me. But, worse than that, I am troubled about the French. O Bob! I am afraid you will be killed, and my mother, and John, and your father, and all of us hunted down!'

'Now I have told you, dear little heart, that it cannot be. We shall drive 'em into the sea after a battle or two, even if they land, which I don't believe they will. We've got ninety sail of the line, and though it is rather unfortunate that we should have declared war against Spain at this ticklish time, there's enough for all.' And

Bob went into elaborate statistics of the navy, army, militia, and volunteers, to prolong the time of holding her. When he had done speaking he drew rather a heavy sigh.

'What's the matter, Bob?'

'I haven't been yet to offer myself as a sea-fencible, and I ought to have done it long ago.'

'You are only one. Surely they can do without you?'

Bob shook his head. She arose from her restful position, her eye catching his with a shamefaced expression of having given way at last. Loveday drew from his pocket a paper, and said, as they slowly walked on, 'Here's something to make us brave and patriotic. I bought it in Budmouth. Isn't it a stirring picture?'

It was a hieroglyphic profile of Napoleon. The hat represented a maimed French eagle; the face was ingeniously made up of human carcases, knotted and writhing together in such directions as to form a physiognomy; a band, or stock, shaped to resemble the English Channel, encircled his throat, and seemed to choke him; his epaulette was a hand tearing a cobweb that represented the treaty of peace with England; and his ear was a woman crouching over a dying child.*

'It is dreadful!' said Anne. 'I don't like to see it.'

She had recovered from her emotion, and walked along beside him with a grave, subdued face. Bob did not like to assume the privileges of an accepted lover and draw her hand through his arm; for, conscious that she naturally belonged to a politer grade than his own, he feared lest her exhibition of tenderness were an impulse which cooler moments might regret. A perfect Paul-and-Virginia[130] life had not absolutely set in for him as yet, and it was not to be hastened by force. When they had passed over the bridge into the mill-front they saw the miller standing at the door with a face of concern.

'Since you have been gone,' he said, 'a Government man has been here, and to all the houses, taking down the numbers of the women and children, and their ages, and the number of horses and waggons that can be mustered, in case they have to retreat inland, out of the way of the invading army.'

The little family gathered themselves together, all feeling the

* Vide Preface.

crisis more seriously than they liked to express. Mrs Loveday thought how ridiculous a thing social ambition was in such a conjuncture as this, and vowed that she would leave Anne to love where she would. Anne, too, forgot the little peculiarities of speech and manner in Bob and his father, which sometimes jarred for a moment upon her more refined sense, and was thankful for their love and protection in this looming trouble.

On going upstairs she remembered the paper which Farmer Derriman had given her, and searched in her bosom for it. She could not find it there. 'I must have left it on the table,' she said to herself. It did not matter; she remembered every word. She took a pen and wrote a duplicate, which she put safely away.

But Anne was wrong. She had, after all, placed the paper where she supposed, and there it ought to have been. But in escaping from Festus, when he feigned apoplexy, it had fallen out upon the grass. Five minutes after that event, when pursuer and pursued were two or three fields ahead, the gaily-dressed woman whom the yeoman had overtaken, peeped cautiously through the stile into the corner of the field which had been the scene of the scramble; and seeing the paper she climbed over, secured it, loosened the wafer without tearing the sheet, and read the memorandum within. Unable to make anything of its meaning, the saunterer put it in her pocket, and, dismissing the matter from her mind, went on by the by-path which led to the back of the mill. Here, behind the hedge, she stood and surveyed the old building for some time, after which she meditatively turned, and retraced her steps towards the Royal watering-place.

# * XXVI *

## The Alarm

THE night which followed was historic and memorable. Mrs Loveday was awakened by the boom of a distant gun: she told the miller, and they listened awhile. The sound was not repeated, but such was the state of their feelings that Mr Loveday went to Bob's room and asked if he had heard it. Bob was wide awake, looking out of the window; he had heard the ominous sound, and was inclined to investigate the matter. While the father and son were dressing they fancied that a glare seemed to be rising in the sky in the direction of the beacon hill. Not wishing to alarm Anne and her mother, the miller assured them that Bob and himself were merely going out of doors to inquire into the cause of the report, after which they plunged into the gloom together. A few steps' progress opened up more of the sky, which, as they had thought, was indeed irradiated by a lurid light; but whether it came from the beacon or from a more distant point they were unable to clearly tell. They pushed on rapidly towards higher ground.

Their excitement was merely of a piece with that of all men at this critical juncture. Everywhere expectation was at fever heat. For the last year or two only five-and-twenty miles of shallow water had divided quiet English homesteads from an enemy's army of a hundred and fifty thousand men. We had taken the matter lightly enough, eating and drinking as in the days of Noe,[131] and singing satires without end. We punned on Buonaparte and his gunboats, chalked his effigy on stage-coaches, and published the same in prints. Still, between these bursts of hilarity, it was sometimes recollected that England was the only European country which had not succumbed to the mighty little man who was less than human in feeling, and more than human in will; that our spirit for resistance was greater than our strength; and that the

Channel was often calm. Boats built of wood which was greenly growing in its native forest three days before it was bent as wales[132] to their sides, were ridiculous enough; but they might be, after all, sufficient for a single trip between two visible shores.

The English watched Buonaparte in these preparations, and Buonaparte watched the English. At the distance of Boulogne details were lost, but we were impressed on fine days by the novel sight of a huge army moving and twinkling like a school of mackerel under the rays of the sun. The regular way of passing an afternoon in the coast towns was to stroll up to the signal posts and chat with the lieutenant on duty there about the latest inimical object seen at sea. About once a week there appeared in the newspapers either a paragraph concerning some adventurous English gentleman who had sailed out in a pleasure-boat till he lay near enough to Boulogne to see Buonaparte standing on the heights among his marshals; or else some lines about a mysterious stranger with a foreign accent, who, after collecting a vast deal of information on our resources, had hired a boat at a southern port, and vanished with it towards France before his intention could be divined.

In forecasting his grand venture, Buonaparte postulated the help of Providence to a remarkable degree. Just at the hour when his troops were on board the flat-bottomed boats and ready to sail, there was to be a great fog, that should spread a vast obscurity over the length and breadth of the Channel, and keep the English blind to events on the other side. The fog was to last twenty-four hours, after which it might clear away. A dead calm was to prevail simultaneously with the fog, with the twofold object of affording the boats easy transit and dooming our ships to lie motionless. Thirdly, there was to be a spring tide, which should combine its manœuvres with those of the fog and calm.

Among the many thousands of minor Englishmen whose lives were affected by these tremendous designs may be numbered our old acquaintance Corporal Tullidge, who sported the crushed arm, and poor old Simon Burden, the dazed veteran who had fought at Minden.[133] Instead of sitting snugly in the settle of the Old Ship, in the village adjoining Overcombe, they were obliged to keep watch on the hill. They made themselves as comfortable as was possible in the circumstances, dwelling in a hut of clods and turf, with a brick chimney for cooking. Here they observed the nightly progress of the moon and stars, grew familiar with the heaving of moles, the dancing of rabbits on the hillocks, the distant hoot of owls, the bark of foxes from woods further inland; but saw not a sign of the enemy. As, night after night, they walked round the two ricks which it was their duty to fire at a signal – one being of furze for a quick flame, the other of turf, for a long, slow radiance – they thought and talked of old times, and drank patriotically from a large wood flagon that was filled every day.

Bob and his father soon became aware that the light was from the beacon. By the time that they reached the top it was one mass of towering flame, from which the sparks fell on the green herbage like a fiery dew; the forms of the two old men being seen passing and repassing in the midst of it. The Lovedays, who came up on the smoky side, regarded the scene for a moment, and then emerged into the light.

'Who goes there?' said Corporal Tullidge, shouldering a pike with his sound arm. 'O, 'tis neighbour Loveday!'

'Did you get your signal to fire it from the east?' said the miller hastily.

'No; from Abbotsea Beach.'

'But you are not to go by a coast signal!'

'Chok' it all, wasn't the Lord-Lieutenant's direction, whenever you see Rainbarrow's Beacon burn to the nor'east'ard, or Haggardon to the nor'west'ard, or the actual presence of the enemy on the shore?'

'But is he here?'

'No doubt o't! The beach light is only just gone down, and Simon heard the guns even better than I.'

'Hark, hark! I hear 'em!' said Bob.

They listened with parted lips, the night wind blowing through Simon Burden's few teeth as through the ruins of Stonehenge. From far down on the lower levels came the noise of wheels and the tramp of horses upon the turnpike road.

'Well, there must be something in it,' said Miller Loveday gravely. 'Bob, we'll go home and make the women-folk safe, and then I'll don my soldier's clothes and be off. God knows where our company will assemble!'

They hastened down the hill, and on getting into the road waited and listened again. Travellers began to come up and pass them in vehicles of all descriptions. It was difficult to attract their attention in the dim light, but by standing on the top of a wall which fenced the road Bob was at last seen.

'What's the matter?' he cried to a butcher who was flying past in his cart, his wife sitting behind him without a bonnet.

'The French have landed!' said the man, without drawing rein.

'Where?' shouted Bob.

'In West Bay; and all Budmouth is in uproar!' replied the voice, now faint in the distance.

Bob and his father hastened on till they reached their own house. As they had expected, Anne and her mother, in common with most of the people, were both dressed, and stood at the door bonneted and shawled, listening to the traffic on the neighbouring highway, Mrs Loveday having secured what money and small valuables they possessed in a huge pocket which extended all round her waist, and added considerably to her weight and diameter.

' 'Tis true enough,' said the miller: 'he's come! You and Anne and the maid must be off to Cousin Jim's at King's-Bere, and when you get there you must do as they do. I must assemble with the company.'

'And I?' said Bob.

'Thou'st better run to the church, and take a pike before they be all gone.'

The horse was put into the gig, and Mrs Loveday, Anne, and the servant-maid were hastily packed into the vehicle, the latter taking the reins; David's duties as a fighting-man forbidding all thought of his domestic offices now. Then the silver tankard, teapot, pair of candlesticks like Ionic columns, and other articles too large to be pocketed were thrown into a basket and put up behind. Then came the leave-taking, which was as sad as it was hurried. Bob kissed Anne, and there was no affectation in her receiving that mark of affection as she said through her tears, 'God bless you!' At last they moved off in the dim light of dawn, neither of the three women knowing which road they were to take, but trusting to chance to find it.

As soon as they were out of sight Bob went off for a pike, and his father, first new-flinting his firelock, proceeded to don his uniform, pipe-claying his breeches with such cursory haste as to bespatter his black gaiters with the same ornamental compound. Finding when he was ready that no bugle had as yet sounded, he went with David to the cart-house, dragged out the waggon, and put therein some of the most useful and easily-handled goods, in case there might be an opportunity for conveying them away. By the time this was done and the waggon pushed back and locked in, Bob had returned with his weapon, somewhat mortified at being doomed to this low form of defence. The miller gave his son a parting grasp of the hand, and arranged to meet him at King's-Bere at the first opportunity if the news were true; if happily false, here at their own house.

'Bother it all!' he exclaimed, looking at his stock of flints.

'What?' said Bob.

'I've got no ammunition: not a blessed round!'

'Then what's the use of going?' asked his son.

The miller paused. 'O, I'll go,' he said. 'Perhaps somebody will lend me a little if I get into a hot corner.'

'Lend ye a little! Father, you was always so simple!' said Bob reproachfully.

'Well – I can bagnet[134] a few, anyhow,' said the miller.

The bugle had been blown ere this, and Loveday the father disappeared towards the place of assembly, his empty cartridge-box behind him. Bob seized a brace of loaded pistols which he had brought home from the ship, and, armed with these and a pike, he locked the door and sallied out again towards the turnpike road.

By this time the yeomanry of the district were also on the move, and among them Festus Derriman, who was sleeping at his uncle's, and had been awakened by Cripplestraw. About the time when Bob and his father were descending from the beacon the stalwart yeoman was standing in the stable-yard adjusting his straps, while Cripplestraw saddled the horse. Festus clanked up and down, looked gloomily at the beacon, heard the retreating carts and carriages, and called Cripplestraw to him, who came from the stable leading the horse at the same moment that Uncle

Benjy peeped unobserved from a mullioned window above their heads, the distant light of the beacon fire touching up his features to the complexion of an old brass clock-face.

'I think that before I start, Cripplestraw,' said Festus, whose lurid visage was undergoing a bleaching process curious to look upon, 'you shall go on to Budmouth, and make a bold inquiry whether the cowardly enemy is on shore as yet, or only looming in the bay.'

'I'd go in a moment, sir,' said the other, 'if I hadn't my bad leg again. I should have joined my company afore this; but they said at last drill that I was too old. So I shall wait up in the hay-loft for tidings as soon as I have packed you off, poor gentleman!'

'Do such alarms as these, Cripplestraw, ever happen without foundation? Buonaparte is a wretch, a miserable wretch, and this may be only a false alarm to disappoint such as me?'

'O no, sir; O no!'

'But sometimes there are false alarms?'

'Well, sir, yes. There was a pretended sally o' gunboats last year.'

'And was there nothing else pretended – something more like this, for instance?'

Cripplestraw shook his head. 'I notice yer modesty, Mr Festus, in making light of things. But there never was, sir. You may depend upon it he's come. Thank God, my duty as a Local don't require me to go to the front, but only the valiant men like my master. Ah, if Boney could only see 'ee now, sir, he'd know too well there is nothing to be got from such a determined skilful officer but blows and musket-balls!'

'Yes, yes, Cripplestraw, if I ride off to Budmouth and meet 'em, all my training will be lost. No skill is required as a forlorn hope.'

'True; that's a point, sir. You would outshine 'em all, and be picked off at the very beginning as a too-dangerous brave man.'

'But if I stay here and urge on the faint-hearted ones, or get up into the turret-stair by that gateway, and pop at the invaders through the loophole, I shouldn't be so completely wasted, should I?'

'You would not, Mr Derriman. But, as you was going to say

next, the fire in yer veins won't let ye do that. You are valiant; very good: you don't want to husband yer valiance at home. The arg'ment is plain.'

'If my birth had been more obscure,' murmured the yeoman, 'and I had only been in the militia, for instance, or among the humble pikemen, so much wouldn't have been expected of me – of my fiery nature. Cripplestraw, is there a drop of brandy to be got at in the house? I don't feel very well.'

'Dear nephew,' said the old gentleman from above, whom neither of the others had as yet noticed, 'I haven't any spirits opened – so unfortunate! But there's a beautiful barrel of crab-apple cider in draught; and there's some cold tea from last night.'

'What, is he listening?' said Festus, staring up. 'Now I warrant how glad he is to see me forced to go – called out of bed without breakfast, and he quite safe, and sure to escape because he's an old man! – Cripplestraw, I like being in the yeomanry cavalry; but I wish I hadn't been in the ranks; I wish I had been only the surgeon, to stay in the rear while the bodies are brought back to him – I mean, I should have thrown my heart at such a time as this more into the labour of restoring wounded men and joining their shattered limbs together – u-u-ugh! – more than I can into causing the wounds – I am too humane, Cripplestraw, for the ranks!'

'Yes, yes,' said his companion, depressing his spirits to a kindred level. 'And yet, such is fate, that, instead of joining men's limbs together, you'll have to get your own joined – poor young sojer! – all through having such a warlike soul.'

'Yes,' murmured Festus, and paused. 'You can't think how strange I feel here, Cripplestraw,' he continued, laying his hand upon the centre buttons of his waistcoat. 'How I do wish I was only the surgeon!'

He slowly mounted, and Uncle Benjy, in the meantime, sang to himself as he looked on, '*Twen-ty-three and a half from N.W. Six-teen and three-quar-ters from N.E.*'

'What's that old mummy singing?' said Festus savagely.

'Only a hymn for preservation from our enemies, dear nephew,' meekly replied the farmer, who had heard the remark. '*Twen-ty-three and a half from N.W.*'

Festus allowed his horse to move on a few paces, and then

turned again, as if struck by a happy invention. 'Cripplestraw,' he began, with an artificial laugh, 'I am obliged to confess, after all – I must see her! 'Tisn't nature that makes me draw back – 'tis love. I must go and look for her.'

'A woman, sir?'

'I didn't want to confess it; but 'tis a woman. Strange that I should be drawn so entirely against my natural wish to rush at 'em!'

Cripplestraw, seeing which way the wind blew, found it advisable to blow in harmony. 'Ah, now at last I see, sir! Spite that few men live that be worthy to command ye; spite that you could rush on, marshal the troops to victory, as I may say; but then – what of it? – there's the unhappy fate of being smit with the eyes of a woman, and you are unmanned! Maister Derriman, who is himself, when he's got a woman round his neck like a millstone?'

'It is something like that.'

'I feel the case. Be you valiant? – I know, of course, the words being a matter of form – be you valiant, I ask? Yes, of course. Then don't you waste it in the open field. Hoard it up, I say, sir, for a higher class of war – the defence of yer adorable lady. Think what you owe her at this terrible time! Now, Maister Derriman, once more I ask ye to cast off that first haughty wish to rush to Budmouth, and to go where your mis'ess is defenceless and alone.'

'I will, Cripplestraw, now you put it like that!'

'Thank ye, thank ye heartily, Maister Derriman. Go now and hide with her.'

'But can I? Now, hang flattery! – can a man hide without a stain? Of course I would not hide in any mean sense; no, not I!'

'If you be in love, 'tis plain you may, since it is not your own life, but another's, that you are concerned for, and you only save your own because it can't be helped.'

' 'Tis true, Cripplestraw, in a sense. But will it be understood that way? Will they see it as a brave hiding?'

'Now, sir, if you had not been in love I own to ye that hiding would look queer, but being to save the tears, groans, fits, swowndings, and perhaps death of a comely young woman, yer principle is good; you honourably retreat because you be too gallant to advance. This sounds strange, ye may say, sir; but it is plain enough to less fiery minds.'

Festus did for a moment try to uncover his teeth in a natural smile, but it died away. 'Cripplestraw, you flatter me; or do you mean it? Well, there's truth in it. I am more gallant in going to her than in marching to the shore. But we cannot be too careful about our good names, we soldiers. I must not be seen. I'm off.'

Cripplestraw opened the hurdle which closed the arch under the portico gateway, and Festus passed under, Uncle Benjamin singing, *Twen-ty-three and a half from N.W.* with a sort of sublime ecstasy, feeling, as Festus had observed, that his money was safe, and that the French would not personally molest an old man in such a ragged, mildewed coat as that he wore, which he had taken the precaution to borrow from a scarecrow in one of his fields for the purpose.

Festus rode on full of his intention to seek out Anne, and under cover of protecting her retreat accompany her to King's-Bere, where he knew the Lovedays had relatives. In the lane he met Granny Seamore, who, having packed up all her possessions in a small basket, was placidly retreating to the mountains till all should be over.

'Well, granny, have ye seen the French?' asked Festus.

'No,' she said, looking up at him through her brazen spectacles. 'If I had I shouldn't ha' seed thee!'

'Faugh!' replied the yeoman, and rode on. Just as he reached the old road, which he had intended merely to cross and avoid, his countenance fell. Some troops of regulars, who appeared to be dragoons, were rattling along the road. Festus hastened towards an opposite gate, so as to get within the field before they should see him; but, as ill-luck would have it, as soon as he got inside, a party of six or seven of his own yeomanry troop were straggling across the same field and making for the spot where he was. The dragoons passed without seeing him; but when he turned out into the road again it was impossible to retreat towards Overcombe village because of the yeomen. So he rode straight on, and heard them coming at his heels. There was no other gate, and the highway soon became as straight as a bowstring. Unable thus to turn without meeting them, and caught like an eel in a water-pipe, Festus drew nearer and nearer to the fateful shore. But he did not relinquish hope. Just ahead there were cross-roads, and he might have a chance of slipping down one of them without being seen. On reaching the spot he found that he was not alone. A horseman had come up the right-hand lane and drawn rein. It was an officer of the German legion, and seeing Festus he held up his hand. Festus rode up to him and saluted.

'It ist false report!' said the officer.

Festus was a man again. He felt that nothing was too much for him. The officer, after some explanation of the cause of alarm, said that he was going across to the road which led by the moor, to stop the troops and volunteers converging from that direction, upon which Festus offered to give information along the Casterbridge road. The German crossed over, and was soon out of sight in the lane, while Festus turned back upon the way by which he had come. The party of yeomanry cavalry was rapidly drawing near, and he soon recognized among them the excited voices of Stubb of Duddle Hole, Noakes of Muckleford, and other comrades of his orgies at the hall. It was a magnificent opportunity, and Festus drew his sword. When they were within speaking distance he reined round his charger's head to Budmouth and shouted, 'On, comrades, on! I am waiting for you. You have been a long time getting up with me, seeing the glorious nature of our deeds today!'

'Well said, Derriman, well said!' replied the foremost of the riders. 'Have you heard anything new?'

'Only that he's here with his tens of thousands, and that we are to ride to meet him sword in hand as soon as we have assembled in the town ahead here.'

'O Lord!' said Noakes, with a slight falling of the lower jaw.

'The man who quails now is unworthy of the name of yeoman,' said Festus, still keeping ahead of the other troopers and holding up his sword to the sun. 'O Noakes, fie, fie! You begin to look pale, man.'

'Faith, perhaps you'd look pale,' said Noakes, with an envious glance upon Festus's daring manner, 'if you had a wife and family depending upon ye!'

'I'll take three frog-eating Frenchmen single-handed!' rejoined Derriman, still flourishing his sword.

'They have as good swords as you; as you will soon find,' said another of the yeomen.

'If they were three times armed,' said Festus – 'ay, thrice three times – I would attempt 'em three to one. How do you feel now, my old friend Stubb?' (turning to another of the warriors). 'O, friend Stubb! no bouncing health to our lady-loves in Oxwell Hall this summer as last. Eh, Brownjohn?'

'I am afraid not,' said Brownjohn gloomily.

'No rattling dinners at Stacie's Hotel, and the King below with his staff. No wrenching off door-knockers and sending 'em to the bakehouse in a pie that nobody calls for. Weeks of cut-and-thrust work rather!'

'I suppose so.'

'Fight how we may we shan't get rid of the cursed tyrant before autumn, and many thousand brave men will lie low before it's done,' remarked a young yeoman with a calm face, who meant to do his duty without much talking.

'No grinning matches at Mai-dun Castle this summer,' Festus resumed; 'no thread-the-needle at Greenhill Fair,[135] and going into shows and driving the showman crazy with cock-a-doodle-doo!'

'I suppose not.'

'Does it make you seem just a trifle uncomfortable, Noakes? Keep up your spirits, old comrade. Come, forward! we are only ambling on like so many donkey-women. We have to get into Budmouth, join the rest of the troop, and then march along the coast west'ard, as I imagine. At this rate we shan't be well into the thick of battle before twelve o'clock. Spur on, comrades. No dancing on the green, Lockham, this year in the moonlight! You was tender upon that girl; gad, what will become o' her in the struggle?'

'Come, come, Derriman,' expostulated Lockham – 'this is all very well, but I don't care for 't. I am as ready to fight as any man, but –'

'Perhaps when you get into battle, Derriman, and see what it's like, your courage will cool down a little,' added Noakes on the same side, but with secret admiration of Festus's reckless bravery.

'I shall be bayoneted first,' said Festus. 'Now let's rally, and on!'

Since Festus was determined to spur on wildly, the rest of the yeomen did not like to seem behindhand, and they rapidly approached the town. Had they been calm enough to reflect, they might have observed that for the last half-hour no carts or carriages had met them on the way, as they had done further back. It was not till the troopers reached the turnpike that they learnt what Festus had known a quarter of an hour before. At the intelligence Derriman sheathed his sword with a sigh; and the party soon fell in with comrades who had arrived there before them, whereupon the source and details of the alarm were boisterously discussed.

'What, didn't you know of the mistake till now?' asked one of these of the new-comers. 'Why, when I was dropping over the hill by the cross-roads I looked back and saw that man talking to the messenger, and he must have told him the truth.' The speaker pointed to Festus. They turned their indignant eyes full upon him. That he had sported with their deepest feelings, while knowing the rumour to be baseless, was soon apparent to all.

'Beat him black and blue with the flat of our blades!' shouted two or three, turning their horses' heads to drop back upon Derriman, in which move they were followed by most of the party.

But Festus, foreseeing danger from the unexpected revelation, had already judiciously placed a few intervening yards between himself and his fellow-yeomen, and now, clapping spurs to his horse, rattled like thunder and lightning up the road homeward. His ready flight added hotness to their pursuit, and as he rode and looked fearfully over his shoulder he could see them following with enraged faces and drawn swords, a position which they kept up for a distance of more than a mile. Then he had the satisfaction of seeing them drop off one by one, and soon he and his panting charger remained alone on the highway.

# XXVII

## Danger to Anne

He stopped and reflected how to turn this rebuff to advantage. Baulked in his project of entering the watering-place and enjoying congratulations upon his patriotic bearing during the advance, he sulkily considered that he might be able to make some use of his enforced retirement by riding to Overcombe and glorifying himself in the eyes of Miss Garland before the truth should have reached that hamlet. Having thus decided he spurred on in a better mood.

By this time the volunteers were on the march, and as Derriman ascended the road he met the Overcombe company, in which trudged Miller Loveday shoulder to shoulder with the other substantial householders of the place and its neighbourhood, duly equipped with pouches, cross-belts, firelocks, flint-boxes, pickers,[136] worms,[137] magazines, priming-horns,[138] heel-ball, and pomatum. There was nothing to be gained by further suppression of the truth, and briefly informing them that the danger was not so immediate as had been supposed, Festus galloped on. At the end of another mile he met a large number of pikemen, including Bob Loveday, whom the yeoman resolved to sound upon the whereabouts of Anne. The circumstances were such as to lead Bob to speak more frankly than he might have done on reflection, and he told Festus the direction in which the women had been sent. Then Festus informed the group that the report of invasion was false, upon which they all turned to go homeward with greatly relieved spirits.

Bob walked beside Derriman's horse for some distance. Loveday had instantly made up his mind to go and look for the women, and ease their anxiety by letting them know the good news as soon as possible. But he said nothing of this to Festus during their return together; nor did Festus tell Bob that he also had resolved to seek them out, and by anticipating everyone else in that enterprise, make of it a glorious opportunity for bringing Miss Garland to her senses about him. He still resented the ducking that he had received at her hands, and was not disposed to let that insult pass without obtaining some sort of sweet revenge.

As soon as they had parted Festus cantered on over the hill, meeting on his way the Longpuddle volunteers, sixty rank and file, under Captain Cunningham; the Casterbridge company, ninety strong (known as the 'Consideration Company' in those days), under Captain Strickland; and others – all with anxious faces and covered with dust. Just passing the word to them and leaving them at halt, he proceeded rapidly onward in the direction of King's-Bere. Nobody appeared on the road for some time, till after a ride of several miles he met a stray corporal of volunteers, who told Festus in answer to his inquiry that he had certainly passed no gig full of women of the kind described. Believing that he had missed them by following the highway, Derriman turned back into a lane along which they might have chosen to journey for privacy's sake, notwithstanding the badness and uncertainty of its track. Arriving again within five miles of Overcombe, he at length heard tidings of the wandering vehicle and its precious burden, which, like the Ark when sent away from the country of Philistines,[139] had apparently been left to the instincts of the beast that drew it. A labouring man, just at daybreak, had seen the helpless party going slowly up a distant drive, which he pointed out.

No sooner had Festus parted from this informant than he beheld Bob approaching, mounted on the miller's second and heavier horse. Bob looked rather surprised, and Festus felt his coming glory in danger.

'They went down that lane,' he said, signifying precisely the opposite direction to the true one. 'I, too, have been on the look-out for missing friends.'

As Festus was riding back there was no reason to doubt his information, and Loveday rode on as misdirected. Immediately that he was out of sight Festus reversed his course, and followed the track which Anne and her companions were last seen to pursue.

This road had been ascended by the gig in question nearly two hours before the present moment. Molly, the servant, held the reins, Mrs Loveday sat beside her, and Anne behind. Their progress was but slow, owing partly to Molly's want of skill, and partly to the steepness of the road, which here passed over downs of some extent, and was rarely or never mended. It was an anxious morning for them all, and the beauties of the early summer day fell upon unheeding eyes. They were too anxious even for conjecture, and each sat thinking her own thoughts, occasionally glancing westward, or stopping the horse to listen to sounds from more frequented roads along which other parties were retreating. Once, while they listened and gazed thus, they saw a glittering in the distance, and heard the tramp of many horses. It was a large body of cavalry going in the direction of the King's watering-place, the same regiment of dragoons, in fact, which Festus had seen further on in its course. The women in the gig had no doubt that these men were marching at once to engage the enemy. By way of varying the monotony of the journey Molly occasionally burst into tears of horror, believing Buonaparte to be in countenance and habits precisely what the caricatures represented him. Mrs Loveday endeavoured to establish cheerfulness by assuring her companions of the natural civility of the French nation, with whom unprotected women were safe from injury, unless through the casual excesses of soldiery beyond control. This was poor consolation to Anne, whose mind was more occupied with Bob than with herself, and a miserable fear that she would never again see him alive so paled her face and saddened her gaze forward, that at last her mother said, 'Who was you thinking of, my dear?' Anne's only reply was a look at her mother, with which a tear mingled.

Molly whipped the horse, by which she quickened his pace for five yards, when he again fell into the perverse slowness that showed how fully conscious he was of being the master-mind and chief personage of the four. Whenever there was a pool of water by the road he turned aside to drink a mouthful, and remained there his own time in spite of Molly's tug at the reins and futile fly-flapping on his rump. They were now in the chalk district, where there were no hedges, and a rough attempt at mending the way had been made by throwing down huge lumps of that glaring material in heaps, without troubling to spread it or break them abroad. The jolting here was most distressing, and seemed about to snap the springs.

'How that wheel do wamble,'[140] said Molly at last. She had scarcely spoken when the wheel came off, and all three were precipitated over it into the road.

Fortunately the horse stood still, and they began to gather themselves up. The only one of the three who had suffered in the least from the fall was Anne, and she was only conscious of a severe shaking which had half stupefied her for the time. The wheel lay flat in the road, so that there was no possibility of driving further in their present plight. They looked around for help. The only friendly object near was a lonely cottage, from its situation evidently the home of a shepherd.

The horse was unharnessed and tied to the back of the gig, and the three women went across to the house. On getting close they found that the shutters of all the lower windows were closed, but on trying the door it opened to the hand. Nobody was within; the house appeared to have been abandoned in some confusion, and the probability was that the shepherd had fled on hearing the alarm. Anne now said that she felt the effects of her fall too severely to be able to go any further just then, and it was agreed that she should be left there while Mrs Loveday and Molly went on for assistance, the elder lady deeming Molly too young and vacant-minded to be trusted to go alone. Molly suggested taking the horse, as the distance might be great, each of them sitting alternately on his back while the other led him by the head. This they did, Anne watching them vanish down the white and lumpy road.

She then looked round the room, as well as she could do so by the light from the open door. It was plain, from the shutters being closed, that the shepherd had left his house before daylight, the candle and extinguisher on the table pointing to the same conclusion. Here she remained, her eyes occasionally sweeping the bare, sunny expanse of down, that was only relieved from absolute emptiness by the overturned gig hard by. The sheep seemed to have gone away, and scarcely a bird flew across to disturb the solitude. Anne had risen early that morning, and leaning back in the withy chair, which she had placed by the door, she soon fell into an uneasy doze, from which she was awakened by the distant tramp of a horse. Feeling much recovered from the effects of the overturn, she eagerly rose and looked out. The horse was not Miller Loveday's, but a powerful bay, bearing a man in full yeomanry uniform.

Anne did not wait to recognize further; instantly re-entering the house, she shut the door and bolted it. In the dark she sat and listened: not a sound. At the end of ten minutes, thinking that the rider if he were not Festus had carelessly passed by, or that if he were Festus he had not seen her, she crept softly upstairs and peeped out of the window. Excepting the spot of shade, formed by the gig as before, the down was quite bare. She then opened the casement and stretched out her neck.

'Ha, young madam! There you are! I knew 'ee! Now you are caught!' came like a clap of thunder from a point three or four feet beneath her, and turning down her frightened eyes she beheld Festus Derriman lurking close to the wall. His attention had first been attracted by her shutting the door of the cottage; then by the overturned gig; and after making sure, by examining the vehicle, that he was not mistaken in her identity, he had dismounted, led his horse round to the side, and crept up to entrap her.

Anne started back into the room, and remained still as a stone. Festus went on – 'Come, you must trust to me. The French have landed. I have been trying to meet with you every hour since that confounded trick you played me. You threw me into the water. Faith, it was well for you I didn't catch ye then! I should have taken a revenge in a better way than I shall now. I mean to have that kiss of ye. Come, Miss Nancy; do you hear? – 'Tis no use for you to lurk inside there. You'll have to turn out as soon as Boney comes over the hill. – Are you going to open the door, I say, and speak to me in a civil way? What do you think I am, then, that you should barricade yourself against me as if I was a wild beast or Frenchman? Open the door, or put out your head, or do something; or 'pon my soul I'll break in the door!'

It occurred to Anne at this point of the tirade that the best policy would be to temporize till somebody should return, and she put out her head and face, now grown somewhat pale.

'That's better,' said Festus. 'Now I can talk to you. Come, my dear, will you open the door? Why should you be afraid of me?'

'I am not altogether afraid of you; I am safe from the French here,' said Anne, not very truthfully, and anxiously casting her eyes over the vacant down.

'Then let me tell you that the alarm is false, and that no landing has been attempted. Now will you open the door and let me in? I am tired. I have been on horseback ever since daylight, and have come to bring you the good tidings.'

Anne looked as if she doubted the news.

'Come,' said Festus.

'No, I cannot let you in,' she murmured, after a pause.

'Dash my wig, then,' he cried, his face flaming up, 'I'll find a way to get in! Now, don't you provoke me! You don't know what I am capable of. I ask you again, will you open the door?'

'Why do you wish it?' she said faintly.

'I have told you I want to sit down; and I want to ask you a question.'

'You can ask me from where you are.'

'I cannot ask you properly. It is about a serious matter: whether you will accept my heart and hand. I am not going to throw myself at your feet; but I ask you to do your duty as a woman, namely, give your solemn word to take my name as soon as the war is over and I have time to attend to you. I scorn to ask it of a haughty hussy who will only speak to me through a window; however, I put it to you for the last time, madam.'

There was no sign on the down of anybody's return, and she said, 'I'll think of it, sir.'

'You have thought of it long enough; I want to know. Will you or won't you?'

'Very well; I think I will.' And then she felt that she might be buying personal safety too dearly by shuffling thus, since he would spread the report that she had accepted him, and cause endless complication. 'No,' she said, 'I have changed my mind. I cannot accept you, Mr Derriman.'

'That's how you play with me!' he exclaimed, stamping. ' "Yes" one moment; "No" the next. Come, you don't know what you refuse. That old hall is my uncle's own, and he has nobody else to leave it to. As soon as he's dead I shall throw up farming and start as a squire. And now,' he added with a bitter sneer, 'what a fool you are to hang back from such a chance!'

'Thank you, I don't value it,' said Anne.

'Because you hate him who would make it yours?'

'It may not lie in your power to do that.'

'What – has the old fellow been telling you his affairs?'

'No.'

'Then why do you mistrust me? Now, after this will you open the door, and show that you treat me as a friend if you won't accept me as a lover? I only want to sit and talk to you.'

Anne thought she would trust him; it seemed almost impossible that he could harm her. She retired from the window and went downstairs. When her hand was upon the bolt of the door, her mind misgave her. Instead of withdrawing it she remained in silence where she was, and he began again –

'Are you going to unfasten it?'

Anne did not speak.

'Now, dash my wig, I will get at you! You've tried me beyond endurance. One kiss would have been enough that day in the mead; now I'll have forty, whether you will or no!'

He flung himself against the door; but as it was bolted, and had in addition a great wooden bar across it, this produced no effect. He was silent for a moment, and then the terrified girl heard him attempt the shuttered window. She ran upstairs and again scanned the down. The yellow gig still lay in the blazing sunshine, and the horse of Festus stood by the corner of the garden – nothing else was to be seen. At this moment there came to her ear the noise of a sword drawn from its scabbard; and, peeping over the window-sill, she saw her tormentor drive his sword between the joints of the shutters, in an attempt to rip them open. The sword snapped off in his hand. With an imprecation he pulled out the piece, and returned the two halves to the scabbard.

'Ha! ha!' he cried, catching sight of the top of her head. ' 'Tis only a joke, you know; but I'll get in all the same. All for a kiss! But never mind, we'll do it yet!' He spoke in an affectedly light tone, as if ashamed of his previous resentful temper; but she could see by the livid back of his neck that he was brimful of suppressed passion. 'Only a jest, you know,' he went on. 'How are we going to do it now? Why, in this way. I go and get a ladder, and enter at the upper window where my love is. And there's the ladder lying under that corn-rick in the first enclosed field. Back in two minutes, dear!'

He ran off, and was lost to her view.

# * XXVIII *

## Anne Does Wonders

ANNE fearfully surveyed her position. The upper windows of the cottage were of flimsiest lead-work, and to keep him out would be hopeless. She felt that not a moment was to be lost in getting away. Running downstairs she opened the door, and then it occurred to her terrified understanding that there would be no chance of escaping him by flight afoot across such an extensive down, since he might mount his horse and easily ride after her. The animal still remained tethered at the corner of the garden; if she could release him and frighten him away before Festus returned, there would not be quite such odds against her. She accordingly unhooked the horse by reaching over the bank, and then, pulling off her muslin neckerchief, flapped it in his eyes to startle him. But the gallant steed did not move or flinch; she tried again, and he seemed rather pleased than otherwise. At this moment she heard a cry from the cottage, and turning, beheld her adversary approaching round the corner of the building.

'I thought I should tole[141] out the mouse by that trick!' cried Festus exultingly. Instead of going for a ladder, he had simply hidden himself at the back to tempt her down.

Poor Anne was now desperate. The bank on which she stood was level with the horse's back, and the creature seemed quiet as a lamb. With a determination of which she was capable in emergencies, she seized the rein, flung herself upon the sheepskin, and held on by the mane. The amazed charger lifted his head, sniffed, wrenched his ears hither and thither, and started off at a frightful speed across the down.

'O, my heart and limbs!' said Festus under his breath, as, thoroughly alarmed, he gazed after her. 'She on Champion! She'll break her neck, and I shall be tried for manslaughter, and disgrace will be brought upon the name of Derriman!'

Champion continued to go at a stretch-gallop, but he did nothing worse. Had he plunged or reared, Derriman's fears might have been verified, and Anne have come with deadly force to the ground. But the course was good, and in the horse's speed lay a comparative security. She was scarcely shaken in her precarious half-horizontal position, though she was awed to see the grass, loose stones, and other objects pass her eyes like strokes whenever she opened them, which was only just for a second at intervals of half a minute; and to feel how wildly the stirrups swung, and that what struck her knee was the bucket of the carbine, [142] and that it was a pistol-holster which hurt her arm.

They quickly cleared the down, and Anne became conscious that the course of the horse was homeward. As soon as the ground began to rise towards the outer belt of upland which lay between her and the coast, Champion, now panting and reeking with moisture, lessened his speed in sheer weariness, and proceeded at a rapid jolting trot. Anne felt that she could not hold on half so well; the gallop had been child's play compared with this. They were in a lane, ascending to a ridge, and she made up her mind for a fall. Over the ridge rose an animated spot, higher and higher; it turned out to be the upper part of a man, and the man to be a soldier. Such was Anne's attitude that she only got an occasional glimpse of him; and, though she feared that he might be a Frenchman, she feared the horse more than the enemy, as she had feared Festus more than the horse. Anne had energy enough left to cry, 'Stop him; stop him!' as the soldier drew near.

He, astonished at the sight of a military horse with a bundle of drapery across his back, had already placed himself in the middle of the lane, and he now held out his arms till his figure assumed the form of a Latin cross [143] planted in the roadway. Champion drew near, swerved, and stood still almost suddenly, a check sufficient to send Anne slipping down his flank to the ground. The timely friend stepped forward and helped her to her feet, when she saw that he was John Loveday.

'Are you hurt?' he said hastily, having turned quite pale at seeing her fall.

'O no; not a bit,' said Anne, gathering herself up with forced briskness, to make light of the misadventure.

'But how did you get in such a place?'

'There, he's gone!' she exclaimed, instead of replying, as Champion swept round John Loveday and cantered off triumphantly in the direction of Oxwell, a performance which she followed with her eyes.

'But how did you come upon his back, and whose horse is it?'

'I will tell you.'

'Well?'

'I – cannot tell you.'

John looked steadily at her, saying nothing.

'How did you come here?' she asked. 'Is it true that the French have not landed at all?'

'Quite true; the alarm was groundless. I'll tell you all about it. You look very tired. You had better sit down a few minutes. Let us sit on this bank.'

He helped her to the slope indicated, and continued, still as if his thoughts were more occupied with the mystery of her recent situation than with what he was saying: 'We arrived at Budmouth Barracks this morning, and are to lie there all the summer. I could not write to tell father we were coming. It was not because of any rumour of the French, for we knew nothing of that till we met the people on the road, and the colonel said in a moment the news was false. Buonaparte is not even at Boulogne just now. I was anxious to know how you had borne the fright, so I hastened to Overcombe at once, as soon as I could get out of barracks.'

Anne, who had not been at all responsive to his discourse, now swayed heavily against him, and looking quickly down he found that she had silently fainted. To support her in his arms was of course the impulse of a moment. There was no water to be had, and he could think of nothing else but to hold her tenderly till she came round again. Certainly he desired nothing more.

Again he asked himself, what did it all mean?

He waited, looking down upon her tired eyelids, and at the row of lashes lying upon each cheek, whose natural roundness showed itself in singular perfection now that the customary pink had given place to a pale luminousness caught from the surrounding atmosphere. The dumpy ringlets about her forehead and behind her poll, which were usually as tight as springs, had been partially uncoiled by the wildness of her ride, and hung in split locks over her forehead and neck. John, who, during the long months of his absence, had lived only to meet her again, was in a state of ecstatic reverence, and bending down he gently kissed her.

Anne was just becoming conscious.

'O, Mr Derriman, never, never!' she murmured, sweeping her face with her hand.

'I thought he was at the bottom of it,' said John.

Anne opened her eyes, and started back from him. 'What is it?' she said wildly.

'You are ill, my dear Miss Garland,' replied John in trembling anxiety, and taking her hand.

'I am not ill, I am wearied out!' she said. 'Can't we walk on? How far are we from Overcombe?'

'About a mile. But tell me, somebody has been hurting you – frightening you. I know who it was; it was Derriman, and that was his horse. Now do you tell me all.'

Anne reflected. 'Then if I tell you,' she said, 'will you discuss with me what I had better do, and not for the present let my mother and your father know? I don't want to alarm them, and I must not let my affairs interrupt the business connection between the mill and the hall that has gone on for so many years.'

The trumpet-major promised, and Anne told the adventure. His brow reddened as she went on, and when she had done she said, 'Now you are angry. Don't do anything dreadful, will you? Remember that this Festus will most likely succeed his uncle at Oxwell, in spite of present appearances, and if Bob succeeds at the mill there should be no enmity between them.'

'That's true. I won't tell Bob. Leave him to me. Where is Derriman now? On his way home, I suppose. When I have seen you into the house I will deal with him – quite quietly, so that he shall say nothing about it.'

'Yes, appeal to him, do! Perhaps he will be better then.'

They walked on together, Loveday seeming to experience much quiet bliss.

'I came to look for you,' he said, 'because of that dear, sweet letter you wrote.'

'Yes, I did write you a letter,' she admitted, with misgiving, now beginning to see her mistake. 'It was because I was sorry I had blamed you.'

'I am almost glad you did blame me,' said John cheerfully, 'since, if you had not, the letter would not have come. I have read it fifty times a day.'

This put Anne into an unhappy mood, and they proceeded without much further talk till the mill chimneys were visible below them. John then said that he would leave her to go in by herself.

'Ah, you are going back to get into some danger on my account?'

'I can't get into much danger with such a fellow as he, can I?' said John, smiling.

'Well, no,' she answered, with a sudden carelessness of tone. It was indispensable that he should be undeceived, and to begin the process by taking an affectedly light view of his personal risks was perhaps as good a way to do it as any. Where friendliness was construed as love, an assumed indifference was the necessary expression for friendliness.

So she let him go; and, bidding him hasten back as soon as he could, went down the hill, while John's feet retraced the upland.

The trumpet-major spent the whole afternoon and evening in that long and difficult search for Festus Derriman. Crossing the down at the end of the second hour he met Molly and Mrs Loveday. The gig had been repaired, they had learnt the ground-lessness of the alarm, and they would have been proceeding happily enough but for their anxiety about Anne. John told them shortly that she had got a lift home, and proceeded on his way.

The worthy object of his search had in the meantime been plodding homeward on foot, sulky at the loss of his charger, encumbered with his sword, belts, high boots, and uniform, and in his own discomfiture careless whether Anne Garland's life had been endangered or not.

At length Derriman reached a place where the road ran between high banks, one of which he mounted and paced along as a change from the hard trackway. Ahead of him he saw an old man sitting down, with eyes fixed on the dust of the road, as if resting and meditating at one and the same time. Being pretty sure that he recognized his uncle in that venerable figure, Festus came forward stealthily, till he was immediately above the old man's back. The latter was clothed in faded nankeen breeches, speckled stockings, a drab hat, and a coat which had once been light blue, but from exposure as a scarecrow had assumed the complexion and fibre of a dried pudding-cloth. The farmer was, in fact, returning to the hall, which he had left in the morning some time later than his nephew, to seek an asylum in a hollow tree about two miles off. The tree was so situated as to command a view of the building, and Uncle Benjy had managed to clamber up inside this natural fortification high enough to watch his residence through a hole in the bark, till, gathering from the words of occasional passers-by that the alarm was at least premature, he had ventured into daylight again.

He was now engaged in abstractedly tracing a diagram in the dust with his walking-stick, and muttered words to himself aloud. Presently he arose and went on his way without turning round. Festus was curious enough to descend and look at the marks. They represented an oblong, with two semi-diagonals, and a little square in the middle. Upon the diagonals were the figures 20 and 17, and on each side of the parallelogram stood a letter signifying the point of the compass.

'What crazy thing is running in his head now?' said Festus to himself, with supercilious pity, recollecting that the farmer had been singing those very numbers earlier in the morning. Being able to make nothing of it, he lengthened his strides, and treading on tiptoe overtook his relative, saluting him by scratching his back like a hen. The startled old farmer danced round like a top, and gasping, said, as he perceived his nephew, 'What, Festy! not thrown from your horse and killed, then, after all!'

'No, nunc. What made ye think that?'

'Champion passed me about an hour ago, when I was in hiding – poor timid soul of me, for I had nothing to lose by the French coming – and he looked awful with the stirrups dangling and the saddle empty. 'Tis a gloomy sight, Festy, to see a horse cantering without a rider, and I thought you had been – feared you had been thrown off and killed as dead as a nit.'

'Bless your dear old heart for being so anxious! And what pretty picture were you drawing just now with your walking-stick?'

'O, that! That is only a way I have of amusing myself. It showed how the French might have advanced to the attack, you know. Such trifles fill the head of a weak old man like me.'

'Or the place where something is hid away – money, for instance?'

'Festy,' said the farmer reproachfully, 'you always know I use the old glove in the bedroom cupboard for any guinea or two I possess.'

'Of course I do,' said Festus ironically.

They had now reached a lonely inn about a mile and a half from the hall, and, the farmer not responding to his nephew's kind invitation to come in and treat him, Festus entered alone. He was dusty, draggled, and weary, and he remained at the tavern long. The trumpet-major, in the meantime, having searched the roads in vain, heard in the course of the evening of the yeoman's arrival at this place, and that he would probably be found there still. He accordingly approached the door, reaching it just as the dusk of evening changed to darkness.

There was no light in the passage, but John pushed on at hazard, inquired for Derriman, and was told that he would be found in the back parlour alone. When Loveday first entered the apartment he was unable to see anything, but following the guidance of a vigorous snoring, he came to the settle, upon which Festus lay asleep, his position being faintly signified by the shine of his buttons and other parts of his uniform. John laid his hand upon the reclining figure and shook him, and by degrees Derriman stopped his snore and sat up.

'Who are you?' he said, in the accents of a man who has been drinking hard. 'Is it you, dear Anne? Let me kiss you; yes, I will.'

'Shut your mouth, you pitiful blockhead; I'll teach you genteeler manners than to persecute a young woman in that way!' and taking Festus by the ear, he gave it a good pull. Festus broke out with an oath, and struck a vague blow in the air with his fist;

whereupon the trumpet-major dealt him a box on the right ear, and a similar one on the left to artistically balance the first. Festus jumped up and used his fists wildly, but without any definite result.

'Want to fight, do ye, eh?' said John. 'Nonsense! you can't fight, you great baby, and never could. You are only fit to be smacked!' and he dealt Festus a specimen of the same on the cheek with the palm of his hand.

'No, sir, no! O, you are Loveday, the young man she's going to be married to, I suppose? Dash me, I didn't want to hurt her, sir.'

'Yes, my name is Loveday; and you'll know where to find me, since we can't finish this tonight. Pistols or swords, whichever you like, my boy. Take that, and that, so that you may not forget to call upon me!' and again he smacked the yeoman's ears and cheeks. 'Do you know what it is for, eh?'

'No, Mr Loveday, sir – yes, I mean, I do.'

'What is it for, then? I shall keep smacking until you tell me. Gad! if you weren't drunk, I'd half kill you here tonight.'

'It is because I served her badly. Damned if I care! I'll do it again, and be hanged to 'ee! Where's my horse Champion? Tell me that,' and he hit at the trumpet-major.

John parried this attack, and taking him firmly by the collar, pushed him down into the seat, saying, 'Here I hold 'ee till you beg pardon for your doings today. Do you want any more of it, do you?' And he shook the yeoman to a sort of jelly.

'I do beg pardon – no, I don't. I say this, that you shall not take such liberties with old Squire Derriman's nephew, you dirty miller's son, you flour-worm, you smut in the corn!'[44] I'll call you out tomorrow morning, and have my revenge.'

'Of course you will; that's what I came for.' And pushing him back into the corner of the settle, Loveday went out of the house, feeling considerable satisfaction at having got himself into the beginning of as nice a quarrel about Anne Garland as the most jealous lover could desire.

But of one feature in this curious adventure he had not the least notion – that Festus Derriman, misled by the darkness, the fumes of his potations, and the constant sight of Anne and Bob together, never once supposed his assailant to be any other man than Bob, believing the trumpet-major miles away.

There was a moon during the early part of John's walk home, but when he had arrived within a mile of Overcombe the sky clouded over, and rain suddenly began to fall with some violence. Near him was a wooden granary on tall stone staddles;[145] and perceiving that the rain was only a thunderstorm which would soon pass away, he ascended the steps and entered the doorway, where he stood watching the half-obscured moon through the streaming rain. Presently, to his surprise, he beheld a female figure running forward with great rapidity, not towards the granary for shelter, but towards open ground. What could she be running for in that direction? The answer came in the appearance of his brother Bob from that quarter, seated on the back of his father's heavy horse. As soon as the woman met him, Bob dismounted and caught her in his arms. They stood locked together, the rain beating into their unconscious forms, and the horse looking on.

The trumpet-major fell back inside the granary, and threw himself on a heap of empty sacks which lay in the corner: he had recognized the woman to be Anne. Here he reclined in a stupor till he was aroused by the sound of voices under him, the voices of Anne and his brother, who, having at last discovered that they were getting wet, had taken shelter under the granary floor.

'I have been home,' said she. 'Mother and Molly have both got back long ago. We were all anxious about you, and I came out to look for you. O, Bob, I am so glad to see you again!'

John might have heard every word of the conversation, which was continued in the same strain for a long time; but he stopped his ears, and would not. Still they remained, and still was he determined that they should not see him. With the conserved hope of more than half a year dashed away in a moment, he could yet feel that the cruelty of a protest would be even greater than its inutility. It was absolutely by his own contrivance that the situation had been shaped. Bob, left to himself, would long ere this have been the husband of another woman.

The rain decreased, and the lovers went on. John looked after them as they strolled, aqua-tinted[146] by the weak moon and mist.

Bob had thrust one of his arms through the rein of the horse, and the other was round Anne's waist. When they were lost behind the declivity the trumpet-major came out, and walked homeward even more slowly than they. As he went on, his face put off its complexion of despair for one of serene resolve. For the first time in his dealings with friends he entered upon a course of counterfeiting, set his features to conceal his thought, and instructed his tongue to do likewise. He threw fictitiousness into his very gait, even now, when there was nobody to see him, and struck at stems of wild parsley with his regimental switch as he had used to do when soldiering was new to him, and life in general a charming experience.

Thus cloaking his sickly thought, he descended to the mill as the others had done before him, occasionally looking down upon the wet road to notice how close Anne's little tracks were to Bob's all the way along, and how precisely a curve in his course was followed by a curve in hers. But after this he erected his head and walked so smartly up to the front door that his spurs rang through the court.

They had all reached home, but before any of them could speak he cried gaily, 'Ah, Bob, I have been thinking of you! By God, how are you, my boy? No French cut-throats after all, you see. Here we are, well and happy together again.'

'A good Providence has watched over us,' said Mrs Loveday cheerfully. 'Yes, in all times and places we are in God's hand.'

'So we be, so we be!' said the miller, who still shone in all the fierceness of uniform. 'Well, now we'll ha'e a drop o' drink.'

'There's none,' said David, coming forward with a drawn face.

'What!' said the miller.

'Afore I went to church for a pike to defend my native country from Boney, I pulled out the spigots of all the barrels, maister; for, thinks I – damn him! – since we can't drink it ourselves, he shan't have it, nor none of his men.'

'But you shouldn't have done it till you was sure he'd come!' said the miller, aghast.

'Chok' it all, I was sure!' said David. 'I'd sooner see churches fall than good drink wasted; but how was I to know better?'

'Well, well; what with one thing and another this day will cost me a pretty penny!' said Loveday, bustling off to the cellar, which he found to be several inches deep in stagnant liquor. 'John, how can I welcome 'ee?' he continued hopelessly, on his return to the room. 'Only go and see what he's done!'

'I've ladled up a drap wi' a spoon, trumpet-major,' said David. ' 'Tisn't bad drinking, though it do taste a little of the floor, that's true.'

John said that he did not require anything at all; and then they all sat down to supper, and were very temperately gay with a drop of mild elder-wine which Mrs Loveday found in the bottom of a jar. The trumpet-major, adhering to the part he meant to play, gave humorous accounts of his adventures since he had last sat there. He told them that the season was to be a very lively one – that the royal family was coming, as usual, and many other interesting things; so that when he left them to return to barracks few would have supposed the British army to contain a lighter-hearted man.

Anne was the only one who doubted the reality of this behaviour. When she had gone up to her bedroom she stood for some time looking at the wick of the candle as if it were a painful object, the expression of her face being shaped by the conviction that John's afternoon words when he helped her out of the way of Champion were not in accordance with his words tonight, and that the dimly-realized kiss during her faintness was no imaginary one. But in the blissful circumstances of having Bob at hand again she took optimist views, and persuaded herself that John would soon begin to see her in the light of a sister.

# * XXIX *

## A Dissembler

To cursory view, John Loveday seemed to accomplish this with amazing ease. Whenever he came from barracks to Overcombe, which was once or twice a week, he related news of all sorts to her and Bob with infinite zest, and made the time as happy a one as had ever been known at the mill, save for himself alone. He said nothing of Festus, except so far as to inform Anne that he had expected to see him and been disappointed. On the evening after the King's arrival at his seaside residence John appeared again, staying to supper and describing the royal entry, the many tasteful illuminations and transparencies[147] which had been exhibited, the quantities of tallow candles burnt for that purpose, and the swarms of aristocracy who had followed the King thither.

When supper was over Bob went outside the house to shut the shutters, which had, as was often the case, been left open some time after lights were kindled within. John still sat at the table when his brother approached the window, though the others had risen and retired. Bob was struck by seeing through the pane how John's face had changed. Throughout the supper-time he had been talking to Anne in the gay tone habitual with him now, which gave greater strangeness to the gloom of his present appearance. He remained in thought for a moment, took a letter from his breast-pocket, opened it, and, with a tender smile at his weakness, kissed the writing before restoring it to its place. The letter was one that Anne had written to him at Exonbury.

Bob stood perplexed; and then a suspicion crossed his mind that John, from brotherly goodness, might be feigning a satisfaction with recent events which he did not feel. Bob now made a noise with the shutters, at which the trumpet-major rose and went out, Bob at once following him.

'Jack,' said the sailor ingenuously, 'I'm terribly sorry that I've done wrong.'

'How?' asked his brother.

'In courting our little Anne. Well, you see, John, she was in the same house with me, and somehow or other I made myself her beau. But I have been thinking that perhaps you had the first claim on her, and if so, Jack, I'll make way for 'ee. I – I don't care for her much, you know – not so very much, and can give her up very well. It is nothing serious between us at all. Yes, John, you try to get her; I can look elsewhere.' Bob never knew how much he loved Anne till he found himself making this speech of renunciation.

'O Bob, you are mistaken!' said the trumpet-major, who was not deceived. 'When I first saw her I admired her, and I admire her now, and like her. I like her so well that I shall be glad to see you marry her.'

'But,' replied Bob, with hesitation, 'I thought I saw you looking very sad, as if you were in love; I saw you take out a letter, in short. That's what it was disturbed me and made me come to you.'

'O, I see your mistake!' said John, laughing forcedly.

At this minute Mrs Loveday and the miller, who were taking a twilight walk in the garden, strolled round near to where the brothers stood. She talked volubly on events in Budmouth, as most people did at this time. 'And they tell me that the theatre has been painted up afresh,' she was saying, 'and that the actors have come for the season, with the most lovely actresses that ever were seen.'

When they had passed by John continued, 'I *am* in love, Bob; but – not with Anne.'

'Ah! who is it then?' said the mate hopefully.

'One of the actresses at the theatre,' John replied, with a concoctive look at the vanishing forms of Mr and Mrs Loveday. 'She is a very lovely woman, you know. But we won't say anything more about it – it dashes a man so.'

'O, one of the actresses!' said Bob, with open mouth.

'But don't you say anything about it!' continued the trumpet-major heartily. 'I don't want it known.'

'No, no – I won't, of course. May I not know her name?'

'No, not now, Bob. I cannot tell 'ee,' John answered, and with truth, for Loveday did not know the name of any actress in the world.

When his brother had gone, Captain Bob hastened off in a state of great animation to Anne, whom he found on the top of a neighbouring hillock which the daylight had scarcely as yet deserted.

'You have been a long time coming, sir,' said she, in sprightly tones of reproach.

'Yes, dearest; and you'll be glad to hear why. I've found out the whole mystery – yes – why he's queer, and everything.'

Anne looked startled.

'He's up to the gunnel[148] in love! We must try to help him on in it, or I fear he'll go melancholy-mad like.'

'We help him?' she asked faintly.

'He's lost his heart to one of the play-actresses at Budmouth, and I think she slights him.'

'O, I am so glad!' she exclaimed.

'Glad that his venture don't prosper?'

'O no; glad he's so sensible. How long is it since that alarm of the French?'

'Six weeks, honey. Why do you ask?'

'Men can forget in six weeks, can't they, Bob?'

The impression that John had really kissed her still remained.

'Well, some men might,' observed Bob judicially. '*I* couldn't. Perhaps John might. I couldn't forget *you* in twenty times as long. Do you know, Anne, I half thought it was you John cared about; and it was a weight off my heart when he said he didn't.'

'Did he say he didn't?'

'Yes. He assured me himself that the only person in the hold of his heart was this lovely play-actress, and nobody else.'

'How I should like to see her!'

'Yes. So should I.'

'I would rather it had been one of our own neighbours' girls, whose birth and breeding we know of; but still, if that is his taste, I hope it will end well for him. How very quick he has been! I certainly wish we could see her.'

'I don't know so much as her name. He is very close, and wouldn't tell a thing about her.'

'Couldn't we get him to go to the theatre with us? and then we could watch him, and easily find out the right one. Then we would learn if she is a good young woman; and if she is, could we not ask her here, and so make it smoother for him? He has been very gay lately; that means budding love: and sometimes between his gaieties he has had melancholy moments; that means there's difficulty.'

Bob thought her plan a good one, and resolved to put it in practice on the first available evening. Anne was very curious as to whether John did really cherish a new passion, the story having quite surprised her. Possibly it was true; six weeks had passed since John had shown a single symptom of the old attachment, and what could not that space of time effect in the heart of a soldier whose very profession it was to leave girls behind him?

After this John Loveday did not come to see them for nearly a month, a neglect which was set down by Bob as an additional proof that his brother's affections were no longer exclusively centred in his old home. When at last he did arrive, and the theatre-going was mentioned to him, the flush of consciousness which Anne expected to see upon his face was unaccountably absent.

'Yes, Bob; I should very well like to go to the theatre,' he replied heartily. 'Who is going besides?'

'Only Anne,' Bob told him, and then it seemed to occur to the trumpet-major that something had been expected of him. He rose and said privately to Bob with some confusion, 'O yes, of course we'll go. As I am connected with one of the – in short I can get you in for nothing, you know. At least let me manage everything.'

'Yes, yes. I wonder you didn't propose to take us before, Jack, and let us have a good look at her.'

'I ought to have. You shall go on a King's night. You won't want me to point her out, Bob; I have my reasons at present for asking it?'

'We'll be content with guessing,' said his brother.

When the gallant John was gone, Anne observed, 'Bob, how he is changed! I watched him. He showed no feeling, even when you burst upon him suddenly with the subject nearest his heart.'

'It must be because his suit don't fay,'[149] said Captain Bob.

# * XXX *

## *At the Theatre Royal*

IN two or three days a message arrived asking them to attend at
the theatre on the coming evening, with the added request that
they would dress in their gayest clothes, to do justice to the places
taken. Accordingly, in the course of the afternoon they drove off,
Bob having clothed himself in a splendid suit, recently purchased
as an attempt to bring himself nearer to Anne's style when they
appeared in public together. As finished off by this dashing and
really fashionable attire, he was the perfection of a beau in the
dog-days;[150] pantaloons and boots of the newest make; yards and
yards of muslin wound round his neck, forming a sort of asylum
for the lower part of his face; two fancy waistcoats, and coat-
buttons like circular shaving glasses. The absurd extreme of female
fashion, which was to wear muslin dresses in January, was at this
time equalled by that of the men, who wore clothes enough in
August to melt them. Nobody would have guessed from Bob's
presentation now that he had ever been aloft on a dark night in the
Atlantic, or knew the hundred ingenuities that could be performed
with a rope's end and a marline-spike as well as his mother
tongue.

It was a day of days. Anne wore her celebrated celestial blue
pelisse, her Leghorn hat,[151] and her muslin dress with the waist
under the arms; the latter being decorated with excellent Honiton
lace bought of the woman who travelled from that place to
Overcombe and its neighbourhood with a basketful of her own
manufacture, and a cushion on which she worked by the wayside.
John met the lovers at the inn outside the town, and after stabling
the horse they entered the town together, the trumpet-major
informing them that the watering-place had never been so full
before, that the Court, the Prince of Wales, and everybody of

consequence was there, and that an attic could scarcely be got for money. The King had gone for a cruise in his yacht, and they would be in time to see him land.

Then drums and fifes were heard, and in a minute or two they saw Sergeant Stanner advancing along the street with a firm countenance, fiery poll, and rigid staring eyes, in front of his recruiting-party. The sergeant's sword was drawn, and at intervals of two or three inches along its shining blade were impaled fluttering one-pound notes, to express the lavish bounty that was offered. He gave a stern, half-suppressed nod of friendship to our people, and passed by. Next they came up to a waggon, bowered over with leaves and flowers, so that the men inside could hardly be seen.

'Come to see the King, hip-hip hurrah!' cried a voice within, and turning they saw through the leaves the nose and face of Cripplestraw. The waggon contained all Derriman's work-people.

'Is your master here?' said John.

'No, trumpet-major, sir. But young maister is coming to fetch us at nine o'clock, in case we should be too blind to drive home.'

'O! where is he now?'

'Never mind,' said Anne impatiently, at which the trumpet-major obediently moved on.

By the time they reached the pier it was six o'clock; the royal yacht was returning; a fact announced by the ships in the harbour firing a salute. The King came ashore with his hat in his hand, and returned the salutations of the well-dressed crowd in his old indiscriminate fashion. While this cheering and waving of hand-kerchiefs was going on Anne stood between the two brothers, who protectingly joined their hands behind her back, as if she were a delicate piece of statuary that a push might damage. Soon the King had passed, and receiving the military salutes of the piquet,[152] joined the Queen and princesses at Gloucester Lodge, the homely house of red brick in which he unostentatiously resided.

As there was yet some little time before the theatre would open, they strayed upon the velvet sands, and listened to the songs of the sailors, one of whom extemporized for the occasion:

Portland Road the King aboard, the King aboard!
Portland Road the King aboard,
We weighed and sailed from Portland Road!★

When they had looked on awhile at the combats at single-stick which were in progress hard by, and seen the sum of five guineas handed over to the modest gentleman who had broken most heads, they returned to Gloucester Lodge, whence the King and other members of his family now reappeared, and drove, at a slow trot, round to the theatre in carriages drawn by the Hanoverian white horses that were so well known in the town at this date.

When Anne and Bob entered the theatre they found that John had taken excellent places, and concluded that he had got them for nothing through the influence of the lady of his choice. As a matter of fact he had paid full prices for those two seats, like any other outsider, and even then had a difficulty in getting them, it being a King's night. When they were settled he himself retired to an obscure part of the pit, from which the stage was scarcely visible.

'We can see beautifully,' said Bob, in an aristocratic voice, as he took a delicate pinch of snuff, and drew out the magnificent pocket-handkerchief brought home from the East for such occasions. 'But I am afraid poor John can't see at all.'

'But we can see him,' replied Anne, 'and notice by his face which of them it is he is so charmed with. The light of that corner candle falls right upon his cheek.'

By this time the King had appeared in his place, which was overhung by a canopy of crimson satin fringed with gold. About twenty places were occupied by the royal family and suite; and beyond them was a crowd of powdered and glittering personages of fashion, completely filling the centre of the little building; though the King so frequently patronized the local stage during these years that the crush was not inconvenient.

The curtain rose and the play began. Tonight it was one of Colman's,[153] who at this time enjoyed great popularity, and Mr Bannister[154] supported the leading character. Anne, with her hand privately clasped in Bob's, and looking as if she did not know it,

★ *Vide* Preface.

partly watched the piece and partly the face of the impressionable John who had so soon transferred his affections elsewhere. She had not long to wait. When a certain one of the subordinate ladies of the comedy entered on the stage the trumpet-major in his corner not only looked conscious, but started and gazed with parted lips.

'This must be the one,' whispered Anne quickly. 'See, he is agitated!'

She turned to Bob, but at the same moment his hand convulsively closed upon hers as he, too, strangely fixed his eyes upon the newly-entered lady.

'What is it?'

Anne looked from one to the other without regarding the stage at all. Her answer came in the voice of the actress who now spoke for the first time. The accents were those of Miss Matilda Johnson.

One thought rushed into both their minds on the instant, and Bob was the first to utter it.

'What – is she the woman of his choice after all?'

'If so, it is a dreadful thing!' murmured Anne.

But, as may be imagined, the unfortunate John was as much surprised by this rencounter as the other two. Until this moment he had been in utter ignorance of the theatrical company and all that pertained to it. Moreover, much as he knew of Miss Johnson, he was not aware that she had ever been trained in her youth as an actress, and that after lapsing into straits and difficulties for a couple of years she had been so fortunate as to again procure an engagement here.

The trumpet-major, though not prominently seated, had been seen by Matilda already, who had observed still more plainly her old betrothed and Anne in the other part of the house. John was not concerned on his own account at being face to face with her, but at the extraordinary suspicion that this conjuncture must revive in the minds of his best beloved friends. After some moments of pained reflection he tapped his knee.

'Gad, I won't explain; it shall go as it is!' he said. 'Let them think her mine. Better that than the truth, after all.'

Had personal prominence in the scene been at this moment

proportioned to intentness of feeling, the whole audience, regal and otherwise, would have faded into an indistinct mist of background, leaving as the sole emergent and telling figures Bob and Anne at one point, the trumpet-major on the left hand, and Matilda at the opposite corner of the stage. But fortunately the deadlock of awkward suspense into which all four had fallen was terminated by an accident. A messenger entered the King's box with dispatches. There was an instant pause in the performance. The dispatch-box being opened the King read for a few moments with great interest, the eyes of the whole house, including those of Anne Garland, being anxiously fixed upon his face; for terrible events fell as unexpectedly as thunderbolts at this critical time of our history. The King at length beckoned to Lord —, who was immediately behind him, the play was again stopped, and the contents of the dispatch were publicly communicated to the audience.

Sir Robert Calder,[155] cruising off Finisterre, had come in sight of Villeneuve, and made the signal for action, which, though checked by the weather, had resulted in the capture of two Spanish line-of-battle ships, and the retreat of Villeneuve into Ferrol.

The news was received with truly national feeling, if noise might be taken as an index of patriotism. 'Rule Britannia' was called for and sung by the whole house. But the importance of the event was far from being recognized at this time; and Bob Loveday, as he sat there and heard it, had very little conception how it would bear upon his destiny.

This parenthetic excitement diverted for a few minutes the eyes of Bob and Anne from the trumpet-major; and when the play proceeded, and they looked back to his corner, he was gone.

'He's just slipped round to talk to her behind the scenes,' said Bob knowingly. 'Shall we go too, and tease him for a sly dog?'

'No, I would rather not.'

'Shall we go home, then?'

'Not unless her presence is too much for you?'

'O – not at all. We'll stay here. Ah, there she is again.'

They sat on, and listened to Matilda's speeches, which she delivered with such delightful coolness that they soon began to considerably interest one of the party.

'Well, what a nerve the young woman has!' he said at last in tones of admiration, and gazing at Miss Johnson with all his might. 'After all, Jack's taste is not so bad. She's really deuced clever.'

'Bob, I'll go home if you wish to,' said Anne quickly.

'O no – let us see how she fleets herself off that bit of a scrape she's playing at now. Well, what a hand she is at it, to be sure!'

Anne said no more, but waited on, supremely uncomfortable, and almost tearful. She began to feel that she did not like life particularly well; it was too complicated: she saw nothing of the scene, and only longed to get away, and to get Bob away with her. At last the curtain fell on the final act, and then began the farce of 'No Song no Supper'.[156] Matilda did not appear in this piece, and Anne again inquired if they should go home. This time Bob agreed, and taking her under his care with redoubled affection, to make up for the species of coma which had seized upon his heart for a time, he quietly accompanied her out of the house.

When they emerged upon the esplanade, the August moon was shining across the sea from the direction of St Aldhelm's Head. Bob unconsciously loitered, and turned towards the pier. Reaching the end of the promenade they surveyed the quivering waters in silence for some time, until a long dark line shot from behind the promontory of the Nothe,[157] and swept forward into the harbour.

'What boat is that?' said Anne.

'It seems to be some frigate lying in the roads,' said Bob carelessly, as he brought Anne round with a gentle pressure of his arm and bent his steps towards the homeward end of the town.

Meanwhile, Miss Johnson, having finished her duties for that evening, rapidly changed her dress, and went out likewise. The prominent position which Anne and Captain Bob had occupied side by side in the theatre, left her no alternative but to suppose that the situation was arranged by Bob as a species of defiance to herself; and her heart, such as it was, became proportionately embittered against him. In spite of the rise in her fortunes, Miss Johnson still remembered – and always would remember – her humiliating departure from Overcombe; and it had been to her even a more grievous thing that Bob had acquiesced in his brother's ruling than that John had determined it. At the time of setting out she was sustained by a firm faith that Bob would follow her, and nullify his brother's scheme; but though she waited Bob never came.

She passed along by the houses facing the sea, and scanned the shore, the footway, and the open road close to her, which, illuminated by the slanting moon to a great brightness, sparkled with minute facets of crystallized salts from the water sprinkled there during the day. The promenaders at the further edge appeared in dark profiles; and beyond them was the grey sea, parted into two masses by the tapering braid of moonlight across the waves.

Two forms crossed this line at a startling nearness to her; she marked them at once as Anne and Bob Loveday. They were walking slowly, and in the earnestness of their discourse were oblivious of the presence of any human beings save themselves. Matilda stood motionless till they had passed.

'How I love them!' she said, treading the initial step of her walk onwards with a vehemence that walking did not demand.

'So do I – especially one,' said a voice at her elbow; and a man wheeled round her, and looked in her face, which had been fully exposed to the moon.

'You – who are you?' she asked.

'Don't you remember, ma'am? We walked some way together towards Overcombe earlier in the summer.' Matilda looked more closely, and perceived that the speaker was Derriman, in plain clothes. He continued, 'You are one of the ladies of the theatre, I know. May I ask why you said in such a queer way that you loved that couple?'

'In a queer way?'

'Well, as if you hated them.'

'I don't mind your knowing that I have good reason to hate them. You do too, it seems?'

'That man,' said Festus savagely, 'came to me one night about that very woman; insulted me before I could put myself on my guard, and ran away before I could come up with him and avenge myself. The woman tricks me at every turn! I want to part 'em.'

'Then why don't you? There's a splendid opportunity. Do you see that soldier walking along? He's a marine; he looks into the gallery of the theatre every night: and he's in connection with the press-gang[158] that came ashore just now from the frigate lying in Portland Roads. They are often here for men.'

'Yes. Our boatmen dread 'em.'

'Well, we have only to tell him that Loveday is a seaman to be clear of him this very night.'

'Done!' said Festus. 'Take my arm and come this way.' They walked across to the footway. 'Fine night, sergeant.'

'It is, sir.'

'Looking for hands, I suppose?'

'It is not to be known, sir. We don't begin till half past ten.'

'It is a pity you don't begin now. I could show 'ee excellent game.'

'What, that little nest of fellows at the "Old Rooms" in Cove Row? I have just heard of 'em.'

'No – come here.' Festus, with Miss Johnson on his arm, led the sergeant quickly along the parade, and by the time they reached the Narrows the lovers, who walked but slowly, were visible in front of them. 'There's your man,' he said.

'That buck in pantaloons and half-boots – a-looking like a squire?'

'Twelve months ago he was mate of the brig *Pewit*; but his father has made money, and keeps him at home.'

'Faith, now you tell of it, there's a hint of sea legs about him. What's the young beau's name?'

'Don't tell!' whispered Matilda, impulsively clutching Festus's arm.

But Festus had already said, 'Robert Loveday, son of the miller at Overcombe. You may find several likely fellows in that neighbourhood.'

The marine said that he would bear it in mind, and they left him.

'I wish you had not told,' said Matilda tearfully. 'She's the worst!'

'Dash my eyes now; listen to that! Why, you chicken-hearted old stager, you was as well agreed as I. Come now; hasn't he used you badly?'

Matilda's acrimony returned. 'I was down on my luck, or he wouldn't have had the chance!' she said.

'Well, then, let things be.'

# XXXI

## *Midnight Visitors*

Miss Garland and Loveday walked leisurely to the inn and called for horse-and-gig. While the hostler was bringing it round, the landlord, who knew Bob and his family well, spoke to him quietly in the passage.

'Is this then because you want to throw dust in the eyes of the *Black Diamond* chaps?' (with an admiring glance at Bob's costume).

'The *Black Diamond*?' said Bob; and Anne turned pale.

'She hove in sight just after dark, and at nine o'clock a boat having more than a dozen marines on board, with cloaks on, rowed into harbour.'

Bob reflected. 'Then there'll be a press tonight; depend upon it,' he said.

'They won't know you, will they, Bob?' said Anne anxiously.

'They certainly won't know him for a seaman now,' remarked the landlord, laughing, and again surveying Bob up and down. 'But if I was you two, I should drive home-along straight and quiet; and be very busy in the mill all tomorrow, Mr Loveday.'

They drove away; and when they got onward out of the town, Anne strained her eyes wistfully towards Portland. Its dark contour, lying like a whale on the sea, was just perceptible in the gloom as the background to half-a-dozen ships' lights nearer at hand.

'They can't make you go, now you are a gentleman tradesman, can they?' she asked.

'If they want me they can have me, dearest. I have often said I ought to volunteer.'

'And not care about me at all?'

'It is just that that keeps me at home. I won't leave you if I can help it.'

'It cannot make such a vast difference to the country whether one man goes or stays! But if you want to go you had better, and not mind us at all!'

Bob put a period to her speech by a mark of affection to which history affords many parallels in every age. She said no more about the *Black Diamond*; but whenever they ascended a hill she turned her head to look at the lights in Portland Roads, and the grey expanse of intervening sea.

Though Captain Bob had stated that he did not wish to volunteer, and would not leave her if he could help it, the remark required some qualification. That Anne was charming and loving enough to chain him anywhere was true; but he had begun to find the mill-work terribly irksome at times. Often during the last month, when standing among the rumbling cogs in his new miller's suit, which ill became him, he had yawned, thought wistfully of the old pea-jacket,[159] and the waters of the deep blue sea. His dread of displeasing his father by showing anything of this change of sentiment was great; yet he might have braved it but for knowing that his marriage with Anne, which he hoped might take place the next year, was dependent entirely upon his adherence to the mill business. Even were his father indifferent, Mrs Loveday would never intrust her only daughter to the hands of a husband who would be away from home five-sixths of his time.

But though, apart from Anne, he was not averse to seafaring in itself, to be smuggled thither by the machinery of a press-gang was intolerable; and the process of seizing, stunning, pinioning, and carrying off unwilling hands was one which Bob as a man had always determined to hold out against to the utmost of his power. Hence, as they went towards home, he frequently listened for sounds behind him, but hearing none he assured his sweetheart that they were safe for that night at least. The mill was still going when they arrived, though old Mr Loveday was not to be seen; he had retired as soon as he heard the horse's hoofs in the lane, leaving Bob to watch the grinding till three o'clock; when the elder would rise, and Bob withdraw to bed – a frequent arrangement between them since Bob had taken the place of grinder.

Having reached the privacy of her own room, Anne threw open the window, for she had not the slightest intention of going to bed just yet. The tale of the *Black Diamond* had disturbed her by a slow, insidious process that was worse than sudden fright. Her window looked into the court before the house, now wrapped in the shadow of the trees and the hill; and she leaned upon its sill listening intently. She could have heard any strange sound distinctly enough in one direction; but in the other all low noises were absorbed in the patter of the mill, and the rush of water down the race.

However, what she heard came from the hitherto silent side, and was intelligible in a moment as being the footsteps of men. She tried to think they were some late stragglers from Budmouth. Alas! no; the tramp was too regular for that of villagers. She hastily turned, extinguished the candle, and listened again. As they were on the main road there was, after all, every probability that the party would pass the bridge which gave access to the mill court without turning in upon it, or even noticing that such an entrance existed. In this again she was disappointed: they crossed into the front without a pause. The pulsations of her heart became a turmoil now, for why should these men, if they were the press-gang, and strangers to the locality, have supposed that a sailor was to be found here, the younger of the two millers Loveday being never seen now in any garb which could suggest that he was other than a miller pure, like his father? One of the men spoke.

'I am not sure that we are in the right place,' he said.

'This is a mill, anyhow,' said another.

'There's lots about here.'

'Then come this way a moment with your light.'

Two of the group went towards the cart-house on the opposite side of the yard, and when they reached it a dark lantern was opened, the rays being directed upon the front of the miller's waggon.

' "Loveday and Son, Overcombe Mill",' continued the man, reading from the waggon. ' "Son", you see, is lately painted in. That's our man.'

He moved to turn off the light, but before he had done so it flashed over the forms of the speakers, and revealed a sergeant, a naval officer, and a file of marines.

Anne waited to see no more. When Bob stayed up to grind, as

he was doing tonight, he often sat in his room instead of remaining all the time in the mill; and this room was an isolated chamber over the bakehouse, which could not be reached without going downstairs and ascending the step-ladder that served for his staircase. Anne descended in the dark, clambered up the ladder, and saw that light strayed through the chink below the door. His window faced towards the garden, and hence the light could not as yet have been seen by the press-gang.

'Bob, dear Bob!' she said, through the keyhole. 'Put out your light, and run out of the back-door!'

'Why?' said Bob, leisurely knocking the ashes from the pipe he had been smoking.

'The press-gang!'

'They have come? By God! who can have blown upon me? All right, dearest. I'm game.'

Anne, scarcely knowing what she did, descended the ladder and ran to the back-door, hastily unbolting it to save Bob's time, and gently opening it in readiness for him. She had no sooner done this than she felt hands laid upon her shoulder from without, and a voice exclaiming, 'That's how we doos it – quite an obleeging young man!'

Though the hands held her rather roughly, Anne did not mind for herself, and turning she cried desperately, in tones intended to reach Bob's ears: 'They are at the back-door; try the front!'

But inexperienced Miss Garland little knew the shrewd habits of the gentlemen she had to deal with, who, well used to this sort of pastime, had already posted themselves at every outlet from the premises.

'Bring the lantern,' shouted the fellow who held her. 'Why – 'tis a girl! I half thought so – Here is a way in,' he continued to his comrades, hastening to the foot of the ladder which led to Bob's room.

'What d'ye want?' said Bob, quietly opening the door, and showing himself still radiant in the full dress that he had worn with such effect at the Theatre Royal, which he had been about to change for his mill suit when Anne gave the alarm.

'This gentleman can't be the right one,' observed a marine, rather impressed by Bob's appearance.

'Yes, yes; that's the man,' said the sergeant. 'Now take it quietly, my young cock-o'-wax. You look as if you meant to, and 'tis wise of ye.'

'Where are you going to take me?' said Bob.

'Only aboard the *Black Diamond*. If you choose to take the bounty and come voluntarily, you'll be allowed to go ashore whenever your ship's in port. If you don't, and we've got to pinion ye, you will not have your liberty at all. As you must come, willy-nilly, you'll do the first if you've any brains whatever.'

Bob's temper began to rise. 'Don't you talk so large, about your pinioning, my man. When I've settled –'

'Now or never, young blow-hard,' interrupted his informant.

'Come, what jabber is this going on?' said the lieutenant, stepping forward. 'Bring your man.'

One of the marines set foot on the ladder, but at the same moment a shoe from Bob's hand hit the lantern with well-aimed directness, knocking it clean out of the grasp of the man who held it. In spite of the darkness they began to scramble up the ladder. Bob thereupon shut the door, which, being but of slight construction, was as he knew only a momentary defence. But it gained him time enough to open the window, gather up his legs upon the sill, and spring across into the apple-tree growing without. He alighted without much hurt beyond a few scratches from the boughs, a shower of falling apples testifying to the force of his leap.

'Here he is!' shouted several below who had seen Bob's figure flying like a raven's across the sky.

There was stillness for a moment in the tree. Then the fugitive made haste to climb out upon a low-hanging branch towards the garden, at which the men beneath all rushed in that direction to catch him as he dropped, saying, 'You may as well come down, old boy. 'Twas a spry jump, and we give ye credit for 't.'

The latter movement of Loveday had been a mere feint. Partly hidden by the leaves he glided back to the other part of the tree, from whence it was easy to jump upon a thatch-covered outhouse. This intention they did not appear to suspect, which gave him the opportunity of sliding down the slope and entering the backdoor of the mill.

'He's here, he's here!' the men exclaimed, running back from the tree.

By this time they had obtained another light, and pursued him closely along the back quarters of the mill. Bob had entered the lower room, seized hold of the chain by which the flour-sacks were hoisted from story to story by connection with the mill-wheel, and pulled the rope that hung alongside for the purpose of throwing it into gear. The foremost pursuers arrived just in time to see Captain Bob's legs and shoe-buckles vanishing through the trap-door in the joists overhead, his person having been whirled up by the machinery like any bag of flour, and the trap falling to behind him.

'He's gone up by the hoist!' said the sergeant, running up the ladder in the corner to the next floor, and elevating the light just in time to see Bob's suspended figure ascending in the same way through the same sort of trap into the second floor. The second trap also fell together behind him, and he was lost to view as before.

It was more difficult to follow now; there was only a flimsy little ladder, and the men ascended cautiously. When they stepped out upon the loft it was empty.

'He must ha' let go here,' said one of the marines, who knew more about mills than the others. 'If he had held fast a moment longer, he would have been dashed against that beam.'

They looked up. The hook by which Bob had held on had ascended to the roof, and was winding round the cylinder. Nothing was visible elsewhere but boarded divisions like the stalls of a stable on each side of the stage they stood upon, these compartments being more or less heaped up with wheat and barley in the grain.

'Perhaps he's buried himself in the corn.'

The whole crew jumped into the corn-bins, and stirred about their yellow contents; but neither arm, leg, nor coat-tail was uncovered. They removed sacks, peeped among the rafters of the roof, but to no purpose. The lieutenant began to fume at the loss of time.

'What cursed fools to let the man go! Why, look here, what's this?' He had opened the door by which sacks were taken in from waggons without, and dangling from the cat-head[160] projecting above it was the rope used in lifting them. 'There's the way he went down,' the officer continued. 'The man's gone.'

Amidst mumblings and curses the gang descended the pair of ladders and came into the open air; but Captain Bob was nowhere to be seen. When they reached the front door of the house the miller was standing on the threshold, half dressed.

'Your son is a clever fellow, miller,' said the lieutenant; 'but it would have been much better for him if he had come quiet.'

'That's a matter of opinion,' said Loveday.

'I have no doubt that he's in the house.'

'He may be; and he may not.'

'Do you know where he is?'

'I do not; and if I did I shouldn't tell.'

'Naturally.'

'I heard steps beating up the road, sir,' said the sergeant.

They turned from the door, and leaving four of the marines to keep watch round the house, the remainder of the party marched into the lane as far as where the other road branched off. While they were pausing to decide which course to take, one of the soldiers held up the light. A black object was discernible upon the ground before them, and they found it to be a hat – the hat of Bob Loveday.

'We are on the track,' cried the sergeant, deciding for this direction.

They tore on rapidly, and the footsteps previously heard became audible again, increasing in clearness, which told that they gained upon the fugitive, who in another five minutes stopped and turned. The rays of the candle fell upon Anne.

'What do you want?' she said, showing her frightened face.

They made no reply, but wheeled round and left her. She sank down on the bank to rest, having done all she could. It was she who had taken down Bob's hat from a nail, and dropped it at the turning with the view of misleading them till he should have got clear off.

# * XXXII *

## *Deliverance*

BUT Anne Garland was too anxious to remain long away from the centre of operations. When she got back she found that the press-gang were standing in the court discussing their next move.

'Waste no more time here,' the lieutenant said. 'Two more villages to visit tonight, and the nearest three miles off. There's nobody else in this place, and we can't come back again.'

When they were moving away, one of the private marines, who had kept his eye on Anne, and noticed her distress, contrived to say in a whisper as he passed her, 'We are coming back again as soon as it begins to get light; that's only said to deceive 'ee. Keep your young man out of the way.'

They went as they had come; and the little household then met together, Mrs Loveday having by this time dressed herself and come down. A long and anxious discussion followed.

'Somebody must have told upon the chap,' Loveday remarked. 'How should they have found him out else, now he's been home from sea this twelvemonth?'

Anne then mentioned what the friendly marine had told her; and fearing lest Bob was in the house, and would be discovered there when daylight came, they searched and called for him everywhere.

'What clothes has he got on?' said the miller.

'His lovely new suit,' said his wife. 'I warrant it is quite spoiled!'

'He's got no hat,' said Anne.

'Well,' said Loveday, 'you two go and lie down now and I'll bide up; and as soon as he comes in, which he'll do most likely in the course of the night, I'll let him know that they are coming again.'

Anne and Mrs Loveday went to their bedrooms, and the miller entered the mill as if he were simply staying up to grind. But he continually left the flour-shoot to go outside and walk round; each time he could see no living being near the spot. Anne meanwhile had lain down dressed upon her bed, the window still open, her ears intent upon the sound of footsteps, and dreading the reappearance of daylight and the gang's return. Three or four times during the night she descended to the mill to inquire of her stepfather if Bob had shown himself; but the answer was always in the negative.

At length the curtains of her bed began to reveal their pattern, the brass handles of the drawers gleamed forth, and day dawned. While the light was yet no more than a suffusion of pallor, she arose, put on her hat, and determined to explore the surrounding premises before the men arrived. Emerging into the raw loneliness of the daybreak, she went upon the bridge and looked up and down the road. It was as she had left it, empty, and the solitude was rendered yet more insistent by the silence of the mill-wheel, which was now stopped, the miller having given up expecting Bob and retired to bed about three o'clock. The footprints of the marines still remained in the dust on the bridge, all the heel-marks towards the house, showing that the party had not as yet returned.

While she lingered she heard a slight noise in the other direction, and, turning, saw a woman approaching. The woman came up quickly, and, to her amazement, Anne recognized Matilda. Her walk was convulsive, face pale, almost haggard, and the cold light of the morning invested it with all the ghostliness of death. She had plainly walked all the way from Budmouth, for her shoes were covered with dust.

'Has the press-gang been here?' she gasped. 'If not they are coming!'

'They have been.'

'And got him – I am too late!'

'No; they are coming back again. Why did you –'

'I came to try to save him. Can we save him? Where is he?'

Anne looked the woman in the face, and it was impossible to doubt that she was in earnest.

'I don't know,' she answered. 'I am trying to find him before they come.'

'Will you not let me help you?' cried the repentant Matilda.

Without either objecting or assenting Anne turned and led the way to the back part of the homestead.

Matilda, too, had suffered that night. From the moment of parting with Festus Derriman a sentiment of revulsion from the act to which she had been a party set in and increased, till at length it reached an intensity of remorse which she could not passively bear. She had risen before day and hastened thitherward to know the worst, and if possible hinder consequences that she had been the first to set in train.

After going hither and thither in the adjoining field, Anne entered the garden. The walks were bathed in grey dew, and as she passed observantly along them it appeared as if they had been brushed by some foot at a much earlier hour. At the end of the garden, bushes of broom, laurel, and yew formed a constantly encroaching shrubbery, that had come there almost by chance and was never trimmed. Behind these bushes was a garden-seat, and upon it lay Bob sound asleep.

The ends of his hair were clotted with damp, and there was a foggy film upon the mirror-like buttons of his coat, and upon the buckles of his shoes. His bunch of new gold seals was dimmed by the same insidious dampness; his shirt-frill and muslin neckcloth were limp as seaweed. It was plain that he had been there a long time. Anne shook him, but he did not awake, his breathing being slow and stertorous.

'Bob, wake; 'tis your own Anne!' she said, with innocent earnestness; and then, fearfully turning her head, she saw that Matilda was close behind her.

'You needn't mind me,' said Matilda bitterly. 'I am on your side now. Shake him again.'

Anne shook him again, but he slept on. Then she noticed that his forehead bore the mark of a heavy wound.

'I fancy I hear something!' said her companion, starting forward and endeavouring to wake Bob herself. 'He is stunned, or drugged!' she said; 'there is no rousing him.'

Anne raised her head and listened. From the direction of the eastern road came the sound of a steady tramp. 'They are coming back!' she said, clasping her hands. 'They will take him, ill as he is! He won't open his eyes – no, it is no use! O, what shall we do?'

Matilda did not reply, but running to the end of the seat on which Bob lay, tried its weight in her arms.

'It is not too heavy,' she said. 'You take that end, and I'll take this. We'll carry him away to some place of hiding.'

Anne instantly seized the other end, and they proceeded with their burden at a slow pace to the lower garden-gate, which they reached as the tread of the press-gang resounded over the bridge that gave access to the mill court, now hidden from view by the hedge and the trees of the garden.

'We will go down inside this field,' said Anne faintly.

'No!' said the other; 'they will see our foot-tracks in the dew. We must go into the road.'

'It is the very road they will come down when they leave the mill.'

'It cannot be helped; it is neck or nothing with us now.'

So they emerged upon the road, and staggered along without speaking, occasionally resting for a moment to ease their arms; then shaking him to arouse him, and finding it useless, seizing the seat again. When they had gone about two hundred yards Matilda betrayed signs of exhaustion, and she asked, 'Is there no shelter near?'

'When we get to that little field of corn,' said Anne.

'It is so very far. Surely there is some place near?'

She pointed to a few scrubby bushes overhanging a little stream, which passed under the road near this point.

'They are not thick enough,' said Anne.

'Let us take him under the bridge,' said Matilda. 'I can go no further.'

Entering the opening by which cattle descended to drink, they waded into the weedy water, which here rose a few inches above their ankles. To ascend the stream, stoop under the arch, and reach the centre of the roadway, was the work of a few minutes.

'If they look under the arch we are lost,' murmured Anne.

'There is no parapet to the bridge, and they may pass over without heeding.'

They waited, their heads almost in contact with the reeking arch, and their feet encircled by the stream, which was at its summer lowness now. For some minutes they could hear nothing but the babble of the water over their ankles, and round the legs of the seat on which Bob slumbered, the sounds being reflected in a musical tinkle from the hollow sides of the arch. Anne's anxiety now was lest he should not continue sleeping till the search was over, but start up with his habitual imprudence, and scorning such means of safety, rush out into their arms.

A quarter of an hour dragged by, and then indications reached their ears that the re-examination of the mill had begun and ended. The well-known tramp drew nearer and reverberated through the ground over their heads, where its volume signified to the listeners that the party had been largely augmented by pressed men since the night preceding. The gang passed the arch, and the noise regularly diminished, as if no man among them had thought of looking aside for a moment.

Matilda broke the silence. 'I wonder if they have left a watch behind?' she said doubtfully.

'I will go and see,' said Anne. 'Wait till I return.'

'No; I can do no more. When you come back I shall be gone. I ask one thing of you. If all goes well with you and him, and he marries you – don't be alarmed; my plans lie elsewhere – when you are his wife tell him who helped to carry him away. But don't mention my name to the rest of your family, either now or at any time.'

Anne regarded the speaker for a moment, and promised; after which she waded out from the archway.

Matilda stood looking at Bob for a moment, as if preparing to go, till moved by some impulse she bent and lightly kissed him once.

'How can you!' cried Anne reproachfully. When leaving the mouth of the arch she had bent back and seen the act.

Matilda flushed. 'You jealous baby!' she said scornfully.

Anne hesitated for a moment, then went out from the water, and hastened towards the mill.

She entered by the garden, and, seeing no one, advanced and

peeped in at the window. Her mother and Mr Loveday were sitting within as usual.

'Are they all gone?' said Anne softly.

'Yes. They did not trouble us much, beyond going into every room, and searching about the garden, where they saw steps. They have been lucky tonight; they have caught fifteen or twenty men at places further on; so the loss of Bob was no hurt to their feelings. I wonder where in the world the poor fellow is!'

'I will show you,' said Anne. And explaining in a few words what had happened, she was promptly followed by David and Loveday along the road. She lifted her dress and entered the arch with some anxiety on account of Matilda; but the actress was gone, and Bob lay on the seat as she had left him.

Bob was brought out, and water thrown upon his face; but though he moved he did not rouse himself until some time after he had been borne into the house. Here he opened his eyes, and saw them standing round, and gathered a little consciousness.

'You are all right, my boy!' said his father. 'What hev happened to ye? Where did ye get that terrible blow?'

'Ah – I can mind now,' murmured Bob, with a stupefied gaze around. 'I fell in slipping down the topsail halyard – the rope, that is, was too short – and I fell upon my head. And then I went away. When I came back I thought I wouldn't disturb ye: so I lay down out there, to sleep out the watch; but the pain in my head was so great that I couldn't get to sleep; so I picked some of the poppy-heads in the border, which I once heard was a good thing for sending folks to sleep when they are in pain. So I munched up all I could find, and dropped off quite nicely.'

'I wondered who had picked 'em!' said Molly. 'I noticed they were gone.'

'Why, you might never have woke again!' said Mrs Loveday, holding up her hands. 'How is your head now?'

'I hardly know,' replied the young man, putting his hand to his forehead and beginning to doze again. 'Where be those fellows that boarded us? With this – smooth water and – fine breeze we ought to get away from 'em. Haul in – the larboard braces, and – bring her to the wind.'

'You are at home, dear Bob,' said Anne, bending over him, 'and the men are gone.'

'Come along upstairs: th' beest hardly awake now,' said his father; and Bob was assisted to bed.

# * XXXIII *

## A Discovery Turns the Scale

In four-and-twenty hours Bob had recovered. But though physically himself again, he was not at all sure of his position as a patriot. He had that practical knowledge of seamanship of which the country stood much in need, and it was humiliating to find that impressment seemed to be necessary to teach him to use it for her advantage. Many neighbouring young men, less fortunate than himself, had been pressed and taken; and their absence seemed a reproach to him. He went away by himself into the mill-roof, and, surrounded by the corn-heaps, gave vent to self-condemnation.

'Certainly, I am no man to lie here so long for the pleasure of sighting that young girl forty times a day, and letting her sight me – bless her eyes! – till I must needs want a press-gang to teach me what I've forgot. And is it then all over with me as a British sailor? We'll see.'

When he was thrown under the influence of Anne's eyes again, which were more tantalizingly beautiful than ever just now (so it seemed to him), his intention of offering his services to the Government would wax weaker, and he would put off his final decision till the next day. Anne saw these fluctuations of his mind between love and patriotism, and being terrified by what she had heard of sea-fights, used the utmost art of which she was capable to seduce him from his forming purpose. She came to him in the mill, wearing the very prettiest of her morning jackets – the one that only just passed the waist, and was laced so tastefully round the collar and bosom. Then she would appear in her new hat, with a bouquet of primroses on one side; and on the following Sunday she walked before him in lemon-coloured boots, so that her feet looked like a pair of yellow-hammers flitting under her dress.

305

But dress was the least of the means she adopted for chaining him down. She talked more tenderly than ever; asked him to begin small undertakings in the garden on her account; she sang about the house, that the place might seem cheerful when he came in. This singing for a purpose required great effort on her part, leaving her afterwards very sad. When Bob asked her what was the matter, she would say, 'Nothing; only I am thinking how you will grieve your father, and cross his purposes, if you carry out your unkind notion of going to sea, and forsaking your place in the mill.'

'Yes,' Bob would say uneasily. 'It will trouble him, I know.'

Being also quite aware how it would trouble her, he would again postpone, and thus another week passed away.

All this time John had not come once to the mill. It appeared as if Miss Johnson absorbed all his time and thoughts. Bob was often seen chuckling over the circumstance. 'A sly rascal!' he said. 'Pretending on the day she came to be married that she was not good enough for me, when it was only that he wanted her for himself. How he could have persuaded her to go away is beyond me to say!'

Anne could not contest this belief of her lover's, and remained silent; but there had more than once occurred to her mind a doubt of its probability. Yet she had only abandoned her opinion that John had schemed for Matilda, to embrace the opposite error; that, finding he had wronged the young lady, he had pitied and grown to love her.

'And yet Jack, when he was a boy, was the simplest fellow alive,' resumed Bob. 'By George, though, I should have been hot against him for such a trick, if in losing her I hadn't found a better! But she'll never come down to him in the world: she has high notions now. I am afraid he's doomed to sigh in vain!'

Though Bob regretted this possibility, the feeling was not reciprocated by Anne. It was true that she knew nothing of Matilda's temporary treachery, and that she disbelieved the story of her lack of virtue; but she did not like the woman. 'Perhaps it will not matter if he is doomed to sigh in vain,' she said. 'But I owe him no ill-will. I have profited by his doings, incomprehensible as they are.' And she bent her fair eyes on Bob and smiled.

Bob looked dubious. 'He thinks he has affronted me, now I have seen through him, and that I shall be against meeting him. But, of course, I am not so touchy. I can stand a practical joke, as can any man who has been afloat. I'll call and see him, and tell him so.'

Before he started, Bob bethought him of something which would still further prove to the misapprehending John that he was entirely forgiven. He went to his room, and took from his chest a packet containing a lock of Miss Johnson's hair, which she had given him during their brief acquaintance, and which till now he had quite forgotten. When, at starting, he wished Anne good-bye, it was accompanied by such a beaming face, that she knew he was full of an idea, and asked what it might be that pleased him so.

'Why, this,' he said, smacking his breast-pocket. 'A lock of hair that Matilda gave me.'

Anne sank back with parted lips.

'I am going to give it to Jack – he'll jump for joy to get it! And it will show him how willing I am to give her up to him, fine piece as she is.'

'Will you see her today, Bob?' Anne asked with an uncertain smile.

'O no – unless it is by accident.'

On reaching the outskirts of the town he went straight to the barracks, and was lucky enough to find John in his room, at the left-hand corner of the quadrangle. John was glad to see him; but to Bob's surprise he showed no immediate contrition, and thus afforded no room for the brotherly speech of forgiveness which Bob had been going to deliver. As the trumpet-major did not open the subject, Bob felt it desirable to begin himself.

'I have brought ye something that you will value, Jack,' he said, as they sat at the window, overlooking the large square barrack-yard. 'I have got no further use for it, and you should have had it before if it had entered my head.'

'Thank you, Bob; what is it?' said John, looking absently at an awkward squad of young men who were drilling in the enclosure.

' 'Tis a young woman's lock of hair.'

'Ah!' said John, quite recovering from his abstraction, and

slightly flushing. Could Bob and Anne have quarrelled? Bob drew the paper from his pocket, and opened it.

'Black!' said John.

'Yes – black enough.'

'Whose?'

'Why, Matilda's.'

'O, Matilda's!'

'Whose did you think then?'

Instead of replying, the trumpet-major's face became as red as sunset, and he turned to the window to hide his confusion.

Bob was silent, and then he, too, looked into the court. At length he arose, walked to his brother, and laid his hand upon his shoulder. 'Jack,' he said, in an altered voice, 'you are a good fellow. Now I see it all.'

'O no – that's nothing,' said John hastily.

'You've been pretending that you care for this woman that I mightn't blame myself for heaving you out from the other – which is what I've done without knowing it.'

'What does it matter?'

'But it does matter! I've been making you unhappy all these weeks and weeks through my thoughtlessness. They seemed to think at home, you know, John, that you had grown not to care for her; or I wouldn't have done it for all the world!'

'You stick to her, Bob, and never mind me. She belongs to you. She loves you. I have no claim upon her, and she thinks nothing about me.'

'She likes you, John, thoroughly well; so does everybody; and if I hadn't come home, putting my foot in it – That coming home of mine has been a regular blight upon the family! I ought never to have stayed. The sea is my home, and why couldn't I bide there?'

The trumpet-major drew Bob's discourse off the subject as soon as he could, and Bob, after some unconsidered replies and remarks, seemed willing to avoid it for the present. He did not ask John to accompany him home, as he had intended; and on leaving the barracks turned southward and entered the town to wander about till he could decide what to do.

It was the 3rd of September, but the King's watering-place still retained its summer aspect. The royal bathing-machine had been drawn out just as Bob reached Gloucester Buildings, and he waited a minute, in the lack of other distraction, to look on. Immediately that the King's machine had entered the water a group of florid men with fiddles, violoncellos, a trombone, and a drum, came forward, packed themselves into another machine that was in waiting, and were drawn out into the waves in the King's rear. All that was to be heard for a few minutes were the slow pulsations of the sea; and then a defeaning noise burst from the interior of the second machine with power enough to split the boards asunder; it was the condensed mass of musicians inside, striking up the strains of 'God save the King', as his Majesty's head rose from the water. Bob took off his hat and waited till the end of the performance, which, intended as a pleasant surprise to George III by the loyal burghers, was possibly in the watery circumstances tolerated rather than desired by that dripping monarch.*

Loveday then passed on to the harbour, where he remained awhile, looking at the busy scene of loading and unloading craft and swabbing the decks of yachts; at the boats and barges rubbing against the quay wall, and at the houses of the merchants, some ancient structures of solid stone, others green-shuttered with heavy wooden bow-windows which appeared as if about to drop into the harbour by their own weight. All these things he gazed upon, and thought of one thing – that he had caused great misery to his brother John.

The town clock struck, and Bob retraced his steps till he again approached the Esplanade and Gloucester Lodge, where the morning sun blazed in upon the house fronts, and not a spot of shade seemed to be attainable. A huzzaing attracted his attention, and he observed that a number of people had gathered before the King's residence, where a brown curricle[161] had stopped, out of which stepped a hale man in the prime of life, wearing a blue uniform, gilt epaulettes, cocked hat, and sword, who crossed the pavement and went in. Bob went up and joined the group. 'What's going on?' he said.

'Captain Hardy,'[162] replied a bystander.

'What of him?'

* *Vide* Preface.

'Just gone in – waiting to see the King.'

'But the captain is in the West Indies?'

'No. The fleet is come home; they can't find the French anywhere.'

'Will they go and look for them again?' asked Bob.

'O yes. Nelson is determined to find 'em. As soon as he's refitted he'll put to sea again. Ah, here's the King coming in.'

Bob was so interested in what he had just heard that he scarcely noticed the arrival of the King, and a body of attendant gentlemen. He went on thinking of his new knowledge; Captain Hardy was come. He was doubtless staying with his family at their small manor-house at Pos'ham, a few miles from Overcombe, where he usually spent the intervals between his different cruises.

Loveday returned to the mill without further delay; and shortly explaining that John was very well, and would come soon, went on to talk of the arrival of Nelson's captain.

'And is he come at last?' said the miller, throwing his thoughts years backward. 'Well can I mind when he first left home to go on board the *Helena* as midshipman!'

'That's not much to remember. I can remember it too,' said Mrs Loveday.

' 'Tis more than twenty years ago anyhow. And more than that, I can mind when he was born; I was a lad, serving my 'prenticeship at the time. He has been in this house often and often when 'a was young. When he came home after his first voyage he stayed about here a long time, and used to look in at the mill whenever he went past. "What will you be next, sir?" said mother to him one day as he stood with his back to the door-post. "A lieutenant, Dame Loveday," says he. "And what next?" says she. "A commander." "And next?" "Next, post-captain." "And then?" "Then adm'l." "And then?" "Then it will be almost time to die." I'd warrant that he'd mind it to this very day if you were to ask him.'

Bob heard all this with a manner of preoccupation, and soon retired to the mill. Thence he went to his room by the back passage, and taking his old seafaring garments from a dark closet in the wall conveyed them to the loft at the top of the mill, where he occupied the remaining spare moments of the day in brushing the mildew from their folds, and hanging each article by the window to get aired. In the evening he returned to the loft, and dressing himself in the old salt suit, went out of the house unobserved by anybody, and ascended the road towards the village of Captain Hardy's infancy, and his present temporary

The shadeless downs were now brown with the droughts of the passing summer, and few living things met his view, the natural rotundity of the elevation being only occasionally disturbed by the presence of a barrow, a thorn-bush, or a piece of dry wall which remained from some attempted enclosure. By the time that he reached the village it was dark, and the larger stars had begun to shine when he walked up to the door of the old-fashioned house which was the family residence of this branch of the South-Wessex Hardys.

'Will the captain allow me to wait on him tonight?' inquired Loveday, explaining who and what he was.

The servant went away for a few minutes, and then told Bob that he might see the captain in the morning.

'If that's the case, I'll come again,' replied Bob, quite cheerful that failure was not absolute.

He had left the door but a few steps when he was called back and asked if he had walked all the way from Overcombe Mill on purpose.

Loveday replied modestly that he had done so.

'Then will you come in?' He followed the speaker into a small study or office, and in a minute or two Captain Hardy entered.

The captain at this time was a bachelor of thirty-five, rather stout in build, with light eyes, bushy eyebrows, a square broad face, plenty of chin, and a mouth whose corners played between humour and grimness. He surveyed Loveday from top to toe.

'Robert Loveday, sir, son of the miller at Overcombe,' said Bob, making a low bow.

'Ah! I remember your father, Loveday,' the gallant seaman replied. 'Well, what do you want to say to me?' Seeing that Bob found it rather difficult to begin, he leant leisurely against the mantelpiece, and went on, 'Is your father well and hearty? I have not seen him for many, many years.'

'Quite well, thank 'ee.'

'You used to have a brother in the army, I think? What was his name – John? A very fine fellow, if I recollect.'

'Yes, cap'n; he's there still.'

'And you are in the merchant-service?'

'Late first mate of the brig *Pewit*.'

'How is it you're not on board a man-of-war?'

'Ay, sir, that's the thing I've come about,' said Bob, recovering confidence. 'I should have been, but 'tis womankind has hampered me. I've waited and waited on at home because of a young woman – lady, I might have said, for she's sprung from a higher class of society than I. Her father was a landscape painter – maybe you've heard of him, sir? The name is Garland.'

'He painted that view of our village here,' said Captain Hardy, looking towards a dark little picture in the corner of the room.

Bob looked, and went on, as if to the picture, 'Well, sir, I have found that – However, the press-gang came a week or two ago, and didn't get hold of me. I didn't care to go aboard as a pressed man.'

'There has been a severe impressment. It is of course a disagreeable necessity, but it can't be helped.'

'Since then, sir, something has happened that makes me wish they had found me, and I have come tonight to ask if I could enter on board your ship the *Victory*.'

The captain shook his head severely, and presently observed: 'I am glad to find that you think of entering the service, Loveday; smart men are badly wanted. But it will not be in your power to choose your ship.'

'Well, well, sir; then I must take my chance elsewhere,' said Bob, his face indicating the disappointment he would not fully express. ' 'Twas only that I felt I would much rather serve under you than anybody else, my father and all of us being known to ye, Captain Hardy, and our families belonging to the same parts.'

Captain Hardy took Bob's altitude[163] more carefully. 'Are you a good practical seaman?' he asked musingly.

'Ay, sir; I believe I am.'

'Active? Fond of skylarking?'

'Well, I don't know about the last. I think I can say I am active enough. I could walk the yard-arm, if required, cross from mast to mast by the stays, and do what most fellows do who call themselves spry.'

The captain then put some questions about the details of navigation, which Loveday, having luckily been used to square rigs, answered satisfactorily. 'As to reefing topsails,' he added, 'if I don't do it like a flash of lightning, I can do it so that they will stand blowing weather. The *Pewit* was not a dull vessel, and when we were convoyed home from Lisbon, she could keep well in sight of the frigate scudding at a distance, by putting on full sail. We had enough hands aboard to reef topsails man-o'-war fashion, which is a rare thing in these days, sir, now that able seamen are so scarce on trading craft. And I hear that men from square-rigged vessels[164] are liked much the best in the navy, as being more ready for use? So that I shouldn't be altogether so raw,' said Bob earnestly, 'if I could enter on your ship, sir. Still, if I can't, I can't.'

'I might ask for you, Loveday,' said the captain thoughtfully, 'and so get you there that way. In short, I think I may say I will ask for you. So consider it settled.'

'My thanks to you, sir,' said Loveday.

'You are aware that the *Victory* is a smart ship, and that cleanliness and order are, of necessity, more strictly insisted upon there than in some others?'

'Sir, I quite see it.'

'Well, I hope you will do your duty as well on a line-of-battle ship as you did when mate of the brig, for it is a duty that may be serious.'

Bob replied that it should be his one endeavour; and receiving a few instructions for getting on board the guard-ship, and being conveyed to Portsmouth, he turned to go away.

'You'll have a stiff walk before you fetch Overcombe Mill this dark night, Loveday,' concluded the captain, peering out of the window. 'I'll send you in a glass of grog to help 'ee on your way.'

The captain then left Bob to himself, and when he had drunk the grog that was brought in he started homeward, with a heart not exactly light, but large with a patriotic cheerfulness, which had not diminished when, after walking so fast in his excitement as to be beaded with perspiration, he entered his father's door.

They were all sitting up for him, and at his approach anxiously raised their sleepy eyes, for it was nearly eleven o'clock.

'There; I knew he'd not be much longer!' cried Anne, jumping up and laughing, in her relief. 'They have been thinking you were very strange and silent today, Bob; you were not, were you?'

'What's the matter, Bob?' said the miller; for Bob's countenance was sublimed by his recent interview, like that of a priest just come from the *penetralia* of the temple.

'He's in his mate's clothes, just as when he came home!' observed Mrs Loveday.

They all saw now that he had something to tell. 'I am going away,' he said when he had sat down. 'I am going to enter on board a man-of-war, and perhaps it will be the *Victory*.'

'Going?' said Anne faintly.

'Now, don't you mind it, there's a dear,' he went on solemnly, taking her hand in his own. 'And you, father, don't you begin to take it to heart' (the miller was looking grave). 'The press-gang has been here, and though I showed them that I was a free man, I am going to show everybody that I can do my duty.'

Neither of the other three answered, Anne and the miller having their eyes bent upon the ground, and the former trying to repress her tears.

'Now don't you grieve, either of you,' he continued; 'nor vex yourselves that this has happened. Please not to be angry with me, father, for deserting you and the mill, where you want me, for I *must go*. For these three years we and the rest of the country have been in fear of the enemy; trade has been hindered; poor folk made hungry; and many rich folk made poor. There must be a deliverance, and it must be done by sea. I have seen Captain Hardy, and I shall serve under him if so be I can.'

'Captain Hardy?'

'Yes. I have been to his house at Pos'ham, where he's staying with his sisters; walked there and back, and I wouldn't have missed it for fifty guineas. I hardly thought he would see me; but he did see me. And he hasn't forgot you.'

Bob then opened his tale in order, relating graphically the conversation to which he had been a party, and they listened with breathless attention.

'Well, if you must go, you must,' said the miller with emotion; 'but I think it somewhat hard that, of my two sons, neither one of 'em can be got to stay and help me in my business as I get old.'

'Don't trouble and vex about it,' said Mrs Loveday soothingly. 'They are both instruments in the hands of Providence, chosen to chastise that Corsican ogre, and do what they can for the country in these trying years.'

'That's just the shape of it, Mrs Loveday,' said Bob.

'And he'll come back soon,' she continued, turning to Anne. 'And then he'll tell us all he has seen, and the glory that he's won, and how he has helped to sweep that scourge Buonaparty off the earth.'

'When be you going, Bob?' his father inquired.

'Tomorrow, if I can. I shall call at the barracks and tell John as I go by. When I get to Portsmouth —'

A burst of sobs in quick succession interrupted his words; they came from Anne, who till that moment had been sitting as before with her hand in that of Bob, and apparently quite calm. Mrs Loveday jumped up, but before she could say anything to soothe the agitated girl she had calmed herself with the same singular suddenness that had marked her giving way. 'I don't mind Bob's going,' she said. 'I think he ought to go. Don't suppose, Bob, that I want you to stay!'

After this she left the apartment, and went into the little side room where she and her mother usually worked. In a few moments Bob followed her. When he came back he was in a very sad and emotional mood. Anybody could see that there had been a parting of profound anguish to both.

'She is not coming back tonight,' he said.

'You will see her tomorrow before you go?' said her mother.

'I may or I may not,' he replied. 'Father and Mrs Loveday, do you go to bed now. I have got to look over my things and get ready; and it will take me some little time. If you should hear noises you will know it is only myself moving about.'

When Bob was left alone he suddenly became brisk, and set himself to overhaul his clothes and other possessions in a business-like manner. By the time that his chest was packed, such things as he meant to leave at home folded into cupboards, and what was useless destroyed, it was past two o'clock. Then he went to bed, so softly that only the creak of one weak stair revealed his passage upward. At the moment that he passed Anne's chamber-door her mother was bending over her as she lay in bed, and saying to her, 'Won't you see him in the morning?'

'No, no,' said Anne. 'I would rather not see him! I have said that I may. But I shall not. I cannot see him again!'

When the family got up next day Bob had vanished. It was his way to disappear like this, to avoid affecting scenes at parting. By the time that they had sat down to a gloomy breakfast, Bob was in the boat of a Budmouth waterman, who pulled him alongside the guardship in the roads, where he laid hold of the man-rope, mounted, and disappeared from external view. In the course of the day the ship moved off, set her royals,[165] and made sail for Portsmouth, with five hundred new hands for the service on board, consisting partly of pressed men and partly of volunteers, among the latter being Robert Loveday.

# * XXXIV *

## *A Speck on the Sea*

IN parting from John, who accompanied him to the quay, Bob had said: 'Now, Jack, these be my last words to you: I give her up. I go away on purpose, and I shall be away a long time. If in that time she should list over towards ye ever so little, mind you take her. You have more right to her than I. You chose her when my mind was elsewhere, and you best deserve her; for I have never known you forget one woman, while I've forgot a dozen. Take her then, if she will come, and God bless both of ye.'

Another person besides John saw Bob go. That was Derriman, who was standing by a bollard[166] a little further up the quay. He did not repress his satisfaction at the sight. John looked towards him with an open gaze of contempt; for the cuffs administered to the yeoman at the inn had not, so far as the trumpet-major was aware, produced any desire to avenge that insult, John being, of course, quite ignorant that Festus had erroneously retaliated upon Bob, in his peculiar though scarcely soldierly way. Finding that he did not even now approach him, John went on his way, and thought over his intention of preserving intact the love between Anne and his brother.

He was surprised when he next went to the mill to find how glad they all were to see him. From the moment of Bob's return to the bosom of the deep Anne had had no existence on land; people might have looked at her human body and said she had flitted thence. The sea and all that belonged to the sea was her daily thought and her nightly dream. She had the whole two-and-thirty winds under her eye, each passing gale that ushered in returning autumn being mentally registered; and she acquired a precise knowledge of the direction in which Portsmouth, Brest, Ferrol, Cadiz, and other such likely places lay. Instead of saying her own familiar prayers at night she substituted, with some confusion of thought, the Forms of Prayer to be used at sea. John at once noticed her lorn, abstracted looks, pitied her – how much he pitied her! – and asked when they were alone if there was anything he could do.

'There are two things,' she said, with almost childish eagerness in her tired eyes.

'They shall be done.'

'The first is to find out if Captain Hardy has gone back to his ship; and the other is – O if you will do it, John! – to get me newspapers whenever possible.'

After this duologue John was absent for a space of three hours, and they thought he had gone back to barracks. He entered, however, at the end of that time, took off his forage-cap, and wiped his forehead.

'You look tired, John,' said his father.

'O no.' He went through the house till he had found Anne Garland.

'I have only done one of those things,' he said to her.

'What, already? I didn't hope for or mean today.'

'Captain Hardy is gone from Pos'ham. He left some days ago. We shall soon hear that the fleet has sailed.'

'You have been all the way to Pos'ham on purpose? How good of you!'

'Well, I was anxious to know myself when Bob is likely to leave. I expect now that we shall soon hear from him.'

Two days later he came again. He brought a newspaper, and what was better, a letter for Anne, franked by the first lieutenant of the *Victory*.

'Then he's aboard her,' said Anne, as she eagerly took the letter.

It was short, but as much as she could expect in the circumstances, and informed them that the captain had been as good as his word, and had gratified Bob's earnest wish to serve under him. The ship, with Admiral Lord Nelson on board, and accompanied by the frigate *Euryalus*, was to sail in two days for Plymouth, where they would be joined by others, and thence proceed to the coast of Spain.

Anne lay awake that night thinking of the *Victory*, and of those who floated in her. To the best of Anne's calculation that ship of war would, during the next twenty-four hours, pass within a few miles of where she herself then lay. Next to seeing Bob, the thing that would give her more pleasure than any other in the world was to see the vessel that contained him – his floating city, his sole dependence in battle and storm – upon whose safety from winds and enemies hung all her hope.

The morrow was market-day at the seaport, and in this she saw her opportunity. A carrier went from Overcombe at six o'clock thither, and having to do a little shopping for herself she gave it as a reason for her intended day's absence, and took a place in the van. When she reached the town it was still early morning, but the borough was already in the zenith of its daily bustle and show. The King was always out-of-doors by six o'clock, and such cock-crow hours at Gloucester Lodge produced an equally forward stir among the population. She alighted, and passed down the esplanade, as fully thronged by persons of fashion at this time of mist and level sunlight as a watering-place in the present day is at four in the afternoon. Dashing bucks and beaux in cocked hats, black feathers, ruffles, and frills, stared at her as she hurried along; the beach was swarming with bathing women, wearing waist-bands that bore the national refrain, 'God save the King', in gilt letters; the shops were all open, and Sergeant Stanner, with his sword-stuck bank-notes and heroic gaze, was beating up[167] at two guineas and a crown, the crown to drink his Majesty's health.

She soon finished her shopping, and then, crossing over into the old town, pursued her way along the coast-road to Portland. At the end of an hour she had been rowed across the Fleet (which then lacked the convenience of a bridge), and reached the base of Portland Hill. The steep incline before her was dotted with houses, showing the pleasant peculiarity of one man's doorstep being behind his neighbour's chimney, and slabs of stone as the common material for walls, roof, floor, pig-sty, stable-manger, door-scraper, and garden-stile. Anne gained the summit, and followed along the central track over the huge lump of freestone which forms the peninsula, the wide sea prospect extending as she went on. Weary with her journey, she approached the extreme southerly peak of rock, and gazed from the cliff at Portland Bill, or Beal,[168] as it was in those days more correctly called.

The wild, herbless, weather-worn promontory was quite a solitude, and, saving the one old lighthouse about fifty yards up the slope, scarce a mark was visible to show that humanity had ever been near the spot. Anne found herself a seat on a stone, and swept with her eyes the tremulous expanse of water around her that seemed to utter a ceaseless unintelligible incantation. Out of the three hundred and sixty degrees of her complete horizon two hundred and fifty were covered by waves, the *coup d'œil* including the area of troubled waters known as the Race, where two seas met to effect the destruction of such vessels as could not be mastered by one. She counted the craft within her view: there were five; no, there were only four; no, there were seven, some of the specks having resolved themselves into two. They were all small coasters, and kept well within sight of land.

Anne sank into a reverie. Then she heard a slight noise on her left hand, and turning beheld an old sailor, who had approached with a glass. He was levelling it over the sea in a direction to the south-east, and somewhat removed from that in which her own eyes had been wandering. Anne moved a few steps thitherward, so as to unclose to her view a deeper sweep on that side, and by this discovered a ship of far larger size than any which had yet dotted the main before her. Its sails were for the most part new and clean, and in comparison with its rapid progress before the wind the small brigs and ketches seemed standing still. Upon this striking object the old man's glass was bent.

'What do you see, sailor?' she asked.

'Almost nothing,' he answered. 'My sight is so gone off lately that things, one and all, be but a November mist to me. And yet I fain would see today. I am looking for the *Victory*.'

'Why?' she said quickly.

'I have a son aboard her. He's one of three from these parts. There's the captain, there's my son Jim, and there's young Loveday of Overcombe – he that lately joined.'

'Shall I look for you?' said Anne, after a pause.

'Certainly, mis'ess, if so be you please.'

Anne took the glass, and he supported it by his arm. 'It is a

large ship,' she said, 'with three masts, three rows of guns along
the side, and all her sails set.'

'I guessed as much.'

'There is a little flag in front – over her bowsprit.'

'The jack.'

'And there's a large one flying at her stern.'

'The ensign.'

'And a white one on her fore-topmast.'

'That's the admiral's flag, the flag of my Lord Nelson. What is
her figure-head, my dear?'

'A coat-of-arms, supported on this side by a sailor.'

Her companion nodded with satisfaction. 'On the other side of
that figure-head is a marine.'

'She is twisting round in a curious way, and her sails sink in like
old cheeks, and she shivers like a leaf upon a tree.'

'She is in stays,[169] for the larboard tack. I can see what she's
been doing. She's been re'ching close in to avoid the flood tide,
as the wind is to the sou'-west, and she's bound down;[170] but as
soon as the ebb made, d'ye see, they made sail to the west'ard.
Captain Hardy may be depended upon for that; he knows every
current about here, being a native.'

'And now I can see the other side; it is a soldier where a sailor
was before. You are *sure* it is the *Victory*?'

'I am sure.'

After this a frigate came into view – the *Euryalus* – sailing in the
same direction. Anne sat down, and her eyes never left the ships.
'Tell me more about the *Victory*,' she said.

'She is the best sailer in the service, and she carries a hundred
guns. The heaviest be on the lower deck, the next size on the
middle deck, the next on the main and upper decks. My son Jim's
place is on the lower deck, because he's short, and they put the
short men below.'

Bob, though not tall, was not likely to be specially selected for
shortness. She pictured him on the upper deck, in his snow-white
trousers and jacket of navy blue, looking perhaps towards the
very point of land where she then was.

The great silent ship, with her population of blue-jackets,
marines, officers, captain, and the admiral who was not to return

alive, passed like a phantom the meridian of the Bill. Sometimes her aspect was that of a large white bat, sometimes that of a grey one. In the course of time the watching girl saw that the ship had passed her nearest point; the breadth of her sails diminished by foreshortening, till she assumed the form of an egg on end. After this something seemed to twinkle, and Anne, who had previously withdrawn from the old sailor, went back to him, and looked again through the glass. The twinkling was the light falling upon the cabin windows of the ship's stern. She explained it to the old man.

'Then we see now what the enemy have seen but once. That was in seventy-nine, when she sighted the French and Spanish fleet off Scilly, and she retreated because she feared a landing. Well, 'tis a brave ship, and she carries brave men!'

Anne's tender bosom heaved, but she said nothing, and again became absorbed in contemplation.

The *Victory* was fast dropping away. She was on the horizon, and soon appeared hull down. That seemed to be like the beginning of a greater end than her present vanishing. Anne Garland could not stay by the sailor any longer, and went about a stone's-throw off, where she was hidden by the inequality of the cliff from his view. The vessel was now exactly end on, and stood out in the direction of the Start,[171] her width having contracted to the proportion of a feather. She sat down again, and mechanically took out some biscuits that she had brought, foreseeing that her waiting might be long. But she could not eat one of them; eating seemed to jar with the mental tenseness of the moment; and her undeviating gaze continued to follow the lessened ship with the fidelity of a balanced needle to a magnetic stone, all else in her being motionless.

The courses[172] of the *Victory* were absorbed into the main, then her topsails went, and then her top-gallants. She was now no more than a dead fly's wing on a sheet of spider's web; and even this fragment diminished. Anne could hardly bear to see the end, and yet she resolved not to flinch. The admiral's flag sank behind the watery line, and in a minute the very truck[173] of the last topmast stole away. The *Victory* was gone.

Anne's lip quivered as she murmured, without removing her wet eyes from the vacant and solemn horizon, ' "They that go down to the sea in ships, that do business in great waters –" '

' "These see the works of the Lord, and His wonders in the deep," '[174] was returned by a man's voice from behind her.

Looking round quickly, she saw a soldier standing there; and the grave eyes of John Loveday bent on her.

' 'Tis what I was thinking,' she said, trying to be composed.

'You were saying it,' he answered gently.

'Was I? – I did not know it . . . How came you here?' she presently added.

'I have been behind you a good while; but you never turned round.'

'I was deeply occupied,' she said in an undertone.

'Yes – I too came to see him pass. I heard this morning that Lord Nelson had embarked, and I knew at once that they would sail immediately. The *Victory* and *Euryalus* are to join the rest of the fleet at Plymouth. There was a great crowd of people assembled to see the admiral off; they cheered him and the ship as she dropped down. He took his coffin on board with him, they say.'

'His coffin!' said Anne, turning deadly pale. 'Something terrible, then, is meant by that! O, why *would* Bob go in that ship? doomed to destruction from the very beginning like this!'

'It was his determination to sail under Captain Hardy, and under no one else,' said John. 'There may be hot work; but we must hope for the best.' And observing how wretched she looked, he added, 'But won't you let me help you back? If you can walk as far as Hope Cove it will be enough. A lerret[175] is going from there across the bay homeward to the harbour in the course of an hour; it belongs to a man I know, and they can take one passenger, I am sure.'

She turned her back upon the Channel, and by his help soon reached the place indicated. The boat was lying there as he had said. She found it to belong to the old man who had been with her at the Bill, and was in charge of his two younger sons. The trumpet-major helped her into it over the slippery blocks of stone, one of the young men spread his jacket for her to sit on, and as soon as they pulled from shore John climbed up the blue-grey cliff, and disappeared over the top, to return to the mainland by road.

Anne was in the town by three o'clock. The trip in the stern of the lerret had quite refreshed her, with the help of the biscuits, which she had at last been able to eat. The van from the port to Overcombe did not start till four o'clock, and feeling no further interest in the gaieties of the place, she strolled on past the King's house to the outskirts, her mind settling down again upon the possibly sad fate of the *Victory* when she found herself alone. She did not hurry on; and finding that even now there wanted another half-hour to the carrier's time, she turned into a little lane to escape the inspection of the numerous passers-by. Here all was quite lonely and still, and she sat down under a willow-tree, absently regarding the landscape, which had begun to put on the rich tones of declining summer, but which to her was as hollow and faded as a theatre by day. She could hold out no longer; burying her face in her hands, she wept without restraint.

Some yards behind her was a little spring of water, having a stone margin round it to prevent the cattle from treading in the sides and filling it up with dirt. While she wept, two elderly gentlemen entered unperceived upon the scene, and walked on to the spring's brink. Here they paused and looked in, afterwards moving round it, and then stooping as if to smell or taste its waters. The spring was, in fact, a sulphurous one,[176] then recently discovered by a physician who lived in the neighbourhood; and it was beginning to attract some attention, having by common report contributed to effect such wonderful cures as almost passed belief. After a considerable discussion, apparently on how the pool might be improved for better use, one of the two elderly gentlemen turned away, leaving the other still probing the spring with his cane. The first stranger, who wore a blue coat with gilt buttons, came on in the direction of Anne Garland, and seeing her sad posture went quickly up to her, and said abruptly, 'What is the matter?'

Anne, who in her grief had observed nothing of the gentlemen's presence, withdrew her handkerchief from her eyes and started to her feet. She instantly recognized her interrogator as the King.[177]

'What, what, crying?' his Majesty inquired kindly. 'How is this!'

'I – have seen a dear friend go away, sir,' she faltered, with downcast eyes.

'Ah! – partings are sad – very sad – for us all. You must hope your friend will return soon. Where is he or she gone?'

'I don't know, your Majesty.'

'Don't know – how is that?'

'He is a sailor on board the *Victory*.'

'Then he has reason to be proud,' said the King with interest. 'He is your brother?'

Anne tried to explain what he was, but could not, and blushed with painful heat.

'Well, well, well; what is his name?'

In spite of Anne's confusion and low spirits, her womanly shrewdness told her at once that no harm could be done by revealing Bob's name; and she answered, 'His name is Robert Loveday, sir.'

'Loveday – a good name. I shall not forget it. Now dry your cheeks, and don't cry any more. Loveday – Robert Loveday.'

Anne curtseyed, the King smiled good-humouredly, and turned to rejoin his companion, who was afterwards heard to be Dr —, the physician in attendance at Gloucester Lodge. This gentleman had in the meantime filled a small phial with the medicinal water, which he carefully placed in his pocket; and on the King coming up they retired together and disappeared. Thereupon Anne, now thoroughly aroused, followed the same way with a gingerly tread, just in time to see them get into a carriage which was in waiting at the turning of the lane.

She quite forgot the carrier, and everything else in connection with riding home. Flying along the road rapidly and unconsciously, when she awoke to a sense of her whereabouts she was so near to Overcombe as to make the carrier not worth waiting for. She had been borne up in this hasty spurt at the end of a weary day by visions of Bob promoted to the rank of admiral, or something equally wonderful, by the King's special command, the chief result of the promotion being, in her arrangement of the piece, that he would stay at home and go to sea no more. But she was not a girl who indulged in extravagant fancies long, and before she reached home she thought that the King had probably forgotten her by that time, and her troubles, and her lover's name.

# * XXXV *

## A Sailor Enters

THE remaining fortnight of the month of September passed away, with a general decline from the summer's excitements. The royal family left the watering-place the first week in October, the German Legion with their artillery about the same time. The dragoons still remained at the barracks just out of the town, and John Loveday brought to Anne every newspaper that he could lay hands on, especially such as contained any fragment of shipping news. This threw them much together; and at these times John was often awkward and confused, on account of the unwonted stress of concealing his great love for her.

Her interests had grandly developed from the limits of Overcombe and the town life hard by, to an extensiveness truly European. During the whole month of October, however, not a single grain of information reached her, or anybody else, concerning Nelson and his blockading squadron off Cadiz. There were the customary bad jokes about Buonaparte, especially when it was found that the whole French army had turned its back upon Boulogne and set out for the Rhine. Then came accounts of his march through Germany and into Austria; but not a word about the *Victory*.

At the beginning of autumn John brought news which fearfully depressed her. The Austrian General Mack[178] had capitulated with his whole army. Then were revived the old misgivings as to invasion. 'Instead of having to cope with him weary with waiting, we shall have to encounter This Man fresh from the fields of victory,' ran the newspaper article.

But the week which had led off with such a dreary piping was to end in another key. On the very day when Mack's army was piling arms at the feet of its conqueror, a blow had been struck by

Bob Loveday and his comrades which eternally shattered the enemy's force by sea. Four days after the receipt of the Austrian news Corporal Tullidge ran into the miller's house to inform him that on the previous Monday, at eleven in the morning, the *Pickle* schooner, with Lieutenant Lapenotiere, had arrived at Falmouth with dispatches from the fleet; that the stage-coaches on the highway through Wessex to London were chalked with the words 'Great Victory!' 'Glorious Triumph!' and so on; and that all the country people were wild to know particulars.

On Friday afternoon John arrived with authentic news of the battle off Cape Trafalgar, and the death of Nelson. Captain Hardy was alive, though his escape had been narrow enough, his shoe-buckle having been carried away by a shot. It was feared that the *Victory* had been the scene of the heaviest slaughter among all the ships engaged, but as yet no returns of killed and wounded had been issued, beyond a rough list of the numbers in some of the ships.

The suspense of the little household in Overcombe Mill was great in the extreme. John came thither daily for more than a week; but no further particulars reached England till the end of that time, and then only the meagre intelligence that there had been a gale immediately after the battle, and that many of the prizes had been lost. Anne said little to all these things, and preserved a superstratum of calmness on her countenance; but some inner voice seemed to whisper to her that Bob was no more. Miller Loveday drove to Pos'ham several times to learn if the Captain's sisters had received any more definite tidings than these flying reports; but that family had heard nothing which could in any way relieve the miller's anxiety. When at last, at the end of November, there appeared a final and revised list of killed and wounded as issued by Admiral Collingwood, it was a useless sheet to the Lovedays. To their great pain it contained no names but those of officers, the friends of ordinary seamen and marines being in those good old days left to discover their losses as best they might.

Anne's conviction of her loss increased with the darkening of the early winter time. Bob was not a cautious man who would avoid needless exposure, and a hundred and fifty of the *Victory's* crew had been disabled or slain. Anybody who had looked into her room at this time would have seen that her favourite reading was the office for the Burial of the Dead at Sea, beginning 'We therefore commit his body to the deep'. In these first days of December several of the victorious fleet came into port; but not the *Victory*. Many supposed that that noble ship, disabled by the battle, had gone to the bottom in the subsequent tempestuous weather; and the belief was persevered in till it was told in the town and port that she had been seen passing up the Channel. Two days later the *Victory* arrived at Portsmouth.

Then letters from survivors began to appear in the public prints which John so regularly brought to Anne; but though he watched the mails with unceasing vigilance there was never a letter from Bob. It sometimes crossed John's mind that his brother might still be alive and well, and that in his wish to abide by his expressed intention of giving up Anne and home life he was deliberately lax in writing. If so, Bob was carrying out the idea too thoughtlessly by half, as could be seen by watching the effects of suspense upon the fair face of the victim, and the anxiety of the rest of the family.

It was a clear day in December. The first slight snow of the season had been sifted over the earth, and one side of the apple-tree branches in the miller's garden was touched with white, though a few leaves were still lingering on the tops of the younger trees. A short sailor of the royal navy, who was not Bob, nor anything like him, crossed the mill court and came to the door. The miller hastened out and brought him into the room, where John, Mrs Loveday, and Anne Garland were all present.

'I'm from aboard the *Victory*,' said the sailor. 'My name's Jim Cornick. And your lad is alive and well.'

They breathed rather than spoke their thankfulness and relief, the miller's eyes being moist as he turned aside to calm himself; while Anne, having first jumped up wildly from her seat, sank back again under the almost insupportable joy that trembled through her limbs to her utmost finger.

'I've come from Spithead to Pos'ham,' the sailor continued, 'and now I am going on to father at Budmouth.'

'Ah! – I know your father,' cried the trumpet-major, 'old James Cornick.'

It was the man who had brought Anne in his lerret from Portland Bill.

'And Bob hasn't got a scratch?' said the miller.

'Not a scratch,' said Cornick.

Loveday then bustled off to draw the visitor something to drink. Anne Garland, with a glowing blush on her face, had gone to the back part of the room, where she was the very embodiment of sweet content as she slightly swayed herself without speaking. A little tide of happiness seemed to ebb and flow through her in listening to the sailor's words, moving her figure with it. The seaman and John went on conversing.

'Bob had a good deal to do with barricading the hawse-holes[179] afore we were in action, and the Adm'l and Cap'n both were very much pleased at how 'twas done. When the Adm'l went up the quarter-deck ladder, Cap'n Hardy said a word or two to Bob, but what it was I don't know, for I was quartered at a gun some ways off. However, Bob saw the Adm'l stagger when 'a was wownded, and was one of the men who carried him to the cockpit. After that he and some other lads jumped aboard the French ship, and I believe they was in her when she struck her flag. What 'a did next I can't say, for the wind had dropped, and the smoke was like a cloud. But 'a got a good deal talked about; and they say there's promotion in store for'n.'

At this point in the story Jim Cornick stopped to drink, and a low unconscious humming came from Anne in her distant corner; the faint melody continued more or less when the conversation between the sailor and the Lovedays was renewed.

'We heard afore that the *Victory* was near knocked to pieces,' said the miller.

'Knocked to pieces? You'd say so if so be you could see her! Gad, her sides be battered like an old penny piece; the shot be still sticking in her wales, and her sails be like so many clap-nets:[180] we have run all the way home under jury topmasts;[181] and as for her decks, you may swab wi' hot water, and you may swab wi' cold, but there's the blood-stains, and there they'll bide . . . The Cap'n had a narrow escape, like many o' the rest – a shot shaved his ankle like a razor. You should have seen that man's face in the het o' battle, his features were as if they'd been cast in steel.'

'We rather expected a letter from Bob before this.'

'Well,' said Jim Cornick, with a smile of toleration, 'you must make allowances. The truth o't is, he's engaged just now at Portsmouth, like a good many of the rest from our ship . . . 'Tis a very nice young woman that he's a-courting of, and I make no doubt that she'll be an excellent wife for him.'

'Ah!' said Mrs Loveday, in a warning tone.

'Courting – wife?' said the miller.

They instinctively looked towards Anne. Anne had started as if shaken by an invisible hand, and a thick mist of doubt seemed to obscure the intelligence of her eyes. This was but for two or three moments. Very pale, she arose and went right up to the seaman. John gently tried to intercept her, but she passed him by.

'Do you speak of Robert Loveday as courting a wife?' she asked, without the least betrayal of emotion.

'I didn't see you, miss,' replied Cornick, turning. 'Yes, your brother hev' his eye on a wife, and he deserves one. I hope you don't mind?'

'Not in the least,' she said, with a stage laugh. 'I am interested, naturally. And what is she?'

'A very nice young master-baker's daughter, honey. A very wise choice of the young man's.'

'Is she fair or dark?'

'Her hair is rather light.'

'I like light hair; and her name?'

'Her name is Caroline. But can it be that my story hurts ye? If so –'

'Yes, yes,' said John, interposing anxiously. 'We don't care for more just at this moment.'

'We *do* care for more!' said Anne vehemently. 'Tell it all, sailor. That is a very pretty name, Caroline. When are they going to be married?'

'I don't know as how the day is settled,' answered Jim, even now scarcely conscious of the devastation he was causing in one fair breast. 'But from the rate the courting is scudding along at, I should say it won't be long first.'

'If you see him when you go back, give him my best wishes,' she lightly said, as she moved away. 'And,' she added, with solemn bitterness, 'say that I am glad to hear he is making such good use of the first days of his escape from the Valley of the Shadow of Death!'[182] She went away, expressing indifference by audibly singing in the distance:

'Shall we go dance the round, the round, the round,
    Shall we go dance the round?'

'Your sister is lively at the news,' observed Jim Cornick.

'Yes,' murmured John gloomily, as he gnawed his lower lip and kept his eyes fixed on the fire.

'Well,' continued the man from the *Victory*, 'I won't say that your brother's intended ha'n't got some ballast, which is very lucky for'n, as he might have picked up with a girl without a single copper nail. To be sure there was a time we had when we got into port! It was open house for us all!' And after mentally regarding the scene for a few seconds Jim emptied his cup and rose to go.

The miller was saying some last words to him outside the house, Anne's voice had hardly ceased singing upstairs, John was standing by the fireplace, and Mrs Loveday was crossing the room to join her daughter, whose manner had given her some uneasiness, when a noise came from above the ceiling, as of some heavy body falling. Mrs Loveday rushed to the staircase, saying, 'Ah, I feared something!' and she was followed by John.

When they entered Anne's room, which they both did almost at one moment, they found her lying insensible upon the floor. The trumpet-major, his lips tightly closed, lifted her in his arms, and laid her upon the bed; after which he went back to the door to give room to her mother, who was bending over the girl with some hartshorn.[183]

Presently Mrs Loveday looked up and said to him, 'She is only in a faint, John, and her colour is coming back. Now leave her to me; I will be downstairs in a few minutes, and tell you how she is.'

John left the room. When he gained the lower apartment his father was standing by the chimney-piece, the sailor having gone. The trumpet-major went up to the fire, and, grasping the edge of the high chimney-shelf, stood silent.

'Did I hear a noise when I went out?' asked the elder, in a tone of misgiving.

'Yes, you did,' said John. 'It was she, but her mother says she is better now. Father,' he added impetuously, 'Bob is a worthless blockhead! If there had been any good in him he would have been drowned years ago!'

'John, John – not too fast,' said the miller. 'That's a hard thing to say of your brother, and you ought to be ashamed of it.'

'Well, he tries me more than I can bear. Good God! what can a man be made of to go on as he does? Why didn't he come home; or if he couldn't get leave why didn't he write? 'Tis scandalous of him to serve a woman like that!'

'Gently, gently. The chap hev done his duty as a sailor; and though there might have been something between him and Anne, her mother, in talking it over with me, has said many times that she couldn't think of their marrying till Bob had settled down in business at home. Folks that gain victories must have a little liberty allowed 'em. Look at the Admiral himself, for that matter.'

John continued looking at the red coals, till hearing Mrs Loveday's foot on the staircase, he went to meet her.

'She is better,' said Mrs Loveday; 'but she won't come down again today.'

Could John have heard what the poor girl was moaning to herself at that moment as she lay writhing on the bed, he would have doubted her mother's assurance. 'If he had been dead I could have borne it, but this I cannot bear!'

# XXXVI

# Derriman Sees Chances

MEANWHILE Sailor Cornick had gone on his way as far as the forking roads, where he met Festus Derriman on foot. The latter, attracted by the seaman's dress, and by seeing him come from the mill, at once accosted him. Jim, with the greatest readiness, fell into conversation, and told the same story as that he had related at the mill.

'Bob Loveday going to be married?' repeated Festus.

'You all seem struck of a heap wi' that.'

'No; I never heard news that pleased me more.'

When Cornick was gone, Festus, instead of passing straight on, halted on the little bridge and meditated. Bob, being now interested elsewhere, would probably not resent the siege of Anne's heart by another; there could, at any rate, be no further possibility of that looming duel which had troubled the yeoman's mind ever since his horse-play on Anne at the house on the down. To march into the mill and propose to Mrs Loveday for Anne before John's interest could revive in her was, to this hero's thinking, excellent discretion.

The day had already begun to darken when he entered, and the cheerful fire shone red upon the floor and walls. Mrs Loveday received him alone, and asked him to take a seat by the chimney-corner, a little of the old hankering for him as a son-in-law having permanently remained with her.

'Your servant, Mrs Loveday,' he said, 'and I will tell you at once what I come for. You will say that I take time by the forelock when I inform you that it is to push on my long-wished-for alliance wi' your daughter, as I believe she is now a free woman again.'

'Thank you, Mr Derriman,' said the mother placably. 'But

she is ill at present. I'll mention it to her when she is better.'

'Ask her to alter her cruel, cruel resolves against me, on the score of – of my consuming passion for her. In short,' continued Festus, dropping his parlour language in his warmth, 'I'll tell thee what, Dame Loveday, I want the maid, and must have her.'

Mrs Loveday replied that that was very plain speaking.

'Well, 'tis. But Bob has given her up. He never meant to marry her. I'll tell you, Mrs Loveday, what I have never told a soul before. I was standing upon Budmouth Quay on that very day in last September that Bob set sail, and I heard him say to his brother John that he gave your daughter up.'

'Then it was very unmannerly of him to trifle with her so,' said Mrs Loveday warmly. 'Who did he give her up to?'

Festus replied with hesitation, 'He gave her up to John.'

'To John? How could he give her up to a man already over head and ears in love with that actress woman?'

'O? You surprise me. Which actress is it?'

'That Miss Johnson. Anne tells me that he loves her hopelessly.'

Festus arose. Miss Johnson seemed suddenly to acquire high value as a sweetheart at this announcement. He had himself felt a nameless attractiveness in her, and John had done likewise. John crossed his path in all possible ways.

Before the yeoman had replied somebody opened the door, and the firelight shone upon the uniform of the person they discussed. Festus nodded on recognizing him, wished Mrs Loveday good evening, and went out precipitately.

'So Bob told you he meant to break off with my Anne when he went away?' Mrs Loveday remarked to the trumpet-major. 'I wish I had known of it before.'

John appeared disturbed at the sudden charge. He murmured that he could not deny it, and then hastily turned from her and followed Derriman, whom he saw before him on the bridge.

'Derriman!' he shouted.

Festus started and looked round. 'Well, trumpet-major,' he said blandly.

'When will you have sense enough to mind your own business, and not come here telling things you have heard by sneaking behind people's backs?' demanded John hotly. 'If you can't learn in any other way, I shall have to pull your ears again, as I did the other day!'

'*You* pull my ears? How can you tell that lie, when you know 'twas somebody else pulled 'em?'

'O no, no. I pulled your ears, and thrashed you in a mild way.'

'You'll swear to it? Surely 'twas another man?'

'It was in the parlour at the public-house; you were almost in the dark.' And John added a few details as to the particular blows, which amounted to proof itself.

'Then I heartily ask your pardon for saying 'twas a lie!' cried Festus, advancing with extended hand and a genial smile. 'Sure, if I had known '*twas* you, I wouldn't have insulted you by denying it.'

'That was why you didn't challenge me, then?'

'That was it! I wouldn't for the world have hurt your nice sense of honour by letting 'ee go unchallenged, if I had known! And now, you see, unfortunately I can't mend the mistake. So long a time has passed since it happened that the heat of my temper is gone off. I couldn't oblige 'ee, try how I might, for I am not a man, trumpet-major, that can butcher in cold blood – no, not I, nor you neither, from what I know of 'ee. So, willy-nilly, we must fain let it pass, eh?'

'We must, I suppose,' said John, smiling grimly. 'Who did you think I was, then, that night when I boxed you all round?'

'No, don't press me,' replied the yeoman. 'I can't reveal; it would be disgracing myself to show how very wide of the truth the mockery of wine was able to lead my senses. We will let it be buried in eternal mixens[184] of forgetfulness.'

'As you wish,' said the trumpet-major loftily. 'But if you ever *should* think you knew it was me, why, you know where to find me?' And Loveday walked away.

The instant that he was gone Festus shook his fist at the evening star, which happened to lie in the same direction as that taken by the dragoon.

'Now for my revenge! Duels? Lifelong disgrace to me if ever I fight with a man of blood below my own! There are other remedies for upper-class souls! . . . Matilda – that's my way.'

Festus strode along till he reached the Hall, where Cripplestraw appeared gazing at him from under the arch of the porter's lodge. Derriman dashed open the entrance-hurdle with such violence that the whole row of them fell flat in the mud.

'Mercy, Maister Festus!' said Cripplestraw. ' "Surely," I says to myself when I see ye a-coming, "surely Maister Festus is fuming like that because there's no chance of the enemy coming this year after all." '

'Cr-r-ripplestraw! I have been wounded to the heart,' replied Derriman, with a lurid brow.

'And the man yet lives, and you wants yer horse-pistols instantly? Certainly, Maister F—'

'No, Cripplestraw, not my pistols, but my new-cut clothes, my heavy gold seals, my silver-topped cane, and my buckles that cost more money than he ever saw! Yes, I must tell somebody, and I'll tell you, because there's no other fool near. He loves her heart and soul. He's poor; she's tip-top genteel, and not rich. I am rich, by comparison. I'll court the pretty play-actress, and win her before his eyes.'

'Play-actress, Maister Derriman?'

'Yes. I saw her this very day, met her by accident, and spoke to her. She's still in the town – perhaps because of him. I can meet her at any hour of the day – But I don't mean to marry her; not I. I will court her for my pastime, and to annoy him. It will be all the more death to him that I don't want her. Then perhaps he will say to me, "You have taken my one ewe lamb" – meaning that I am the king, and he's the poor man, as in the church verse;[185] and he'll beg for mercy when 'tis too late – unless, meanwhile, I shall have tired of my new toy. Saddle the horse, Cripplestraw, tomorrow at ten.'

Full of this resolve to scourge John Loveday to the quick through his passion for Miss Johnson, Festus came out booted and spurred at the time appointed, and set off on his morning ride.

Miss Johnson's theatrical engagement having long ago terminated, she would have left the Royal watering-place with the rest of the visitors had not matrimonial hopes detained her there. These had nothing whatever to do with John Loveday, as may be imagined, but with a stout, staid boat-builder in Cove Row by the quay, who had shown much interest in her impersonations. Unfortunately this substantial man had not been quite so attentive since the end of the season as his previous manner led her to expect; and it was a great pleasure to the lady to see Mr Derriman leaning over the harbour bridge with his eyes fixed upon her as she came towards it after a stroll past her elderly wooer's house.

' 'Od take it, ma'am, you didn't tell me when I saw you last that the tooting man with the blue jacket and lace was yours devoted?' began Festus.

'Who do you mean?' In Matilda's ever-changing emotional interests, John Loveday was a stale and unprofitable[186] personality.

'Why, that trumpet-major man.'

'O! What of him?'

'Come; he loves you, and you know it, ma'am.'

She knew, at any rate, how to take the current when it served.[187] So she glanced at Festus, folded her lips meaningly, and nodded.

'I've come to cut him out.'

She shook her head, it being unsafe to speak till she knew a little more of the subject.

'What!' said Festus, reddening, 'do you mean to say that you think of him seriously – you, who might look so much higher?'

'Constant dropping will wear away a stone; and you should only hear his pleading! His handsome face is impressive, and his manners are – O, so genteel! I am not rich; I am, in short, a poor lady of decayed family, who has nothing to boast of but my blood and ancestors, and they won't find a body in food and clothing! – I hold the world but as the world, Derrimanio – a stage where every man must play a part, and mine a sad one!'[188] She dropped her eyes thoughtfully and sighed.

'We will talk of this,' said Festus, much affected. 'Let us walk to the Look-out.'

She made no objection, and said, as they turned that way, 'Mr Derriman, a long time ago I found something belonging to you; but I have never yet remembered to return it.' And she drew from her bosom the paper which Anne had dropped in the meadow when eluding the grasp of Festus on that summer day.

'Zounds, I smell fresh meat!' cried Festus when he had looked it over. ' 'Tis in my uncle's writing, and 'tis what I heard him singing on the day the French didn't come, and afterwards saw him marking in the road. 'Tis something he's got hid away. Give me the paper, there's a dear; 'tis worth sterling gold!'

'Halves, then?' said Matilda tenderly.

'Gad, yes – anything!' replied Festus, blazing into a smile, for she had looked up in her best new manner at the possibility that he might be worth the winning. They went up the steps to the summit of the cliff, and dwindled over it against the sky.

# XXXVII

# Reaction

THERE was no letter from Bob, though December had passed, and the new year was two weeks old. His movements were, however, pretty accurately registered in the papers, which John still brought, but which Anne no longer read. During the second week in December the *Victory* sailed for Sheerness, and on the 9th of the following January the public funeral of Lord Nelson took place in St Paul's.

Then there came a meagre line addressed to the family in general. Bob's new Portsmouth attachment was not mentioned, but he told them he had been one of the eight-and-forty seamen who walked two-and-two in the funeral procession, and that Captain Hardy had borne the banner of emblems on the same occasion. The crew was soon to be paid off at Chatham, when he thought of returning to Portsmouth for a few days to see a valued friend. After that he should come home.

But the spring advanced without bringing him, and John watched Anne Garland's desolation with augmenting desire to do something towards consoling her. The old feelings, so religiously held in check, were stimulated to rebelliousness, though they did not show themselves in any direct manner as yet.

The miller, in the meantime, who seldom interfered in such matters, was observed to look meaningly at Anne and the trumpet-major from day to day; and by and by he spoke privately to John.

His words were short and to the point: Anne was very melancholy; she had thought too much of Bob. Now 'twas plain that they had lost him for many years to come. Well; he had always felt that of the two he would rather John married her. Now John might settle down there, and succeed where Bob had failed. 'So if you could get her, my sonny, to think less of him and more of thyself, it would be a good thing for all.'

An inward excitement had risen in John; but he suppressed it and said firmly –

'Fairness to Bob before everything!'

'He hev forgot her, and there's an end on't.'

'She's not forgot him.'

'Well, well; think it over.'

This discourse was the cause of his penning a letter to his brother. He begged for a distinct statement whether, as John at first supposed, Bob's verbal renunciation of Anne on the quay had been only a momentary ebullition of friendship, which it would be cruel to take literally; or whether, as seemed now, it had passed from a hasty resolve to a standing purpose, persevered in for his own pleasure, with not a care for the result on poor Anne.

John waited anxiously for the answer, but no answer came; and the silence seemed even more significant than a letter of assurance could have been of his absolution from further support to a claim which Bob himself had so clearly renounced. Thus it happened that paternal pressure, brotherly indifference, and his own released impulse operated in one delightful direction, and the trumpet-major once more approached Anne as in the old time.

But it was not till she had been left to herself for a full five months, and the blue-bells and ragged-robins of the following year were again making themselves common to the rambling eye, that he directly addressed her. She was tying up a group of tall flowering plants in the garden: she knew that he was behind her, but she did not turn. She had subsided into a placid dignity which enabled her when watched to perform any little action with seeming composure – very different from the flutter of her inexperienced days.

'Are you never going to turn round?' he at length asked good-humouredly.

She then did turn, and looked at him for a moment without speaking; a certain suspicion looming in her eyes, as if suggested by his perceptible want of ease.

'How like summer it is getting to feel, is it not?' she said.

John admitted that it was getting to feel like summer; and,

bending his gaze upon her with an earnestness which no longer left any doubt of his subject, went on to ask –

'Have you ever in these last weeks thought of how it used to be between us?'

She replied quickly, 'O, John, you shouldn't begin that again. I am almost another woman now!'

'Well, that's all the more reason why I should, isn't it?'

Anne looked thoughtfully to the other end of the garden, faintly shaking her head; 'I don't quite see it like that,' she returned.

'You feel yourself quite free, don't you?'

'*Quite* free!' she said instantly, and with proud distinctness; her eyes fell, and she repeated more slowly, 'Quite free.' Then her thoughts seemed to fly from herself to him. 'But you are not?'

'I am not?'

'Miss Johnson!'

'O – that woman! You know as well as I that was all make-up, and that I never for a moment thought of her.'

'I had an idea you were acting; but I wasn't sure.'

'Well, that's nothing now. Anne, I want to relieve your life; to cheer you in some way; to make some amends for my brother's bad conduct. If you cannot love me, liking will be well enough. I have thought over every side of it so many times – for months have I been thinking it over – and I am at last sure that I do right to put it to you in this way. That I don't wrong Bob I am quite convinced. As far as he is concerned we be both free. Had I not been sure of that I would never have spoken. Father wants me to take on the mill, and it will please him if you can give me one little hope; it will make the house go on altogether better if you can think o' me.'

'You are generous and good, John,' she said, as a big round tear bowled helter-skelter down her face and hat-strings.

'I am not that; I fear I am quite the opposite,' he said, without looking at her. 'It would be all gain to me – But you have not answered my question.'

She lifted her eyes. 'John, I cannot!' she said, with a cheerless smile. 'Positively I cannot. Will you make me a promise?'

'What is it?'

'I want you to promise first – Yes, it is dreadfully unreasonable,' she added, in a mild distress. 'But do promise!'

John by this time seemed to have a feeling that it was all up with him for the present. 'I promise,' he said listlessly.

'It is that you won't speak to me about this for *ever* so long,' she returned, with emphatic kindliness.

'Very good,' he replied; 'very good. Dear Anne, you don't think I have been unmanly or unfair in starting this anew?'

Anne looked into his face without a smile. 'You have been perfectly natural,' she murmured. 'And so I think have I.'

John, mournfully: 'You will not avoid me for this, or be afraid of me? I will not break my word. I will not worry you any more.'

'Thank you, John. You need not have said worry; it isn't that.'

'Well, I am very blind and stupid. I have been hurting your heart all the time without knowing it. It is my fate, I suppose. Men who love women the very best always blunder and give more pain than those who love them less.'

Anne laid one of her hands on the other as she softly replied, looking down at them, 'No one loves me as well as you, John; nobody in the world is so worthy to be loved; and yet I cannot anyhow love you rightly.' And lifting her eyes, 'But I do so feel for you that I will try as hard as I can to think about you.'

'Well, that is something,' he said, smiling. 'You say I must not speak about it again for ever so long; how long?'

'Now that's not fair,' Anne retorted, going down the garden, and leaving him alone.

About a week passed. Then one afternoon the miller walked up to Anne indoors, a weighty topic being expressed in his tread.

'I was so glad, my honey,' he began, with a knowing smile, 'to see that from the mill-window last week.' He flung a nod in the direction of the garden.

Anne innocently inquired what it could be.

'Jack and you in the garden together,' he continued, laying his hand gently on her shoulder and stroking it. 'It would so please me, my dear little girl, if you could get to like him better than that weathercock, Master Bob.'

Anne shook her head; not in forcible negation, but to imply a kind of neutrality.

'Can't you? Come now,' said the miller.

She threw back her head with a little laugh of grievance. 'How you all beset me!' she expostulated. 'It makes me feel very wicked in not obeying you, and being faithful – faithful to –' But she could not trust that side of the subject to words. 'Why would it please you so much?' she asked.

'John is as steady and staunch a fellow as ever blowed a trumpet. I've always thought you might do better with him than with Bob. Now I've a plan for taking him into the mill, and letting him have a comfortable time o't after his long knocking about; but so much depends upon you that I must bide a bit till I see what your pleasure is about the poor fellow. Mind, my dear, I don't want to force ye; I only just ask ye.'

Anne meditatively regarded the miller from under her shady eyelids, the fingers of one hand playing a silent tattoo on her bosom. 'I don't know what to say to you,' she answered brusquely, and went away.

But these discourses were not without their effect upon the extremely conscientious mind of Anne. They were, moreover, much helped by an incident which took place one evening in the autumn of this year, when John came to tea. Anne was sitting on a low stool in front of the fire, her hands clasped across her knee. John Loveday had just seated himself on a chair close behind her, and Mrs Loveday was in the act of filling the teapot from the kettle which hung in the chimney exactly above Anne. The kettle slipped forward suddenly; whereupon John jumped from the chair and put his own two hands over Anne's just in time to shield them, and the precious knee she clasped, from the jet of scalding water which had directed itself upon that point. The accidental overflow was instantly checked by Mrs Loveday; but what had come was received by the devoted trumpet-major on the back of his hands.

Anne, who had hardly been aware that he was behind her, started up like a person awakened from a trance. 'What have you done to yourself, poor John, to keep it off me!' she cried, looking at his hands.

John reddened emotionally at her words, 'It is a bit of a scald, that's all,' he replied, drawing a finger across the back of one hand, and bringing off the skin by the touch.

'You are scalded painfully, and I not at all!' She gazed into his kind face as she had never gazed there before, and when Mrs Loveday came back with oil and other liniments for the wound Anne would let nobody dress it but herself. It seemed as if her coyness had all gone, and when she had done all that lay in her power she still sat by him. At his departure she said what she had never said to him in her life before: 'Come again soon!'

In short, that impulsive act of devotion, the last of a series of the same tenor, had been the added drop which finally turned the wheel. John's character deeply impressed her. His determined steadfastness to his lodestar won her admiration, the more especially as that star was herself. She began to wonder more and more how she could have so persistently held out against his advances before Bob came home to renew girlish memories which had by that time got considerably weakened. Could she not, after all, please the miller, and try to listen to John? By so doing she would make a worthy man happy, the only sacrifice being at worst that of her unworthy self, whose future was no longer valuable. 'As for Bob, the woman is to be pitied who loves him,' she reflected indignantly, and persuaded herself that, whoever the woman might be, she was not Anne Garland.

After this there was something of recklessness and something of pleasantry in the young girl's manner of making herself an example of the triumph of pride and common sense over memory and sentiment. Her attitude had been epitomized in her defiant singing at the time she learnt that Bob was not leal and true. John, as was inevitable, came again almost immediately, drawn thither by the sun of her first smile on him, and the words which had accompanied it. And now instead of going off to her little pursuits upstairs, downstairs, across the room, in the corner, or to any place except where he happened to be, as had been her custom hitherto, she remained seated near him, returning interesting answers to his general remarks, and at every opportunity letting him know that at last he had found favour in her eyes.

The day was fine, and they went out of doors, where Anne

endeavoured to seat herself on the sloping stone of the window-sill.

'How good you have become lately,' said John, standing over her and smiling in the sunlight which blazed against the wall. 'I fancy you have stayed at home this afternoon on my account.'

'Perhaps I have,' she said gaily –

'Do whatever we may for him, dame, we cannot do too much!
For he's one that has guarded our land.

And he has done more than that: he has saved me from a dreadful scalding. The back of your hand will not be well for a long time, John, will it?'

He held out his hand to regard its condition, and the next natural thing was to take hers. There was a glow upon his face when he did it: his star was at last on a fair way towards the zenith after its long and weary declination. The least penetrating eye could have perceived that Anne had resolved to let him woo, possibly in her temerity to let him win. Whatever silent sorrow might be locked up in her, it was by this time thrust a long way down from the light.

'I want you to go somewhere with me if you will,' he said, still holding her hand.

'Yes? Where is it?'

He pointed to a distant hill-side which, hitherto green, had within the last few days begun to show scratches of white on its face. 'Up there,' he said.

'I see little figures of men moving about. What are they doing?'

'Cutting out a huge picture of the king on horseback in the earth of the hill. The king's head is to be as big as our mill-pond and his body as big as this garden; he and the horse will cover more than an acre. When shall we go?'

'Whenever you please,' said she.

'John!' cried Mrs Loveday from the front door. 'Here's a friend come for you.'

John went round, and found his trusty lieutenant, Trumpeter Buck, waiting for him. A letter had come to the barracks for John in his absence, and the trumpeter, who was going for a walk, had brought it along with him. Buck then entered the mill to discuss, if possible, a mug of last year's mead with the miller; and John proceeded to read his letter, Anne being still round the corner where he had left her. When he had read a few words he turned as pale as a sheet, but he did not move, and perused the writing to the end.

Afterwards he laid his elbow against the wall, and put his palm to his head, thinking with painful intentness. Then he took himself vigorously in hand, as it were, and gradually became natural again. When he parted from Anne to go home with Buck she noticed nothing different in him.

In barracks that evening he read the letter again. It was from Bob; and the agitating contents were these:

> DEAR JOHN, I have drifted off from writing till the present time because I have not been clear about my feelings; but I have discovered them at last, and can say beyond doubt that I mean to be faithful to my dearest Anne after all. The fact is, John, I've got into a bit of a scrape, and I've a secret to tell you about it (which must go no further on any account). On landing last autumn I fell in with a young woman, and we got rather warm as folks do; in short, we liked one another well enough for a while. But I have got into shoal water[189] with her, and have found her to be a terrible take-in. Nothing in her at all – no sense, no niceness, all tantrums and empty noise, John, though she seemed monstrous clever at first. So my heart comes back to its old anchorage. I hope my return to faithfulness will make no difference to you. But as you showed by your looks at our parting that you should not accept my offer to give her up – made in too much haste, as I have since found – I feel that you won't mind that I have returned to the path of honour. I dare not write to Anne as yet, and please do not let her know a word about the other young woman, or there will be the devil to pay. I shall come home and make all things right, please God. In the meantime I should take it as a kindness, John, if you would keep a brotherly eye upon Anne, and guide her mind back to me. I shall die of sorrow if anybody sets her against me, for my hopes are getting bound up in her again quite strong. Hoping you are jovial, as times go, I am, – Your affectionate brother,
>
> ROBERT.

When the cold daylight fell upon John's face, as he dressed himself next morning, the incipient yesterday's wrinkle in his forehead had become permanently graven there. He had resolved, for the sake of that only brother whom he had nursed as a baby, instructed as a child, and protected and loved always, to pause in his procedure for the present, and at least do nothing to hinder Bob's restoration to favour, if a genuine, even though temporarily smothered, love for Anne should still hold possession of him. But having arranged to take her to see the excavated figure of the king, he started for Overcombe during the day, as if nothing had occurred to check the smooth course of his love.

# * XXXVIII *

## A Delicate Situation

'I AM ready to go,' said Anne, as soon as he arrived.

He paused as if taken aback by her readiness, and replied with much uncertainty, 'Would it – wouldn't it be better to put it off till there is less sun?'

The very slightest symptom of surprise arose in her as she rejoined, 'But the weather may change; or had we better not go at all?'

'O no! – it was only a thought. We will start at once.'

And along the vale they went, John keeping himself about a yard from her right hand. When the third field had been crossed they came upon half-a-dozen little boys at play.

'Why don't he clipse her to his side, like a man?' said the biggest and rudest boy.

'Why don't he clipse her to his side, like a man?' echoed all the rude smaller boys in a chorus.

The trumpet-major turned, and, after some running, succeeded in smacking two of them with his switch, returning to Anne breathless. 'I am ashamed they should have insulted you so,' he said, blushing for her.

'They said no harm, poor boys,' she replied reproachfully.

Poor John was dumb with perception. The gentle hint upon which he would have eagerly spoken only one short day ago was now like fire to his wound.

They presently came to some stepping-stones across a brook. John crossed first without turning his head, and Anne, just lifting the skirt of her dress, crossed behind him. When they had reached the other side a village girl and a young shepherd approached the brink to cross. Anne stopped and watched them. The shepherd took a hand of the young girl in each of his own, and walked backward over the stones, facing her, and keeping her upright by his grasp, both of them laughing as they went.

'What are you staying for, Miss Garland?' asked John.

'I was only thinking how happy they are,' she said quietly; and withdrawing her eyes from the tender pair, she turned and followed him, not knowing that the seeming sound of a passing bumble-bee was a suppressed groan from John.

When they reached the hill they found forty navvies at work removing the dark sod so as to lay bare the chalk beneath. The equestrian figure that their shovels were forming was scarcely intelligible to John and Anne now they were close, and after pacing from the horse's head down his breast to his hoof, back by way of the king's bridle-arm, past the bridge of his nose, and into his cocked-hat, Anne said that she had had enough of it, and stepped out of the chalk clearing upon the grass. The trumpet-major had remained all the time in a melancholy attitude within the rowel[190] of his Majesty's right spur.

'My shoes are caked with chalk,' she said as they walked downwards again; and she drew back her dress to look at them. 'How can I get some of it cleared off?'

'If you was to wipe them in the long grass there,' said John, pointing to a spot where the blades were rank and dense, 'some of it would come off.' Having said this, he walked on with religious firmness.

Anne raked her little feet on the right side, on the left side, over the toe, and behind the heel; but the tenacious chalk held its own. Panting with her exertion, she gave it up, and at length overtook him.

'I hope it is right now?' he said, looking gingerly over his shoulder.

'No, indeed!' said she. 'I wanted some assistance – someone to steady me. It is so hard to stand on one foot and wipe the other without support. I was in danger of toppling over, and so gave it up.'

'Merciful stars, what an opportunity!' thought the poor fellow while she waited for him to offer help. But his lips remained closed, and she went on with a pouting smile –

'You seem in such a hurry! Why are you in such a hurry? After all the fine things you have said about – about caring so much for me, and all that, you won't stop for anything!'

It was too much for John. 'Upon my heart and life, my dea—' he began. Here Bob's letter crackled warningly in his waistcoat pocket as he laid his hand asseveratingly upon his breast, and he became suddenly sealed up to dumbness and gloom as before.

When they reached home Anne sank upon a stool outside the door, fatigued with her excursion. Her first act was to try to pull off her shoe – it was a difficult matter; but John stood beating with his switch the leaves of the creeper on the wall.

'Mother – David – Molly, or somebody – do come and help me pull off these dirty shoes!' she cried aloud at last. 'Nobody helps me in anything!'

'I am very sorry,' said John, coming towards her with incredible slowness and an air of unutterable depression.

'O, I can do without *you*. David is best,' she returned as the old man approached and removed the obnoxious shoes in a trice.

Anne was amazed at this sudden change from devotion to crass indifference. On entering her room she flew to the glass, almost expecting to learn that some extraordinary change had come over her pretty countenance, rendering her intolerable for evermore. But it was, if anything, fresher than usual, on account of the exercise. 'Well!' she said retrospectively. For the first time since their acquaintance she had this week encouraged him; and for the first time he had shown that encouragement was useless. 'But perhaps he does not clearly understand,' she added serenely.

When he next came it was, to her surprise, to bring her newspapers, now for some time discontinued. As soon as she saw them she said, 'I do not care for newspapers.'

'The shipping news is very full and long today, though the print is rather small.'

'I take no further interest in the shipping news,' she replied with cold dignity.

She was sitting by the window, inside the table, and hence when, in spite of her negations, he deliberately unfolded the paper and began to read about the Royal Navy she could hardly rise and go away. With a stoical mien he read on to the end of the report, bringing out the name of Bob's ship with tremendous force.

'No,' she said at last, 'I'll hear no more! Let me read to you.'

The trumpet-major sat down. Anne turned to the military news, delivering every detail with much apparent enthusiasm. 'That's the subject *I* like!' she said fervently.

'But – but Bob is in the navy now, and will most likely rise to be an officer. And then –'

'What is there like the army?' she interrupted. 'There is no smartness about sailors. They waddle like ducks, and they only fight stupid battles that no one can form any idea of. There is no science nor stratagem in sea-fights – nothing more than what you see when two rams run their heads together in a field to knock each other down. But in military battles there is such art, and such splendour, and the men are so smart, particularly the horse-soldiers. O, I shall never forget what gallant men you all seemed when you came and pitched your tents on the downs! I like the cavalry better than anything I know; and the dragoons the best of the cavalry – and the trumpeters the best of the dragoons!'

'O, if it had but come a little sooner!' moaned John within him. He replied as soon as he could regain self-command, 'I am glad Bob is in the navy at last – he is so much more fitted for that than the merchant-service – so brave by nature, ready for any daring deed. I have heard ever so much more about his doings on board the *Victory*. Captain Hardy took special notice that when he –'

'I don't want to know anything more about it,' said Anne impatiently: 'of course sailors fight; there's nothing else to do in a ship, since you can't run away! You may as well fight and be killed as be killed not fighting.'

'Still it is his character to be careless of himself where the honour of his country is concerned,' John pleaded. 'If you had only known him as a boy you would own it. He would always risk his own life to save anybody else's. Once when a cottage was afire up the lane he rushed in for a baby, although he was only a boy himself, and he had the narrowest escape. We have got his hat now with the hole burnt in it. Shall I get it and show it to you?'

'No – I don't wish it. It has nothing to do with me.' But as he persisted in his course towards the door, she added, 'Ah! you are leaving because I am in your way. You want to be alone while you read the paper – I will go at once. I did not see that I was interrupting you.' And she rose as if to retreat.

'No, no! I would rather be interrupted by *you* than – O, Miss Garland, excuse me! I'll just speak to father in the mill, now I am here.'

It is scarcely necessary to state that Anne (whose unquestionable gentility amid somewhat homely surroundings has been many times insisted on in the course of this history) was usually the reverse of a woman with a coming-on disposition; but, whether from pique at his manner, or from wilful adherence to a course rashly resolved on, or from coquettish maliciousness in reaction from long depression, or from any other thing, – so it was that she would not let him go.

'Trumpet-major,' she said, recalling him.

'Yes?' he replied timidly.

'The bow of my cap-ribbon has come untied, has it not?' She turned and fixed her bewitching glance upon him.

The bow was just over her forehead, or, more precisely, at the point where the organ of comparison merges in that of benevolence, according to the phrenological theory of Gall. [19] John, thus brought to, endeavoured to look at the bow in a skimming, duck-and-drake fashion, so as to avoid dipping his own glance as far as to the plane of his interrogator's eyes. 'It is untied,' he said, drawing back a little.

She came nearer, and asked, 'Will you tie it for me, please?'

As there was no help for it, he nerved himself and assented. As her head only reached to his fourth button she necessarily looked up for his convenience, and John began fumbling at the bow. Try as he would, it was impossible to touch the ribbon without getting his finger tips mixed with the curls of her forehead.

'Your hand shakes – ah! you have been walking fast,' she said.

'Yes – yes.'

'Have you almost done it?' She inquiringly directed her gaze upward through his fingers.

'No – not yet,' he faltered in a warm sweat of emotion, his heart going like a flail.

'Then be quick, please.'

'Yes, I will, Miss Garland! B-B-Bob is a very good fel—'

'Not that man's name to me!' she interrupted.

John was silent instantly, and nothing was to be heard but the rustling of the ribbon; till his hands once more blundered among the curls, and then touched her forehead.

'O good God!' ejaculated the trumpet-major in a whisper, turning away hastily to the corner-cupboard, and resting his face upon his hand.

'What's the matter, John?' said she.

'I can't do it!'

'What?'

'Tie your cap-ribbon.'

'Why not?'

'Because you are so – Because I am clumsy, and never could tie a bow.'

'You are clumsy indeed,' answered Anne, and went away.

After this she felt injured, for it seemed to show that he rated her happiness as of meaner value than Bob's; since he had persisted in his idea of giving Bob another chance when she had implied that it was her wish to do otherwise. Could Miss Johnson have anything to do with his firmness? An opportunity of testing him in this direction occurred some days later. She had been up the village, and met John at the mill-door.

'Have you heard the news? Matilda Johnson is going to be married to young Derriman.'

Anne stood with her back to the sun, and as he faced her, his features were searchingly exhibited. There was no change whatever in them, unless it were that a certain light of interest kindled by her question turned to complete and blank indifference. 'Well, as times go, it is not a bad match for her,' he said, with a phlegm which was hardly that of a lover.

John on his part was beginning to find these temptations almost more than he could bear. But being quartered so near to his father's house it was unnatural not to visit him, especially when at any moment the regiment might be ordered abroad, and a separation of years ensue; and as long as he went there he could not help seeing her.

The year changed from green to gold, and from gold to grey, but little change came over the house of Loveday. During the last twelve months Bob had been occasionally heard of as upholding his country's honour in Denmark, the West Indies, Gibraltar, Malta, and other places about the globe, till the family received a short letter stating that he had arrived again at Portsmouth. At Portsmouth Bob seemed disposed to remain, for though some time elapsed without further intelligence, the gallant seaman never appeared at Overcombe. Then on a sudden John learnt that Bob's long-talked-of promotion for signal services rendered was to be an accomplished fact. The trumpet-major at once walked off to Overcombe, and reached the village in the early afternoon. Not one of the family was in the house at the moment, and John strolled onwards over the hill towards Casterbridge, without much thought of direction till, lifting his eyes, he beheld Anne Garland wandering about with a little basket upon her arm.

At first John blushed with delight at the sweet vision; but, recalled by his conscience, the blush of delight was at once mangled and slain. He looked for a means of retreat. But the field was open, and a soldier was a conspicuous object: there was no escaping her.

'It was kind of you to come,' she said, with an inviting smile.

'It was quite by accident,' he answered, with an indifferent laugh. 'I thought you was at home.'

Anne blushed and said nothing, and they rambled on together. In the middle of the field rose a fragment of stone wall in the form of a gable, known as Faringdon Ruin;[192] and when they had reached it John paused and politely asked her if she were not a little tired with walking so far. No particular reply was returned by the young lady, but they both stopped, and Anne seated herself on a stone, which had fallen from the ruin to the ground.

'A church once stood here,' observed John in a matter-of-fact tone.

'Yes, I have often shaped it out in my mind,' she returned. 'Here where I sit must have been the altar.'

'True; this standing bit of wall was the chancel end.'

Anne had been adding up her little studies of the trumpet-major's character, and was surprised to find how the brightness of that character increased in her eyes with each examination. A kindly and gentle sensation was aroused in her. Here was a neglected heroic man, who, loving her to distraction, deliberately doomed himself to pensive shade to avoid even the appearance of standing in a brother's way.

'If the altar stood here, hundreds of people have been made man and wife just there, in past times,' she said, with calm deliberateness, throwing a little stone on a spot about a yard westward.

John annihilated another tender burst and replied, 'Yes, this field used to be a village. My grandfather could call to mind when there were houses here. But the squire pulled 'em down, because poor folk were an eyesore to him.'

'Do you know, John, what you once asked me to do?' she continued, not accepting the digression, and turning her eyes upon him.

'In what sort of way?'

'In the matter of my future life, and yours.'

'I am afraid I don't.'

'John Loveday!'

He turned his back upon her for a moment, that she might not see his face. 'Ah! – I do remember,' he said at last, in a dry, small, repressed voice.

'Well – need I say more? Isn't it sufficient?'

'It would be sufficient,' answered the unhappy man. 'But –'

She looked up with a reproachful smile, and shook her head. 'That summer,' she went on, 'you asked me ten times if you asked me once. I am older now; much more of a woman, you know; and my opinion is changed about some people; especially about one.'

'O Anne, Anne!' he burst out as, racked between honour and desire, he snatched up her hand. The next moment it fell heavily to her lap. He had absolutely relinquished it half-way to his lips.

'I have been thinking lately,' he said, with preternaturally sudden calmness, 'that men of the military profession ought not to m— – ought to be like St Paul, I mean.'

'Fie, John; pretending religion!' she said sternly. 'It isn't that at all. *It's Bob!*'

'Yes!' cried the miserable trumpet-major. 'I have had a letter from him today.' He pulled out a sheet of paper from his breast. 'That's it! He's promoted – he's a lieutenant, and appointed to a sloop that only cruises on our own coast, so that he'll be at home on leave half his time – he'll be a gentleman some day, and worthy of you!'

He threw the letter into her lap, and drew back to the other side of the gable-wall. Anne jumped up from her seat, flung away the letter without looking at it, and went hastily on. John did not attempt to overtake her. Picking up the letter, he followed in her wake at a distance of a hundred yards.

But, though Anne had withdrawn from his presence thus precipitately, she never thought more highly of him in her life then she did five minutes afterwards, when the excitement of the moment had passed. She saw it all quite clearly; and his self-sacrifice impressed her so much that the effect was just the reverse of what he had been aiming to produce. The more he pleaded for Bob, the more her perverse generosity pleaded for John. Today the crisis had come – with what results she had not foreseen.

As soon as the trumpet-major reached the nearest pen-and-ink he flung himself into a seat and wrote wildly to Bob:

> DEAR ROBERT, I write these few lines to let you know that if you want Anne Garland you must come at once – you must come instantly, and post-haste – *or she will be gone!* Somebody else wants her, and she wants him! It is your last chance, in the opinion of –
> Your faithful brother and well-wisher,
> JOHN.
>
> P.S. Glad to hear of your promotion. Tell me the day and I'll meet the coach.

# * XXXIX *

## Bob Loveday Struts Up and Down

ONE night, about a week later, two men were walking in the dark along the turnpike road towards Overcombe, one of them with a bag in his hand.

'Now,' said the taller of the two, the squareness of whose shoulders signified that he wore epaulettes, 'now you must do the best you can for yourself, Bob. I have done all I can; but th'hast thy work cut out, I can tell thee.'

'I wouldn't have run such a risk for the world,' said the other, in a tone of ingenuous contrition. 'But thou'st see, Jack, I didn't think there was any danger, knowing you was taking care of her, and keeping my place warm for me. I didn't hurry myself, that's true; but, thinks I, if I get this promotion I am promised I shall naturally have leave, and then I'll go and see 'em all. Gad, I shouldn't have been here now but for your letter!'

'You little think what risks you've run,' said his brother. 'However, try to make up for lost time.'

'All right. And whatever you do, Jack, don't say a word about this other girl. Hang the girl! – I was a great fool, I know; still, it is over now, and I am come to my senses. I suppose Anne never caught a capful of wind from that quarter?'

'She knows all about it,' said John seriously.

'Knows? By George, then, I'm ruined!' said Bob, standing stock-still in the road as if he meant to remain there all night.

'That's what I meant by saying it would be a hard battle for 'ee,' returned John, with the same quietness as before.

Bob sighed and moved on. 'I don't deserve that woman!' he cried passionately, thumping his three upper ribs with his fist.

'I've thought as much myself,' observed John, with a dryness which was almost bitter. 'But it depends on how thou'st behave in future.'

'John,' said Bob, taking his brother's hand, 'I'll be a new man. I solemnly swear by that eternal milestone staring at me there that I'll never look at another woman with the thought of marrying her whilst that darling is free – no, not if she be a mermaiden of light! It's a lucky thing that I'm slipped in on the quarter-deck! it may help me with her – hey?'

'It may with her mother; I don't think it will make much difference with Anne. Still, it is a good thing; and I hope that some day you'll command a big ship.'

Bob shook his head. 'Officers are scarce; but I'm afraid my luck won't carry me so far as that.'

'Did she ever tell you that she mentioned your name to the King?'

The seaman stood still again. 'Never!' he said. 'How did such a thing as that happen, in Heaven's name?'

John described in detail, and they walked on, lost in conjecture.

As soon as they entered the house the returned officer of the navy was welcomed with acclamation by his father and David, with mild approval by Mrs Loveday, and by Anne not at all – that discreet maiden having carefully retired to her own room some time earlier in the evening. Bob did not dare to ask for her in any positive manner; he just inquired about her health, and that was all.

'Why, what's the matter with thy face, my son?' said the miller, staring. 'David, show a light here.' And a candle was thrust against Bob's cheek, where there appeared a jagged streak like the geological remains of a lobster.

'O – that's where that rascally Frenchman's grenade busted and hit me from the *Redoubtable*, you know, as I told 'ee in my letter.'

'Not a word!'

'What, didn't I tell 'ee? Ah, no; I meant to, but I forgot it.'

'And here's a sort of dint in yer forehead too; what do that mean, my dear boy?' said the miller, putting his finger in a chasm in Bob's skull.

'That was done in the Indies. Yes, that was rather a troublesome chop – a cutlass did it. I should have told 'ee, but I found 'twould make my letter so long that I put it off, and put it off; and at last thought it wasn't worth while.'

John soon rose to take his departure.

'It's all up with me and her, you see,' said Bob to him outside the door. 'She's not even going to see me.'

'Wait a little,' said the trumpet-major.

It was easy enough on the night of the arrival, in the midst of excitement, when blood was warm, for Anne to be resolute in her avoidance of Bob Loveday. But in the morning determination is apt to grow invertebrate; rules of pugnacity are less easily acted up to, and a feeling of live and let live takes possession of the gentle soul. Anne had not meant even to sit down to the same breakfast-table with Bob; but when the rest were assembled, and had got some way through the substantial repast which was served at this hour in the miller's house, Anne entered. She came silently as a phantom, her eyes cast down, her cheeks pale. It was a good long walk from the door to the table, and Bob made a full inspection of her as she came up to a chair at the remotest corner, in the direct rays of the morning light, where she dumbly sat herself down.

It was altogether different from how she had expected. Here was she, who had done nothing, feeling all the embarrassment; and Bob, who had done the wrong, feeling apparently quite at ease.

'You'll speak to Bob, won't you, honey?' said the miller after a silence. To meet Bob like this after an absence seemed irregular in his eyes.

'If he wish me to,' she replied, so addressing the miller that no part, scrap, or outlying beam whatever of her glance passed near the subject of her remark.

'He's a lieutenant, you know, dear,' said her mother on the same side; 'and he's been dreadfully wounded.'

'Oh?' said Anne, turning a little towards the false one; at which Bob felt it to be time for him to put in a spoke for himself.

'I am glad to see you,' he said contritely; 'and how do you do?'

'Very well, thank you.'

He extended his hand. She allowed him to take hers, but only to the extent of a niggardly inch or so. At the same moment she glanced up at him, when their eyes met, and hers were again withdrawn.

The hitch between the two younger members of the household tended to make the breakfast a dull one. Bob was so depressed by her unforgiving manner that he could not throw that sparkle into his stories which their substance naturally required; and when the meal was over, and they went about their different businesses, the pair resembled the two Dromios[193] in seldom or never being, thanks to Anne's subtle contrivances, both in the same room at the same time.

This kind of performance repeated itself during several days. At last, after dogging her hither and thither, leaning with a wrinkled forehead against door-posts, taking an oblique view into the room where she happened to be, picking up worsted balls and getting no thanks, placing a splinter from the *Victory*, several bullets from the *Redoubtable*, a strip of the flag, and other interesting relics, carefully labelled, upon her table, and hearing no more about them than if they had been pebbles from the nearest brook, he hit upon a new plan. To avoid him she frequently sat upstairs in a window overlooking the garden. Lieutenant Loveday carefully dressed himself in a new uniform, which he had caused to be sent some days before, to dazzle admiring friends, but which he had never as yet put on in public or mentioned to a soul. When arrayed he entered the sunny garden, and there walked slowly up and down as he had seen Nelson and Captain Hardy do on the quarter-deck; but keeping his right shoulder, on which his one epaulette was fixed, as much towards Anne's window as possible.

But she made no sign, though there was not the least question that she saw him. At the end of half-an-hour he went in, took off his clothes, and gave himself up to doubt and the best tobacco.

He repeated the programme on the next afternoon, and on the next, never saying a word within doors about his doings or his notice.

Meanwhile the results in Anne's chamber were not uninteresting. She had been looking out on the first day, and was duly amazed to see a naval officer in full uniform promenading in the path. Finding it to be Bob, she left the window with a sense that the scene was not for her; then, from mere curiosity, peeped out from behind the curtain. Well, he was a pretty spectacle, she admitted, relieved as his figure was by a dense mass of sunny, close-trimmed hedge, over which nasturtiums climbed in wild luxuriance; and if she could care for him one bit, which she couldn't, his form would have been a delightful study, surpassing in interest even its splendour on the memorable day of their visit to the town theatre. She called her mother; Mrs Loveday came promptly.

'O, it is nothing,' said Anne indifferently; 'only that Bob has got his uniform.'

Mrs Loveday peeped out, and raised her hands with delight. 'And he has not said a word to us about it! What a lovely epaulette! I must call his father.'

'No, indeed. As I take no interest in him I shall not let people come into my room to admire him.'

'Well, you called me,' said her mother.

'It was because I thought you liked fine clothes. It is what I don't care for.'

Notwithstanding this assertion she again looked out at Bob the next afternoon when his footsteps rustled on the gravel, and studied his appearance under all the varying angles of the sunlight, as if fine clothes and uniforms were not altogether a matter of indifference. He certainly was a splendid, gentlemanly, and gallant sailor from end to end of him; but then, what were a dashing presentment, a naval rank, and telling scars, if a man was fickle-hearted? However, she peeped on till the fourth day, and then she did not peep. The window was open, she looked right out, and Bob knew that he had got a rise to his bait at last. He touched his hat to her, keeping his right shoulder forwards, and said, 'Good-day, Miss Garland,' with a smile.

Anne replied, 'Good-day,' with funereal seriousness; and the acquaintance thus revived led to the interchange of a few words at supper-time, at which Mrs Loveday nodded with satisfaction. But Anne took especial care that he should never meet her alone, and to insure this her ingenuity was in constant exercise. There were so many nooks and windings on the miller's rambling premises that she could never be sure he would not turn up within a foot of her, particularly as his thin shoes were almost noiseless.

One fine afternoon she accompanied Molly in search of elderberries for making the family wine which was drunk by Mrs Loveday, Anne, and anybody who could not stand the rougher and stronger liquors provided by the miller. After walking rather a long distance over the down they came to a grassy hollow, where elder-bushes in knots of twos and threes rose from an uneven bank and hung their heads towards the south, black and heavy with bunches of fruit. The charm of fruit-gathering to girls is enhanced in the case of elderberries by the inoffensive softness of the leaves, boughs, and bark, which makes getting into the branches easy and pleasant to the most indifferent climbers. Anne and Molly had soon gathered a basketful, and sending the servant home with it, Anne remained in the bush picking and throwing down bunch by bunch upon the grass. She was so absorbed in her occupation of pulling the twigs towards her, and the rustling of their leaves so filled her ears, that it was a great surprise when, on turning her head, she perceived a similar movement to her own among the boughs of the adjoining bush.

At first she thought they were disturbed by being partly in contact with the boughs of her bush; but in a moment Robert Loveday's face peered from them, at a distance of about a yard from her own. Anne uttered a little indignant 'Well!', recovered herself, and went on plucking. Bob thereupon went on plucking likewise.

'I am picking elderberries for your mother,' said the lieutenant at last, humbly.

'So I see.'

'And I happen to have come to the next bush to yours.'

'So I see; but not the reason why.'

Anne was now in the westernmost branches of the bush, and Bob had leant across into the eastern branches of his. In gathering he swayed towards her, back again, forward again.

'I beg pardon,' he said, when a further swing than usual had taken him almost in contact with her.

'Then why do you do it?'

'The wind rocks the bough, and the bough rocks me.' She expressed by a look her opinion of this statement in the face of the gentlest breeze; and Bob pursued: 'I am afraid the berries will stain your pretty hands.'

'I wear gloves.'

'Ah, that's a plan I should never have thought of. Can I help you?'

'Not at all.'

'You are offended: that's what that means.'

'No,' she said.

'Then will you shake hands?'

Anne hesitated; then slowly stretched out her hand, which he took at once. 'That will do,' she said, finding that he did not relinquish it immediately. But as he still held it, she pulled, the effect of which was to draw Bob's swaying person, bough and all, towards her, and herself towards him.

'I am afraid to let go your hand,' said that officer; 'for if I do your spar will fly back, and you will be thrown upon the ground with great violence.'

'I wish you to let me go!'

He accordingly did, and she flew back, but did not by any means fall.

'It reminds me of the times when I used to be aloft clinging to a yard not much bigger than this tree-stem, in the mid-Atlantic, and thinking about you. I could see you in my fancy as plain as I see you now.'

'Me, or some other woman!' retorted Anne haughtily.

'No!' declared Bob, shaking the bush for emphasis. 'I'll protest that I did not think of anybody but you all the time we were dropping down Channel all the time we were off Cadiz, all the time through battles and bombardments. I seemed to see you in the smoke, and, thinks I, if I go to Davy's locker, what will she do?'

'You didn't think that when you landed after Trafalgar.'

'Well, now,' said the lieutenant in a reasoning tone; 'that was a curious thing. You'll hardly believe it, maybe; but when a man is away from the woman he loves best in the port – world, I mean – he can have a sort of temporary feeling for another without disturbing the old one, which flows along under the same as ever.'

'I can't believe it, and won't,' said Anne firmly.

Molly now appeared with the empty basket, and when it had been filled from the heap on the grass, Anne went home with her, bidding Loveday a frigid adieu.

The same evening, when Bob was absent, the miller proposed that they should all three go to an upper window of the house, to get a distant view of some rockets and illuminations which were to be exhibited in the town and harbour in honour of the King, who had returned this year as usual. They accordingly went upstairs to an empty attic, placed chairs against the window, and put out the light, Anne sitting in the middle, her mother close by, and the miller behind, smoking. No sign of any pyrotechnic display was visible over the port as yet, and Mrs Loveday passed the time by talking to the miller, who replied in monosyllables. While this was going on Anne fancied that she heard someone approach, and presently felt sure that Bob was drawing near her in the surrounding darkness; but as the other two had noticed nothing she said not a word.

All at once the swarthy expanse of southward sky was broken by the blaze of several rockets simultaneously ascending from different ships in the roads. At the very same moment a warm mysterious hand slipped round her own, and gave it a gentle squeeze.

'O dear!' said Anne, with a sudden start away.

'How nervous you are, child, to be startled by fireworks so far off,' said Mrs Loveday.

'I never saw rockets before,' murmured Anne, recovering from her surprise.

Mrs Loveday presently spoke again. 'I wonder what has become of Bob?'

Anne did not reply, being much exercised in trying to get her hand away from the one that imprisoned it; and whatever the miller thought he kept to himself, because it disturbed his smoking to speak.

Another batch of rockets went up. 'O I never!' said Anne, in a half-suppressed tone, springing in her chair. A second hand had with the rise of the rockets leapt round her waist.

'Poor girl, you certainly must have change of scene at this rate,' said Mrs Loveday.

'I suppose I must,' murmured the dutiful daughter.

For some minutes nothing further occurred to disturb Anne's serenity. Then a slow, quiet 'a-hem' came from the obscurity of the apartment.

'What, Bob? How long have you been there?' inquired Mrs Loveday.

'Not long,' said the lieutenant coolly. 'I heard you were all here, and crept up quietly, not to disturb ye.'

'Why don't you wear heels to your shoes like Christian people, and not creep about so like a cat?'

'Well, it keeps your floor clean to go slip-shod.'[194]

'That's true.'

Meanwhile Anne was gently but firmly trying to pull Bob's arm from her waist, her distressful difficulty being that in freeing her waist she enslaved her hand, and in getting her hand free she enslaved her waist. Finding the struggle a futile one, owing to the invisibility of her antagonist, and her wish to keep its nature secret from the other two, she arose, and saying that she did not care to see any more, felt her way downstairs. Bob followed, leaving Loveday and his wife to themselves.

'Dear Anne,' he began, when he had got down, and saw her in the candle-light of the large room. But she adroitly passed out at the other door, at which he took a candle and followed her to the small room. 'Dear Anne, do let me speak,' he repeated, as soon as the rays revealed her figure. But she passed into the bakehouse before he could say more; whereupon he perseveringly did the same. Looking round for her here he perceived her at the end of the room, where there were no means of exit whatever.

'Dear Anne,' he began again, setting down the candle, 'you must try to forgive me; really you must. I love you the best of anybody in the wide, wide world. Try to forgive me; come!' And he imploringly took her hand.

Anne's bosom began to surge and fall like a small tide, her eyes remaining fixed upon the floor; till, when Loveday ventured to draw her slightly towards him, she burst out crying. 'I don't like you, Bob; I don't!' she suddenly exclaimed between her sobs. 'I did once, but I don't now – I can't, I can't; you have been very cruel to me!' She violently turned away, weeping.

'I have, I have been terribly bad, I know,' answered Bob, conscience-stricken by her grief. 'But – if you could only forgive me – I promise that I'll never do anything to grieve 'ee again. Do you forgive me, Anne?'

Anne's only reply was crying and shaking her head.

'Let's make it up. Come, say we have made it up, dear.'

She withdrew her hand, and still keeping her eyes buried in her handkerchief, said 'No.'

'Very well, then!' exclaimed Bob, with sudden determination. 'Now I know my doom! And whatever you hear of as happening to me, mind this, you cruel girl, that it is all your causing!' Saying this he strode with a hasty tread across the room into the passage and out at the door, slamming it loudly behind him.

Anne suddenly looked up from her handkerchief, and stared with round wet eyes and parted lips at the door by which he had gone. Having remained with suspended breath in this attitude for a few seconds she turned round, bent her head upon the table, and burst out weeping anew with thrice the violence of the former time. It really seemed now as if her grief would overwhelm her, all the emotions which had been suppressed, bottled up, and concealed since Bob's return having made themselves a sluice at last.

But such things have their end; and left to herself in the large, vacant, old apartment, she grew quieter, and at last calm. At length she took the candle and ascended to her bedroom, where she bathed her eyes and looked in the glass to see if she had made herself a dreadful object. It was not so bad as she had expected, and she went downstairs again.

Nobody was there, and, sitting down, she wondered what Bob had really meant by his words. It was too dreadful to think that he intended to go straight away to sea without seeing her again, and frightened at what she had done she waited anxiously for his return.

# XL

# A Call on Business

HER suspense was interrupted by a very gentle tapping at the door, and then the rustle of a hand over its surface, as if searching for the latch in the dark. The door opened a few inches, and the alabaster face of Uncle Benjy appeared in the slit.

'O, Squire Derriman, you frighten me!'

'All alone?' he asked in a whisper.

'My mother and Mr Loveday are somewhere about the house.'

'That will do,' he said, coming forward. 'I be wherried out of my life, and I have thought of you again – you yourself, dear Anne, and not the miller. If you will only take this and lock it up for a few days till I can find another good place for it – if you only would!' And he breathlessly deposited the tin box on the table.

'What, obliged to dig it up from the cellar?'

'Ay; my nephew hath a scent of the place – how, I don't know! but he and a young woman he's met with are searching everywhere. I worked like a wire-drawer to get it up and away while they were scraping in the next cellar. Now where could ye put it, dear? 'Tis only a few documents, and my will, and such like, you know. Poor soul 'o me, I'm worn out with running and fright!'

'I'll put it here till I can think of a better place,' said Anne, lifting the box. 'Dear me, how heavy it is!'

'Yes, yes,' said Uncle Benjy hastily; 'the box is iron, you see. However, take care of it, because I am going to make it worth your while. Ah, you are a good girl, Anne. I wish you was mine!'

Anne looked at Uncle Benjy. She had known for some time that she possessed all the affection he had to bestow.

'Why do you wish that?' she said simply.

'Now don't ye argue with me. Where d'ye put the coffer?'

'Here,' said Anne, going to the window-seat, which rose as

a flap, disclosing a boxed receptacle beneath, as in many old houses.

' 'Tis very well for the present,' he said dubiously, and they dropped the coffer in, Anne locking down the seat, and giving him the key. 'Now I don't want ye to be on my side for nothing,' he went on. 'I never did now, did I? This is for you.' He handed her a little packet of paper, which Anne turned over and looked at curiously. 'I always meant to do it,' continued Uncle Benjy, gazing at the packet as it lay in her hand, and sighing. 'Come, open it, my dear; I always meant to do it!'

She opened it and found twenty new guineas snugly packed within.

'Yes, they are for you. I always meant to do it!' he said, sighing again.

'But you owe me nothing!' returned Anne, holding them out.

'Don't say it!' cried Uncle Benjy, covering his eyes. 'Put 'em away . . . Well, if you *don't* want 'em – But put 'em away, dear Anne; they are for you, because you have kept my counsel. Good night t' ye. Yes, they are for you.'

He went a few steps, and turning back added anxiously, 'You won't spend 'em in clothes, or waste 'em in fairings,[195] or ornaments of any kind, my dear girl?'

'I will not,' said Anne. 'I wish you would have them.'

'No, no,' said Uncle Benjy, rushing off to escape their shine. But he had got no further than the passage when he returned again.

'And you won't lend 'em to anybody, or put 'em into the bank – for no bank is safe in these troublous times? . . . If I was you I'd keep them *exactly* as they be, and not spend 'em on any account. Shall I lock them into my box for ye?'

'Certainly,' said she; and the farmer rapidly unlocked the window-bench, opened the box, and locked them in.

' 'Tis much the best plan,' he said with great satisfaction as he returned the keys to his pocket. 'There they will always be safe, you see, and you won't be exposed to temptation.'

When the old man had been gone a few minutes, the miller and his wife came in, quite unconscious of all that had passed. Anne's anxiety about Bob was again uppermost now, and she spoke but meagrely of old Derriman's visit, and nothing of what he had left. She would fain have asked them if they knew were Bob was, but that she did not wish to inform them of the rupture. She was forced to admit to herself that she had somewhat tried his patience, and that impulsive men had been known to do dark things with themselves at such times.

They sat down to supper, the clock ticked rapidly on, and at length the miller said, 'Bob is later than usual. Where can he be?'

As they both looked at her, she could no longer keep the secret. 'It is my fault,' she cried; 'I have driven him away! What shall I do?'

The nature of the quarrel was at once guessed, and her two elders said no more. Anne rose and went to the front door, where she listened for every sound with a palpitating heart. Then she went in; then she went out: and on one occasion she heard the miller say, 'I wonder what hath passed between Bob and Anne. I hope the chap will come home.'

Just about this time light footsteps were heard without, and Bob bounced into the passage. Anne, who stood back in the dark while he passed, followed him into the room, where her mother and the miller were on the point of retiring to bed, candle in hand.

'I have kept ye up, I fear,' began Bob cheerily, and apparently without the faintest recollection of his tragic exit from the house. 'But the truth on't is, I met with Fess Derriman at the "Duke of York" as I went from here, and there we have been playing Put[196] ever since, not noticing how the time was going. I haven't had a good chat with the fellow for years and years, and really he is an out and out good comrade – a regular hearty! Poor fellow, he's been very badly used. I never heard the rights of the story till now; but it seems that old uncle of his treats him shamefully. He has been hiding away his money, so that poor Fess might not have a farthing, till at last the young man has turned, like any other worm, and is now determined to ferret out what he has done with it. The poor young chap hadn't a farthing of ready money till I lent him a couple of guineas – a thing I never did more willingly in my life. But the man was very honourable. "No; no," says he, "don't let me deprive ye." He's going to marry, and what may you think he is going to do it for?'

'For love, I hope,' said Anne's mother.

'For money, I suppose, since he's so short,' said the miller.

'No,' said Bob, 'for *spite*. He has been badly served – deuced badly served – by a woman. I never heard of a more heartless case in my life. The poor chap wouldn't mention names, but it seems this young woman has trifled with him in all manner of cruel ways – pushed him into the river, tried to steal his horse when he was called out to defend his country – in short, served him rascally. So I gave him the two guineas and said, "Now let's drink to the hussy's downfall!"'

'O!' said Anne, having approached behind him.

Bob turned and saw her, and at the same moment Mr and Mrs Loveday discreetly retired by the other door.

'Is it peace?' he asked tenderly.

'O yes,' she anxiously replied. 'I – didn't mean to make you think I had no heart.' At this Bob inclined his countenance towards hers. 'No,' she said, smiling through two incipient tears as she drew back. 'You are to show good behaviour for six months, and you must promise not to frighten me again by running off when I – show you how badly you have served me.'

'I am yours obedient – in anything,' cried Bob, 'But am I pardoned?'

Youth is foolish; and does a woman often let her reasoning in favour of the worthier stand in the way of her perverse desire for the less worthy at such times as these? She murmured some soft words, ending with 'Do you repent?'

It would be superfluous to transcribe Bob's answer.

Footsteps were heard without.

'O begad; I forgot!' said Bob. 'He's waiting out there for a light.'

'Who?'

'My friend Derriman.'

'But, Bob, I have to explain.'

But Festus had by this time entered the lobby, and Anne, with a hasty 'Get rid of him at once!', vanished upstairs.

Here she waited and waited, but Festus did not seem inclined to depart; and at last, foreboding some collision of interests from Bob's new friendship for this man, she crept into a storeroom which was over the apartment into which Loveday and Festus had gone. By looking through a knot-hole in the floor it was easy to command a view of the room beneath, this being unceiled, with moulded beams and rafters.

Festus had sat down on the hollow window-bench, and was continuing the statement of his wrongs. 'If he only knew what he was sitting upon, she thought apprehensively, 'how easily he could tear up the flap, lock and all, with his strong arm, and seize upon poor Uncle Benjy's possessions!' But he did not appear to know, unless he were acting, which was just possible. After a while he rose, and going to the table lifted the candle to light his pipe. At the moment when the flame began diving into the bowl the door noiselessly opened and a figure slipped across the room to the window-bench, hastily unlocked it, withdrew the box, and beat a retreat. Anne in a moment recognized the ghostly intruder as Festus Derriman's uncle. Before he could get out of the room Festus set down the candle and turned.

'What – Uncle Benjy – haw, haw! Here at this time of night?'

Uncle Benjy's eyes grew paralysed, and his mouth opened and shut like a frog's in a drought, the action producing no sound.

'What have we got here – a tin box – the box of boxes? Why, I'll carry it for 'ee, uncle! – I am going home.'

'N-no-no, thanky, Festus: it is n-n-not heavy at all, thanky,' gasped the squireen.

'O but I must,' said Festus, pulling at the box.

'Don't let him have it, Bob!' screamed the excited Anne through the hole in the floor.'

'No, don't let him!' cried the uncle. ' 'Tis a plot – there's a woman at the window waiting to help him!'

Anne's eyes flew to the window, and she saw Matilda's face pressed against the pane.

Bob, though he did not know whence Anne's command proceeded, obeyed with alacrity, pulled the box from the two relatives, and placed it on the table beside him.

'Now, look here, hearties; what's the meaning o' this?' he said.

'He's trying to rob me of all I possess!' cried the old man. 'My heart-strings seem as if they were going crack, crack, crack!'

At this instant the miller in his shirt-sleeves entered the room, having got thus far in his undressing when he heard the noise. Bob and Festus turned to him to explain; and when the latter had had his say Bob added, 'Well, all I know is that this box' – here he stretched out his hand to lay it upon the lid for emphasis. But as nothing but thin air met his fingers where the box had been, he turned, and found that the box had gone, Uncle Benjy having vanished also.

Festus, with an imprecation, hastened to the door, but though the night was not dark Farmer Derriman and his burden were nowhere to be seen. On the bridge Festus joined a shadowy female form, and they went along the road together, followed for some distance by Bob, lest they should meet with and harm the old man. But the precaution was unnecessary: nowhere on the road was there any sign of Farmer Derriman, or of the box that belonged to him. When Bob re-entered the house Anne and Mrs Loveday had joined the miller downstairs, and then for the first time he learnt who had been the heroine of Festus's lamentable story, with many other particulars of that yeoman's history which he had never before known. Bob swore that he would not speak to the traitor again, and the family retired.

The escape of old Mr Derriman from the annoyances of his nephew not only held good for that night, but for next day, and for ever. Just after dawn on the following morning a labouring man, who was going to his work, saw the old farmer and landowner leaning over a rail in a mead near his house, apparently engaged in contemplating the water of a brook before him. Drawing near, the man spoke, but Uncle Benjy did not reply. His head was hanging strangely, his body being supported in its erect position entirely by the rail that passed under each arm. On after-examination it was found that Uncle Benjy's poor withered heart had cracked and stopped its beating from damages inflicted on it by the excitements of his life, and of the previous night in particular. The unconscious carcass was little more than a light empty husk, dry and fleshless as that of a dead heron found on a moor in January.

But the tin box was not discovered with or near him. It was searched for all the week, and all the month. The mill-pond was dragged, quarries were examined, woods were threaded, rewards were offered; but in vain.

At length one day in the spring, when the mill-house was about to be cleaned throughout, the chimney-board of Anne's bedroom, concealing a yawning fire-place, had to be taken down. In the chasm behind it stood the missing deed-box of Farmer Derriman.

Many were the conjectures as to how it had got there. Then Anne remembered that on going to bed on the night of the collision between Festus and his uncle in the room below, she had seen mud on the carpet of her room, and the miller remembered that he had seen footprints on the back staircase. The solution of the mystery seemed to be that the late Uncle Benjy, instead of running off from the house with his box, had doubled on getting out of the front door, entered at the back, deposited his box in Anne's chamber where it was found, and then leisurely pursued his way home at the heels of Festus, intending to tell Anne of his trick the next day – an intention that was for ever frustrated by the stroke of death.

Mr Derriman's solicitor was a Casterbridge man, and Anne placed the box in his hands. Uncle Benjy's will was discovered within; and by this testament Anne's queer old friend appointed her sole executrix of his said will, and, more than that, gave and bequeathed to the same young lady all his real and personal estate, with the solitary exception of five small freehold houses in a back street in Budmouth, which were devised to his nephew Festus, as a sufficient property to maintain him decently, without affording any margin for extravagances. Oxwell Hall, with its muddy quadrangle, archways, mullioned windows, cracked battlements, and weed-grown garden, passed with the rest into the hands of Anne.

# * XLI *

## John Marches into the Night

DURING this exciting time John Loveday seldom or never appeared at the mill. With the recall of Bob, in which he had been sole agent, his mission seemed to be complete.

One mid-day, before Anne had made any change in her manner of living on account of her unexpected acquisition, Lieutenant Bob came in rather suddenly. He had been to Budmouth, and announced to the arrested senses of the family that the —th Dragoons were ordered to join Sir Arthur Wellesley[197] in the Peninsula.

These tidings produced a great impression on the household. John had been so long in the neighbourhood, either at camp or in barracks, that they had almost forgotten the possibility of his being sent away; and they now began to reflect upon the singular infrequency of his calls since his brother's return. There was not much time, however, for reflection, if they wished to make the most of John's farewell visit, which was to be paid the same evening, the departure of the regiment being fixed for next day. A hurried valedictory supper was prepared during the afternoon, and shortly afterwards John arrived.

He seemed to be more thoughtful and a trifle paler than of old, but beyond these traces, which might have been due to the natural wear and tear of time, he showed no signs of gloom. On his way through the town that morning a curious little incident had occurred to him. He was walking past one of the churches when a wedding-party came forth, the bride and bridegroom being Matilda and Festus Derriman. At sight of the trumpet-major the yeoman had glared triumphantly; Matilda, on her part, had winked at him slily, as much as to say —. But what she meant heaven knows; the trumpet-major did not trouble himself to think, and passed on without returning the mark of confidence with which she had favoured him.

Soon after John's arrival at the mill several of his friends dropped in for the same purpose of bidding adieu. They were mostly the men who had been entertained there on the occasion of the regiment's advent on the down, when Anne and her mother were coaxed in to grace the party by their superior presence; and the soldiers' well-trained, gallant manners were such as to make them interesting visitors now as at all times. For it was a period when romance had not so greatly faded out of military life as it has done in these days of short service, heterogeneous mixing, and transient campaigns; when the *esprit de corps* was strong, and long experience stamped noteworthy professional characteristics even on rank and file; while the miller's visitors had the additional advantage of being picked men.

They could not stay so long tonight as on that earlier and more cheerful occasion, and the final adieus were spoken at an early hour. It was no mere playing at departure, as when they had gone to Exonbury barracks, and there was a warm and prolonged shaking of hands all round.

'You'll wish the poor fellows good-bye?' said Bob to Anne, who had not come forward for that purpose like the rest. 'They are going away, and would like to have your good word.'

She then shyly advanced, and every man felt that he must make some pretty speech as he shook her by the hand.

'Good-bye! May you remember us as long as it makes ye happy, and forget us as soon as it makes ye sad,' said Sergeant Brett.

'Good night! Health, wealth, and long life to ye!' said Sergeant-major Wills, taking her hand from Brett.

'I trust to meet ye again as the wife of a worthy man,' said Trumpeter Buck.

'We'll drink your health throughout the campaign, and so good-bye t'ye,' said Saddler-sergeant Jones, raising her hand to his lips.

Three others followed with similar remarks, to each of which Anne blushingly replied as well as she could, wishing them a prosperous voyage, easy conquest, and a speedy return.

But, alas, for that! Battles and skirmishes, advances and retreats, fevers and fatigues, told hard on Anne's gallant friends in the coming time. Of the seven upon whom these wishes were bestowed, five, including the trumpet-major, were dead men within the few following years, and their bones left to moulder in the land of their campaigns.

John lingered behind. When the others were outside, expressing a final farewell to his father, Bob, and Mrs Loveday, he came to Anne, who remained within.

'But I thought you were going to look in again before leaving?' she said gently.

'No; I find I cannot. Good-bye!'

'John,' said Anne, holding his right hand in both hers, 'I must tell you something. You were wise in not taking me at my word that day. I was greatly mistaken about myself. Gratitude is not love, though I wanted to make it so for the time. You don't call me thoughtless for what I did?'

'My dear Anne,' cried John, with more gaiety than truthfulness, 'don't let yourself be troubled! What happens is for the best. Soldiers love here today and there tomorrow. Who knows that you won't hear of my attentions to some Spanish maid before a month is gone by? 'Tis the way of us, you know; a soldier's heart is not worth a week's purchase – ha, ha! Good-bye, good-bye!'

Anne felt the expediency of his manner, received the affectation as real, and smiled her reply, not knowing that the adieu was for evermore. Then with a tear in his eye he went out of the door, where he bade farewell to the miller, Mrs Loveday, and Bob, who said at parting, 'It's all right, Jack, my dear fellow. After a coaxing that would have been enough to win three ordinary English-women, five French, and ten Mulotters,[198] she has today agreed to bestow her hand upon me at the end of six months. Good-bye, Jack, good-bye!'

The candle held by his father shed its waving light upon John's face and uniform as with a farewell smile he turned on the doorstone, backed by the black night; and in another moment he had plunged into the darkness, the ring of his smart step dying away upon the bridge as he joined his companions-in-arms, and went off to blow his trumpet till silenced for ever upon one of the bloody battle-fields of Spain.

# APPENDIX: 'THE ALARM'

THE memories of Hardy's paternal grandmother, Mary Hardy, née Head (1772–1857), made an indelible impression upon the writer as a boy. Living with the family at Higher Bockhampton, she would recount stories of her unhappy childhood at Fawley in Berkshire and of her removal to Dorset. She could recall hearing news of the execution of the French royal family, and told vivid stories about the invasion scare. The poem, published first in *Wessex Poems* in 1898, is fuelled by those and other memories. It records the dilemma of Hardy's grandfather when, as a Volunteer, he was compelled to leave his pregnant wife at home. He had left instructions that, in the event of an invasion, his wife was to drive with the nurse inland to Bere Regis. The first beacon was lit on the downs above Weymouth; the one described in the poem was sited on Egdon Heath at Rainbarrow, close to the Hardy cottage. In the first edition of *Wessex Poems* the date for the action of the narrative is 1803, but the actual date would seem to have been 1 May 1804.

## The Alarm

(*Traditional*)

IN MEMORY OF ONE OF THE WRITER'S FAMILY WHO WAS A
VOLUNTEER DURING THE WAR WITH NAPOLEON

IN a ferny byway
        Near the great South-Wessex Highway,
A homestead raised its breakfast-smoke aloft;
The dew-damps still lay steamless, for the sun had made no

skyway,
And twilight cloaked the croft.

It was almost past conceiving
Here, where woodbines hung inweaving,
That quite closely hostile armaments might steer,
Save from seeing in the porchway a fair woman mutely grieving,
And a harnessed Volunteer.

In haste he'd flown there
To his comely wife alone there,
While marching south hard by, to still her fears,
For she soon would be a mother, and few messengers were known
there
In these campaigning years.

'Twas time to be Good-bying,
Since the assembly-hour was nighing
In royal George's town at six that morn;
And betwixt its wharves and this retreat were ten good miles of
hieing
Ere ring of bugle-horn.

'I've laid in food, Dear,
And broached the spiced and brewed, Dear;
And if our July hope should antedate,
Let the char-wench mount and gallop by the halterpath and wood,
Dear,
And fetch assistance straight.

'As for Buonaparte, forget him;
He's not like to land! But let him,
Those strike with aim who strike for wives and sons!
And the war-boats built to float him; 'twere but wanted to upset
him
A slat from Nelson's guns!

'But, to assure thee,
And of creeping fears to cure thee,
If he *should* be rumoured anchoring in the Road,

Drive with the nurse in Kingsbere; and let nothing thence allure
thee
  Till we have him safe-bestowed.

  'Now, to turn to marching matters: –
  I've my knapsack, firelock, spatters,
Crossbelts, priming-horn, stock, bay'net, blackball, clay,
Pouch, magazine, and flint-box that at every quick-step clatters; –
  My heart, Dear; that must stay!'

  – With breathings broken
  Farewell was kissed unspoken,
And they parted there as morning stroked the panes;
And the Volunteer went on, and turned, and twirled his glove for
token,
  And took the coastward lanes.

  When above He'th Hills he found him,
  He saw, on gazing round him,
The Barrow-Beacon burning – burning low,
As if, perhaps, enkindled ever since he'd homeward bound him;
  And it meant: Expect the Foe!

  Leaving the byway,
  He entered on the highway,
Where were cars and chariots, faring fast inland;
'He's anchored, Soldier!' shouted some: 'God save thee,
marching thy way,
  Th'lt front him on the strand!'

  He slowed; he stopped; he paltered
  Awhile with self, and faltered,
'Why courting misadventure shoreward roam?
To Molly, surely! Seek the woods with her till times have altered;
  Charity favours home.

  'Else, my denying
  He'd come, she'll read as lying –
Think the Barrow-Beacon must have met my eyes –
That my words were not unwareness, but deceit of her, while
vying
  In deeds that jeopardize.

'At home is stocked provision,
And to-night, without suspicion,
We might bear it with us to a covert near;
Such sin, to save a childing wife, would earn it Christ's remission,
Though none forgive it here!'

While he stood thinking,
A little bird, perched drinking
Among the crowfoot tufts the river bore,
Was tangled in their stringy arms and fluttered, almost sinking
Near him, upon the moor.

He stepped in, reached, and seized it,
And, preening, had released it
But that a thought of Holy Writ occurred,
And Signs Divine ere battle, till it seemed him Heaven had pleased it
As guide to send the bird.

'O Lord, direct me! . . .
Doth Duty now expect me
To march a-coast, or guard my weak ones near?
Give this bird a flight according, that I thence learn to elect me
The southward or the rear.'

He loosed his clasp; when, rising,
The bird – as if surmising –
Bore due to southward, crossing by the Froom,
And Durnover Great Field and Fort, the soldier clear advising –
Prompted he deemed by Whom.

Then on he panted
By grim Mai-Don, and slanted
Up the steep Ridge-way, hearkening between whiles;
Till nearing coast and harbour he beheld the shore-line planted
With Foot and Horse for miles.

Mistrusting not the omen,
He gained the beach, where Yeomen,
Militia, Fencibles and Pikemen bold,
With Regulars in thousands, were enmassed to meet the Foemen,

Whose fleet had not yet shoaled.

Captain and Colonel,
    Sere Generals, Ensigns vernal,
  Were there; of neighbour-natives, Michel, Smith,
Meggs, Bingham, Gambier, Cunningham, to face the said
        nocturnal
    Swoop on their land and kith.

But Buonapart still tarried:
    His project had miscarred;
  At the last hour, equipped for victory,
The fleet had paused; his subtle combinations had been parried
    By British strategy.

Homeward returning
    Anon, no beacons burning,
  No alarms, the Volunteer, in modest bliss,
Te Deum sang with wife and friends: 'We praise Thee, Lord,
        discerning
    That Thou hast helped in this!'

# NOTES

1 (p. 57). *trumpet-major*: senior trumpeter in a cavalry regiment, ranking as a sergeant and responsible for instructing other trumpeters.

2 (p. 57). *firelock*: musket equipped with a flintlock.

3 (p. 60). *diapason*: a diapason is one of the two principal notes of an organ. When stopped it sounds more softly an octave higher.

4 (p. 60). *bolting*: sifting the grain.

5 (p. 60). *hopper*: a tunnel-shaped receptacle which opens to allow grain to be passed into the machinery.

6 (p. 64). *picket their horses*: hitch their horses to pointed staves knocked into the ground.

7 (p. 64). *shakos*: conical hats decorated with a plume, deriving from the Hungarian *csako*.

8 (p. 64). *pelisse*: long, fur-lined cloak.

9 (p. 65). *kerseymere*: fine woollen cloth.

10 (p. 67). *Gothic*: descended from the early Germanic tribes.

11 (p. 67). *Ceorls or villeins*: ceorls were the lowest-ranking freemen in Anglo-Saxon society; villeins were serfs in the feudal system.

12 (p. 70). *mampus*: crowd (dialect).

13 (p. 70). *yeomanry*: a mounted volunteer force. Such corps were established in 1794 for the defence of the realm to replace cavalry regiments drafted overseas.

14 (p. 72). *Arcadian hat*: simplified classical styles were fashionable from the middle of the 1790s.

15 (p. 72). *sarcenet*: a soft, silken material of Middle Eastern origin.

16 (p. 73). *quarter-guard*: sentries guarding the camp or quarters.

17 (p. 73). *Hanoverians*: George II began the practice of enlisting soldiers from his father's native state of Hanover into the British army.

18 (p. 73). *tattoo*: a summons to soldiers by drum beat or bugle call.

19 (p. 73). *Charles's Wain*: a constellation also known as the Plough or the Great Bear.

20 (p. 75). *mill-tail*: a passage through which the water runs from the mill-wheel.

21 (p. 76). *German Legion*: during his reign George III was both a German and a British monarch.

22 (p. 76). *queues*: pigtails.

23 (p. 82). *toss-potting*: drinking heavily.

24 (p. 82). *Volunteers*: the first volunteer units were formed in 1794.

25 (p. 83). *chiel*: child (dialect).

26 (p. 84). *Valenciennes*: Valenciennes in northern France was captured by Anglo-Austrian forces on 28 July 1793.

27 (p. 84). *morticed*: a term from carpentry here applied to bone surgery. The joining together of two pieces by the insertion of a projecting tongue into a slot.

28 (p. 84). *pummy*: pomace, the pulp of apples crushed in cider-making (dialect).

29 (p. 86). *Fencible*: local defence volunteer.

30 (p. 87). *brig*: brigantine, a two-masted, square-rigged sailing ship.

31 (p. 88). *'When lawyers strive to heal a breach . . . Rol'-li cum ro'-rum, &c.*: Hardy expanded this song in successive editions.

32 (p. 88). *Albuera*: a battle in Spain when, on 16 May 1811, Beresford's forces defeated the French under Marshal Soult.

33 (p. 88). *Beresford*: William Carr Beresford (1768–1854), British general.

34 (p. 89). *Farnese Hercules*: a statue portraying a muscular Hercules, once located in the Farnese Palace in Rome.

35 (p. 89). *spud*: small spade.

36 (p. 90). *barton*: farmyard.

37 (p. 90). *Dutch cabbage*: Red cabbage.

38 (p. 91). *Rufus*: 'red' in Latin.

39 (p. 92). *'Vittoria'*: a battle in the Peninsular War, where Wellington defeated the French on 21 June 1813.

40 (p. 92). *'Waterloo'*: Wellington finally defeated Napoleon at this battle in Belgium on 18 June 1815.

41 (p. 95). *the excellent county history*: John Hutchins's *History and Antiquities of the Count of Dorset* (1774). Hardy read the third edition, published 1861–73.

42 (p. 96). *iron stanchions*: upright iron rods acting as supports in window-frames.

43 (p. 96). *gnomon*: a triangular projection on a sundial, the shadow of which indicates the time of day.

44 (p. 97). *'Duty of Man'*: The Whole Duty of Man (1658) by Richard Allestree. Allestree (1619–1681) was a royalist divine who took an active role

in the Civil War, and later became provost of Eton College. *The Whole Duty* is a handbook of Christian ethics.

45 (p. 98). *Carlton House*: the home of the Prince of Wales, and hence a centre for fashionable society.

46 (p. 98). *lamiger*: a cripple (dialect).

47 (p. 102). *fare*: a litter (dialect).

48 (p. 102). *sniche*: greedy (dialect).

49 (p. 104). *'Brighton Camp'*: An alternative name for the song 'The Girl I Left Behind Me'.

50 (p. 105). *giltycups*: buttercups (dialect).

51 (p. 106). *Blenheim*: a village in south-west Germany where the Duke of Marlborough gained a crushing victory over the French in 1704.

52 (p. 106). *third guard, low point . . . second guard*: defensive positions in sword-drill.

53 (p. 107). *priming-pan*: small plate in a matchlock or flintlock gun for holding the gunpowder which ignites the charge.

54 (p. 108). *wicket*: a small door or gate, usually in a wall.

55 (p. 110). *put on the big pot*: behaved as if he were an important person.

56 (p. 110). *ipso facto*: by that very fact (Latin).

57 (p. 114). *sutlers*: sellers of provisions who followed the army.

58 (p. 117). *the Royal watering-place*: Budmouth (Weymouth).

59 (p. 120). *eltrot*: cow-parsley (dialect).

60 (p. 120). *serpent*: an obsolete brass wind instrument, about eight feet long and coiled like a snake.

61 (p. 124). *twenties*: small candles, twenty to the pound.

62 (p. 124). *rummers*: large drinking glasses.

63 (p. 124). *tear-brass*: rowdy, boisterous.

64 (p. 124). *scram*: puny, emaciated (dialect).

65 (p. 124). *blue-vinnied*: Mouldy blue.

66 (p. 124). *gallicrow*: Scarecrow (dialect).

67 (p. 127). *knap*: low hill.

68 (p. 131). *the land of Lot*: the fertile plain of the Jordan. See Genesis 13:1–12.

69 (p. 132). *dun-fly*: gadfly.

70 (p. 137). *Gloucester Lodge*: George III's residence at Weymouth, later the Gloucester Hotel.

71 (p. 141). *Peter's, Casterbridge*: the parish church of Dorchester.

72 (p. 144). *cortège*: procession.

73 (p. 144). *the bucolic tastes of the King*: George III was colloquially known as 'Farmer George'.

74 (p. 144). *roads*: a sheltered stretch of water near the shore.

75 (p. 145). *the adjoining Isle*: Portland is a rocky peninsular, often called 'the Isle', projecting into the English Channel south of Weymouth.

76 (p. 146). In the serial version, all except the first sentence of this paragraph appeared at the end of the previous chapter. For the first edition Hardy excised the following from the end of Chapter II:

> Anne, who had that romantic interest in court people and pageantry which was natural to an imaginative girl of her tastes, frequently bent her eyes on this microscopic spectacle from the field near the front of her house, and allowed her fancy to paint the portraits and histories of those who moved therein. That speck was a coach, perchance full of ladies of resplendent charms, leading fairy lives in some gorgeous palace, and accustomed to walk in gardens of bewildering beauty. Those rattling dots of horsemen were perhaps gallant nobles and knights who had the privilege of jesting with kings; that figure on the horizon about the size of a pin's head, was perhaps composed throughout of royal blood. That, as a matter of fact, the several coaches contained the elderly countess of A—, of placid nature, plain features, and dowdy dress; the virtuous and homely Lady B—; the strange-tempered Marchioness of C—, and so on: that the horsemen were puffy, red-faced, General D—, a couple of grey and bald-headed colonels, a diminutive diplomatist, and numbers of commonplace attendants on the court, made no difference whatever to the transcendency of her mental impressions. (*Good Words*, 1880, p. 253.)

77 (p. 147). *the monument*: a large stone pillar erected on Blackdown in 1846 in memory of Admiral Hardy, who had lived at nearby Portisham.

78 (p. 147). *the Dukes of Cambridge and Cumberland*: the fourth and fifth sons of George III.

79 (p. 147). *three of the princesses . . . the two remaining princesses* : the five daughters of George III.

80. (p. 149). *a letter in the candle*: a spark in the candle was thought to indicate that the person to whom it pointed was about to receive a letter.

81 (p. 150). *Talavera, Albuera, Salamanca, Vittoria, Toulouse, and Waterloo*: various battles in the campaign against Napoleon: Talavera (22 April 1809), Albuera (16 May 1811), Salamanca (22 July 1812) and Vittoria (21 June 1813) were fought in Spain; Toulouse (10 April 1814) in France, and Waterloo (18 June 1815) in Belgium.

82 (p. 153). *the First Consul*: Napoleon was elected First Consul in imitation of the Roman Republic in 1799.

83 (p. 156). *turnip-lantern*: A hollowed-out turnip containing a lantern.

84 (p. 160). *Scrounch it all*: A dialect expletive, having the literal meaning, 'to tread heavily'.

85 (p. 162). *the chord*: the straight line between two intersections of a curve.

86 (p. 163). *nadir*: the lowest point in the heavens.

87 (p. 163). *plinth*: here indicating the base of a wall.

88 (p. 163). *Barbary ape*: apes from the north-west coast of Africa.

89 (p. 165). *chimney-crook*: an ajdustable hook for suspending a pot or kettle over the fire.

90 (p. 165). *Hollands*: gin.

91 (p. 165). *the scroff*: odds and ends (dialect).

92 (p. 173). *diachylon plaister*: sticking plaster made up with olive oil and lead oxide.

93 (p. 174). *clock-line*: cord from which the weights of a large clock are hung.

94 (p. 174). *rocked*: cleaned.

95 (p. 174). *skitty boots*: high boots laced in front.

96 (p. 175). *barrow-pig*: a castrated boar.

97 (p. 175). *black-pot*: black pudding.

98 (p. 175). *white-pot*: a pudding made up with cream, raisins, sugar and spices.

99 (p. 175). *chitterlings*: the small intestine of a pig.

100 (p. 175). *milts*: spleens.

101 (p. 175). *Falstaff's favourite beverage*: in Shakespeare's *Henry IV, Parts I and II*, Falstaff's favourite drink is sack, a white Spanish wine.

102 (p. 176). *did not colour*: did not add artificial colouring.

103 (p. 177). *the Bow*: an old name for the curved corner at the street-crossing in the centre of Dorchester.

104 (p. 177). *bakehouses*: it was common practice to take one's own pies to the local bakehouse to be cooked.

105 (p. 177). *road-waggon*: a heavy, slow transport cart used for goods and for passengers who could not afford the stage-coach fare.

106 (p. 181). *Elliston*: Robert William Elliston (1774–1831), a well-known actor and theatre manager.

107 (p. 185). *Pharoah's baker*: Pharoah dismissed, then arrested and hanged his baker. See Genesis 40.

108 (p. 189). *a face as impassible as Talleyrand's*: Charles Maurice de Talleyrand–Périgord (1754–1838), French foreign minister after the deposition of Napoleon and the restoration of the Bourbons. A notoriously impassive individual.

109 (p. 189). *Flemish-ladder*: rope ladder.

110 (p. 193). *burr-stones*: millstones of rough, uneven texture.

111 (p. 195). *culverts*: stone conduits for water passing under a road.

112 (p. 196). *to yaw*: the motion of a sailing ship turning from side to side.

113 (p. 197). *unreaves*: unravels.

114 (p. 197). *marline-spike*: pointed iron tool used by seamen for separating the strands of a rope.

115 (p. 210). *The Route*: detailed marching orders.

116 (p. 215). *ewe-lease*: a meadow set aside for sheep.

117 (p. 218). *bolter*: the sieve through which meal is sifted.

118 (p. 219). *Æolian harp*: a stringed instrument which, when blown upon by the wind, emits musical sounds. Aeolus was the Roman god of the winds.

119 (p. 225). *heel-balled*: a ball of wax mixed with lamp-black which was used for polishing shoes and metals.

120 (p. 226). *Frederick William's Patagonians*: Frederick William I of Prussia (1657–1713) recruited a regiment of exceptionally tall soldiers. The natives of Patagonia had a reputation for large stature.

121 (p. 226). *Martinmas*: St Martin's Day, 11 November.

122 (p. 228). *a lion and a unicorn*: the royal coat of arms.

123 (p. 229). *the Tything-man*: Originally, the head man of a tithing of ten households; more generally, a parish officer.

124 (p. 231). *fawlocks*: firelocks (dialect).

125 (p. 231). *rammer*: ramrod.

126 (p. 233). *benefit-club staves:* Benefit clubs were organizations which insured members against sickness or old age. Staves were the wands the club members carried on their Whitsun walk.

127 (p. 238). *carved finials*: ornaments in stone or plaster projecting from the ends of pinnacles.

128 (p. 240). *spencer*: a short woollen jacket worn by women.

129 (p. 240). *'Mameluke' sleeves*: a full sleeve with a deep cuff named after the rulers of Egypt.

130 (p. 244). *A perfect Paul-and-Virginia life*: Bernardin de Saint-Pierre's novel *Paul et Virginie* (1787) contains a portrayal of idyllic love.

131 (p. 246). *in the days of Noe*: in the time of Noah – i.e., before the catastrophe of the Flood. See Matthew 24:37–8.

132 (p. 247). *wales*: the planks along the side of a boat.

133 (p. 247). *Minden*: a battle in Germany in August 1759 when the British and Hanoverians defeated the French.

134 (p. 250). *bagnet*: bayonet (dialect).

135 (p. 256). *Greenhill Fair*: Greenhill is Woodbury Castle near Bere Regis,

where a fair was held annually in September. Thread-the-needle is a game in which the 'cat' pursues the 'mouse' in and out of a ring of players.

136 (p. 258). *pickers*: needle-like objects used to clear the vent of a musket.

137 (p. 258). *worms*: screws fixed to the end of a rod, used for taking out the charge from a gun.

138 (p. 258). *priming-horns*: horn-shaped containers for gunpowder.

139 (p. 259). *like the Ark when sent away from the country of the Philistines*: the Philistines captured the Ark of the Israelites, but when they suffered misfortune they placed it on a cart drawn by two cattle and allowed the animals to wander away with it. See I Samuel 6.

140 (p. 261). *wamble*: to move about shakily (dialect).

141 (p. 266). *tole*: to entice (dialect).

142 (p. 267). *the bucket of the carbine*: a leather socket to hold a carbine or small rifle.

143 (p. 267). *Latin cross*: a cross with a horizontal bar two thirds of the way up.

144 (p. 273). *smut in the corn*: a fungus disease.

145 (p. 274). *stone staddles*: pillars supporting a granary.

146 (p. 274). *Aqua-tinted*: an aquatint is produced by etching on copper with resin and nitric acid. This process gives the print a delicate monochromatic tone.

147 (p. 277). *illuminations and transparencies*: pictures made visible by lighting behind.

148 (p. 279). *gunnel*: gunwale, the side of the ship (dialect).

149 (p. 281). *fay*: prosper (dialect).

150 (p. 282). *dog-days*: the hottest days of the year, when Sirius, the dog-star, rises and sets with the sun.

151 (p. 282). *Leghorn hat*: a plaited straw hat named after the Italian resort.

152 (p. 283). *piquet*: a small body of troops on guard.

153 (p. 284). *Colman*: George Colman the Younger (1762–1836), a prolific playwright.

154 (p. 284). *Bannister*: Jack Bannister (1760–1836), an actor famed for his good looks.

155 (p. 286). *Sir Robert Calder*: Admiral Sir Robert Calder (1745–1818). Villeneuve had been ordered to decoy the British fleet under Nelson into sailing towards the West Indies, then to return and escort Napoleon's flat-bottomed boats across the Channel for the invasion of England. In 1805 the first part of the plan was effected, but Nelson discovered it and notified the Admiralty. Villeneuve was intercepted off Cape Finisterre in north-west Spain, defeated by a small fleet under Calder and forced to take refuge in Spanish ports.

156 (p. 287). *'No Song No Supper'*: a farce by Prince Hoare (1755–1834), with musical numbers composed by Stephen Storace (1763–1796), first performed at the Theatre Royal, Drury Lane, in 1790.

157 (p. 287). *the Nothe*: a small promontory at Weymouth which at that time housed a fort commanding the bay.

158 (p. 289). *press-gang*: a body of marines sent ashore to force likely recruits to serve in the Royal Navy.

159 (p. 292). *pea-jacket*: a sailor's short woollen overcoat.

160 (p. 297). *cat-head*: a projection from the outer wall of a mill used for lifting sacks.

161 (p. 309). *curricle*: a light two-wheeled carriage drawn by two horses.

162 (p. 309). *Captain Hardy*: Sir Thomas Masterman Hardy (1769–1839), captain of Nelson's flagship the *Victory* at Trafalgar, and later an admiral. A remote relation of the novelist.

163 (p. 312). *altitude*: as with a sextant.

164 (p. 313). *square-rigged vessels*: ships with sails suspended from yards fixed horizontally across the masts.

165 (p. 316). *royals*: small sails hoisted above the top-gallants.

166 (p. 317). *bollard*: a post on the quayside used for mooring boats.

167 (p. 319). *beating up*: canvassing for recruits.

168 (p. 320). *Portland Bill, or Beal*: beal is normally the mouth of a river valley, but here it refers to Portland Bill, the most southerly point of the peninsula.

169 (p. 321). *in stays*: when a ship is turned against the wind for the purpose of tacking.

170 (p. 321). *bound down*: heading down the English Channel towards the Atlantic.

171 (p. 322). *the Start*: The southernmost tip of Devon.

172 (p. 322). *the courses*: the lower sails of a ship.

173 (p. 322). *truck*: a wooden cap fixed to the top of a mast.

174 (p. 323). ' *"These see the works of the Lord, and His wonders in the deep,"* ': Psalm 57:23–4.

175 (p. 323). *lerret*: a small boat specially designed to cope with the heavy seas around Portland.

176 (p. 324). *The spring was, in fact, a sulphurous one*: Hardy refers here to a medicinal spring at Nottington, near Weymouth. Treatises were published in the late eighteenth century extolling the virtues of its waters, and in 1830 a pavilion was erected for the use of patrons. The spa failed soon afterwards.

177 (p. 325). *She instantly recognized her interrogator as the King*: George III was renowned for his habit of walking around incognito. Here, and in the

interview between Bob Loveday and Captain Hardy, Hardy successfully ignored Leslie Stephen's advice to keep historical personages 'round the corner' in his story.

178 (p. 327). *General Mack*: Karl, Baron von Leiberich (1752–1828), a leading strategist in the Austrian army; his forces capitulated to Napoleon at the Battle of Ulm in 1805.

179 (p. 330). *hawse-holes*: holes in the bows of large ships of the period through which the anchor-cable passed.

180 (p. 330). *clap-nets*: nets with jointed rims which could be closed by pulling a string, utilized to catch birds.

181 (p. 330). *topmasts*: temporary masts rigged up to replace those shot away in battle.

182 (p. 332). *the Valley of the Shadow of Death*: See Psalm 23:4.

183 (p. 332). *hartshorn*: ammonia, used as smelling-salts.

184 (p. 336). *mixens*: refuse-heaps.

185 (p. 337). *Then perhaps . . . as in the church verse*: the prophet Nathan reproached David for causing Uriah's death and taking his wife Bathsheba. In Nathan's parable a rich man with many sheep made a poor man sacrifice his one ewe-lamb to feed the rich man's guest. See II Samuel 12.

186 (p. 338). *a stale and unprofitable personality*: an echo from Shakespeare's *Hamlet*, I.ii.133–4:

> How weary, stale, flat, and unprofitable,
> Seem to me all the uses of this world!

187 (p. 338). *She knew . . . when it served*: an echo of Shakespeare's *Julius Caesar*, IV.iii.221–2:

> And we must take the current when it serves,
> Or lose our ventures.

188 (p. 338). *I hold the world . . . a sad one*; an echo of Shakespeare's *The Merchant of Venice*, I.i.77–9:

> I hold the world but as the world, Gratiano –
> A stage, where every man must play a part,
> And mine a sad one.

189 (p. 347). *shoal water*: shallow water.

190 (p. 350). *rowel*: the spiked wheel on the end of a spur.

191 (p. 353). *Gall*: Franz Joseph Gall (1758–1828), the founder of phrenology.

192 (p. 355). *Faringdon Ruin*: the remaining end wall of a ruined church near Dorchester.

193 (p. 361). *the two Dromios*: the identical twin servants in Shakespeare's *Comedy of Errors*.

194 (p. 366). *to go slip-shod*: wearing slippers.

195 (p. 369). *fairings*: presents bought at fairs.

196 (p. 370). *Put*: a card game involving the winning of tricks.

197 (p. 375). *Sir Arthur Wellesley*: Sir Arthur Wellesley (1769–1852), commander of the British army in the Peninsular Wars, later created Duke of Wellington.

198 (p. 377). *Mulotters*: mulattos.

# FOR THE BEST IN PAPERBACKS, LOOK FOR THE

In every corner of the world, on every subject under the sun, Penguins represent quality and variety – the very best in publishing today.

For complete information about books available from Penguin and how to order them, write to us at the appropriate address below. Please note that for copyright reasons the selection of books varies from country to country.

**In the United Kingdom:** For a complete list of books available from Penguin in the U.K., please write to *Dept EP, Penguin Books Ltd, Harmondsworth, Middlesex, UB7 0DA*

**In the United States:** For a complete list of books available from Penguin in the U.S., please write to *Dept BA, Viking Penguin, 299 Murray Hill Parkway, East Rutherford, New Jersey 07073*

**In Canada:** For a complete list of books available from Penguin in Canada, please write to *Penguin Books Canada Limited, 2801 John Street, Markham, Ontario L3R 1B4*

**In Australia:** For a complete list of books available from Penguin in Australia, please write to the *Marketing Department, Penguin Books Australia Ltd, P.O. Box 257, Ringwood, Victoria 3134*

**In New Zealand:** For a complete list of books available from Penguin in New Zealand, please write to the *Marketing Department, Penguin Books (N.Z.) Ltd, Private Bag, Takapuna, Auckland 9*

**In India:** For a complete list of books available from Penguin in India, please write to *Penguin Overseas Ltd, 706 Eros Apartments, 56 Nehru Place, New Delhi 110019*

## PENGUIN CLASSICS

## THE LIBRARY OF EVERY CIVILIZED PERSON

| | |
|---|---|
| Matthew Arnold | Selected Prose |
| Jane Austen | Emma |
| | Lady Susan, The Watsons, Sanditon |
| | Mansfield Park |
| | Northanger Abbey |
| | Persuasion |
| | Pride and Prejudice |
| | Sense and Sensibility |
| Anne Brontë | The Tenant of Wildfell Hall |
| Charlotte Brontë | Jane Eyre |
| | Shirley |
| | Villette |
| Emily Brontë | Wuthering Heights |
| Samuel Butler | Erewhon |
| | The Way of All Flesh |
| Thomas Carlyle | Selected Writings |
| Wilkie Collins | The Moonstone |
| | The Woman in White |
| Charles Darwin | The Origin of the Species |
| Charles Dickens | American Notes for General Circulation |
| | Barnaby Rudge |
| | Bleak House |
| | The Christmas Books |
| | David Copperfield |
| | Dombey and Son |
| | Great Expectations |
| | Hard Times |
| | Little Dorrit |
| | Martin Chuzzlewit |
| | The Mystery of Edwin Drood |
| | Nicholas Nickleby |
| | The Old Curiosity Shop |
| | Oliver Twist |
| | Our Mutual Friend |
| | The Pickwick Papers |
| | Selected Short Fiction |
| | A Tale of Two Cities |

# THE LIBRARY OF EVERY CIVILIZED PERSON

| | |
|---|---|
| Benjamin Disraeli | **Sybil** |
| George Eliot | **Adam Bede** |
| | **Daniel Deronda** |
| | **Felix Holt** |
| | **Middlemarch** |
| | **The Mill on the Floss** |
| | **Romola** |
| | **Scenes of Clerical Life** |
| | **Silas Marner** |
| Elizabeth Gaskell | **Cranford and Cousin Phillis** |
| | **The Life of Charlotte Brontë** |
| | **Mary Barton** |
| | **North and South** |
| | **Wives and Daughters** |
| Edward Gibbon | **The Decline and Fall of the Roman Empire** |
| George Gissing | **New Grub Street** |
| Edmund Gosse | **Father and Son** |
| Richard Jefferies | **Landscape with Figures** |
| Thomas Macaulay | **The History of England** |
| Henry Mayhew | **Selections from London Labour and The London Poor** |
| John Stuart Mill | **On Liberty** |
| William Morris | **News from Nowhere and Selected Writings and Designs** |
| Walter Pater | **Marius the Epicurean** |
| John Ruskin | **'Unto This Last' and Other Writings** |
| Sir Walter Scott | **Ivanhoe** |
| Robert Louis Stevenson | **Dr Jekyll and Mr Hyde** |
| William Makepeace Thackeray | **The History of Henry Esmond** |
| | **Vanity Fair** |
| Anthony Trollope | **Barchester Towers** |
| | **Framley Parsonage** |
| | **Phineas Finn** |
| | **The Warden** |
| Mrs Humphrey Ward | **Helbeck of Bannisdale** |
| Mary Wollstonecraft | **Vindication of the Rights of Women** |

# THE LIBRARY OF EVERY CIVILIZED PERSON

| | |
|---|---|
| John Aubrey | **Brief Lives** |
| Francis Bacon | **The Essays** |
| James Boswell | **The Life of Johnson** |
| Sir Thomas Browne | **The Major Works** |
| John Bunyan | **The Pilgrim's Progress** |
| Edmund Burke | **Reflections on the Revolution in France** |
| Thomas de Quincey | **Confessions of an English Opium Eater** |
| | **Recollections of the Lakes and the Lake Poets** |
| Daniel Defoe | **A Journal of the Plague Year** |
| | **Moll Flanders** |
| | **Robinson Crusoe** |
| | **Roxana** |
| | **A Tour Through the Whole Island of Great Britain** |
| Henry Fielding | **Jonathan Wild** |
| | **Joseph Andrews** |
| | **The History of Tom Jones** |
| Oliver Goldsmith | **The Vicar of Wakefield** |
| William Hazlitt | **Selected Writings** |
| Thomas Hobbes | **Leviathan** |
| Samuel Johnson/<br>James Boswell | **A Journey to the Western Islands of<br>Scotland/The Journal of a Tour to the<br>Hebrides** |
| Charles Lamb | **Selected Prose** |
| Samuel Richardson | **Clarissa** |
| | **Pamela** |
| Adam Smith | **The Wealth of Nations** |
| Tobias Smollet | **Humphry Clinker** |
| Richard Steele and<br>Joseph Addison | Selections from the **Tatler** and the **Spectator** |
| Laurence Sterne | **The Life and Opinions of Tristram Shandy,<br>Gentleman** |
| | **A Sentimental Journey Through France and Italy** |
| Jonathan Swift | **Gulliver's Travels** |
| Dorothy and William<br>Wordsworth | **Home at Grasmere** |

# Thomas Hardy in Penguin

'Hardy is one of the relatively few writers who produced, by common consent, both major fiction and major poetry' – Martin Seymour-Smith

## Jude the Obscure

Jude Fawley, the stone-mason, whose academic ambitions are thwarted by poverty and the indifference of the authorities at Christminster, appears to find fulfilment in his relationship with Sue Brideshead. Ironically, when tragedy strikes it is Sue who is unequal to the challenge.

## Far From the Madding Crowd

Perhaps the best-known and most humorous of Hardy's novels even though the familiar themes of suffering and betrayal are evident, *Far from the Madding Crowd* is the product of Hardy's intimate and first-hand knowledge of the attitudes, habits, inconsistencies and idiosyncrasies of rural men and women.

## Tess of the D'Urbervilles

In a novel full of poetry and mysteriously luminous settings, Hardy unfolds the story of his beautiful suffering Tess with peculiar and unforgettable tenderness and intensity.

## The Mayor of Casterbridge

In depicting Michael Henchard, a man who overreaches the limits, Hardy once again demonstrates his uncanny psychological grasp and his deeply rooted knowledge of mid-nineteenth-century Dorset.

## The Selected Poems

Hardy's poetry offers a kaleidoscope of forms, metres and subjects, and in his poems of love and marriage he is unparalleled in any language.